Bang Tango

image

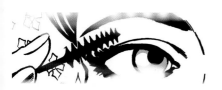

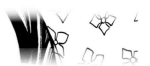

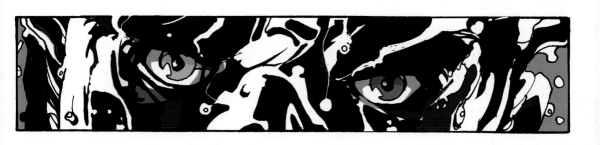

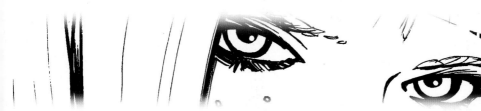

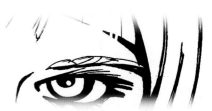

Image Comics, Inc.

Robert Kirkman — *Chief Operating Officer*
Erik Larsen — *Chief Financial Officer*
Todd McFarlane — *President*
Marc Silvestri — *Chief Executive Officer*
Jim Valentino — *Vice President*

Eric Stephenson — *Publisher*
Ron Richards — *Director of Business Development*
Jennifer de Guzman — *Director of Trade Book Sales*
Kat Salazar — *Director of PR & Marketing*
Corey Murphy — *Director of Retail Sales*
Jeremy Sullivan — *Director of Digital Sales*
Emilio Bautista — *Sales Assistant*
Branwyn Bigglestone — *Senior Accounts Manager*
Emily Miller — *Accounts Manager*
Jessica Ambriz — *Administrative Assistant*
Tyler Shainline — *Events Coordinator*
David Brothers — *Content Manager*
Jonathan Chan — *Production Manager*
Drew Gill — *Art Director*
Meredith Wallace — *Print Manager*
Addison Duke — *Production Artist*
Vincent Kukua — *Production Artist*
Tricia Ramos — *Production Assistant*

www.imagecomics.com

International Rights / Foreign Licensing

foreignlicensing@imagecomics.com

www.manofaction.tv

BANG!TANGO
ISBN: 978-1-63215-250-3
First Printing

JOE KELLY
Writer

ADRIÁN SIBAR
Artist

THOMAS MAUER
Lettering & Design

RODNEY RAMOS
Additional Inks

Created By
JOE KELLY & ADRIÁN SIBAR

BOB SCHRECK
Original Series Editor

BRANDON MONTCLARE
Original Series Asst. Editor

Special thanks to

KAREN BERGER
PAUL LEVITZ
JACK MAHAN
&
BOB SCHRECK

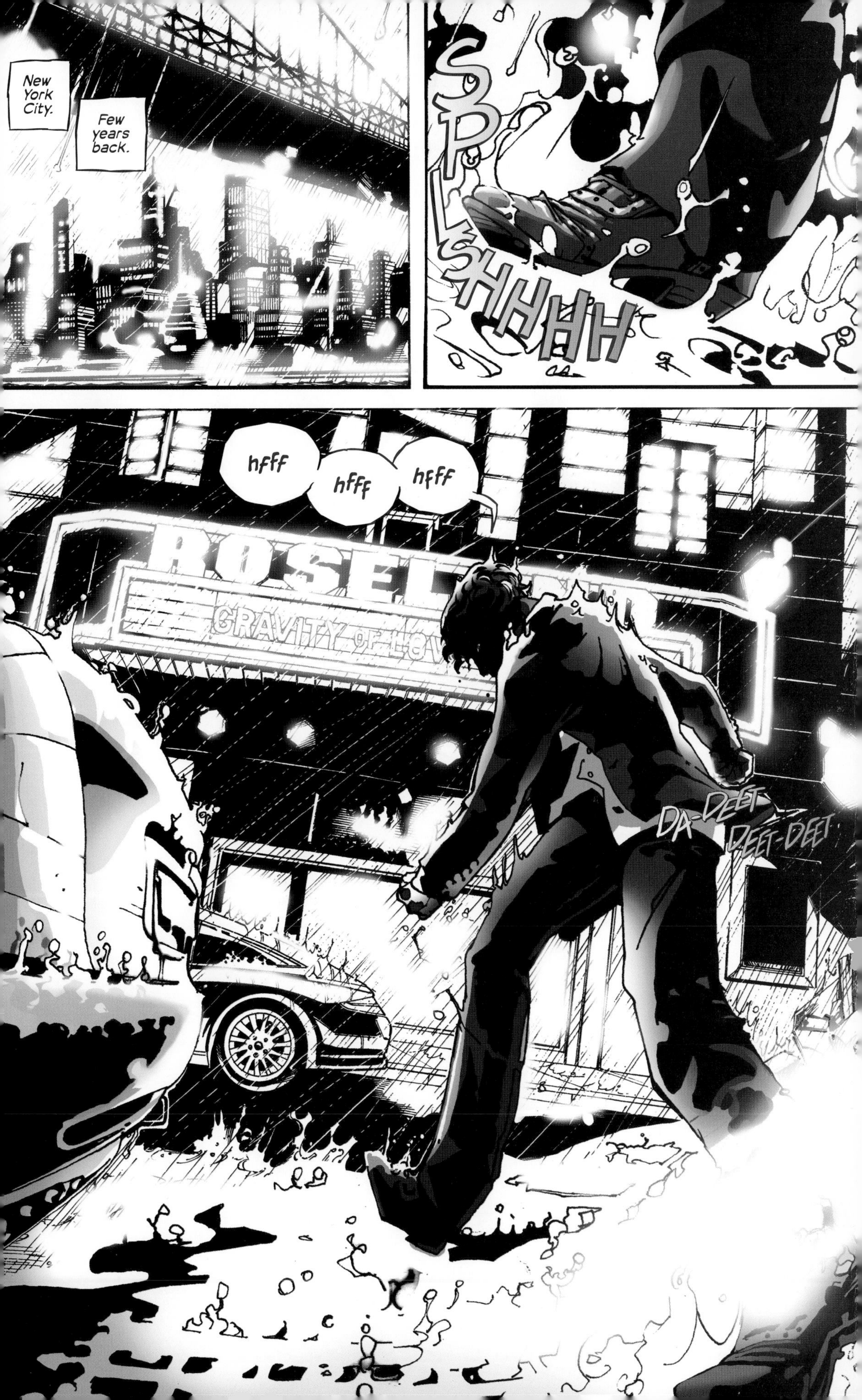
New York City.
Few years back.
SPLSHHHH
hfff
hfff
hfff
ROSEL
GRAVITY OF LOV
DA-DEET DEET-DEET

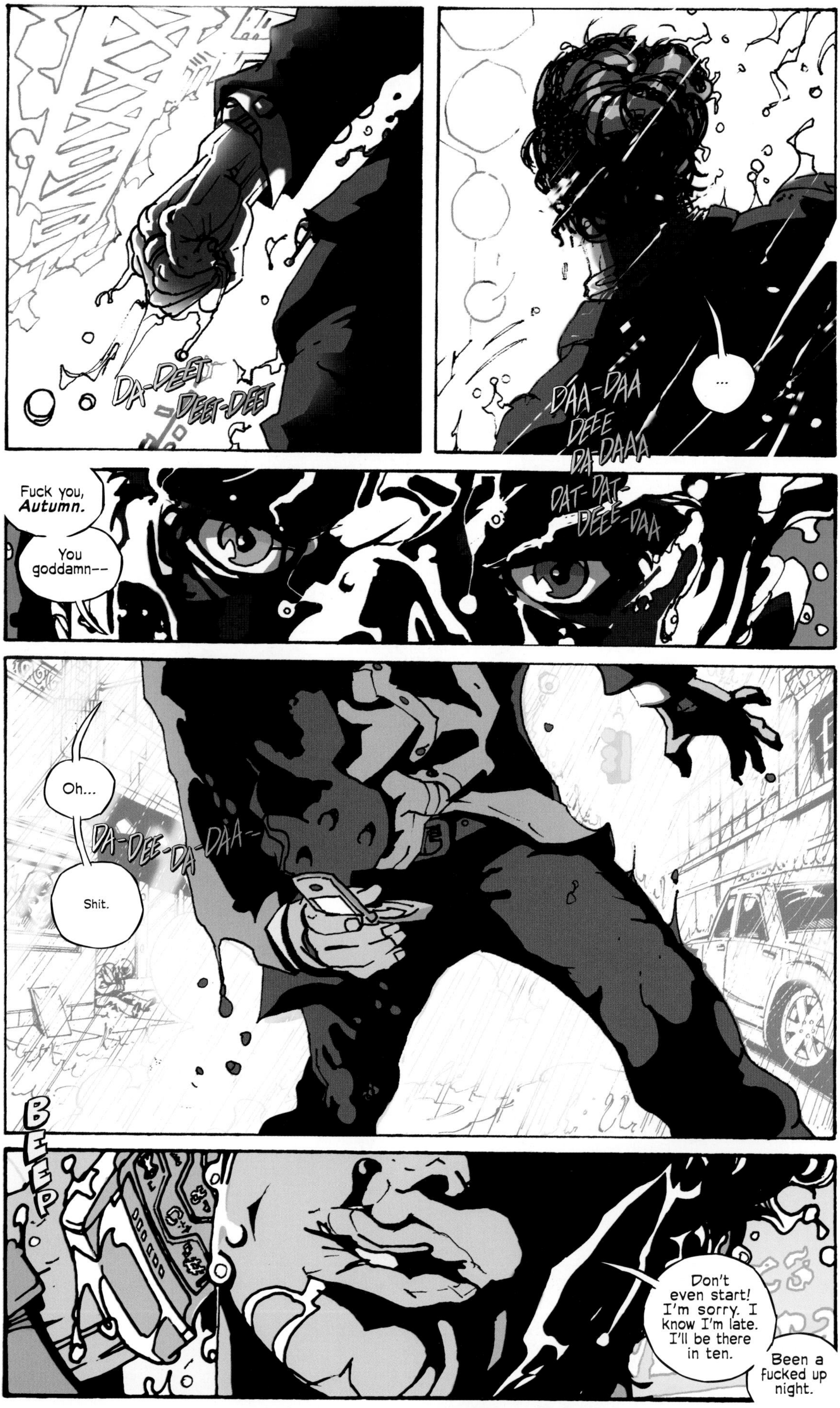
DA-DEET DEET-DEET
...
DAA-DAA DEEE DA-DAAA DAT-DAT-DEEE-DAA
Fuck you, *Autumn.*
You goddamn--
Oh...
DA-DEE-DA-DAA--
Shit.
BEEP
Don't even start! I'm sorry. I know I'm late. I'll be there in ten.
Been a fucked up night.

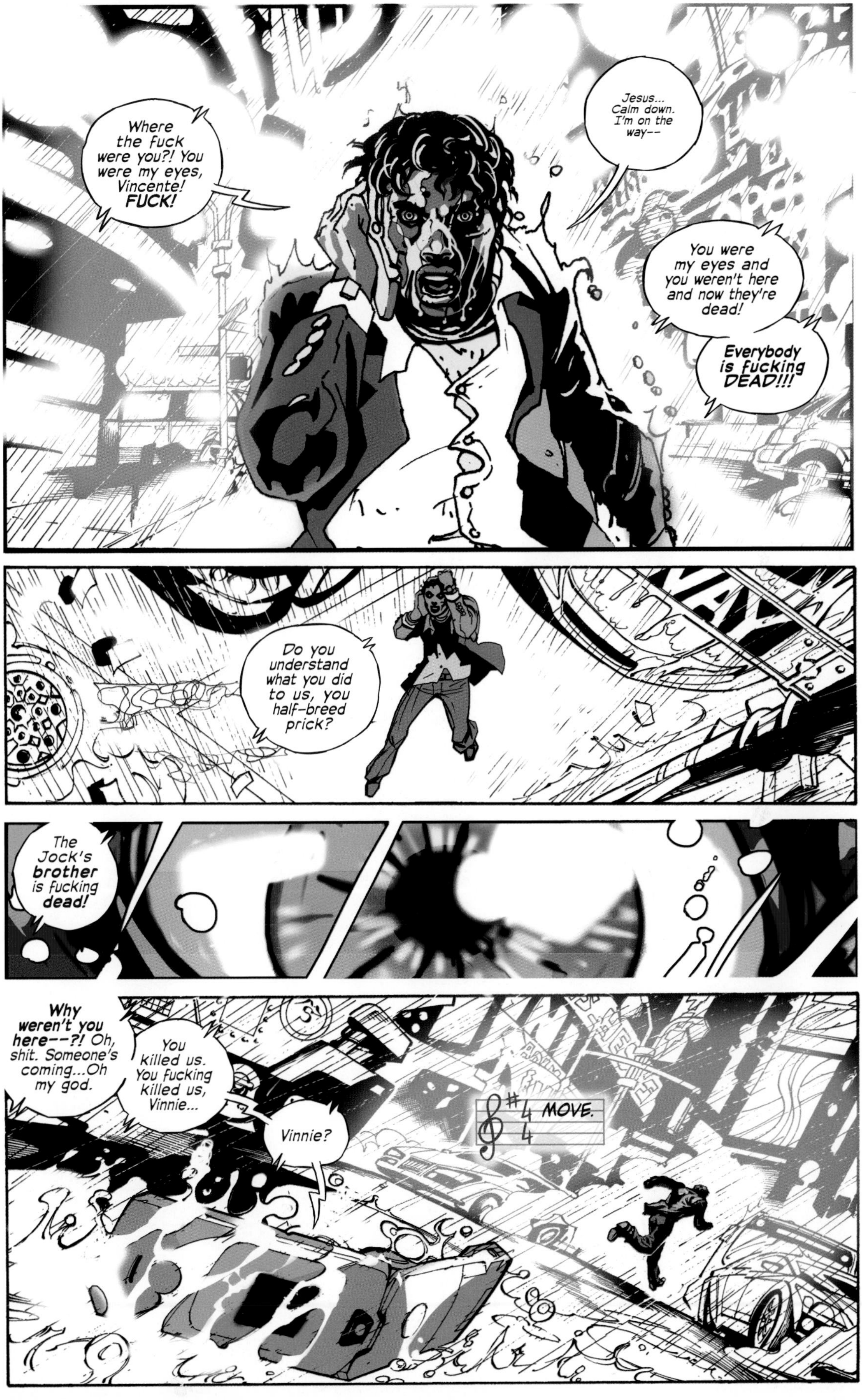
Where the fuck were you?! You were my eyes, Vincente! FUCK!
Jesus... Calm down. I'm on the way--
You were my eyes and you weren't here and now they're dead!
Everybody is fucking DEAD!!!
Do you understand what you did to us, you half-breed prick?
The Jock's brother is fucking dead!
Why weren't you here--?! Oh, shit. Someone's coming...Oh my god.
You killed us. You fucking killed us, Vinnie...
Vinnie?
4/4 MOVE.

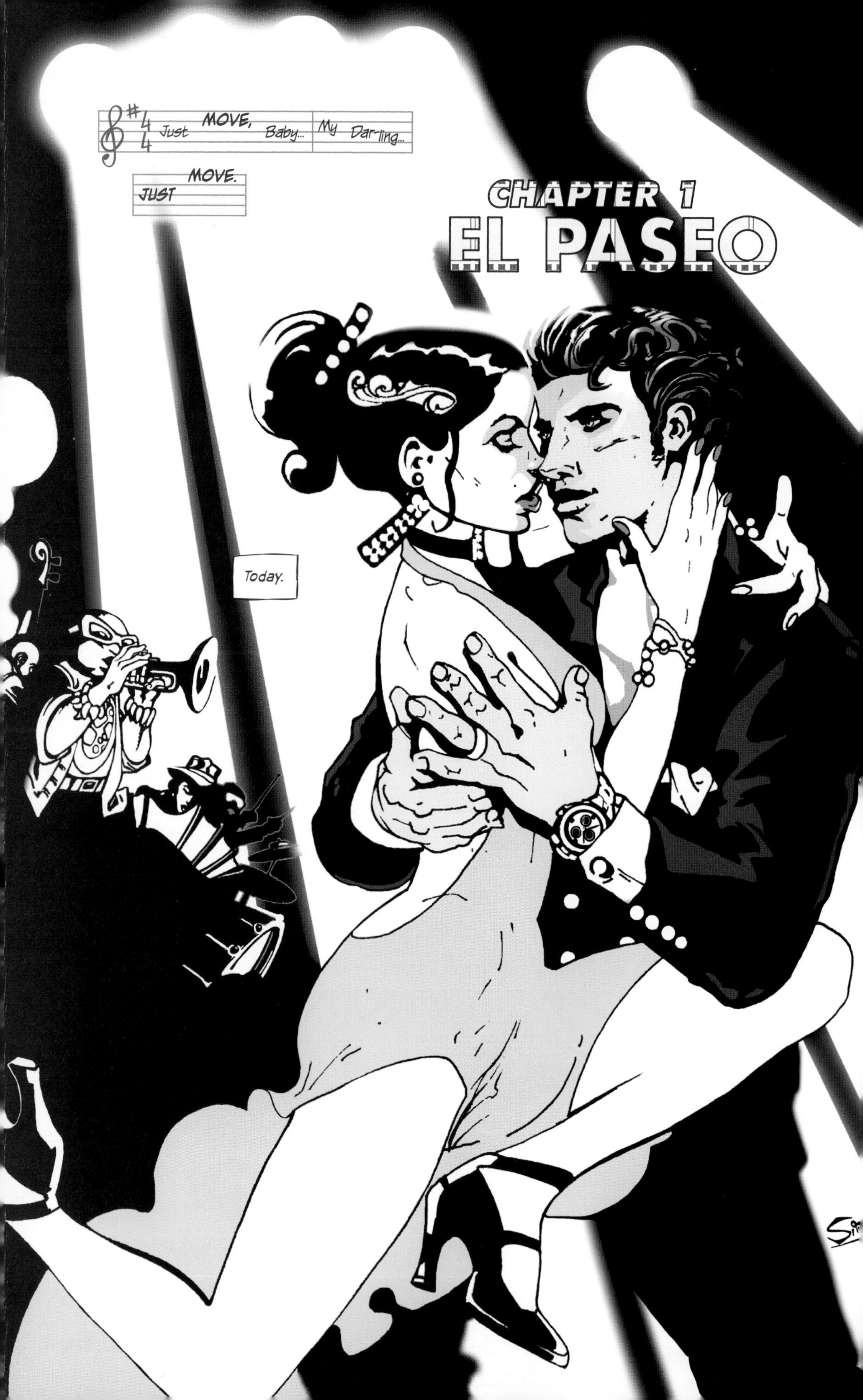
Just MOVE, Baby... My Dar-ling...
JUST MOVE.
CHAPTER 1
EL PASEO
Today.

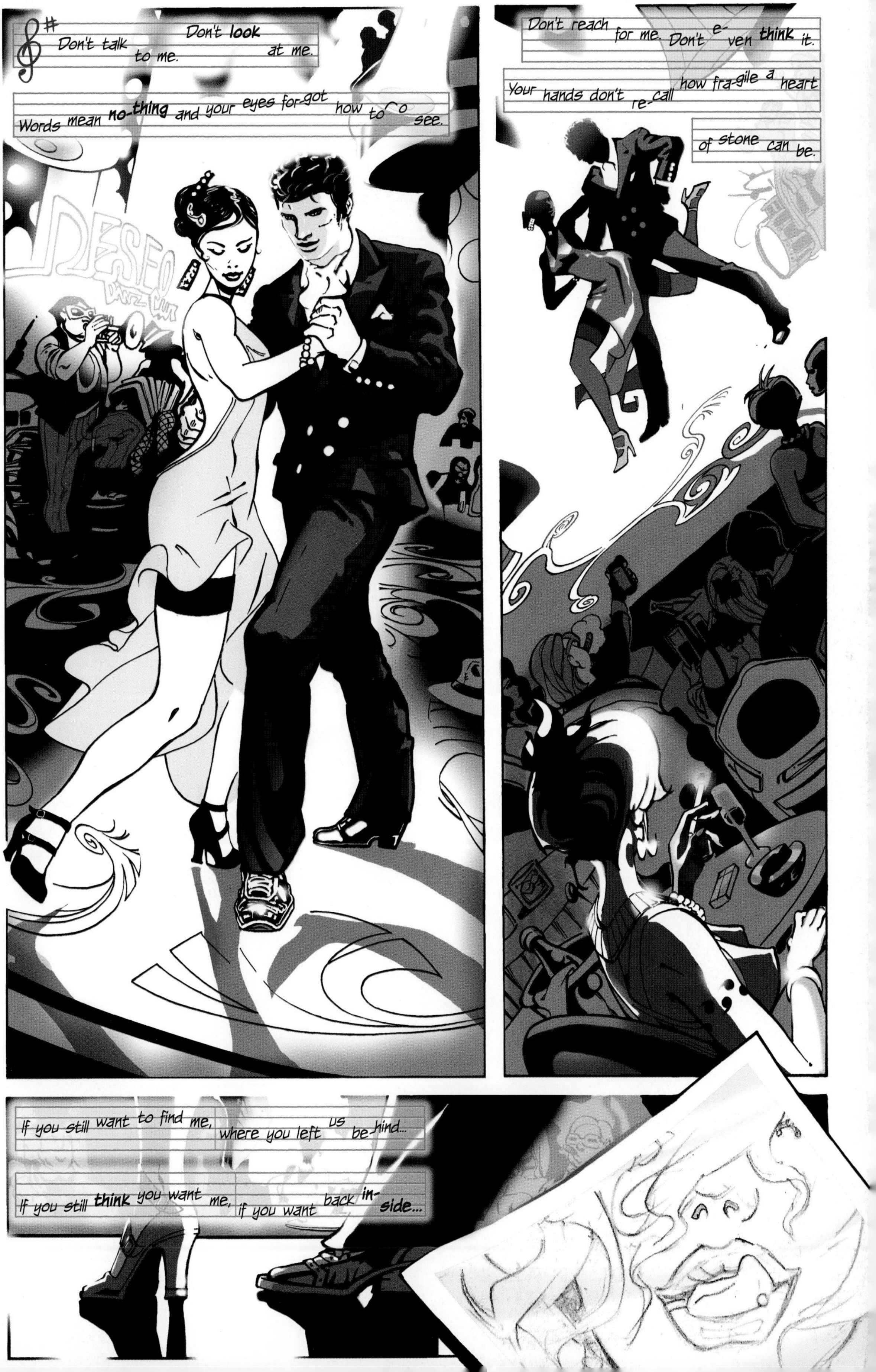
Don't talk to me. Don't look at me.
Words mean no-thing and your eyes for-got how to see.
DESEO
Don't reach for me. Don't e-ven think it.
Your hands don't re-call how fra-gile a heart
of stone can be.
If you still want to find me, where you left us be-hind...
If you still think you want me, if you want back in-side...

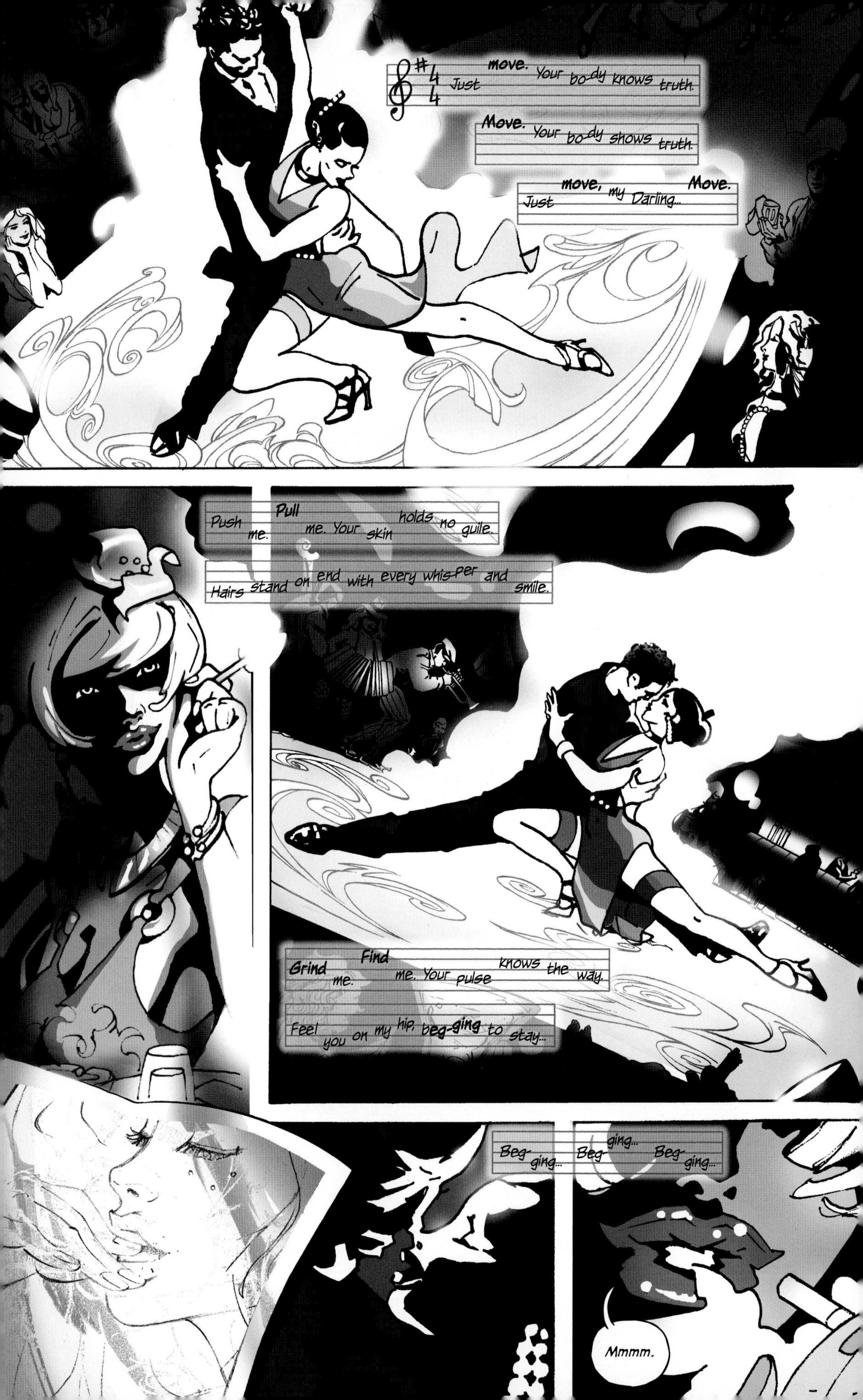
Just move. Your body knows truth.
Move. Your body shows truth.
Just move, my Darling... Move.
Push me. Pull me. Your skin holds no guile.
Hairs stand on end with every whisper and smile.
Grind me. Find me. Your pulse knows the way.
Feel you on my hip, begging to stay...
Beg-ging... Beg-ging... Beg-ging...
Mmmm.

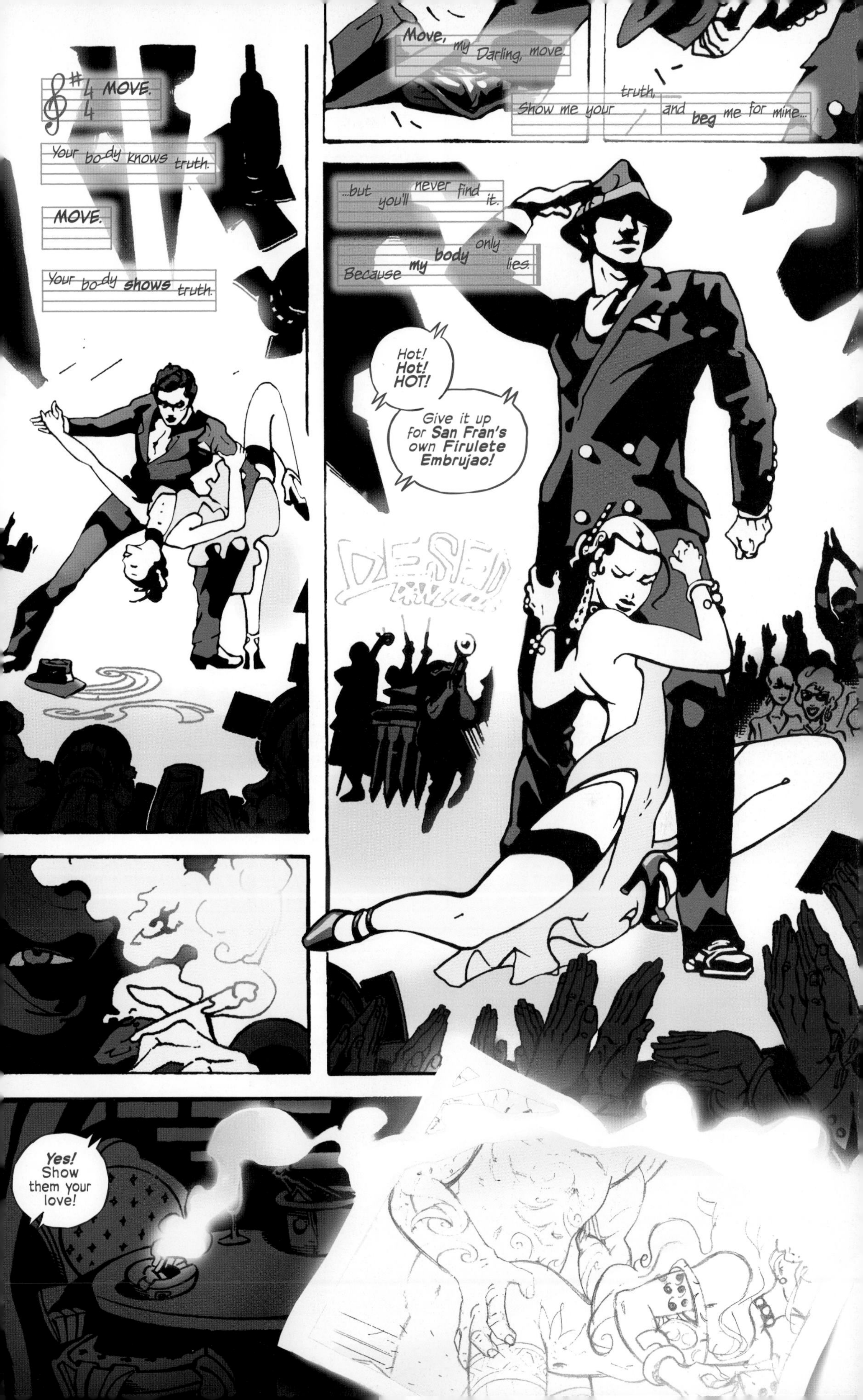
MOVE.
Your body knows truth.
MOVE.
Your body shows truth.
Move, my Darling, move.
Show me your truth, and beg me for mine...
...but you'll never find it.
Because my body only lies.
Hot! Hot! HOT!
Give it up for San Fran's own Firulete Embrujao!
Yes! Show them your love!

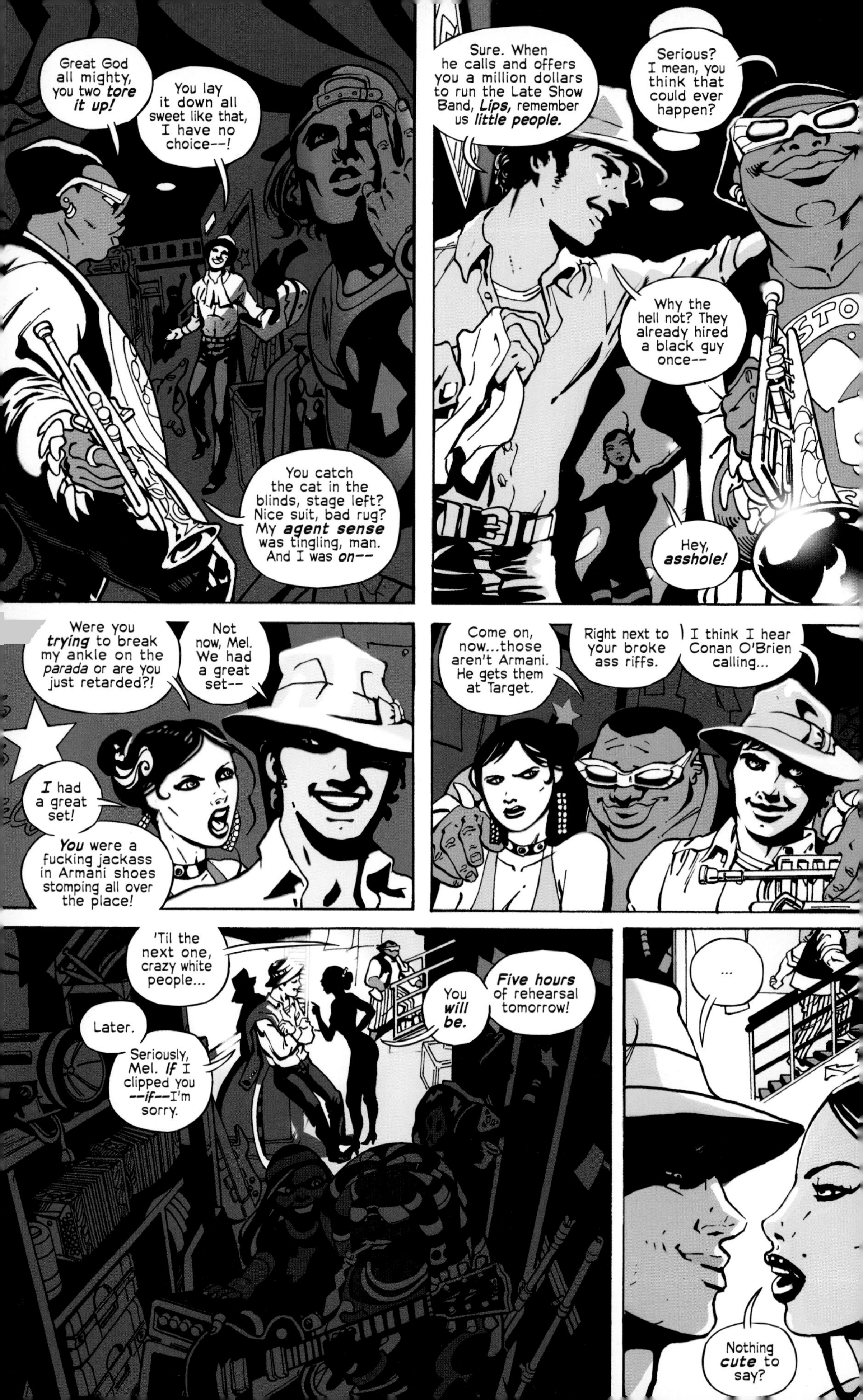

Great God all mighty, you two *tore it up!*
You lay it down all sweet like that, I have no choice--!
You catch the cat in the blinds, stage left? Nice suit, bad rug? My ***agent sense*** was tingling, man. And I was *on*--
Sure. When he calls and offers you a million dollars to run the Late Show Band, ***Lips,*** remember us ***little people.***
Serious? I mean, you think that could ever happen?
Why the hell not? They already hired a black guy once--
Hey, ***asshole!***
Were you ***trying*** to break my ankle on the *parada* or are you just retarded?!
Not now, Mel. We had a great set--
I had a great set!
You were a fucking jackass in Armani shoes stomping all over the place!
Come on, now...those aren't Armani. He gets them at Target.
Right next to your broke ass riffs.
I think I hear Conan O'Brien calling...
'Til the next one, crazy white people...
Later.
Seriously, Mel. ***If*** I clipped you ***--if--***I'm sorry.
You ***will be.***
Five hours of rehearsal tomorrow!
...
Nothing ***cute*** to say?

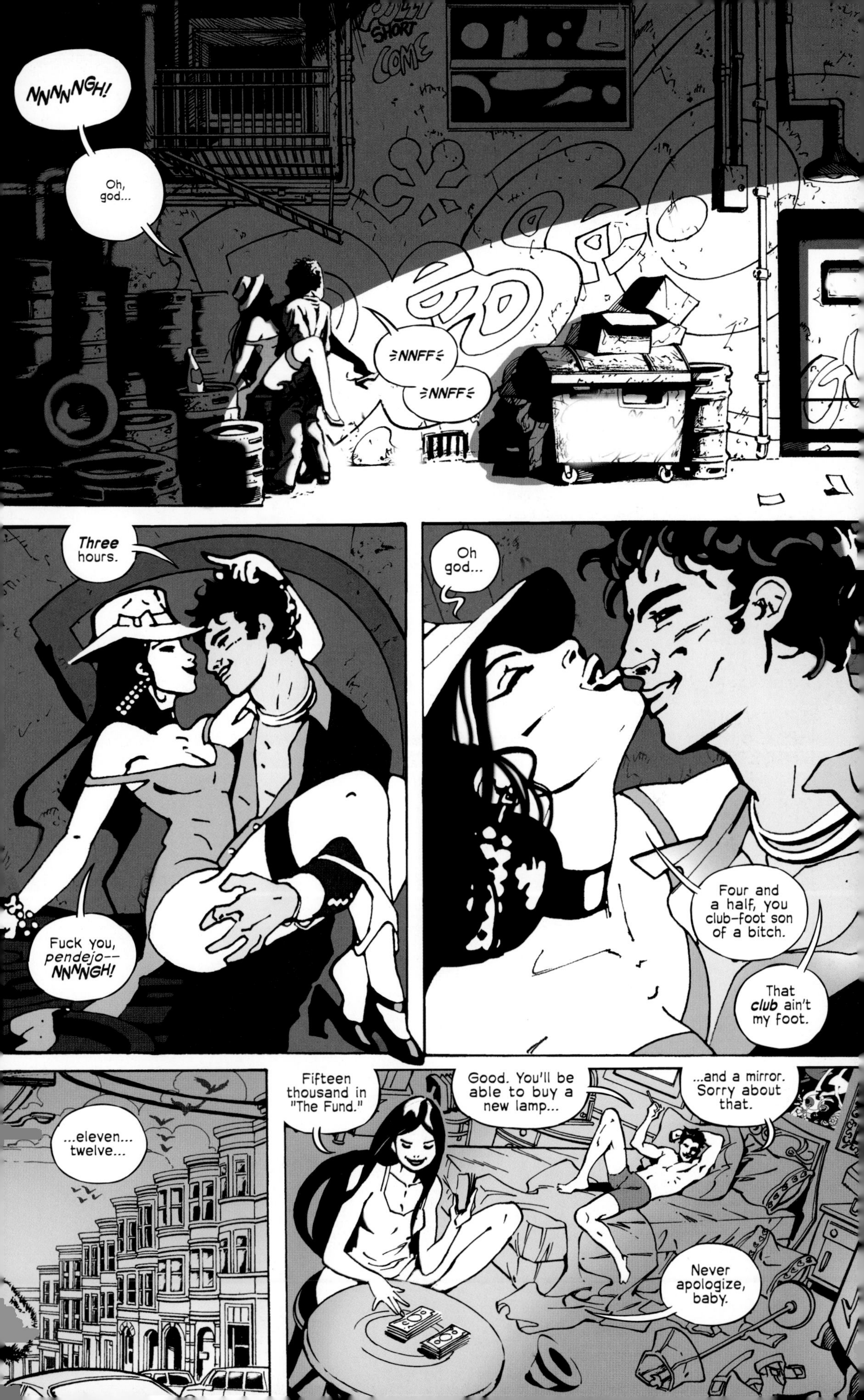
NNNNNGH!
Oh, god...
SHORT
COME
NNFF
NNFF
Three hours.
Fuck you, pendejo-- NNNNGH!
Oh god...
Four and a half, you club-foot son of a bitch.
That club ain't my foot.
...eleven... twelve...
Fifteen thousand in "The Fund."
Good. You'll be able to buy a new lamp...
...and a mirror. Sorry about that.
Never apologize, baby.

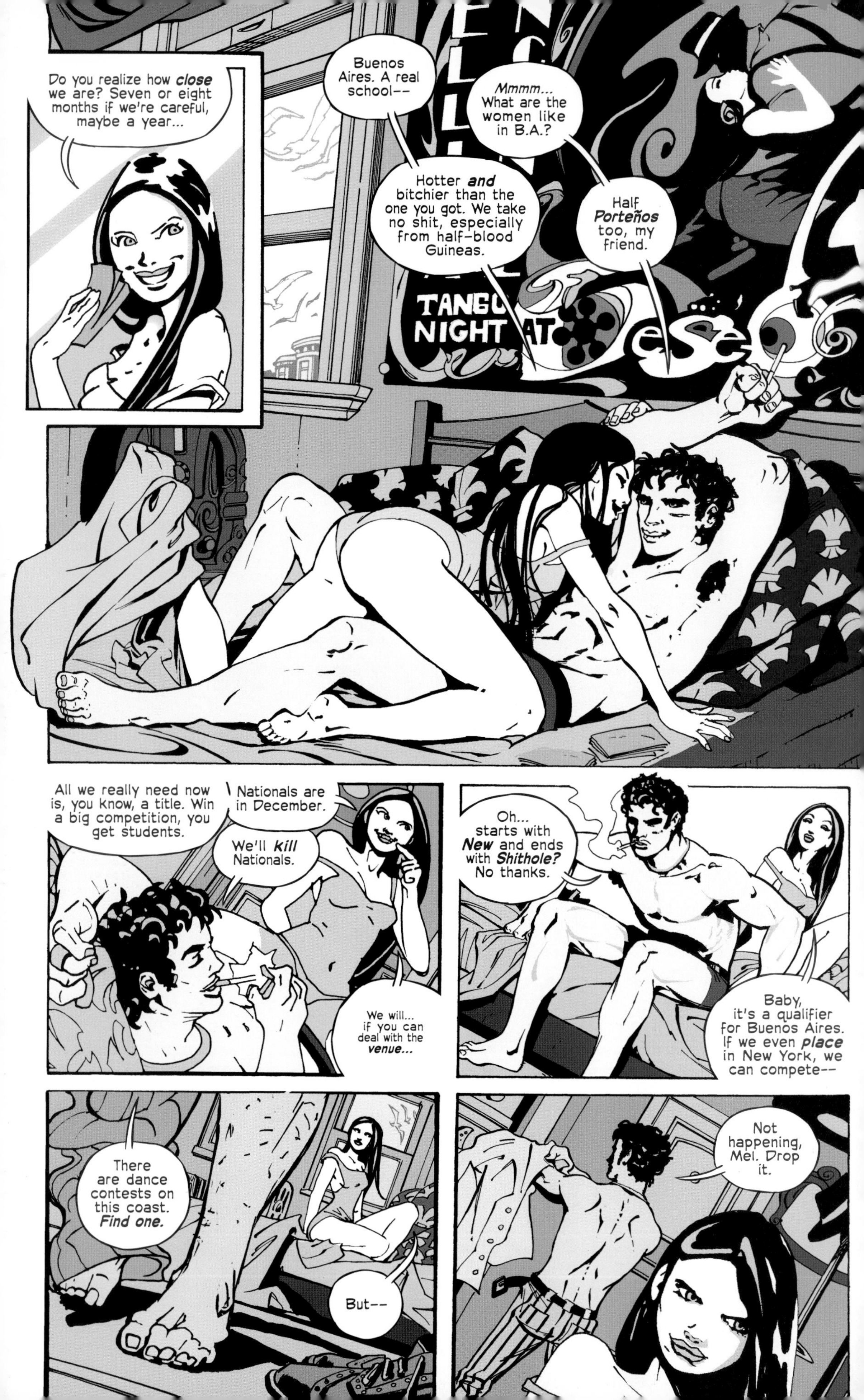

Do you realize how *close* we are? Seven or eight months if we're careful, maybe a year...
Buenos Aires. A real school--
Mmmm... What are the women like in B.A.?
Hotter *and* bitchier than the one you got. We take no shit, especially from half-blood Guineas.
Half *Porteños* too, my friend.
All we really need now is, you know, a title. Win a big competition, you get students.
Nationals are in December.
We'll *kill* Nationals.
We will... if you can deal with the *venue...*
Oh... starts with *New* and ends with *Shithole?* No thanks.
Baby, it's a qualifier for Buenos Aires. If we even *place* in New York, we can compete--
There are dance contests on this coast. *Find one.*
But--
Not happening, Mel. Drop it.

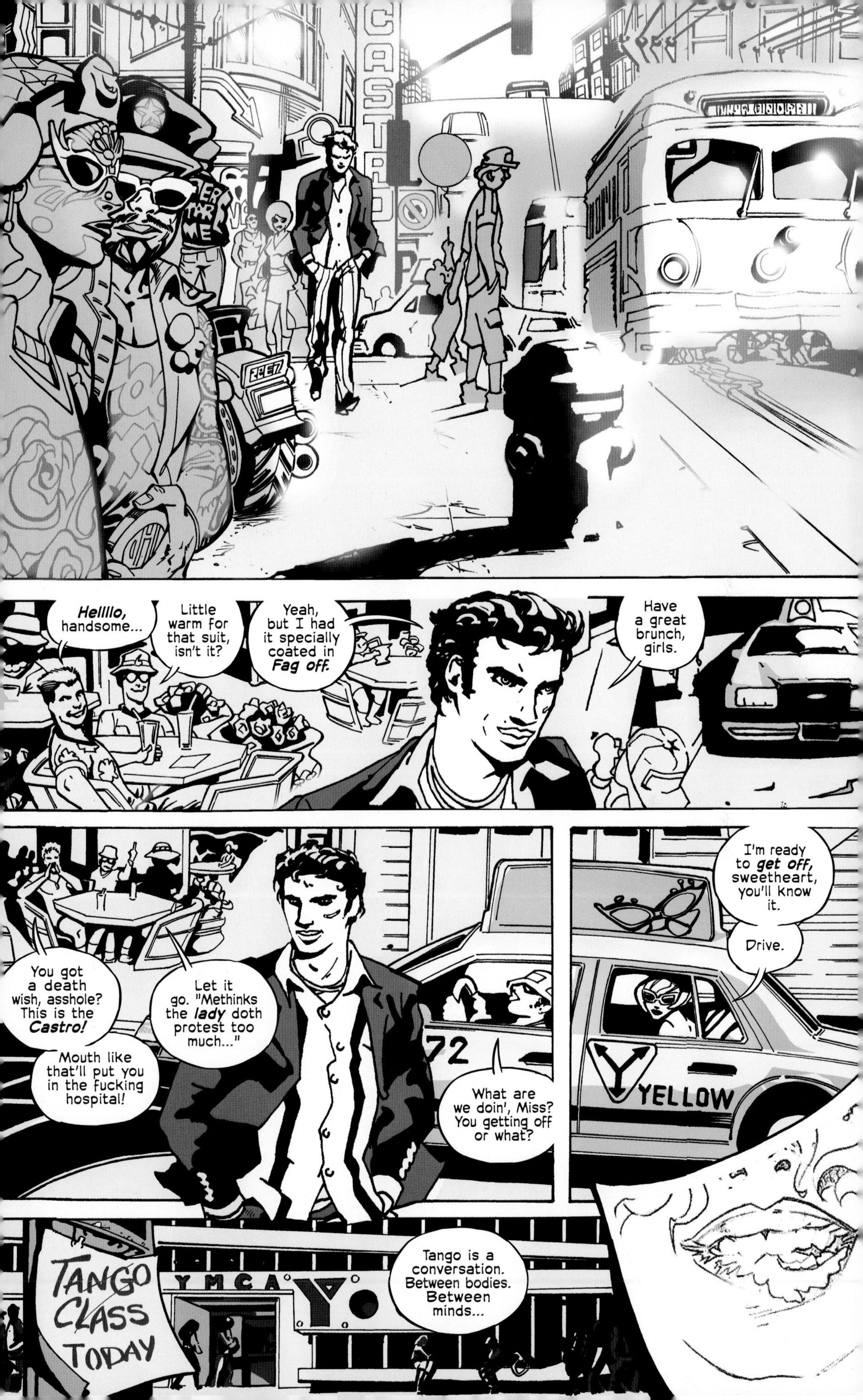
CASTRO
Hellllo, handsome...
Little warm for that suit, isn't it?
Yeah, but I had it specially coated in Fag off.
Have a great brunch, girls.
You got a death wish, asshole? This is the Castro!
Mouth like that'll put you in the fucking hospital!
Let it go. "Methinks the lady doth protest too much..."
72
YELLOW
What are we doin', Miss? You getting off or what?
I'm ready to get off, sweetheart, you'll know it.
Drive.
TANGO CLASS TODAY
YMCA
Tango is a conversation. Between bodies. Between minds...

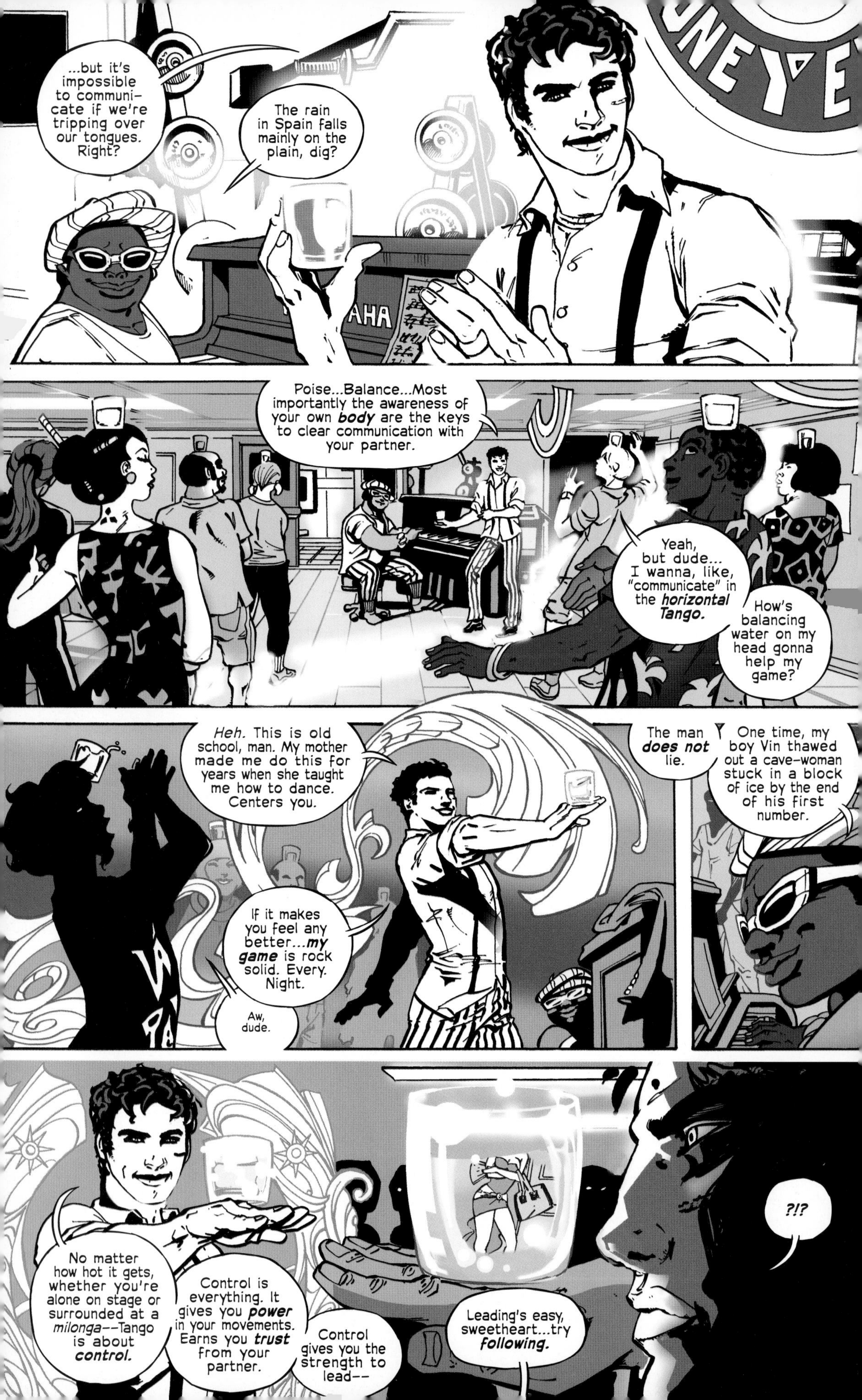

...but it's impossible to communicate if we're tripping over our tongues. Right?
The rain in Spain falls mainly on the plain, dig?
Poise...Balance...Most importantly the awareness of your own *body* are the keys to clear communication with your partner.
Yeah, but dude... I wanna, like, "communicate" in the *horizontal Tango.*
How's balancing water on my head gonna help my game?
Heh. This is old school, man. My mother made me do this for years when she taught me how to dance. Centers you.
If it makes you feel any better...*my game* is rock solid. Every. Night.
Aw, dude.
The man *does not* lie.
One time, my boy Vin thawed out a cave-woman stuck in a block of ice by the end of his first number.
No matter how hot it gets, whether you're alone on stage or surrounded at a *milonga*--Tango is about *control.*
Control is everything. It gives you *power* in your movements. Earns you *trust* from your partner.
Control gives you the strength to lead--
Leading's easy, sweetheart...try *following.*
?!?

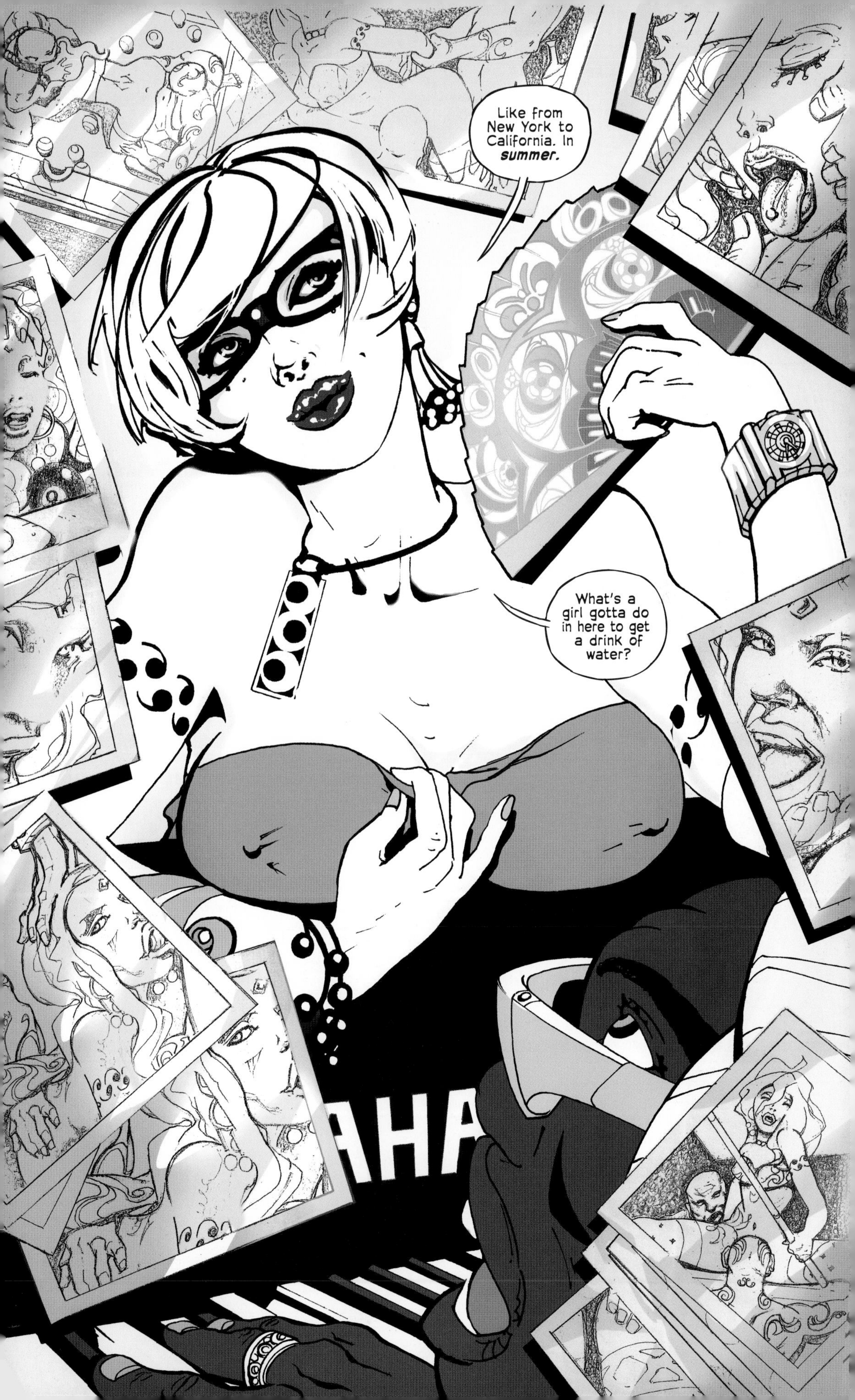
Like from New York to California. In *summer.*
What's a girl gotta do in here to get a drink of water?

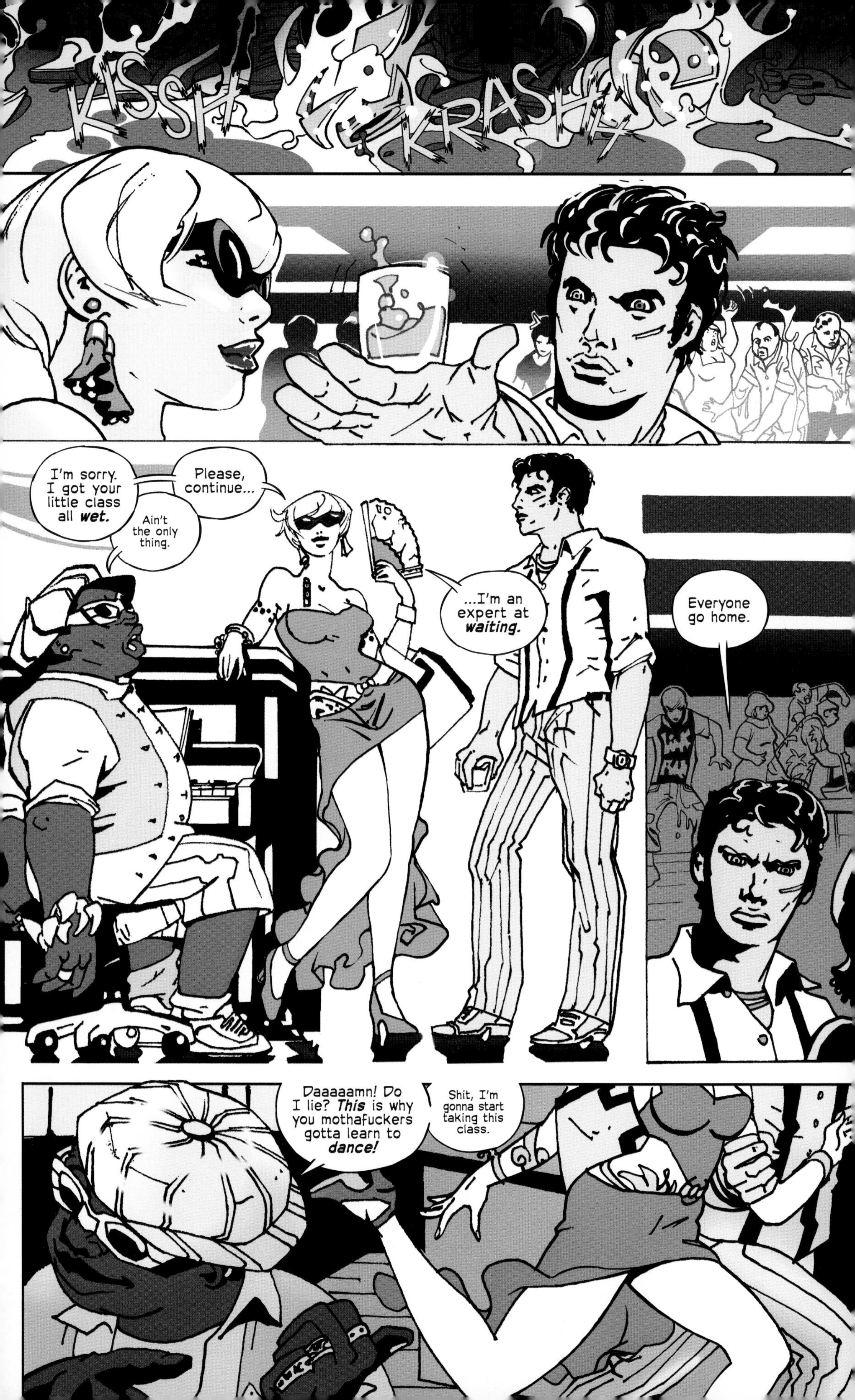
KISSH
KRASHH
I'm sorry. I got your little class all *wet.*
Please, continue...
Ain't the only thing.
...I'm an expert at *waiting.*
Everyone go home.
Daaaaamn! Do I lie? *This* is why you mothafuckers gotta learn to *dance!*
Shit, I'm gonna start taking this class.

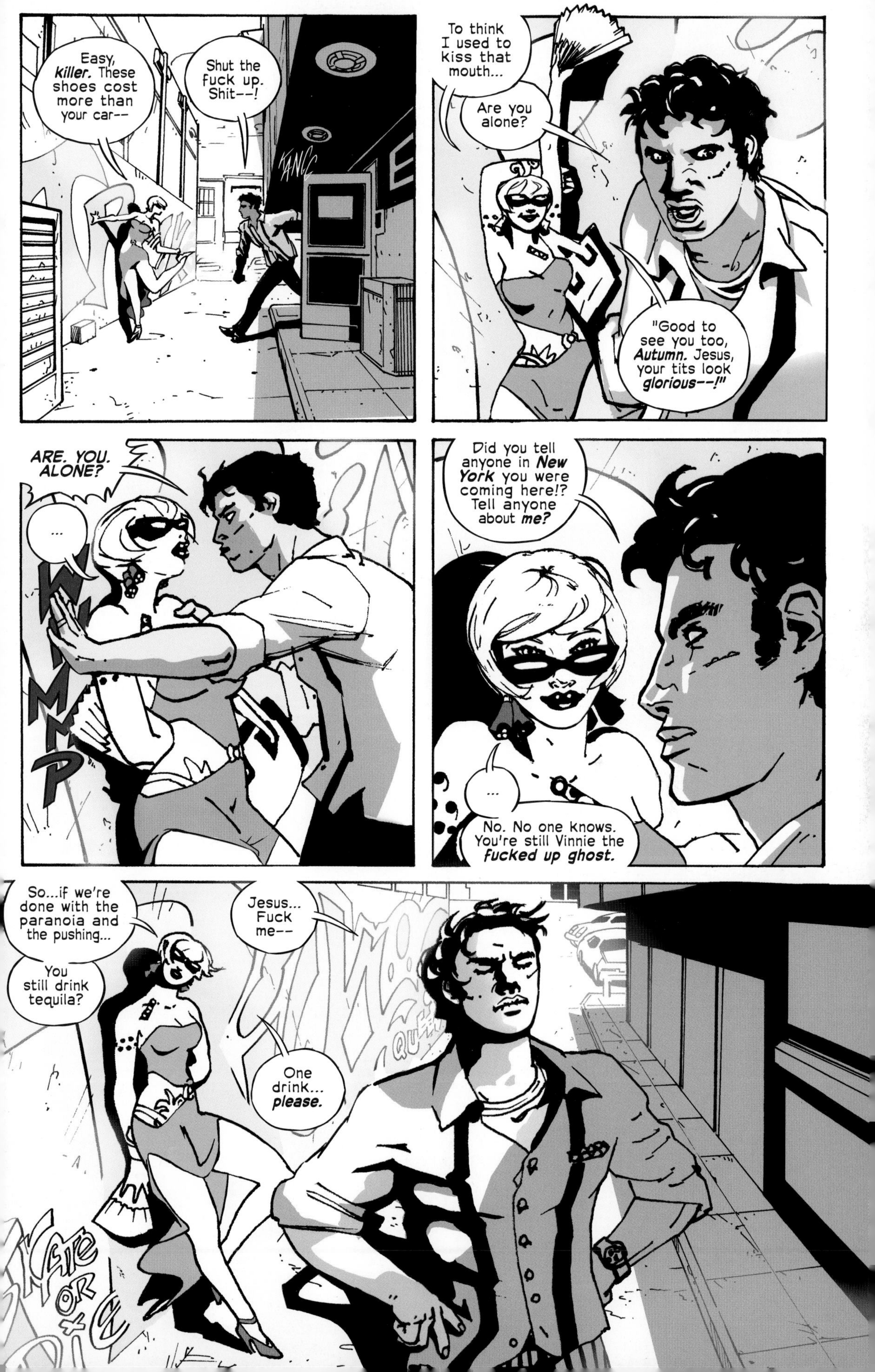
Easy, *killer.* These shoes cost more than your car--
Shut the fuck up. Shit--!
KANG
To think I used to kiss that mouth...
Are you alone?
"Good to see you too, *Autumn.* Jesus, your tits look *glorious--!"*
ARE. YOU. ALONE?
...
Did you tell anyone in *New York* you were coming here!? Tell anyone about *me?*
...
No. No one knows. You're still Vinnie the *fucked up ghost.*
So...if we're done with the paranoia and the pushing...
You still drink tequila?
Jesus... Fuck me--
One drink... *please.*

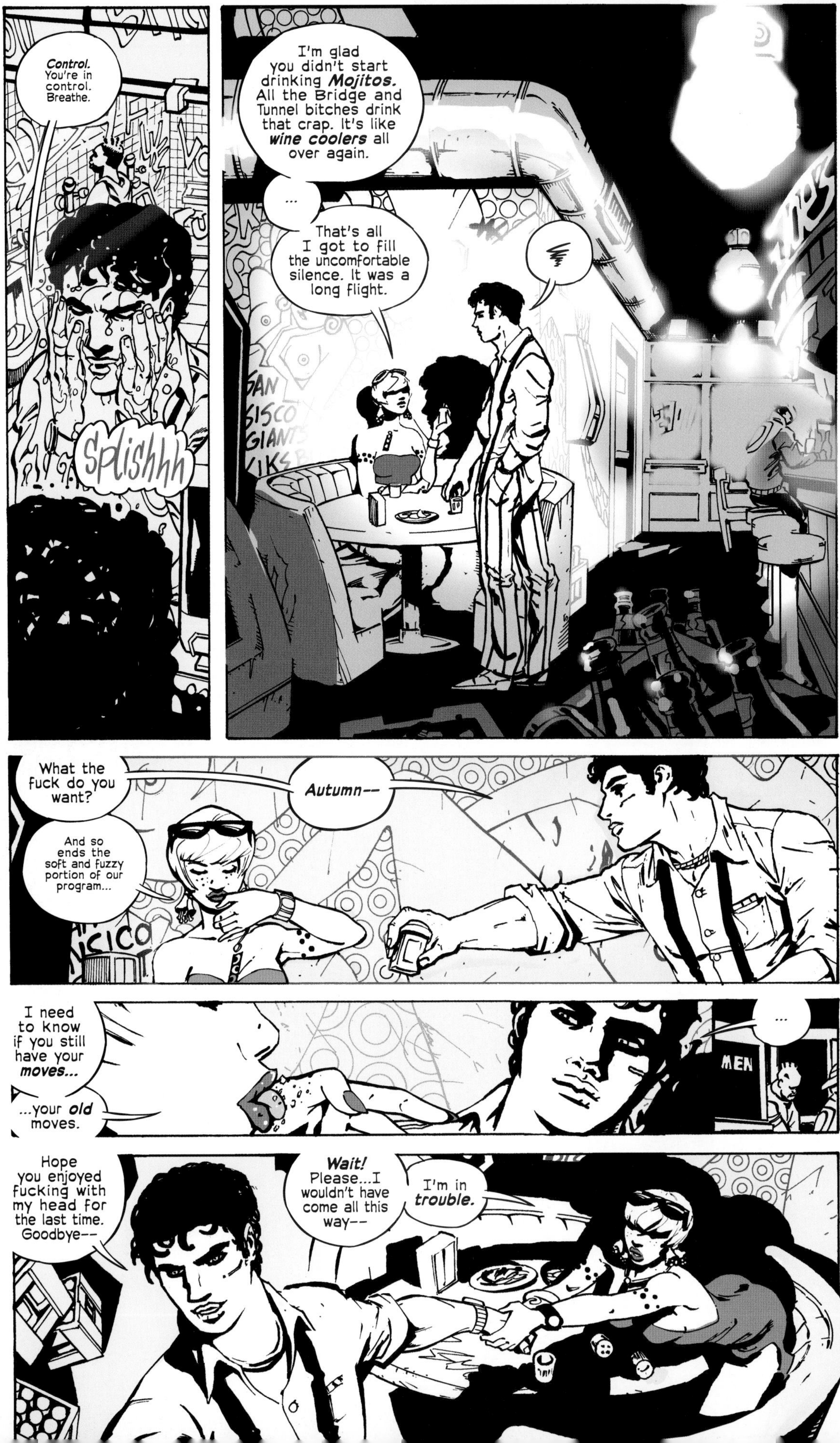

Control. You're in control. Breathe.
Splishhh
I'm glad you didn't start drinking Mojitos. All the Bridge and Tunnel bitches drink that crap. It's like wine coolers all over again.
...
That's all I got to fill the uncomfortable silence. It was a long flight.
What the fuck do you want?
Autumn--
And so ends the soft and fuzzy portion of our program...
I need to know if you still have your moves...
...your old moves.
...
MEN
Hope you enjoyed fucking with my head for the last time. Goodbye--
Wait! Please...I wouldn't have come all this way--
I'm in trouble.

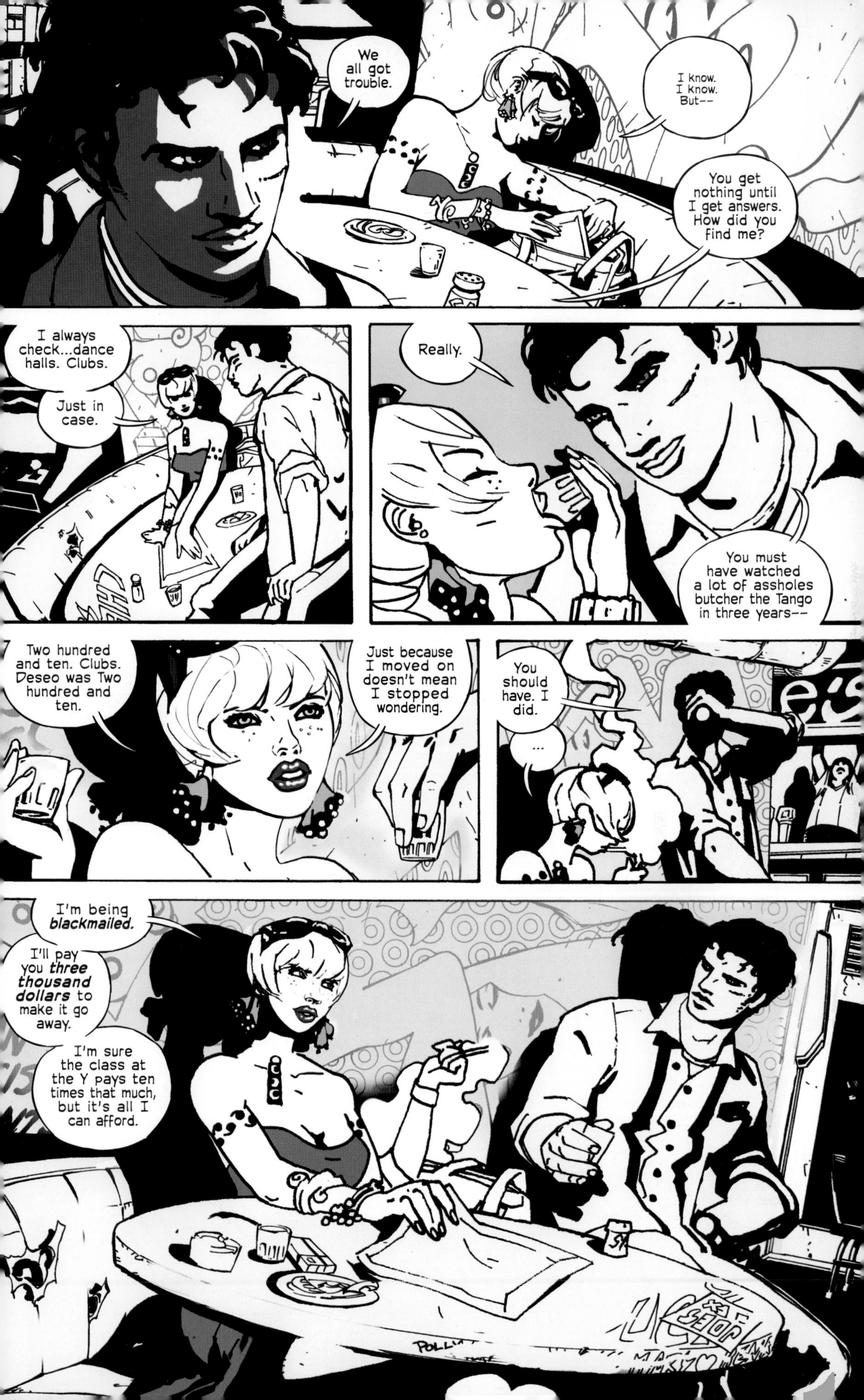

We all got trouble.
I know. I know. But--
You get nothing until I get answers. How did you find me?
I always check...dance halls. Clubs.
Just in case.
Really.
You must have watched a lot of assholes butcher the Tango in three years--
Two hundred and ten. Clubs. Deseo was Two hundred and ten.
Just because I moved on doesn't mean I stopped wondering.
You should have. I did.
...
I'm being *blackmailed.*
I'll pay you ***three thousand dollars*** to make it go away.
I'm sure the class at the Y pays ten times that much, but it's all I can afford.

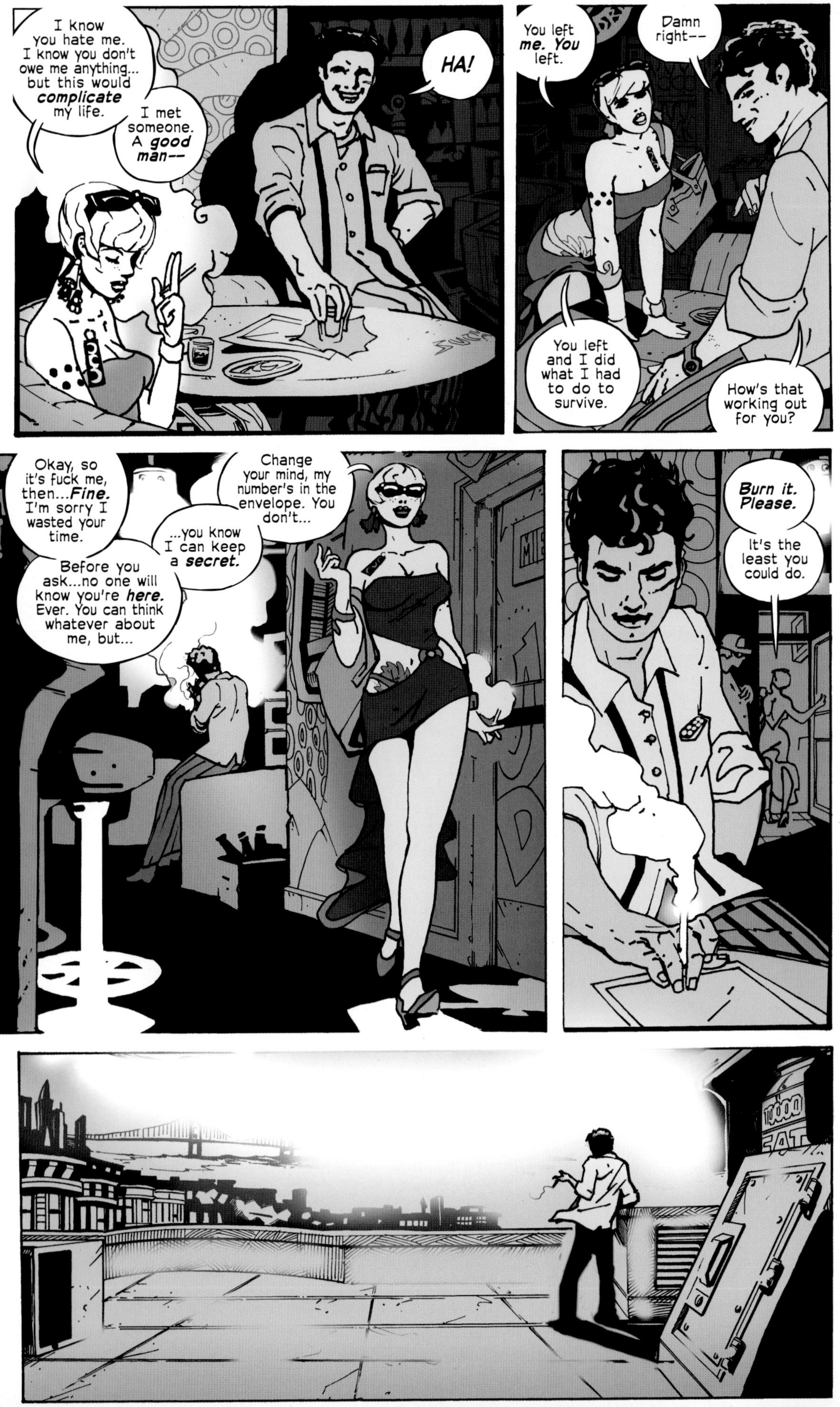
I know you hate me. I know you don't owe me anything... but this would *complicate* my life.
I met someone. A *good man--*
HA!
You left *me. You* left.
Damn right--
You left and I did what I had to do to survive.
How's that working out for you?
Okay, so it's fuck me, then... *Fine.* I'm sorry I wasted your time.
Before you ask...no one will know you're *here.* Ever. You can think whatever about me, but...
...you know I can keep a *secret.*
Change your mind, my number's in the envelope. You don't...
Burn it. Please.
It's the least you could do.

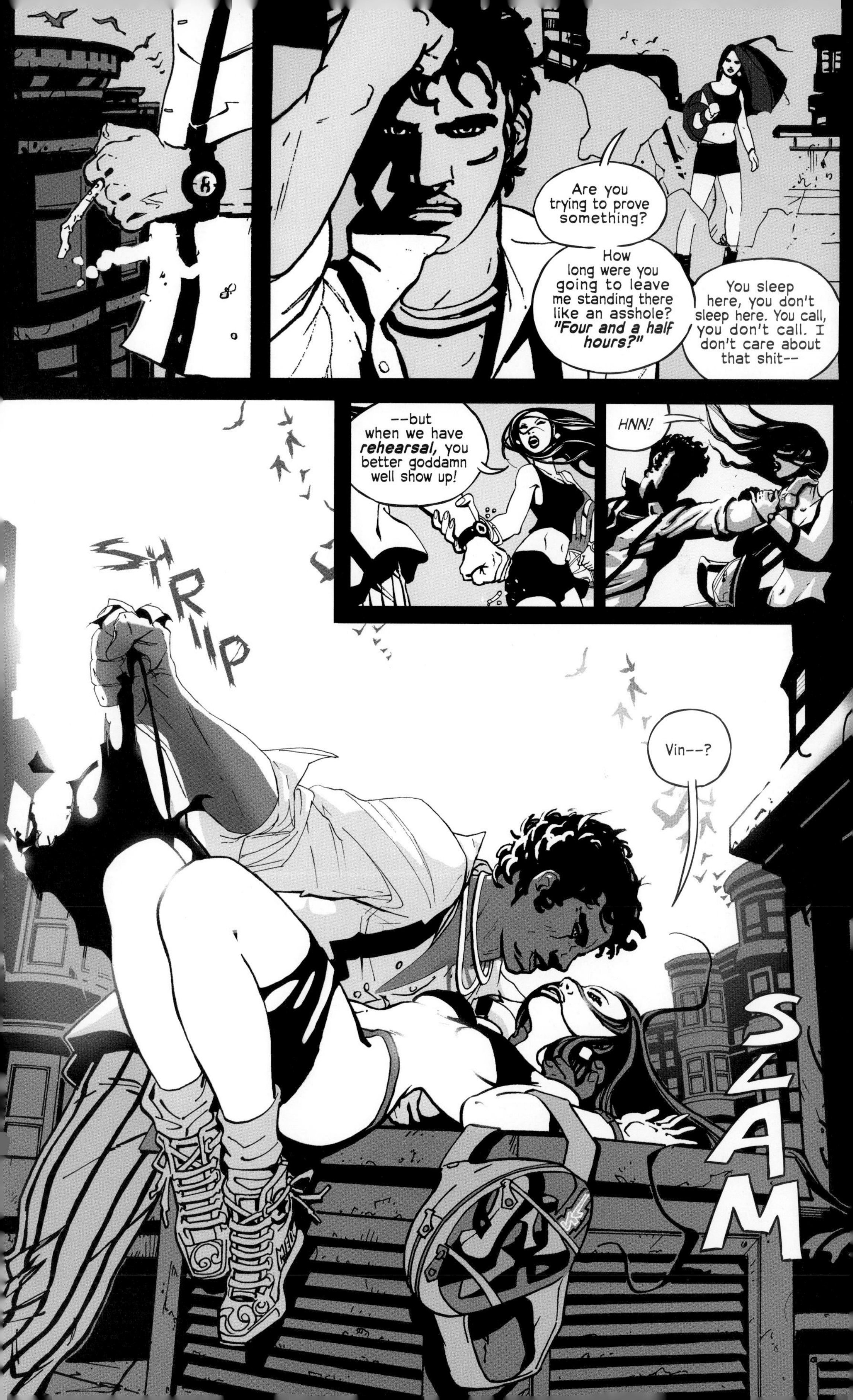
Are you trying to prove something?
How long were you going to leave me standing there like an asshole? "Four and a half hours?"
You sleep here, you don't sleep here. You call, you don't call. I don't care about that shit--
--but when we have rehearsal, you better goddamn well show up!
HNN!
SHRIIP
Vin--?
SLAM

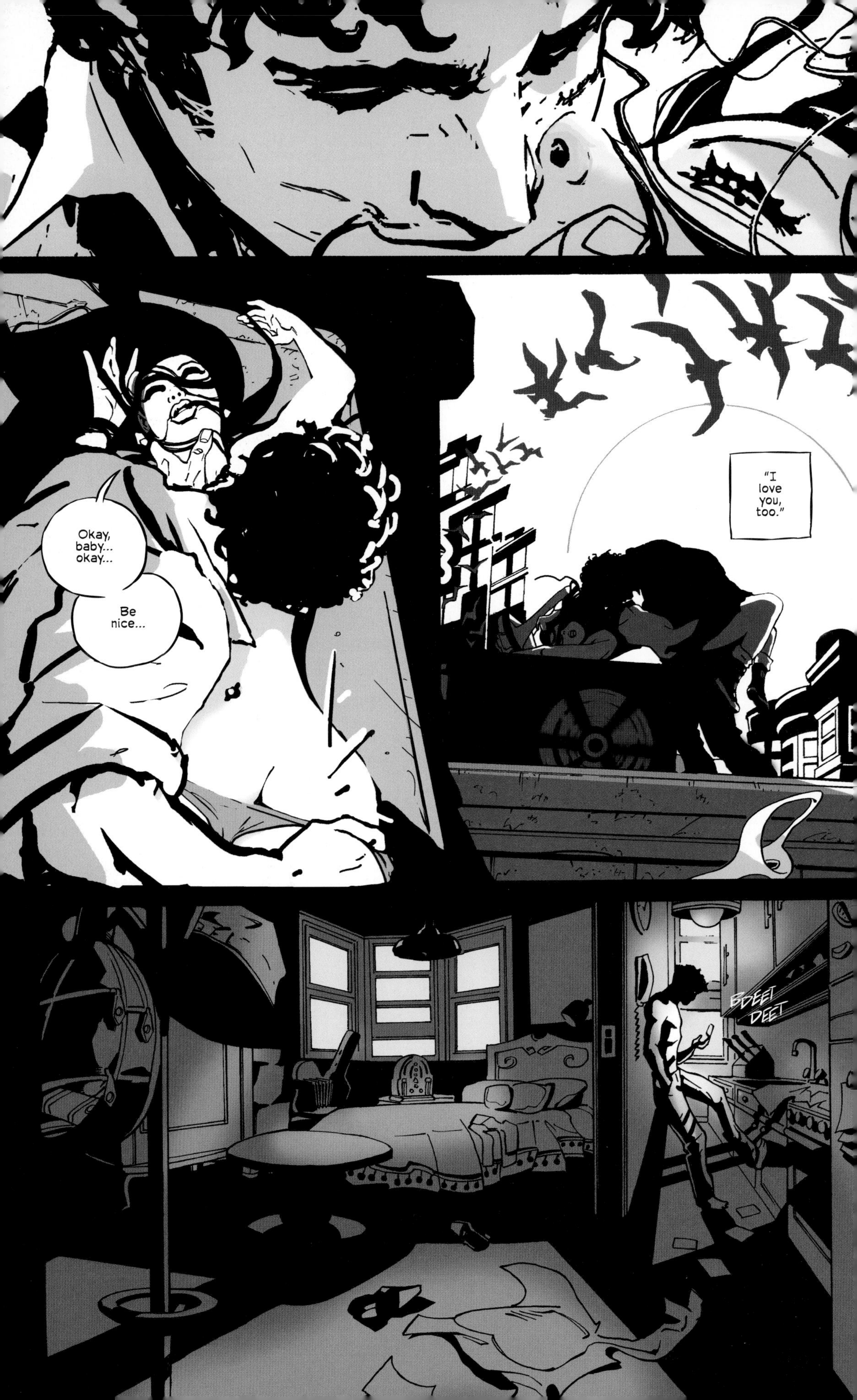

Okay, baby... okay...
Be nice...
"I love you, too."
BDEET DEET

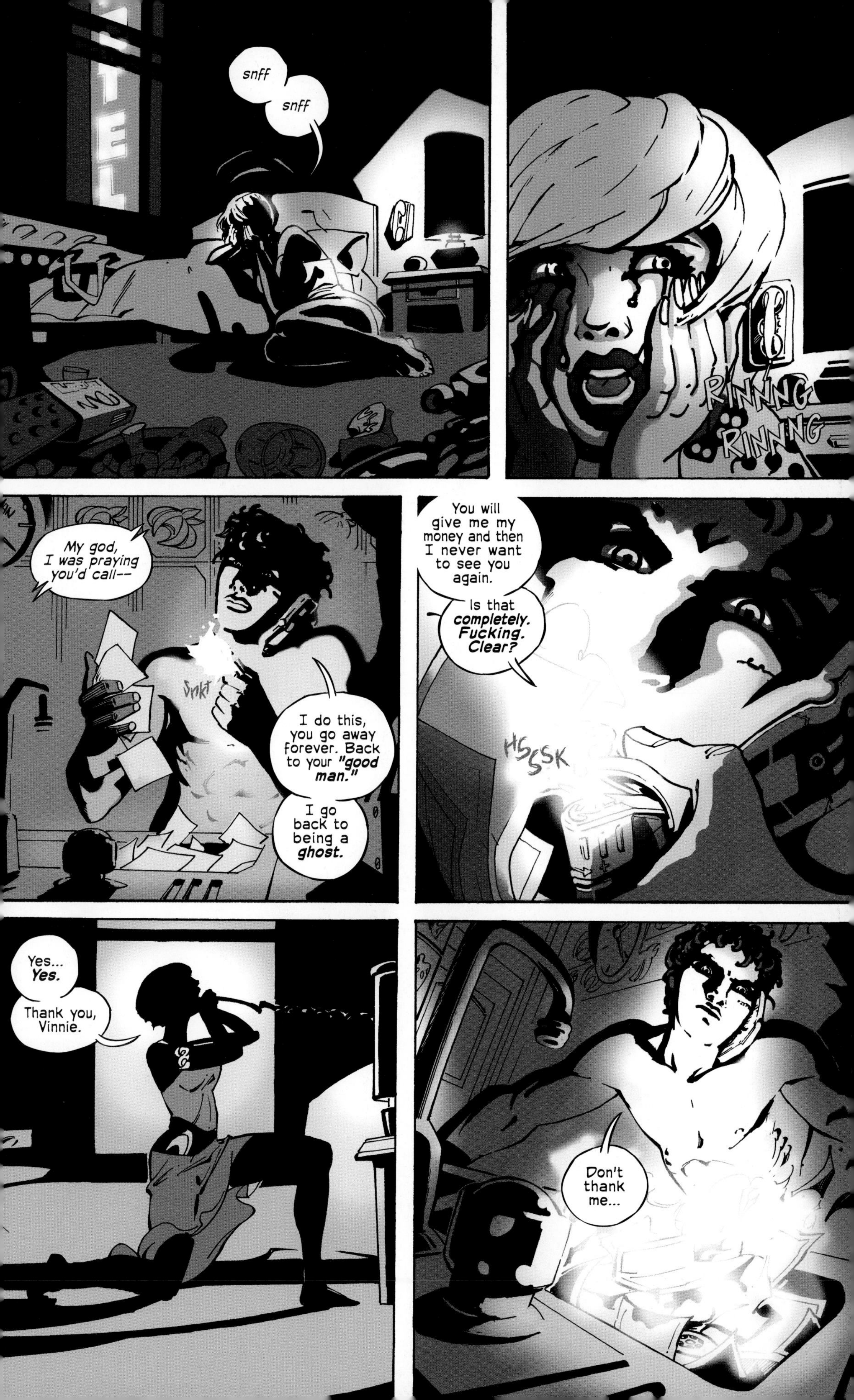

TEL
snff
snff
RINNNG
RINNNG
My god, I was praying you'd call--
SNKT
I do this, you go away forever. Back to your *"good man."*
I go back to being a ***ghost.***
You will give me my money and then I never want to see you again.
Is that ***completely. Fucking. Clear?***
HSSSK
Yes... ***Yes.***
Thank you, Vinnie.
Don't thank me...

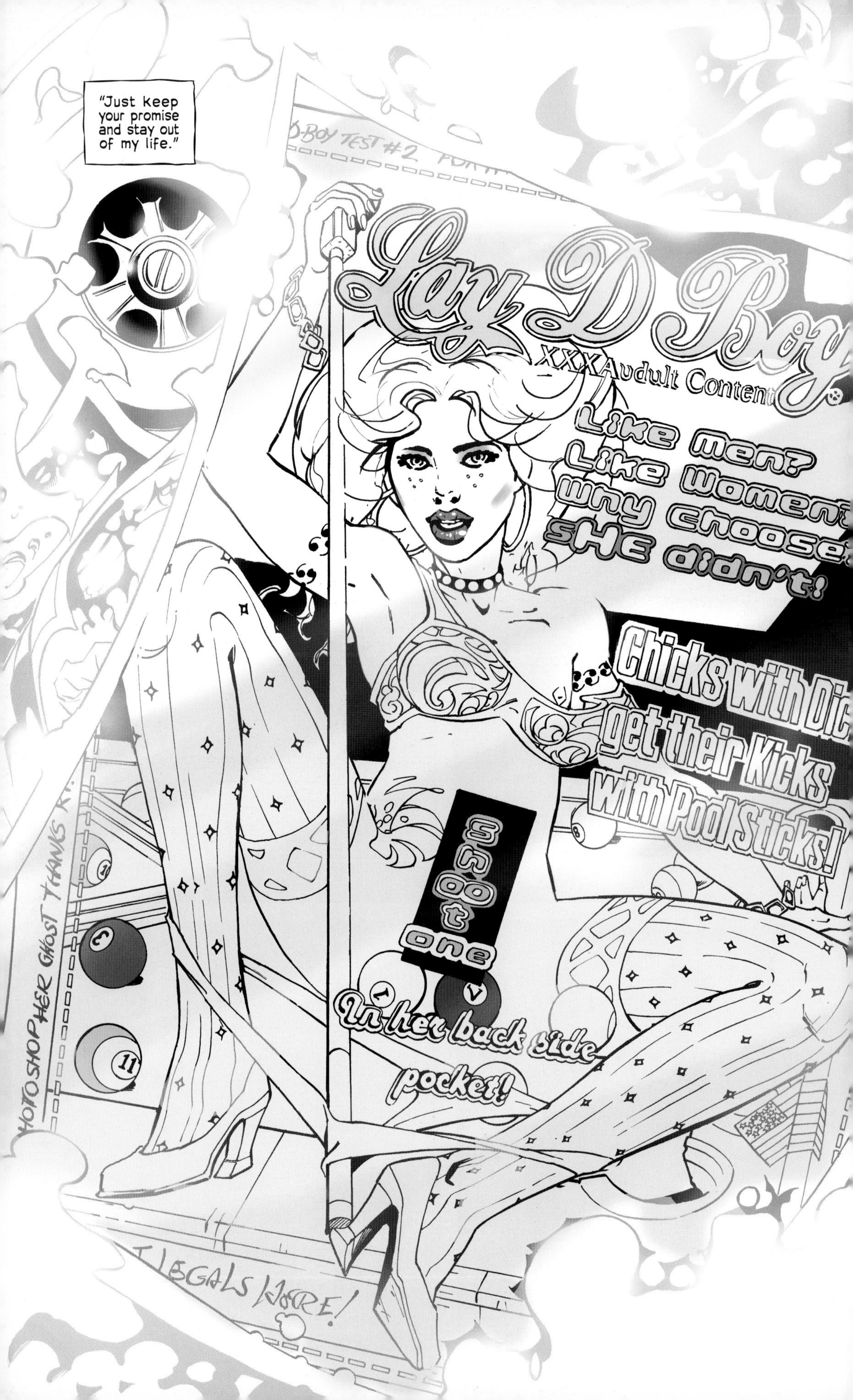
"Just keep your promise and stay out of my life."
D-BOY TEST #2 FOR
Lay D Boy
XXXAudult Content
Like men?
Like women
why choose
sHE didn't!
Chicks with Dic
get their Kicks
with Pool Sticks!
shoot one
In her back side pocket!
HOTOSHOP HER GHOST THANKS
LEGALS WERE!

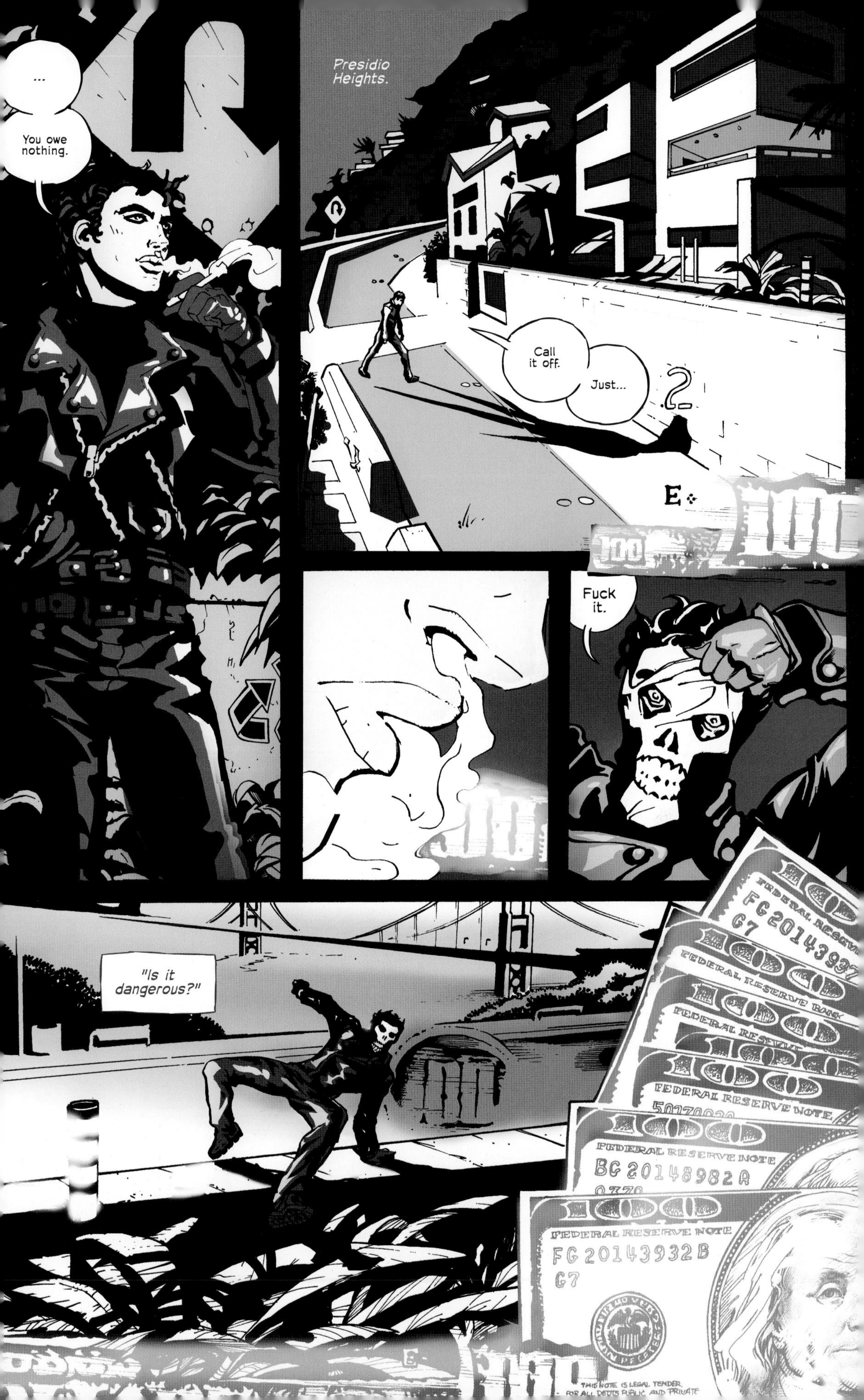
...
You owe nothing.
Presidio Heights.
Call it off.
Just...
Fuck it.
"Is it dangerous?"
FEDERAL RESERVE NOTE
FG 20143932 B
G7
BG 20148982 A
THIS NOTE IS LEGAL TENDER FOR ALL DEBTS PUBLIC AND PRIVATE

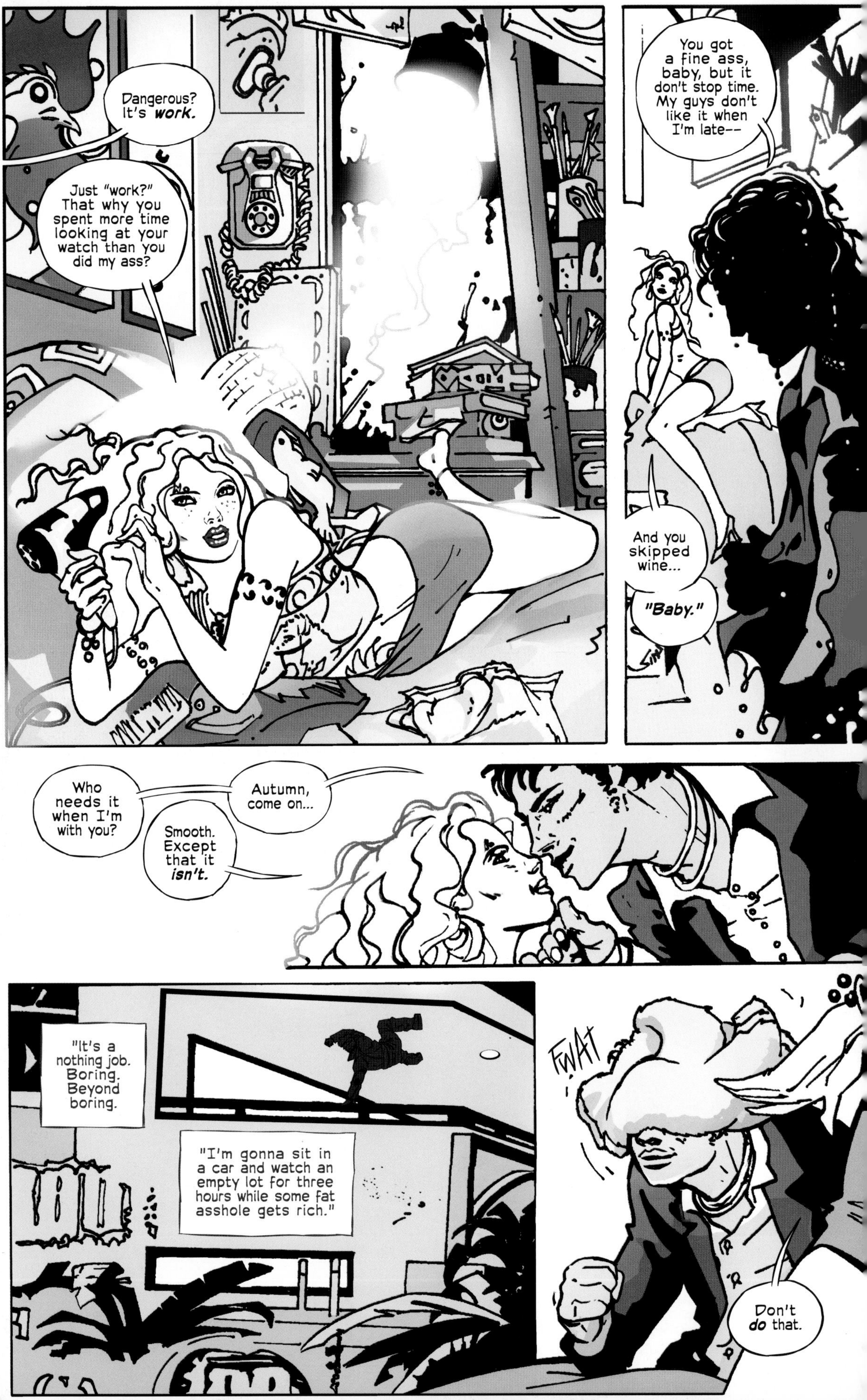
Dangerous? It's *work.*
Just "work?" That why you spent more time looking at your watch than you did my ass?
You got a fine ass, baby, but it don't stop time. My guys don't like it when I'm late--
And you skipped wine...
"Baby."
Who needs it when I'm with you?
Autumn, come on...
Smooth. Except that it *isn't.*
"It's a nothing job. Boring. Beyond boring.
"I'm gonna sit in a car and watch an empty lot for three hours while some fat asshole gets rich."
FWAT
Don't *do* that.

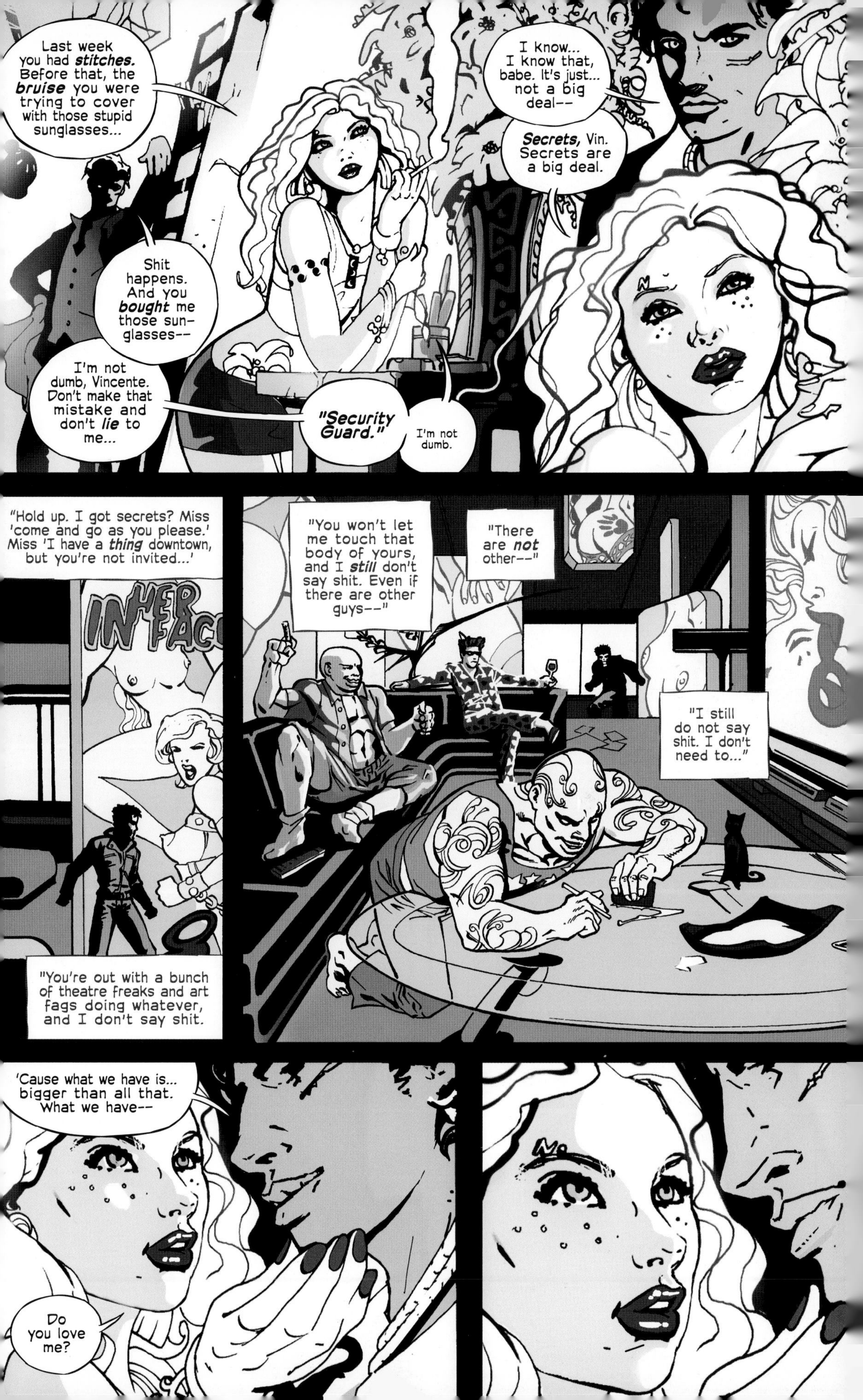

Last week you had *stitches.* Before that, the *bruise* you were trying to cover with those stupid sunglasses...
I know... I know that, babe. It's just... not a big deal--
Secrets, Vin. Secrets are a big deal.
Shit happens. And you *bought* me those sun-glasses--
I'm not dumb, Vincente. Don't make that mistake and don't *lie* to me...
"Security Guard."
I'm not dumb.
"Hold up. I got secrets? Miss 'come and go as you please.' Miss 'I have a *thing* downtown, but you're not invited...'
IN HER FACE
"You're out with a bunch of theatre freaks and art fags doing whatever, and I don't say shit.
"You won't let me touch that body of yours, and I *still* don't say shit. Even if there are other guys--"
"There are *not* other--"
"I still do not say shit. I don't need to..."
'Cause what we have is... bigger than all that. What we have--
Do you love me?

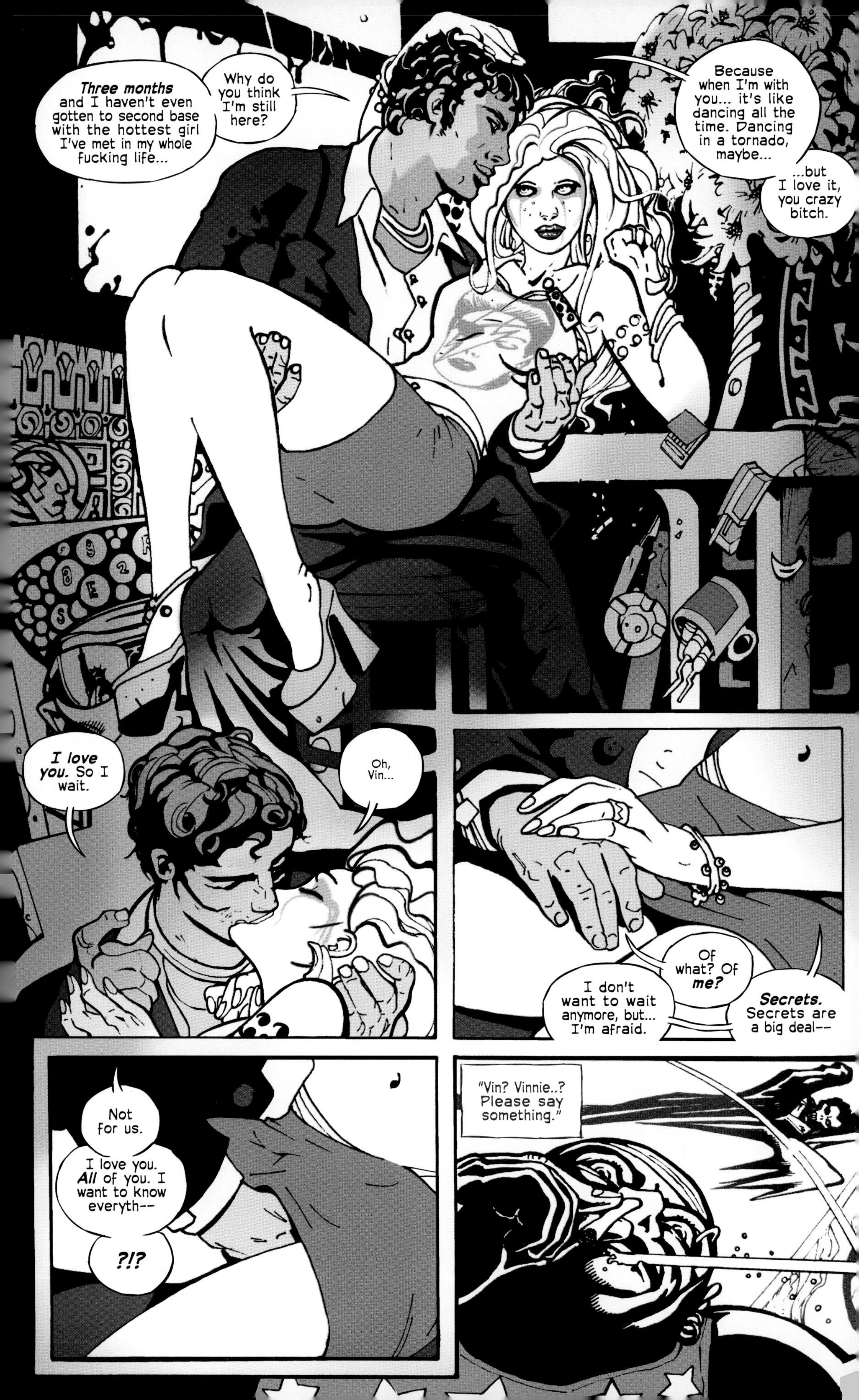

Three months and I haven't even gotten to second base with the hottest girl I've met in my whole fucking life...
Why do you think I'm still here?
Because when I'm with you... it's like dancing all the time. Dancing in a tornado, maybe...
...but I love it, you crazy bitch.
I love you. So I wait.
Oh, Vin...
I don't want to wait anymore, but... I'm afraid.
Of what? Of *me?*
Secrets. Secrets are a big deal--
Not for us.
I love you. *All* of you. I want to know everyth--
?!?
"Vin? Vinnie..? Please say something."

CHAPTER 2
MORDIDA

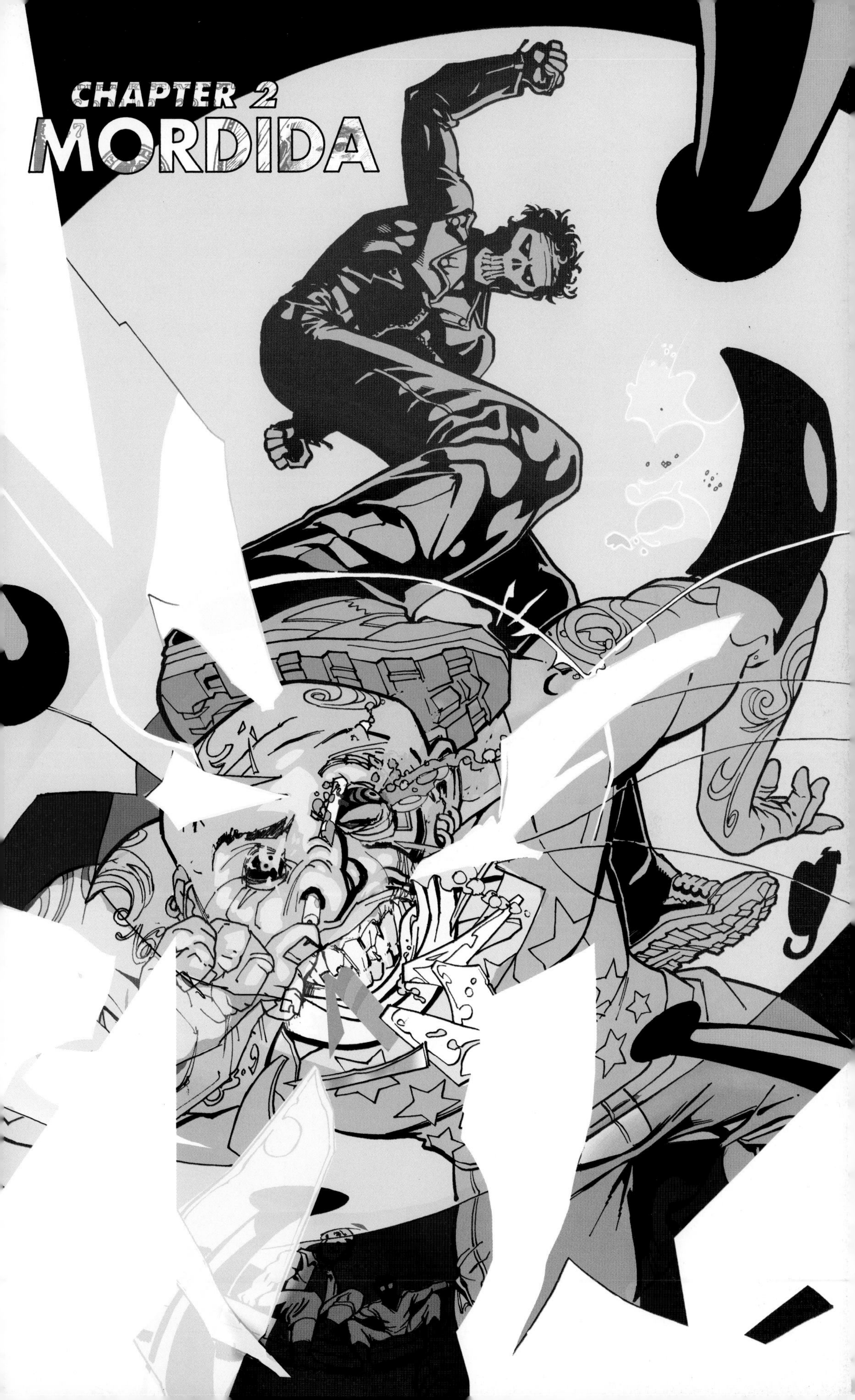

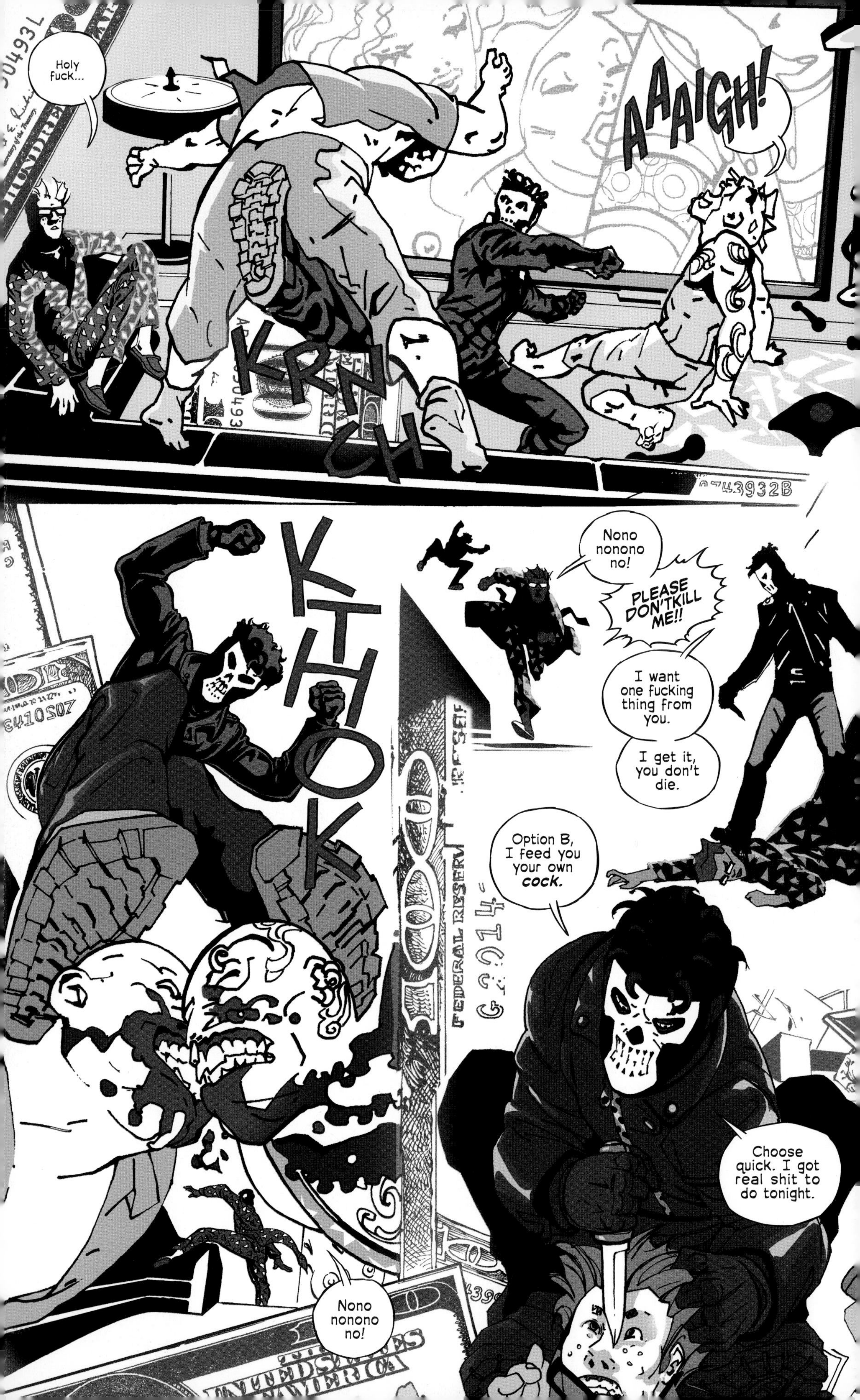
Holy fuck...
AAAIGH!
KRNCH
KTHOOK
Nono nonono no!
PLEASE DON'TKILL ME!!
I want one fucking thing from you.
I get it, you don't die.
Option B, I feed you your own cock.
Choose quick. I got real shit to do tonight.
Nono nonono no!

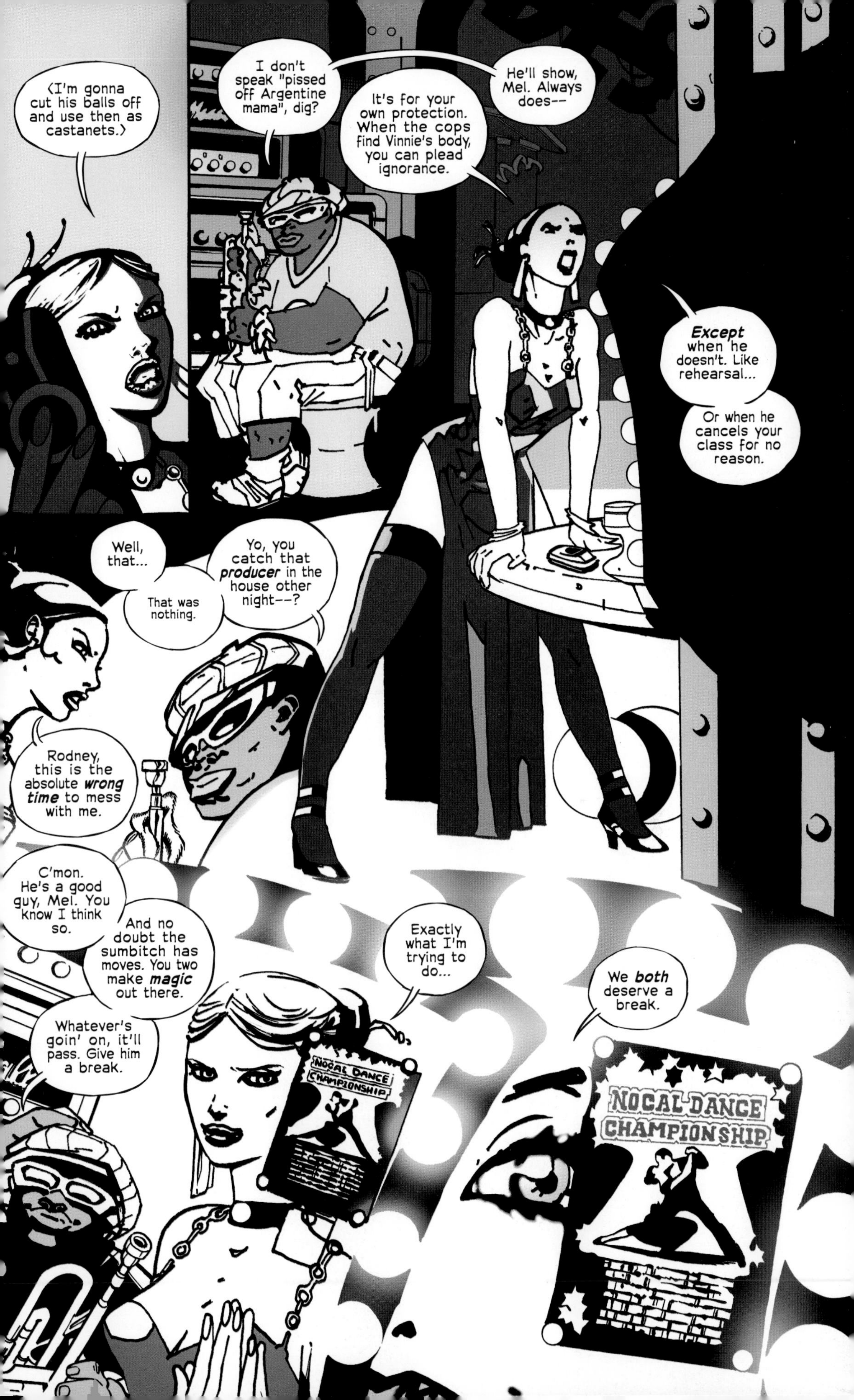

‹I'm gonna cut his balls off and use then as castanets.›
I don't speak "pissed off Argentine mama", dig?
He'll show, Mel. Always does--
It's for your own protection. When the cops find Vinnie's body, you can plead ignorance.
Except when he doesn't. Like rehearsal...
Or when he cancels your class for no reason.
Well, that...
That was nothing.
Yo, you catch that producer in the house other night--?
Rodney, this is the absolute wrong time to mess with me.
C'mon. He's a good guy, Mel. You know I think so.
And no doubt the sumbitch has moves. You two make magic out there.
Whatever's goin' on, it'll pass. Give him a break.
Exactly what I'm trying to do...
We both deserve a break.
NOCAL DANCE CHAMPIONSHIP
NOCAL DANCE CHAMPIONSHIP

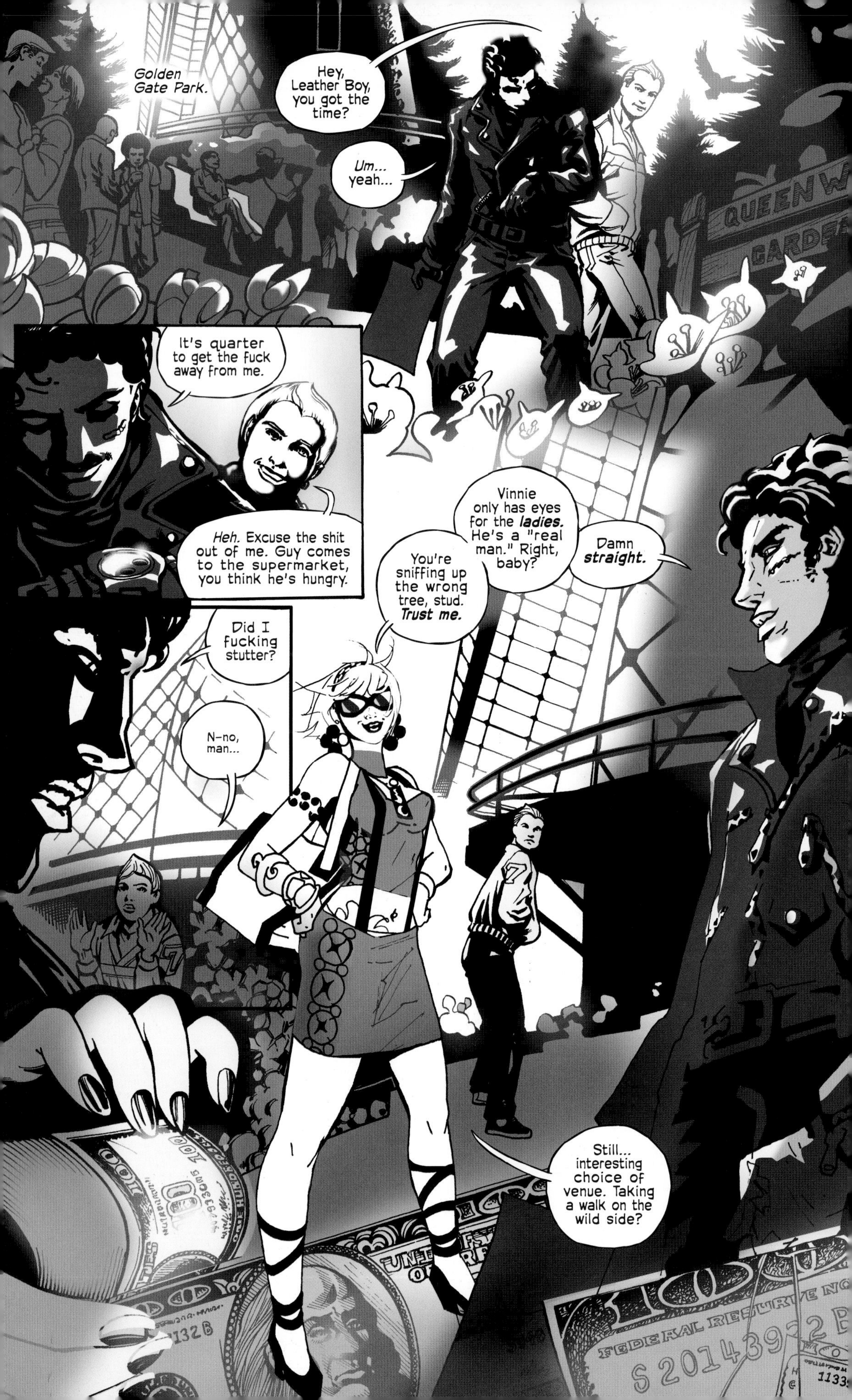

Golden Gate Park.
Hey, Leather Boy, you got the time?
Um... yeah...
QUEEN W
GARDE
It's quarter to get the fuck away from me.
Heh. Excuse the shit out of me. Guy comes to the supermarket, you think he's hungry.
Did I fucking stutter?
N-no, man...
You're sniffing up the wrong tree, stud. Trust me.
Vinnie only has eyes for the ladies. He's a "real man." Right, baby?
Damn straight.
Still... interesting choice of venue. Taking a walk on the wild side?

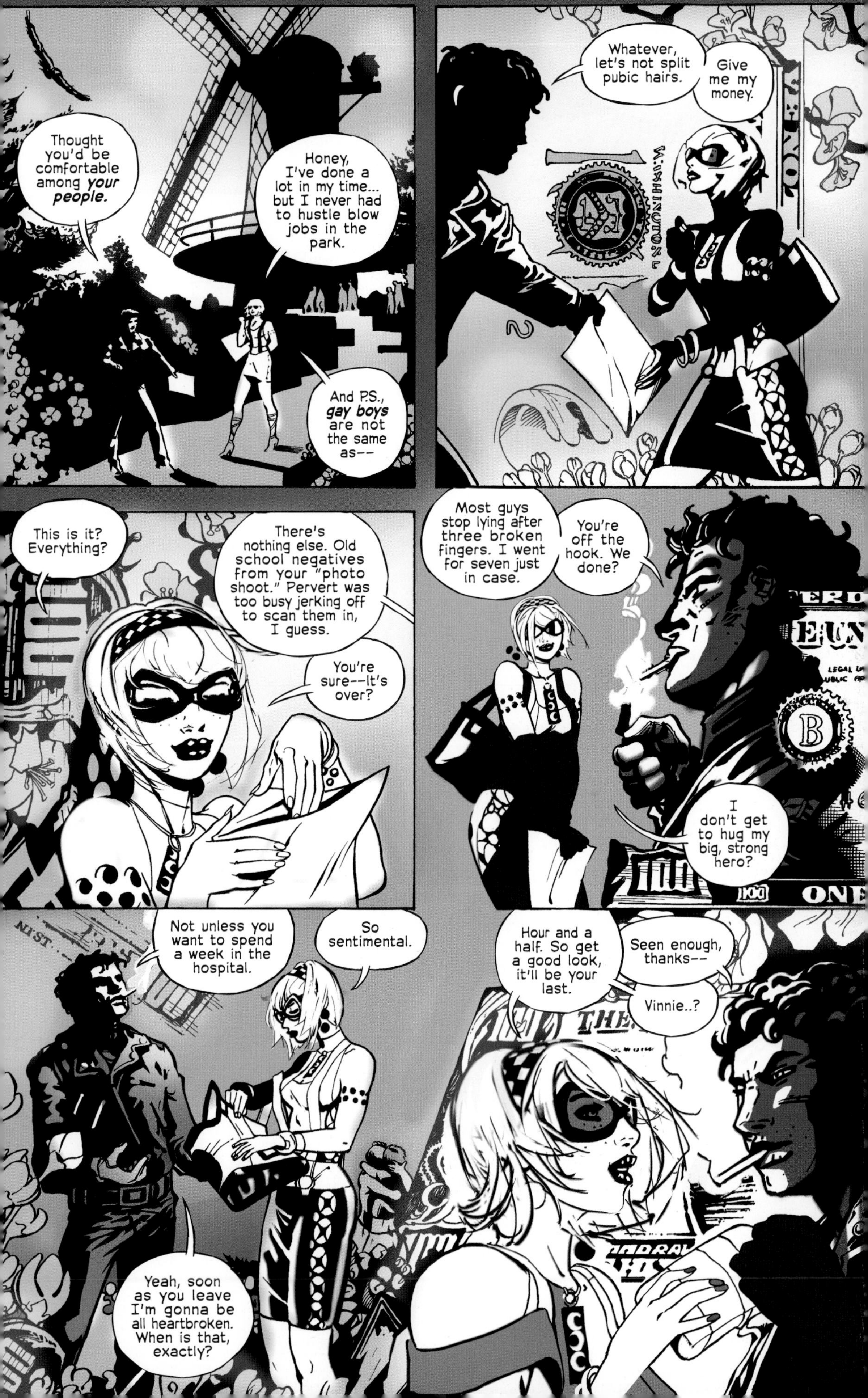
Thought you'd be comfortable among *your people.*
Honey, I've done a lot in my time... but I never had to hustle blow jobs in the park.
And P.S., *gay boys* are not the same as--
Whatever, let's not split pubic hairs.
Give me my money.
This is it? Everything?
There's nothing else. Old school negatives from your "photo shoot." Pervert was too busy jerking off to scan them in, I guess.
You're sure--it's over?
Most guys stop lying after three broken fingers. I went for seven just in case.
You're off the hook. We done?
I don't get to hug my big, strong hero?
Not unless you want to spend a week in the hospital.
So sentimental.
Yeah, soon as you leave I'm gonna be all heartbroken. When is that, exactly?
Hour and a half. So get a good look, it'll be your last.
Seen enough, thanks--
Vinnie..?

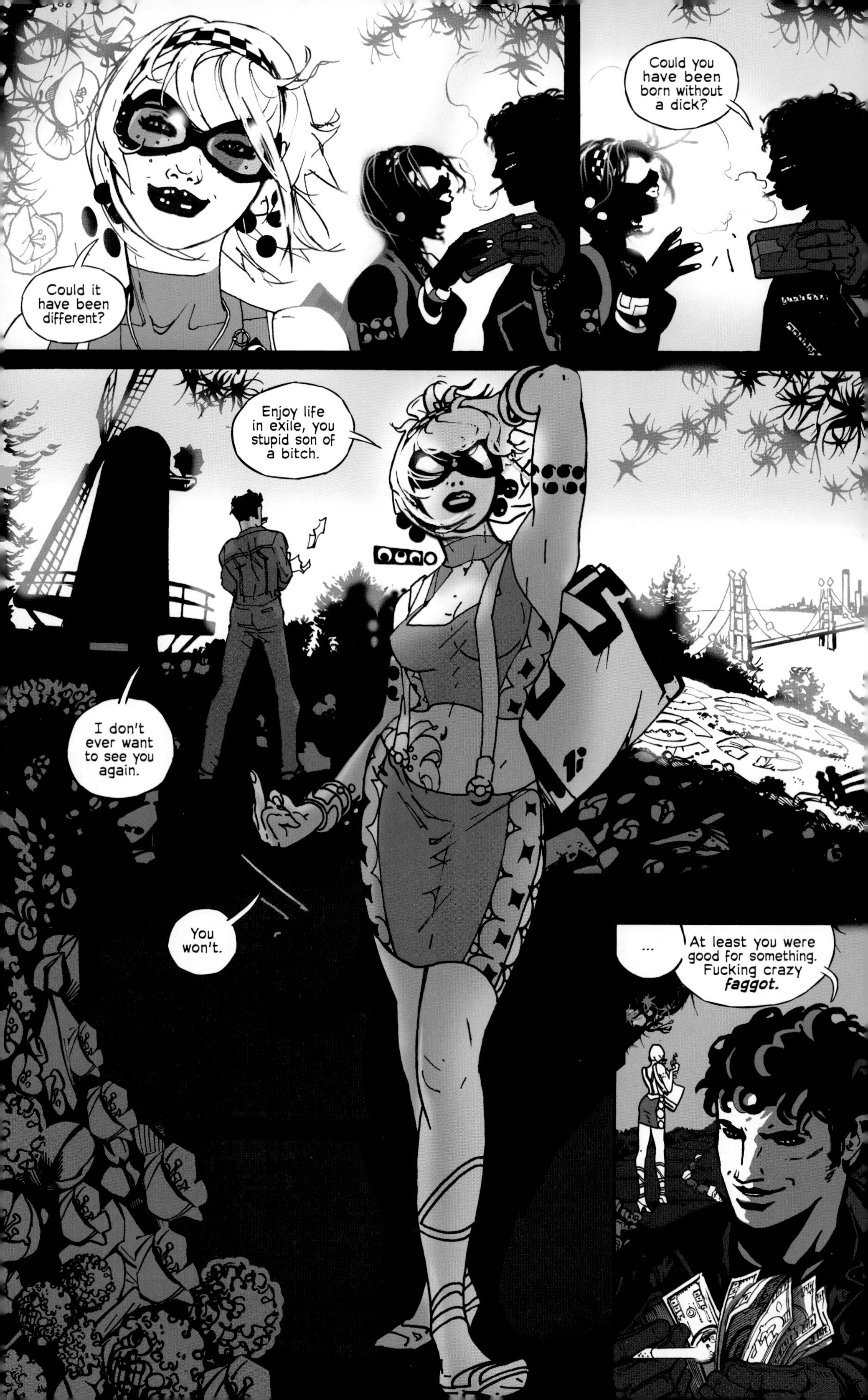
Could it have been different?
Could you have been born without a dick?
Enjoy life in exile, you stupid son of a bitch.
I don't ever want to see you again.
You won't.
...
At least you were good for something. Fucking crazy *faggot.*

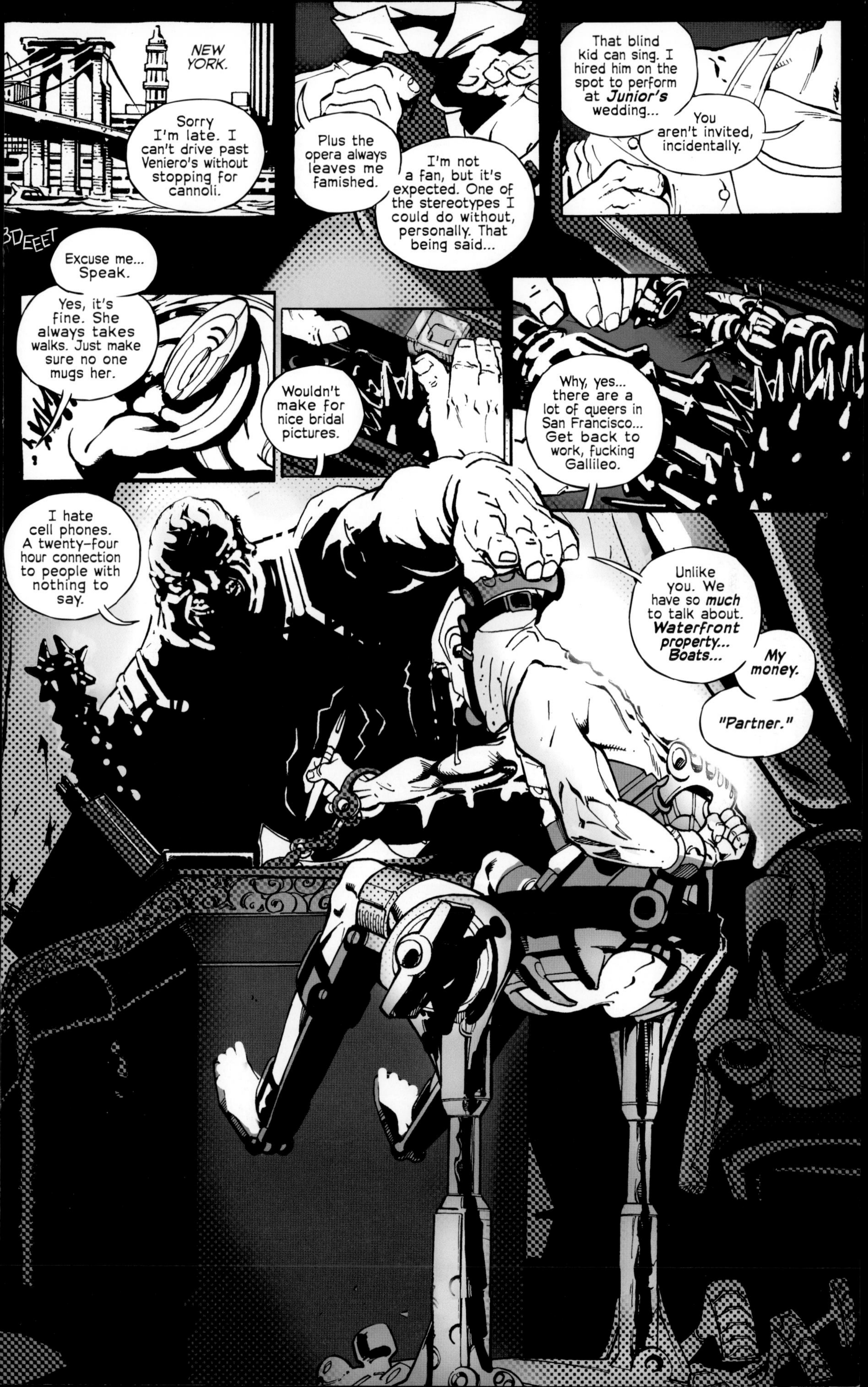

NEW YORK.
Sorry I'm late. I can't drive past Veniero's without stopping for cannoli.
Plus the opera always leaves me famished.
I'm not a fan, but it's expected. One of the stereotypes I could do without, personally. That being said...
That blind kid can sing. I hired him on the spot to perform at *Junior's* wedding...
You aren't invited, incidentally.
BDEEET
Excuse me... Speak.
Yes, it's fine. She always takes walks. Just make sure no one mugs her.
Wouldn't make for nice bridal pictures.
Why, yes... there are a lot of queers in San Francisco... Get back to work, fucking Gallileo.
I hate cell phones. A twenty-four hour connection to people with nothing to say.
Unlike you. We have so *much* to talk about. ***Waterfront property... Boats...***
My money.
"Partner."

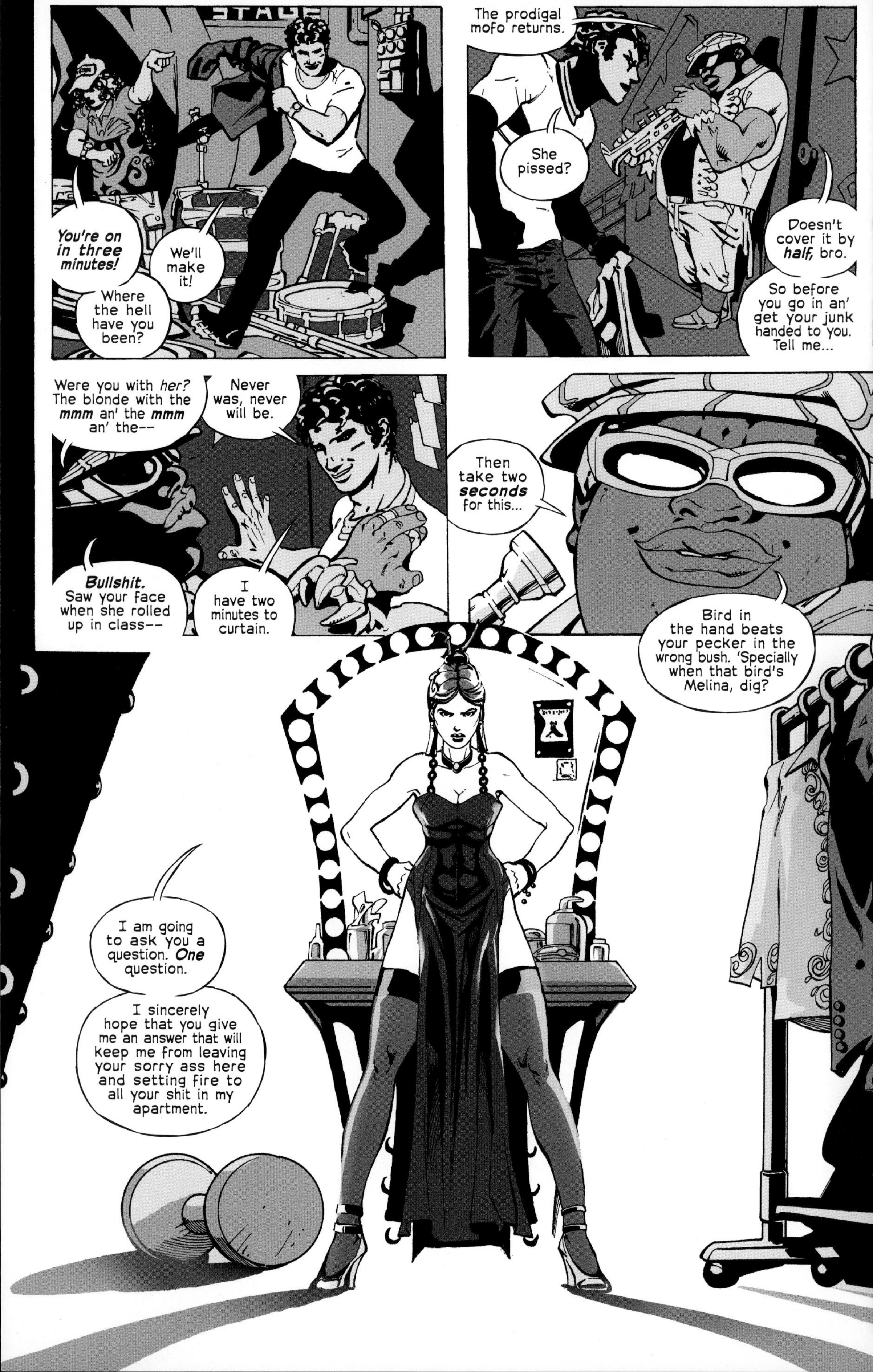
STAGE
You're on in three minutes!
Where the hell have you been?
We'll make it!
The prodigal mofo returns.
She pissed?
Doesn't cover it by *half,* bro.
So before you go in an' get your junk handed to you. Tell me...
Were you with *her?* The blonde with the ***mmm*** an' the ***mmm*** an' the--
Never was, never will be.
Bullshit. Saw your face when she rolled up in class--
I have two minutes to curtain.
Then take two ***seconds*** for this...
Bird in the hand beats your pecker in the wrong bush. 'Specially when that bird's Melina, dig?
I am going to ask you a question. *One* question.
I sincerely hope that you give me an answer that will keep me from leaving your sorry ass here and setting fire to all your shit in my apartment.

Let's do this *after* the set-- Mel--

In three years, I will be living in Buenos Aires running a small but *well respected* dance school.

In a year and a half, when I will *leave* San Francisco, it will be as a national champion... with endorsements and the *money* to open that school.

In less than a month, I will take a major step on this journey when I win the *NoCal* Dance championships.

A national qualifier. Prize Money. *Prestige.*

So my question is... Will you be *with* me or *not?*

Some rich girl wanted to dance the Tango at her wedding. Paid extra for me to wait in the wings until she pulled it off.

Then a fucking bridesmaid got her period and the whole thing got pushed back fifty minutes. I was trying to surprise you--

BULL--

...shit.

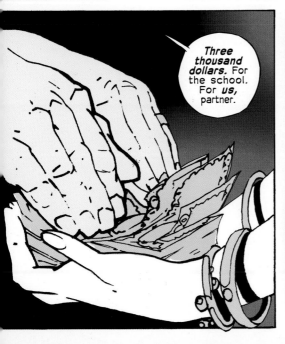

Three *thousand dollars.* For the school. For *us,* partner.

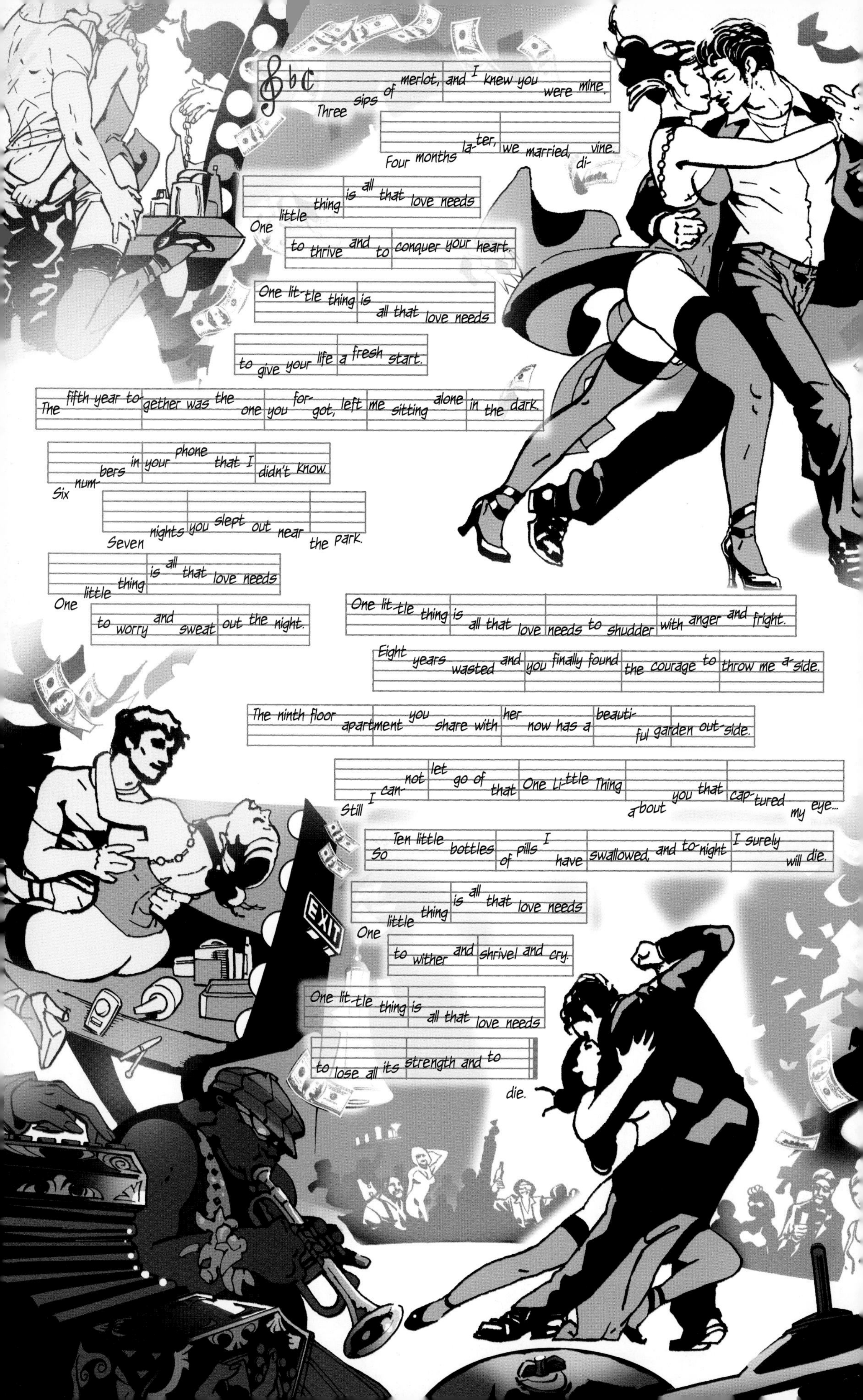

Three sips of merlot, and I knew you were mine.
Four months la-ter, we married, di-vine.
One little thing is all that love needs
to thrive and to conquer your heart.
One lit-tle thing is all that love needs
to give your life a fresh start.
The fifth year to-gether was the one you for-got, left me sitting alone in the dark.
Six num-bers in your phone that I didn't know.
Seven nights you slept out near the park.
One little thing is all that love needs
to worry and sweat out the night.
One lit-tle thing is all that love needs to shudder with anger and fright.
Eight years wasted and you finally found the courage to throw me a-side.
The ninth floor apartment you share with her now has a beauti-ful garden out-side.
Still I can-not let go of that One Li-ttle Thing about you that cap-tured my eye...
So Ten little bottles of pills I have swallowed, and to-night I surely will die.
One little thing is all that love needs
to wither and shrivel and cry.
One lit-tle thing is all that love needs
to lose all its strength and to die.
EXIT

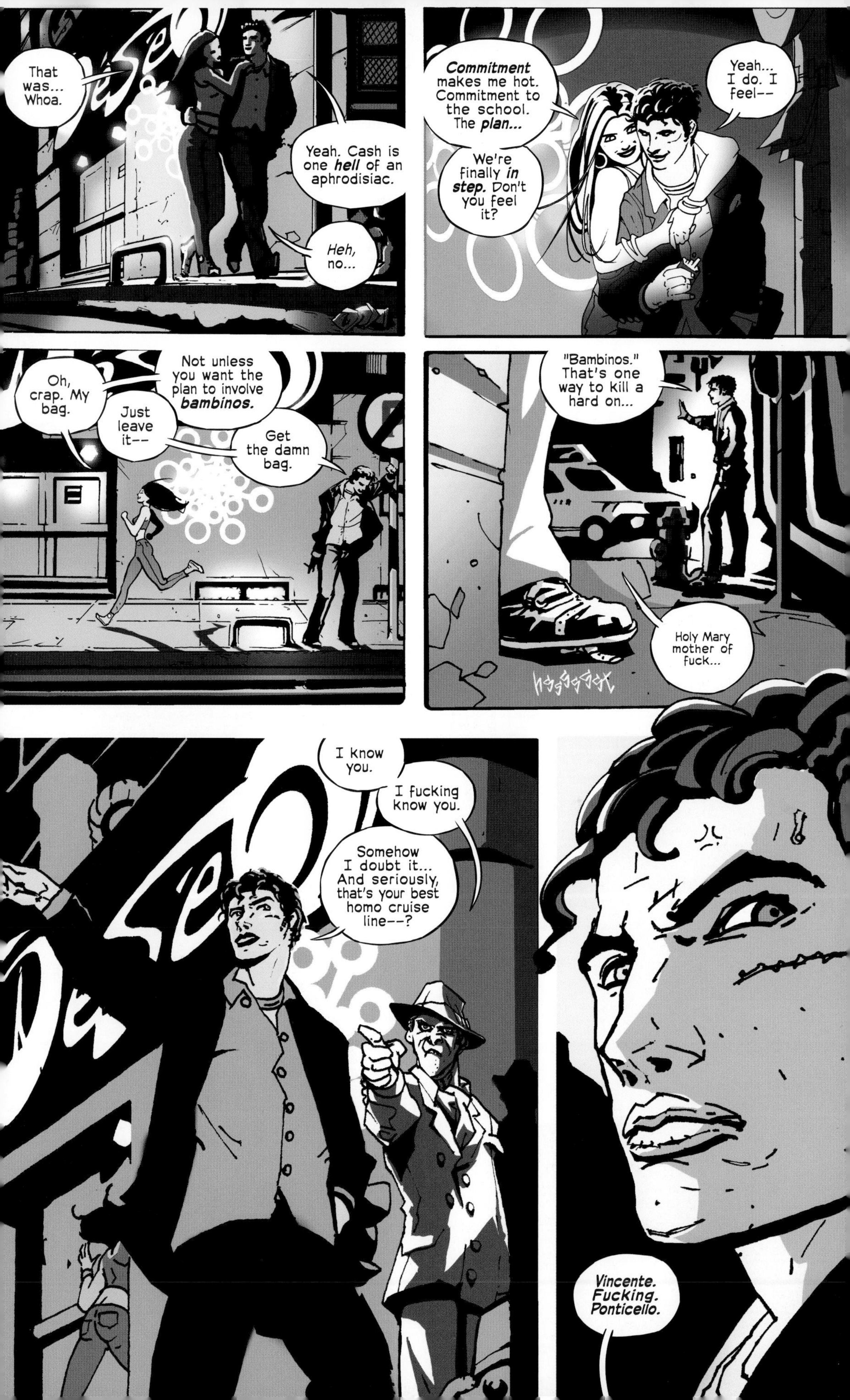

That was... Whoa.
Yeah. Cash is one **hell** of an aphrodisiac.
Heh, no...
Commitment makes me hot. Commitment to the school. The **plan...**
We're finally **in step.** Don't you feel it?
Yeah... I do. I feel--
Oh, crap. My bag.
Not unless you want the plan to involve **bambinos.**
Just leave it--
Get the damn bag.
"Bambinos." That's one way to kill a hard on...
Holy Mary mother of fuck...
I know you.
I fucking know you.
Somehow I doubt it... And seriously, that's your best homo cruise line--?
Vincente. Fucking. Ponticello.

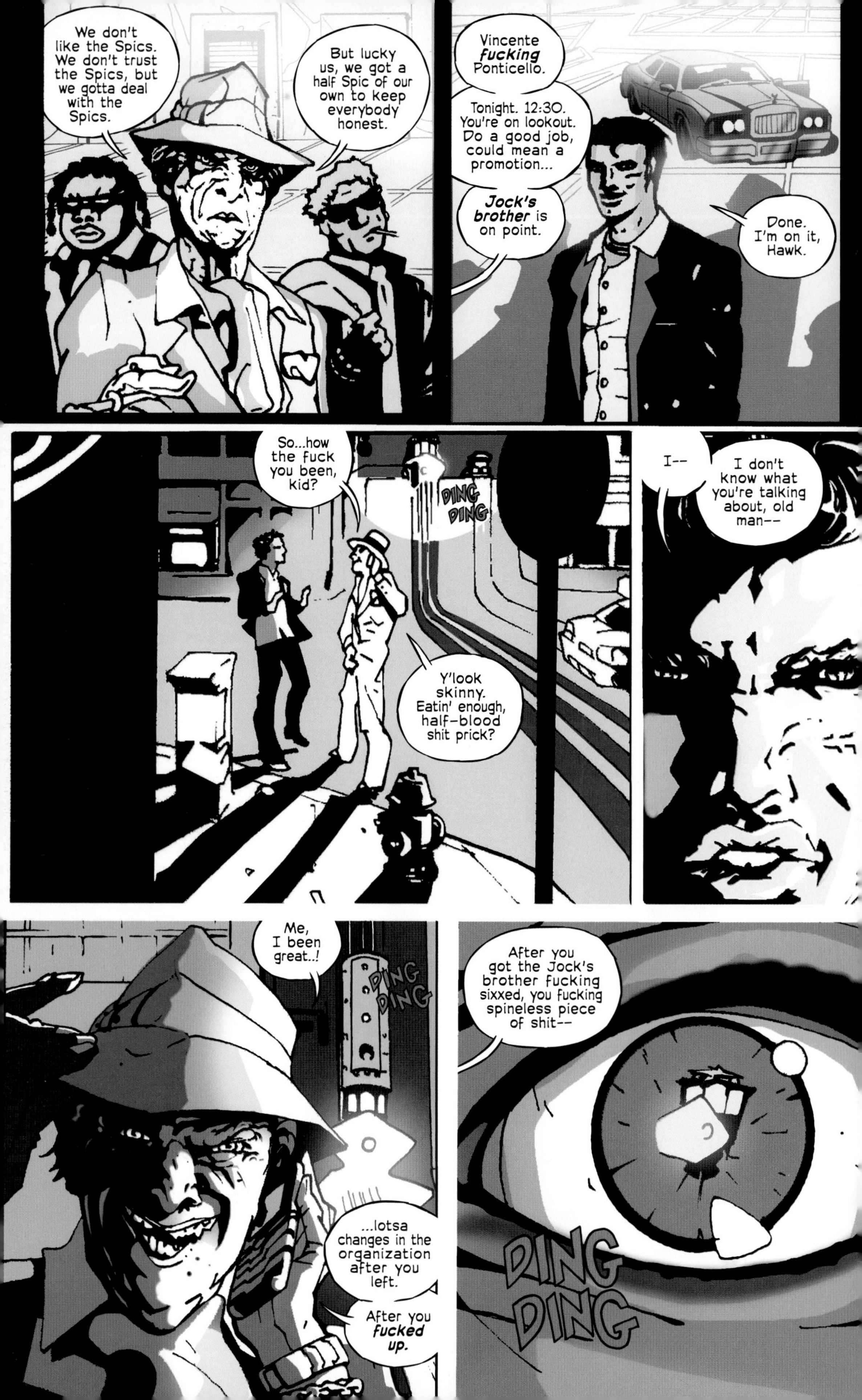
We don't like the Spics. We don't trust the Spics, but we gotta deal with the Spics.
But lucky us, we got a half Spic of our own to keep everybody honest.
Vincente *fucking* Ponticello.
Tonight. 12:30. You're on lookout. Do a good job, could mean a promotion...
Jock's brother is on point.
Done. I'm on it, Hawk.
So...how the fuck you been, kid?
DING DING
Y'look skinny. Eatin' enough, half-blood shit prick?
I--
I don't know what you're talking about, old man--
Me, I been great..!
DING DING
...lotsa changes in the organization after you left.
After you ***fucked up.***
After you got the Jock's brother fucking sixxed, you fucking spineless piece of shit--
DING DING

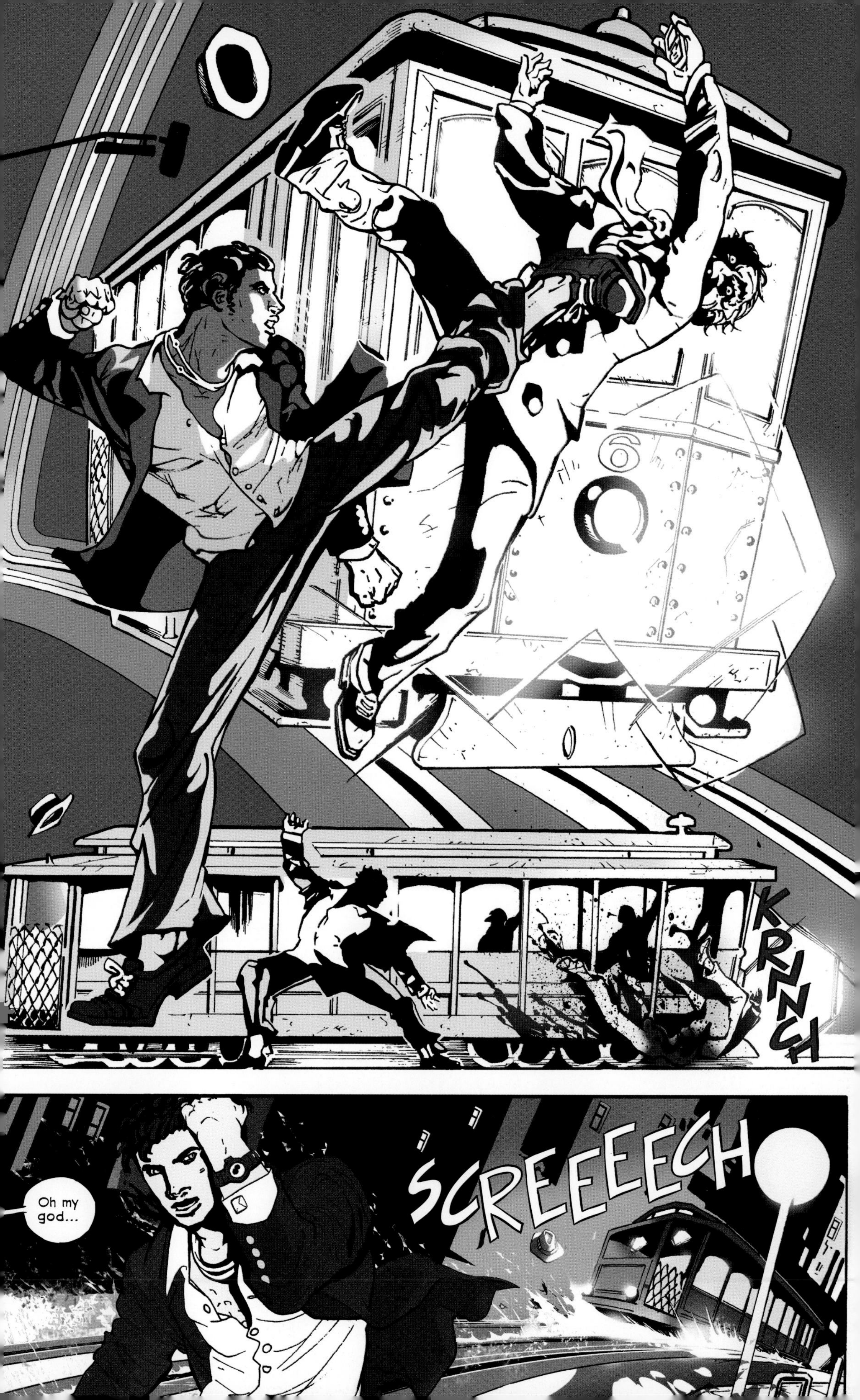
KRNNCH
Oh my god...
SCREEEECH

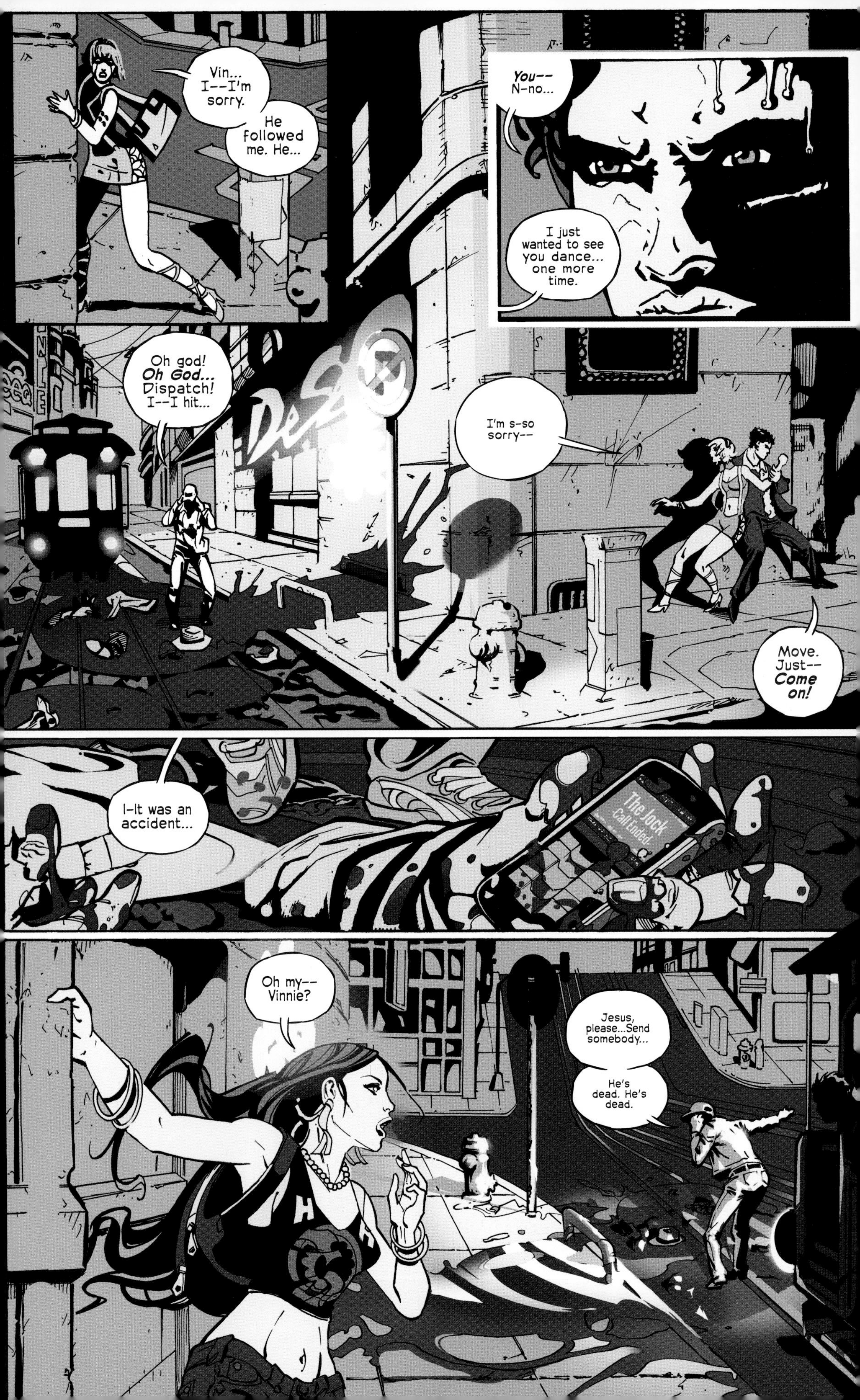

Vin... I--I'm sorry.
He followed me. He...
You-- N-no...
I just wanted to see you dance... one more time.
Oh god! Oh God... Dispatch! I--I hit...
I'm s-so sorry--
Move. Just-- Come on!
I-It was an accident...
The Jock
Call Ended
Oh my-- Vinnie?
Jesus, please...Send somebody...
He's dead. He's dead.

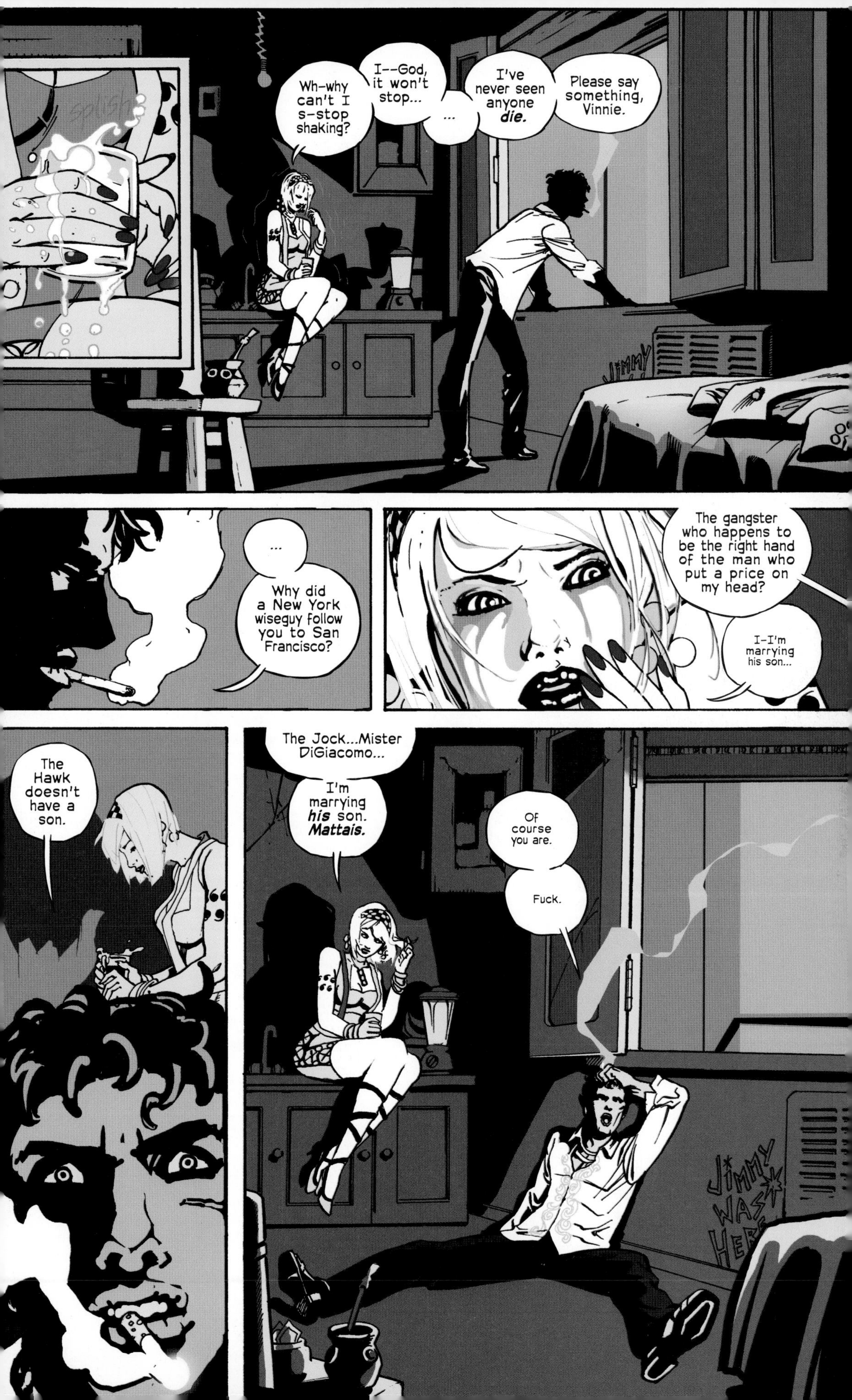
Wh-why can't I s-stop shaking?
I--God, it won't stop...
...
I've never seen anyone *die.*
Please say something, Vinnie.
JIMMY
...
Why did a New York wiseguy follow you to San Francisco?
The gangster who happens to be the right hand of the man who put a price on my head?
I-I'm marrying his son...
The Hawk doesn't have a son.
The Jock...Mister DiGiacomo...
I'm marrying *his* son. *Mattais.*
Of course you are.
Fuck.

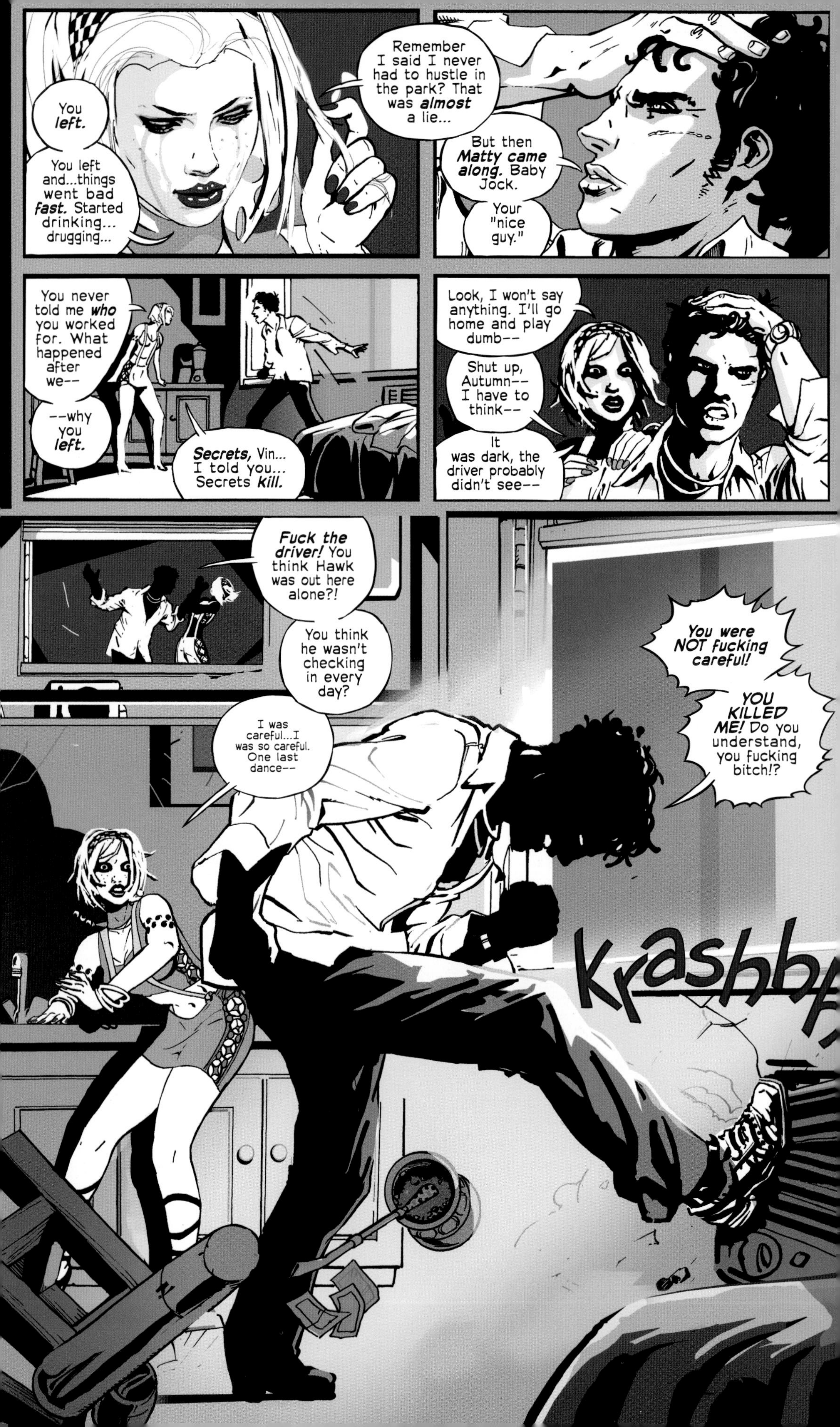
You left.
You left and...things went bad fast. Started drinking... drugging...
Remember I said I never had to hustle in the park? That was almost a lie...
But then Matty came along. Baby Jock.
Your "nice guy."
You never told me who you worked for. What happened after we--
--why you left.
Secrets, Vin... I told you... Secrets kill.
Look, I won't say anything. I'll go home and play dumb--
Shut up, Autumn-- I have to think--
It was dark, the driver probably didn't see--
Fuck the driver! You think Hawk was out here alone?!
You think he wasn't checking in every day?
I was careful...I was so careful. One last dance--
You were NOT fucking careful!
YOU KILLED ME! Do you understand, you fucking bitch!?
Krashh

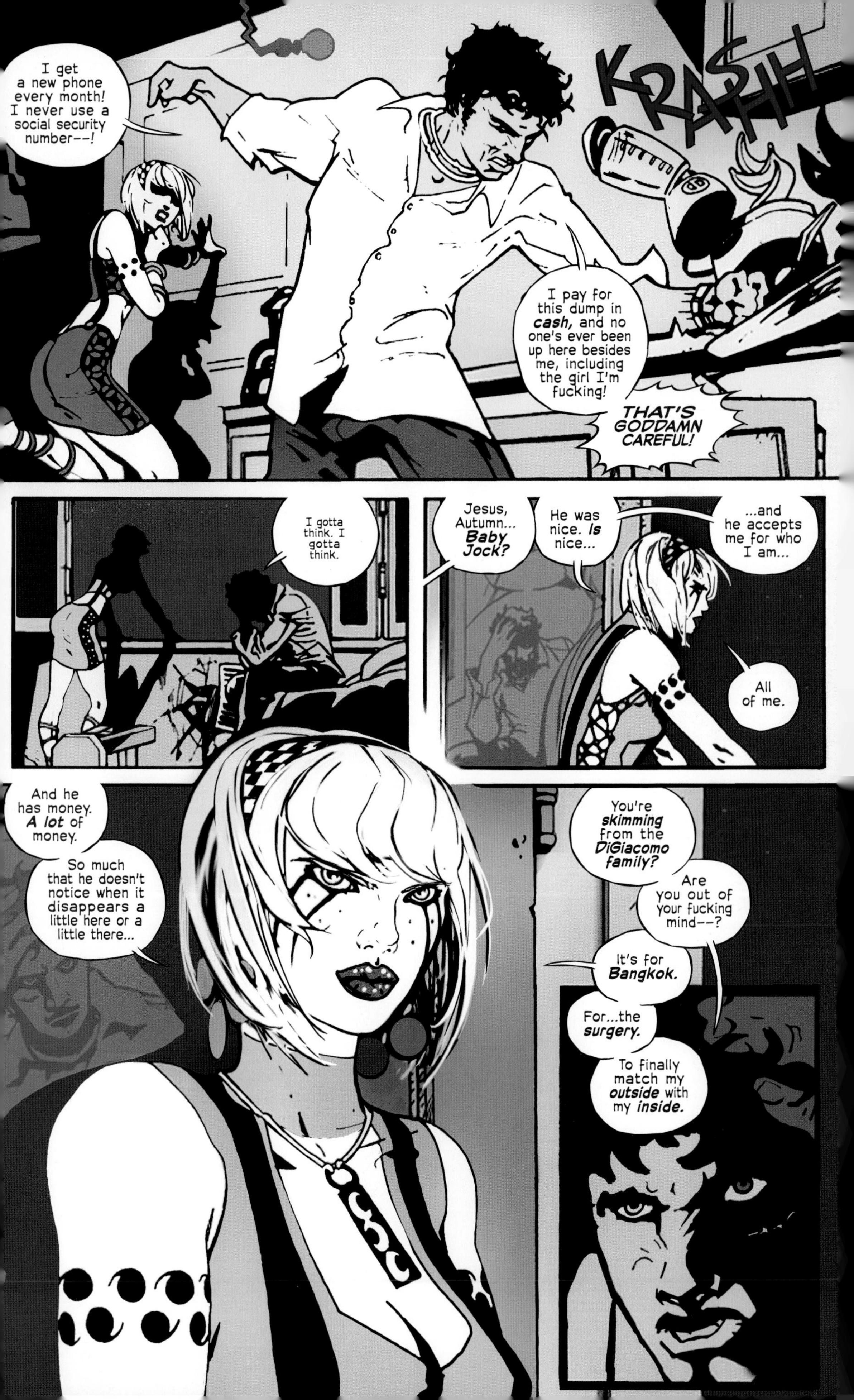
KRASHH
I get a new phone every month! I never use a social security number--!
I pay for this dump in *cash,* and no one's ever been up here besides me, including the girl I'm fucking!
THAT'S GODDAMN CAREFUL!
I gotta think. I gotta think.
Jesus, Autumn... *Baby Jock?*
He was nice. *Is* nice...
...and he accepts me for who I am...
All of me.
And he has money. *A lot* of money.
So much that he doesn't notice when it disappears a little here or a little there...
You're *skimming* from the *DiGiacomo family?*
Are you out of your fucking mind--?
It's for *Bangkok.*
For...the *surgery.*
To finally match my *outside* with my *inside.*

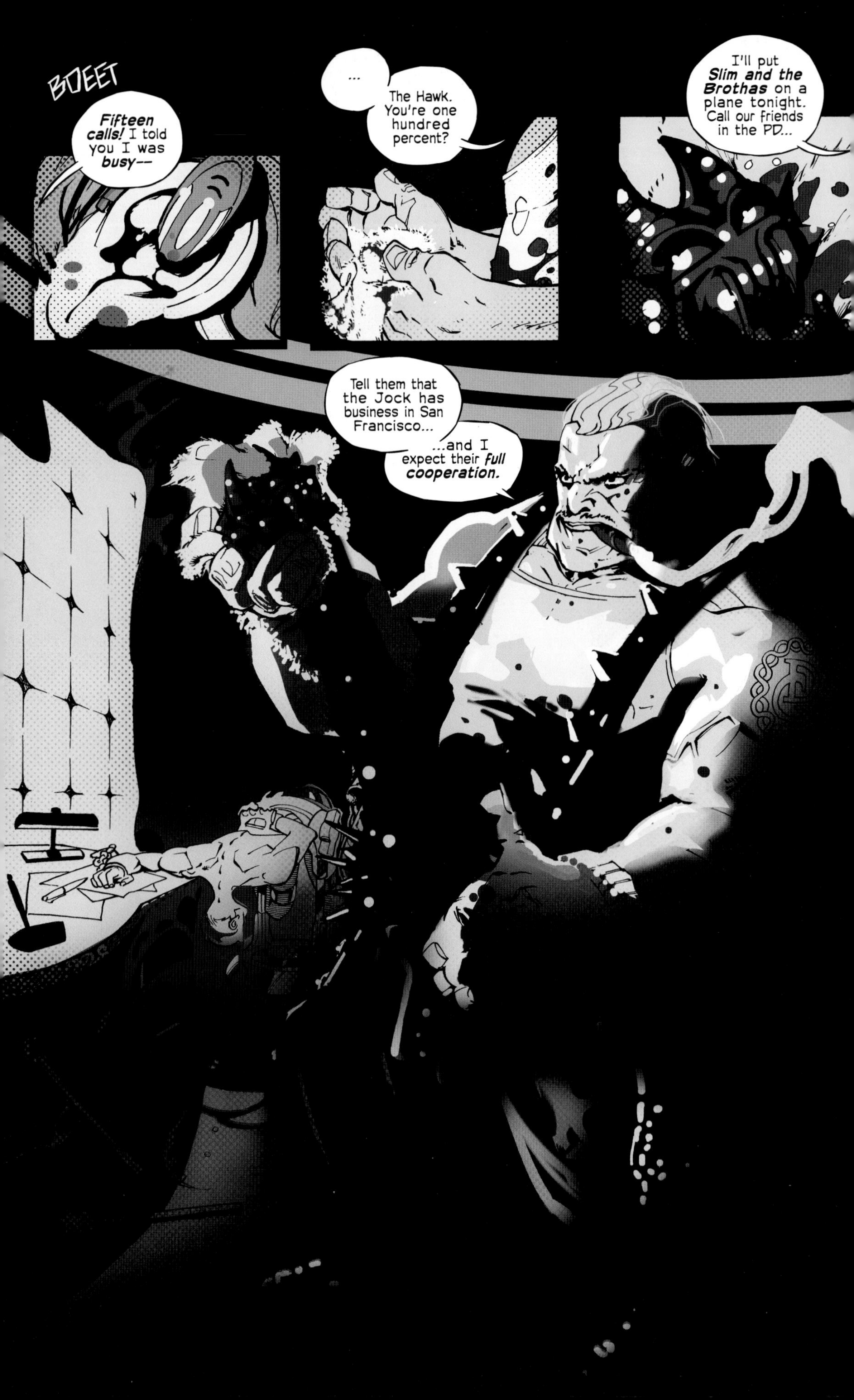
BOEET
Fifteen calls! I told you I was busy--
...
The Hawk. You're one hundred percent?
I'll put Slim and the Brothas on a plane tonight. Call our friends in the PD...
Tell them that the Jock has business in San Francisco...
...and I expect their full cooperation.

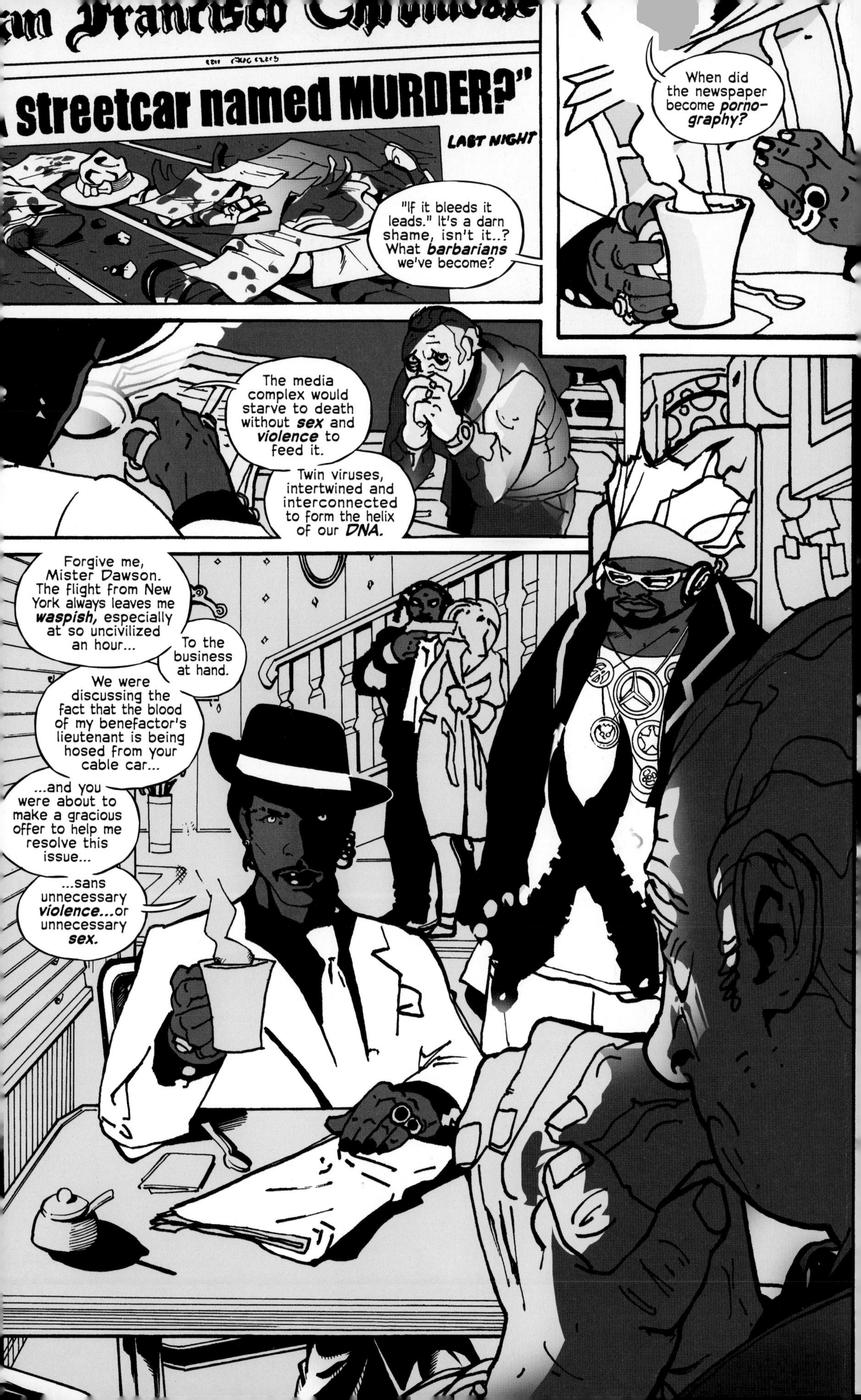
San Francisco Chronicle
A streetcar named MURDER?"
LAST NIGHT
"If it bleeds it leads." It's a darn shame, isn't it..? What *barbarians* we've become?
When did the newspaper become *pornography?*
The media complex would starve to death without *sex* and *violence* to feed it.
Twin viruses, intertwined and interconnected to form the helix of our *DNA.*
Forgive me, Mister Dawson. The flight from New York always leaves me *waspish,* especially at so uncivilized an hour...
To the business at hand.
We were discussing the fact that the blood of my benefactor's lieutenant is being hosed from your cable car...
...and you were about to make a gracious offer to help me resolve this issue...
...sans unnecessary *violence...*or unnecessary *sex.*

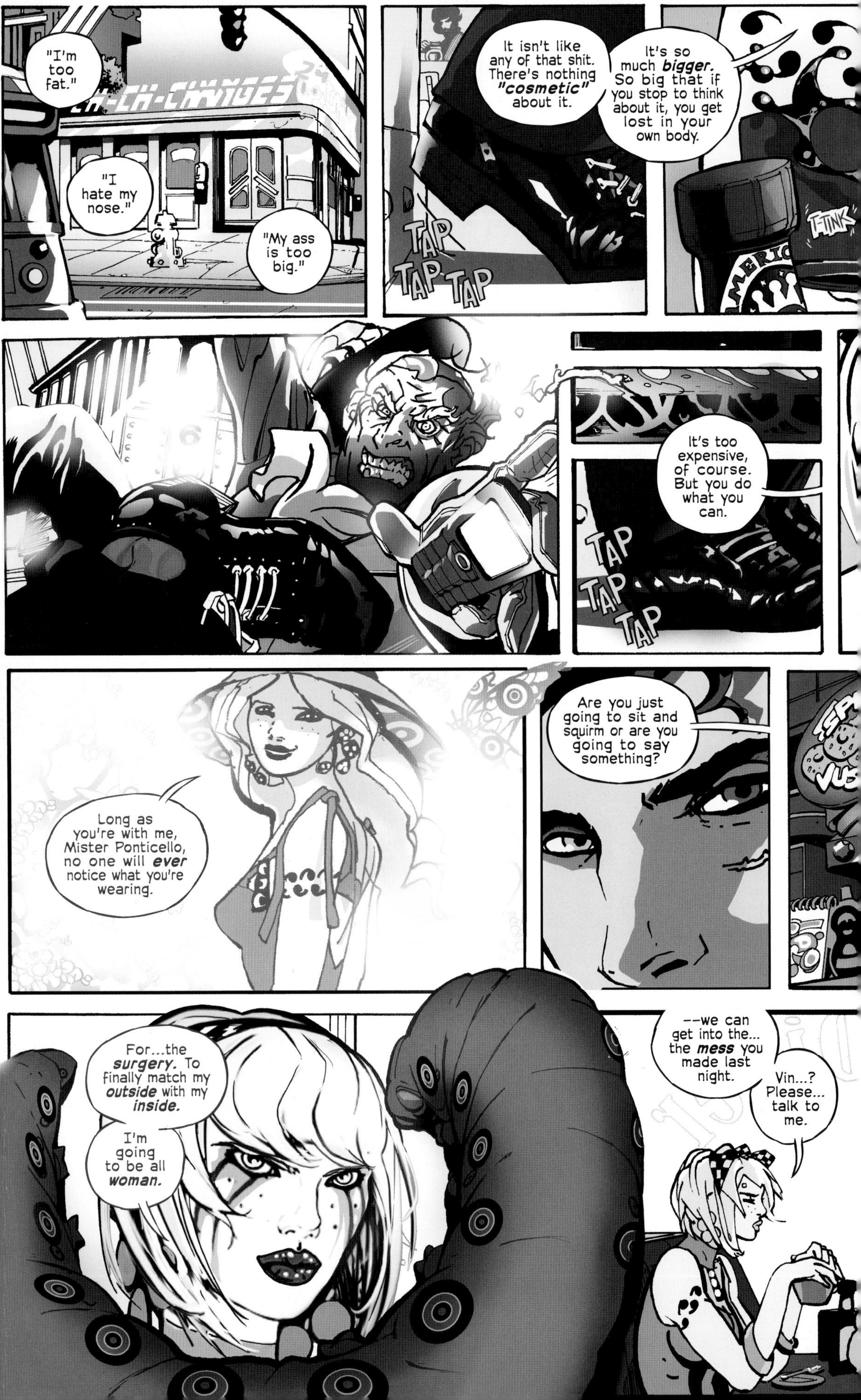
"I'm too fat."
CH-CH-CHANGES
"I hate my nose."
"My ass is too big."
It isn't like any of that shit. There's nothing "cosmetic" about it.
It's so much bigger. So big that if you stop to think about it, you get lost in your own body.
TAP TAP TAP TAP
T-TINK
It's too expensive, of course. But you do what you can.
TAP TAP TAP
Long as you're with me, Mister Ponticello, no one will ever notice what you're wearing.
Are you just going to sit and squirm or are you going to say something?
For...the surgery. To finally match my outside with my inside.
I'm going to be all woman.
--we can get into the... the mess you made last night.
Vin...? Please... talk to me.

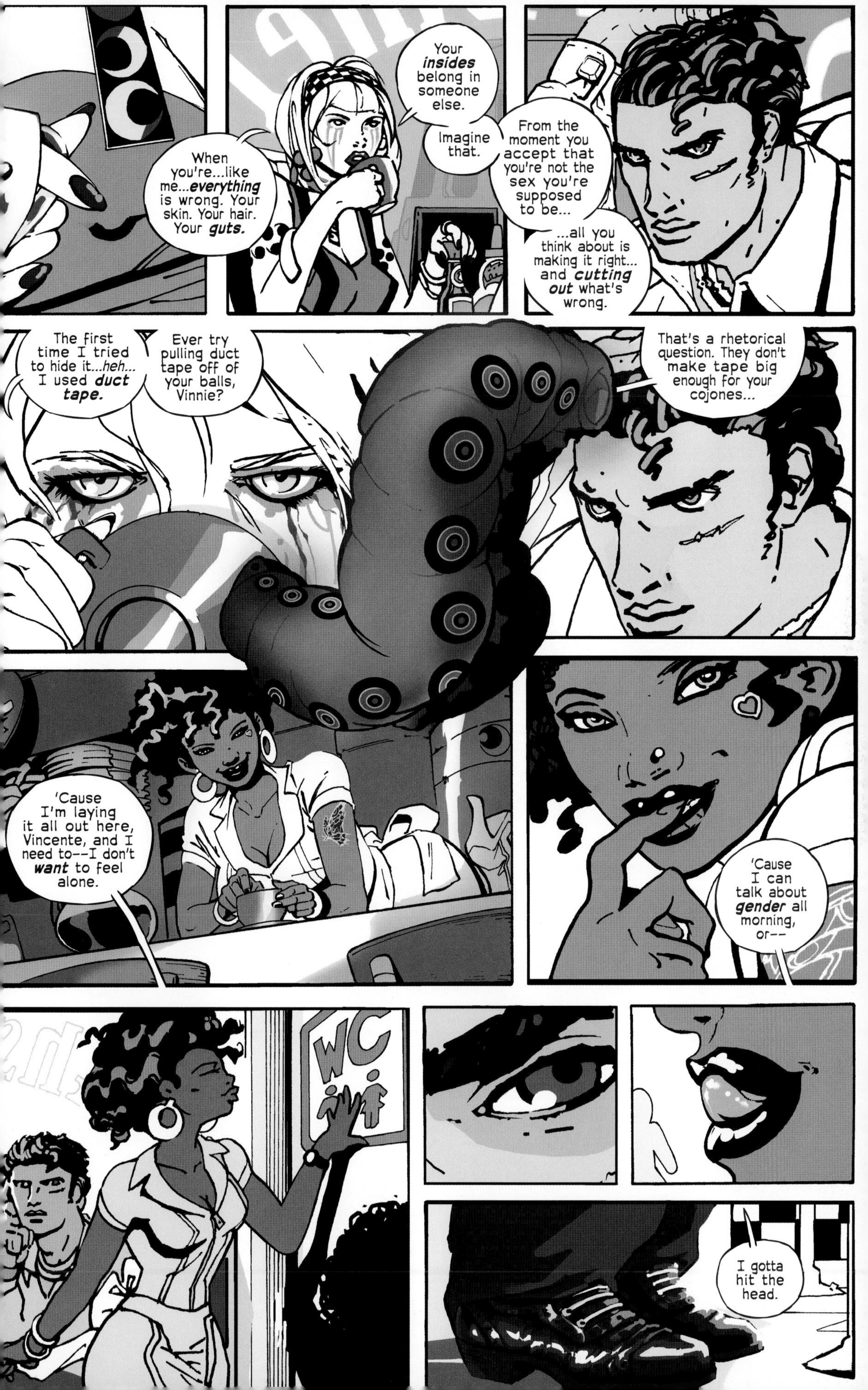

When you're...like me...*everything* is wrong. Your skin. Your hair. Your *guts.*
Your *insides* belong in someone else.
Imagine that.
From the moment you accept that you're not the sex you're supposed to be...
...all you think about is making it right... and *cutting out* what's wrong.
The first time I tried to hide it...*heh...* I used *duct tape.*
Ever try pulling duct tape off of your balls, Vinnie?
That's a rhetorical question. They don't make tape big enough for your cojones...
'Cause I'm laying it all out here, Vincente, and I need to--I don't *want* to feel alone.
'Cause I can talk about *gender* all morning, or--
WC
I gotta hit the head.

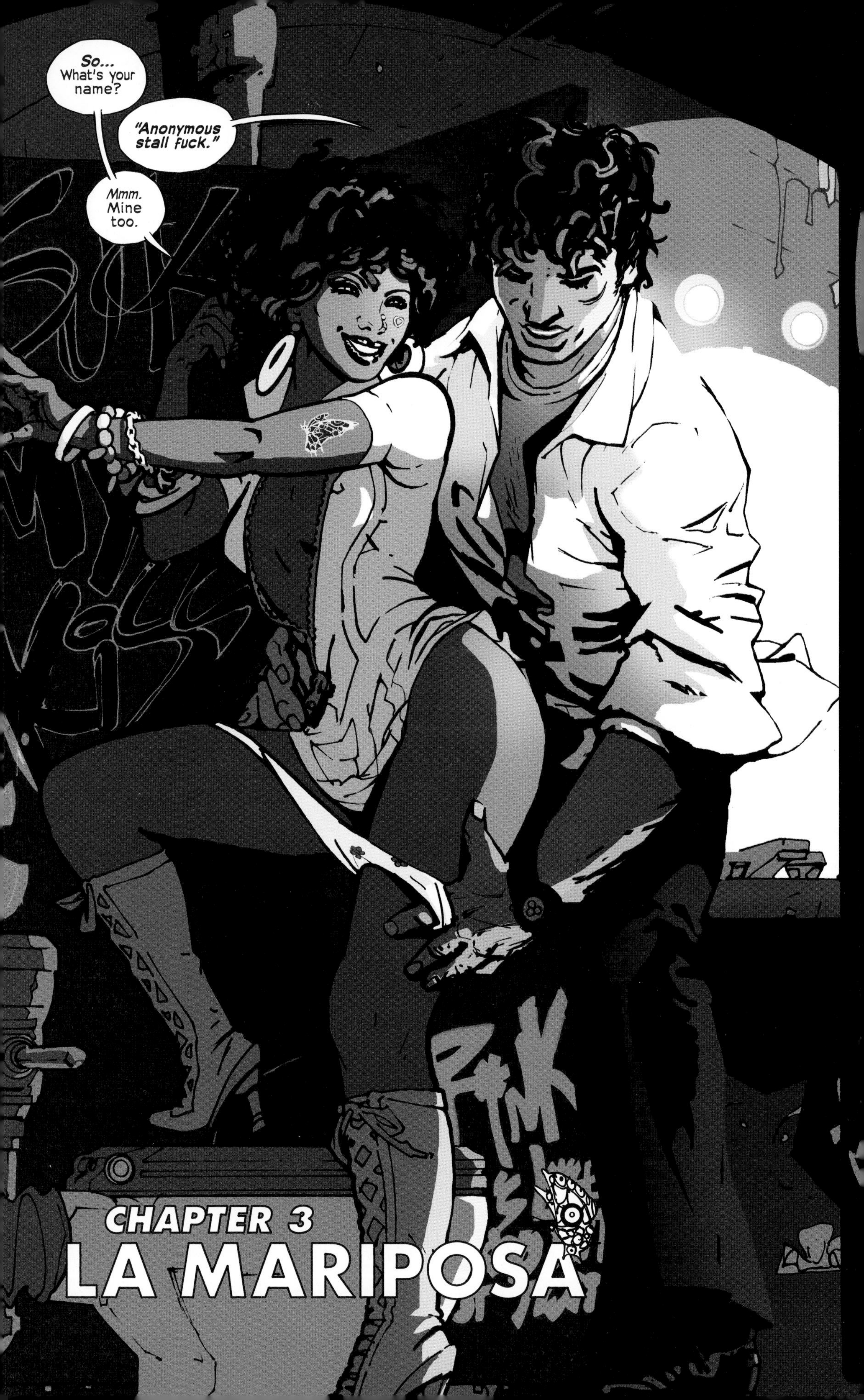
So... What's your name?
"Anonymous stall fuck."
Mmm. Mine too.

CHAPTER 3
LA MARIPOSA

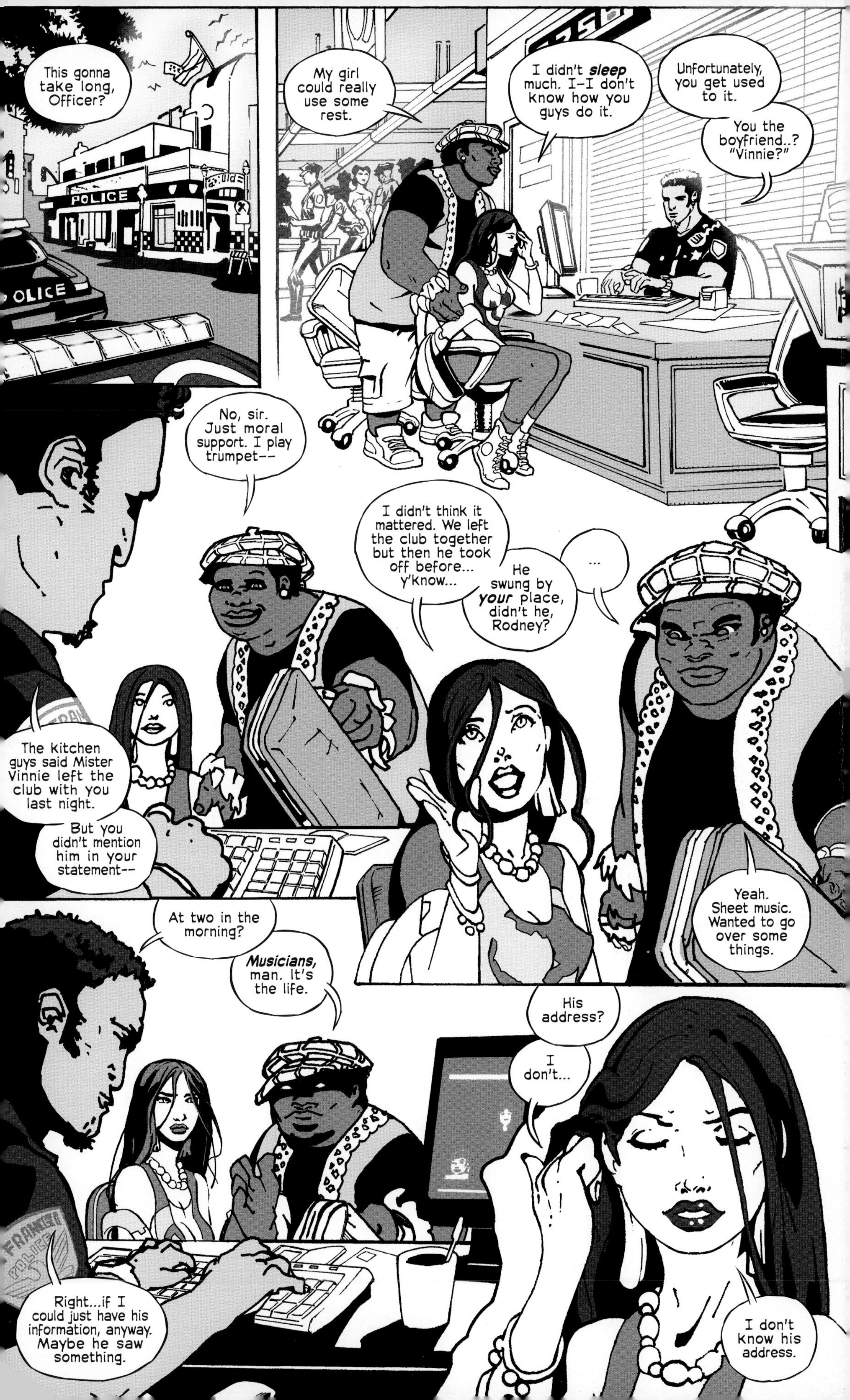
This gonna take long, Officer?
POLICE
POLICE
My girl could really use some rest.
I didn't *sleep* much. I--I don't know how you guys do it.
Unfortunately, you get used to it.
You the boyfriend..? "Vinnie?"
No, sir. Just moral support. I play trumpet--
The kitchen guys said Mister Vinnie left the club with you last night.
But you didn't mention him in your statement--
I didn't think it mattered. We left the club together but then he took off before... y'know...
He swung by *your* place, didn't he, Rodney?
...
Yeah. Sheet music. Wanted to go over some things.
At two in the morning?
Musicians, man. It's the life.
Right...if I could just have his information, anyway. Maybe he saw something.
His address?
I don't...
I don't know his address.

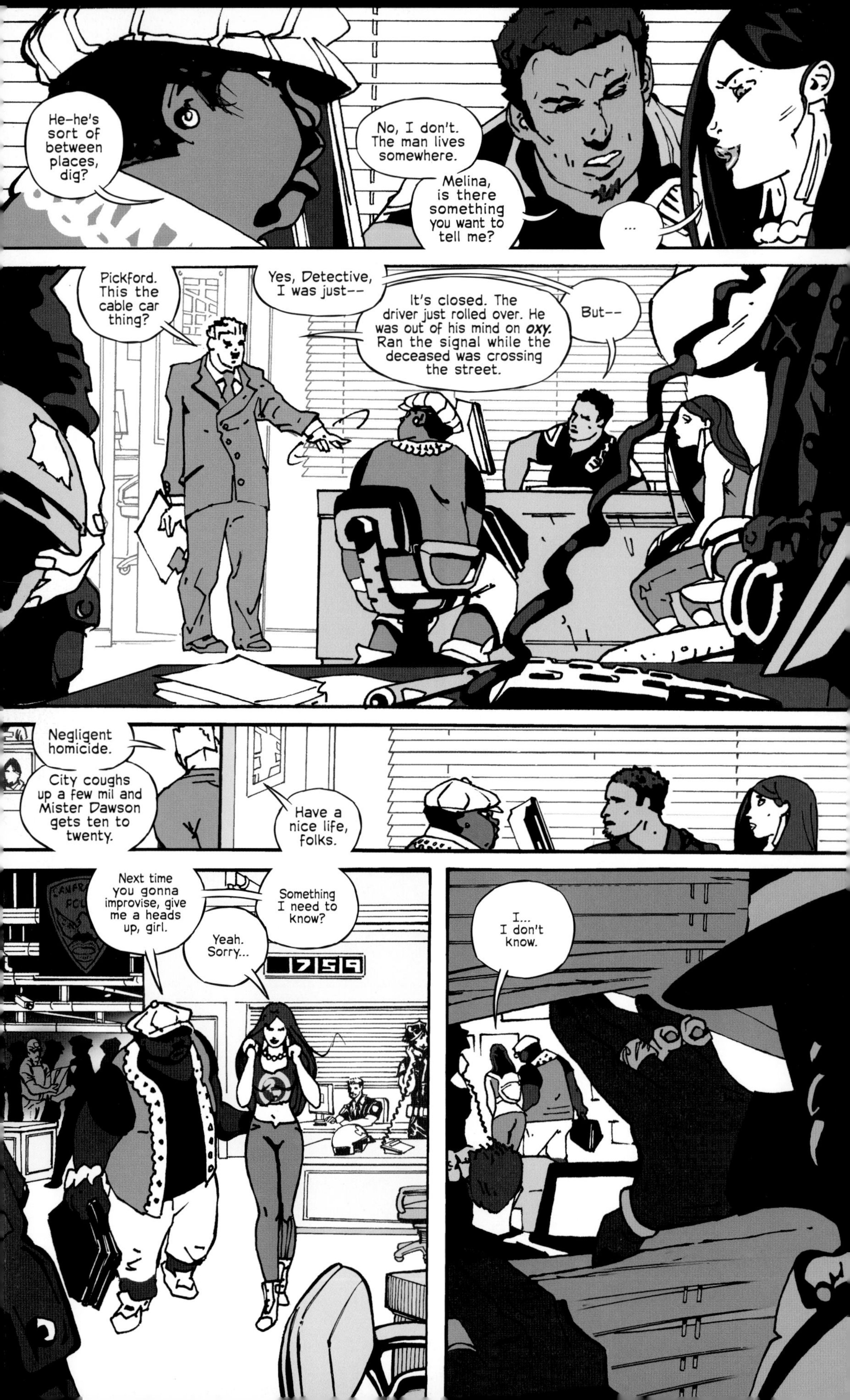
He–he's sort of between places, dig?
No, I don't. The man lives somewhere.
Melina, is there something you want to tell me?
...
Pickford. This the cable car thing?
Yes, Detective, I was just--
It's closed. The driver just rolled over. He was out of his mind on *oxy.* Ran the signal while the deceased was crossing the street.
But--
Negligent homicide.
City coughs up a few mil and Mister Dawson gets ten to twenty.
Have a nice life, folks.
Next time you gonna improvise, give me a heads up, girl.
Something I need to know?
Yeah. Sorry...
7 5 9
I... I don't know.

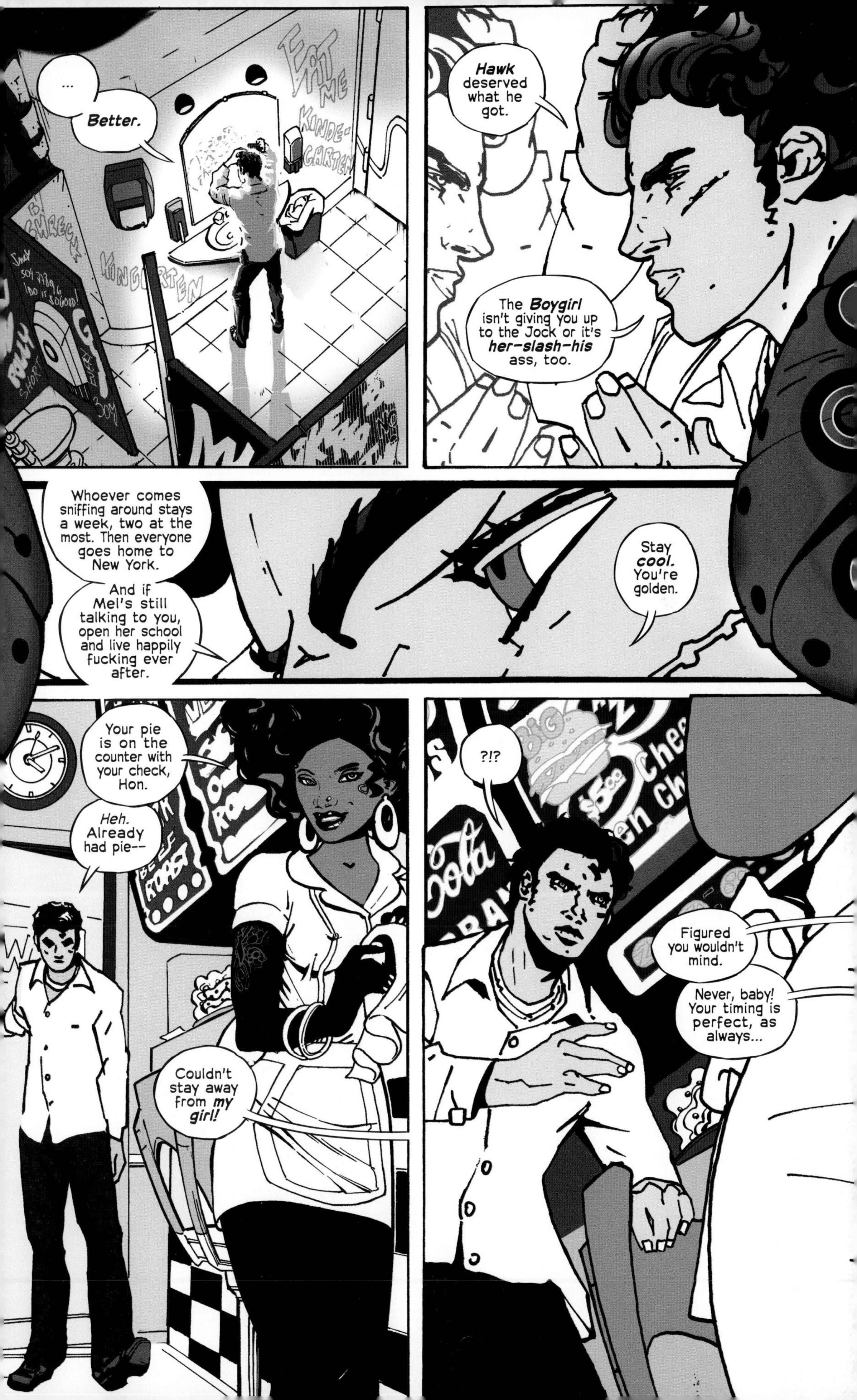
...
Better.
Hawk deserved what he got.
The Boygirl isn't giving you up to the Jock or it's her-slash-his ass, too.
Whoever comes sniffing around stays a week, two at the most. Then everyone goes home to New York.
And if Mel's still talking to you, open her school and live happily fucking ever after.
Stay cool. You're golden.
Your pie is on the counter with your check, Hon.
Heh. Already had pie--
Couldn't stay away from my girl!
?!?
Figured you wouldn't mind.
Never, baby! Your timing is perfect, as always...

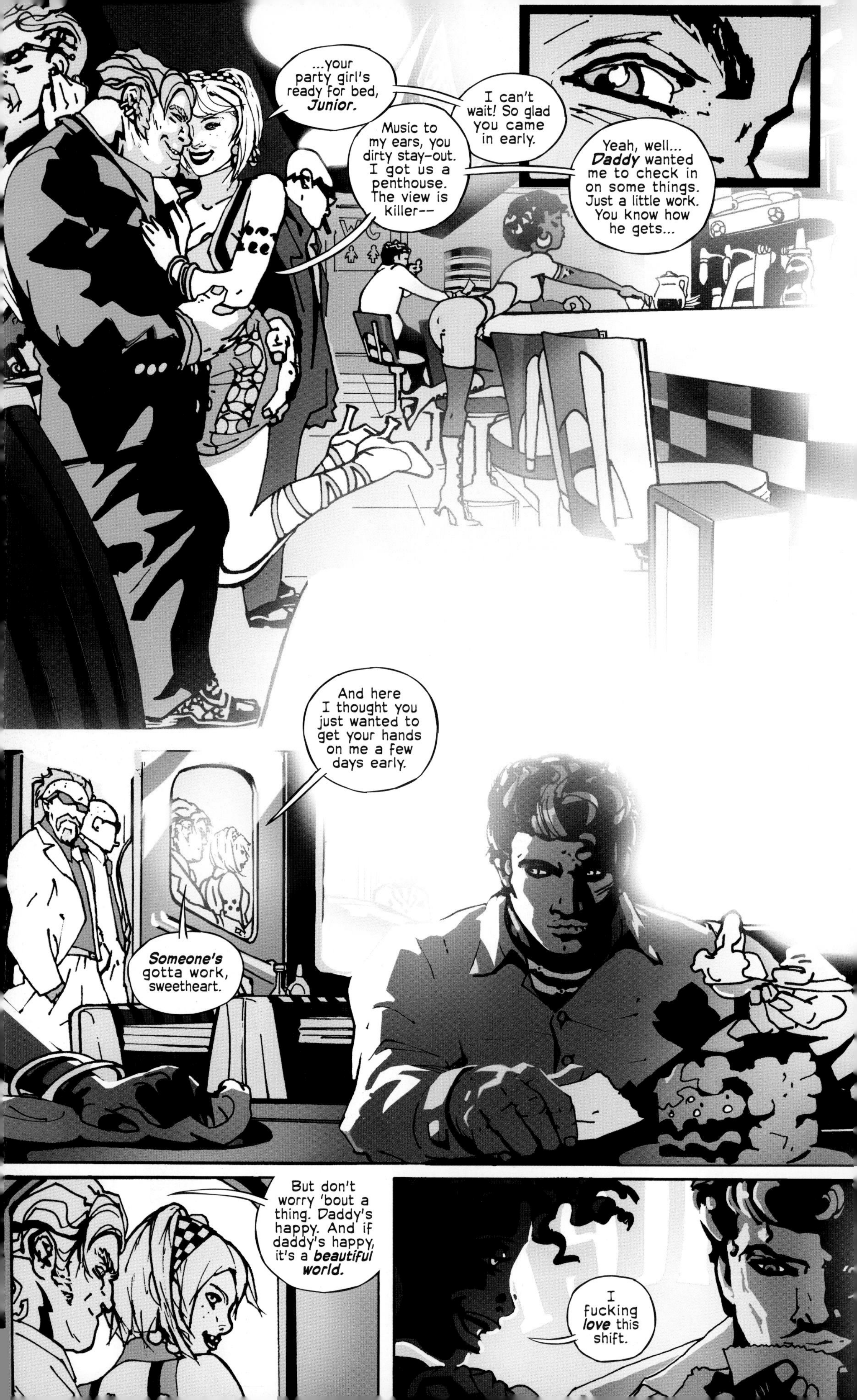
...your party girl's ready for bed, *Junior.*
I can't wait! So glad you came in early.
Music to my ears, you dirty stay-out. I got us a penthouse. The view is killer--
Yeah, well... *Daddy* wanted me to check in on some things. Just a little work. You know how he gets...
And here I thought you just wanted to get your hands on me a few days early.
Someone's gotta work, sweetheart.
But don't worry 'bout a thing. Daddy's happy. And if daddy's happy, it's a *beautiful world.*
I fucking *love* this shift.

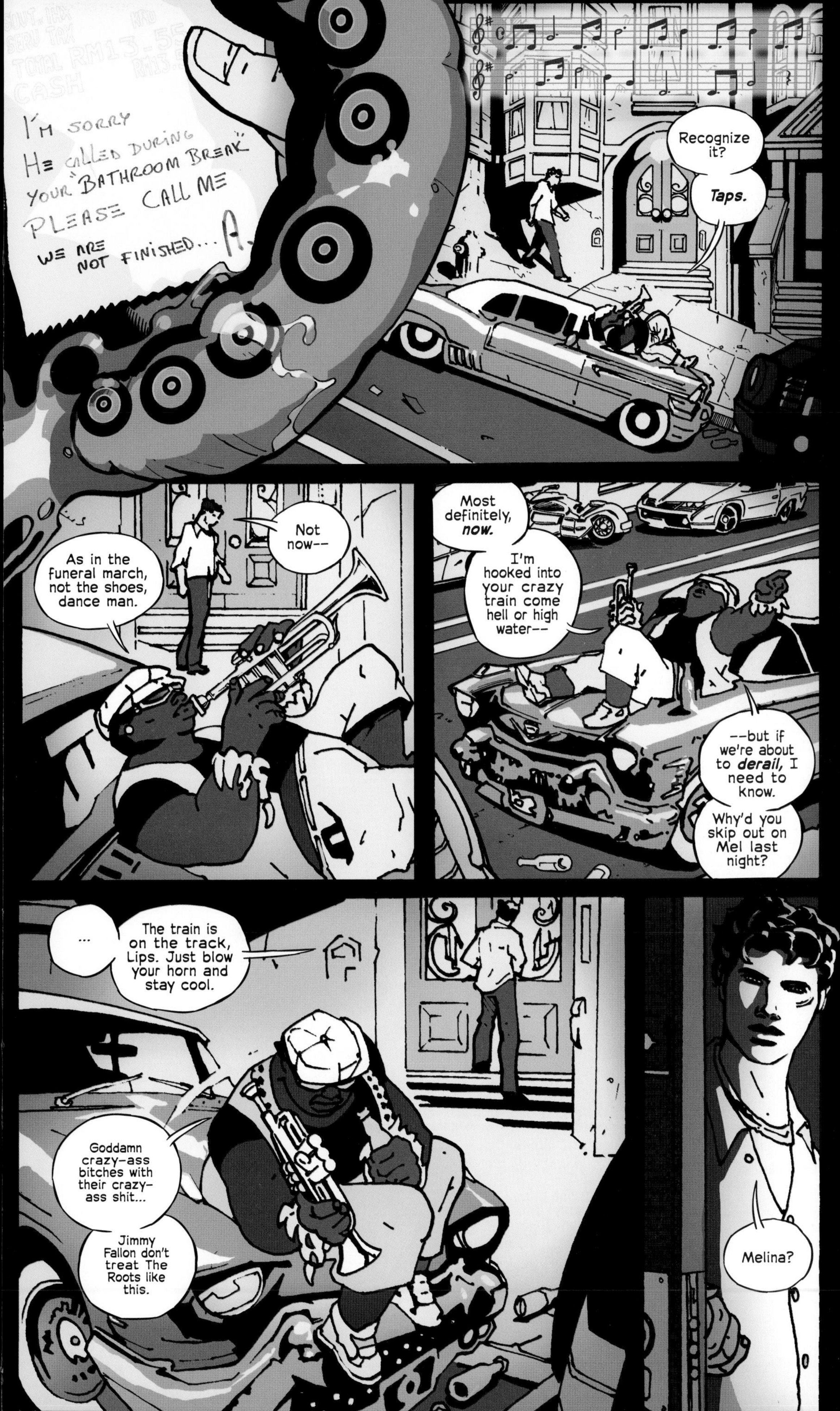
I'M SORRY
HE CALLED DURING YOUR "BATHROOM BREAK"
PLEASE CALL ME
WE ARE NOT FINISHED... A.
Recognize it?
Taps.
Not now--
As in the funeral march, not the shoes, dance man.
Most definitely, now.
I'm hooked into your crazy train come hell or high water--
--but if we're about to derail, I need to know.
Why'd you skip out on Mel last night?
...
The train is on the track, Lips. Just blow your horn and stay cool.
Goddamn crazy-ass bitches with their crazy-ass shit...
Jimmy Fallon don't treat The Roots like this.
Melina?

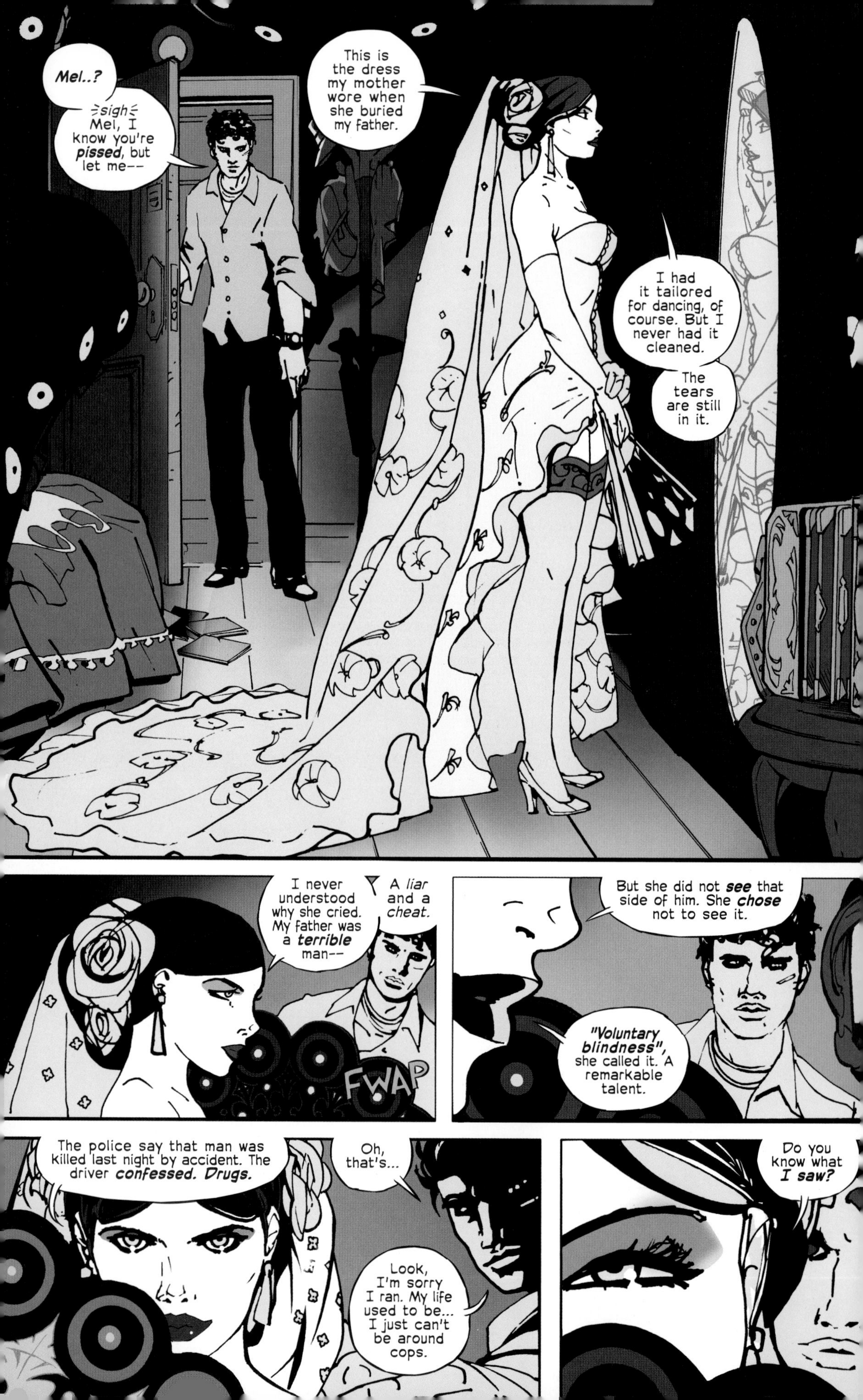
Mel..?
sigh Mel, I know you're ***pissed***, but let me--
This is the dress my mother wore when she buried my father.
I had it tailored for dancing, of course. But I never had it cleaned.
The tears are still in it.
I never understood why she cried. My father was a ***terrible*** man--
A *liar* and a *cheat*.
FWAP
But she did not ***see*** that side of him. She ***chose*** not to see it.
"Voluntary blindness", she called it. A remarkable talent.
The police say that man was killed last night by accident. The driver ***confessed. Drugs.***
Oh, that's...
Look, I'm sorry I ran. My life used to be... I just can't be around cops.
Do you know what ***I saw?***

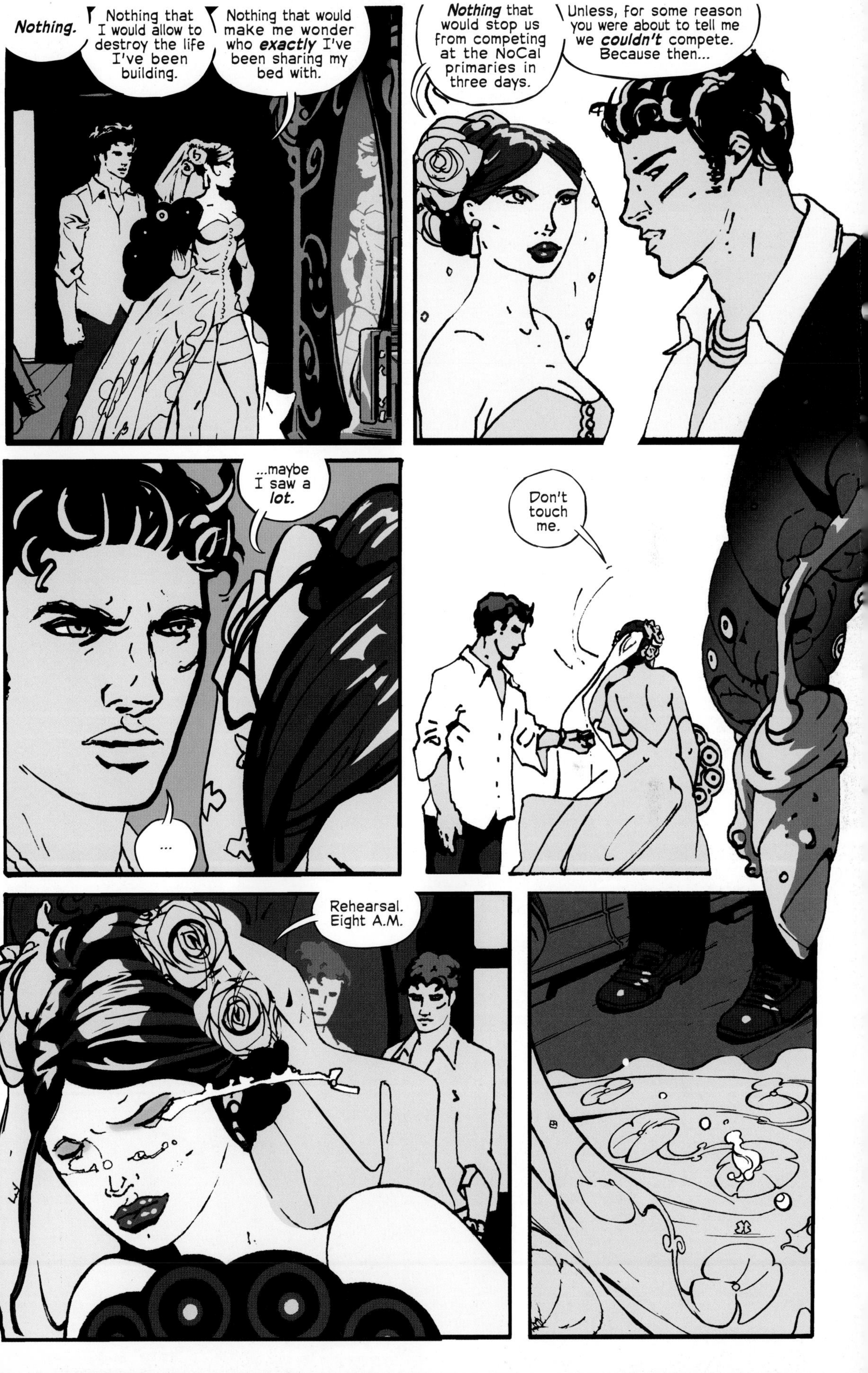

Nothing.
Nothing that I would allow to destroy the life I've been building.
Nothing that would make me wonder who exactly I've been sharing my bed with.
Nothing that would stop us from competing at the NoCal primaries in three days.
Unless, for some reason you were about to tell me we couldn't compete. Because then...
...maybe I saw a lot.
...
Don't touch me.
Rehearsal. Eight A.M.

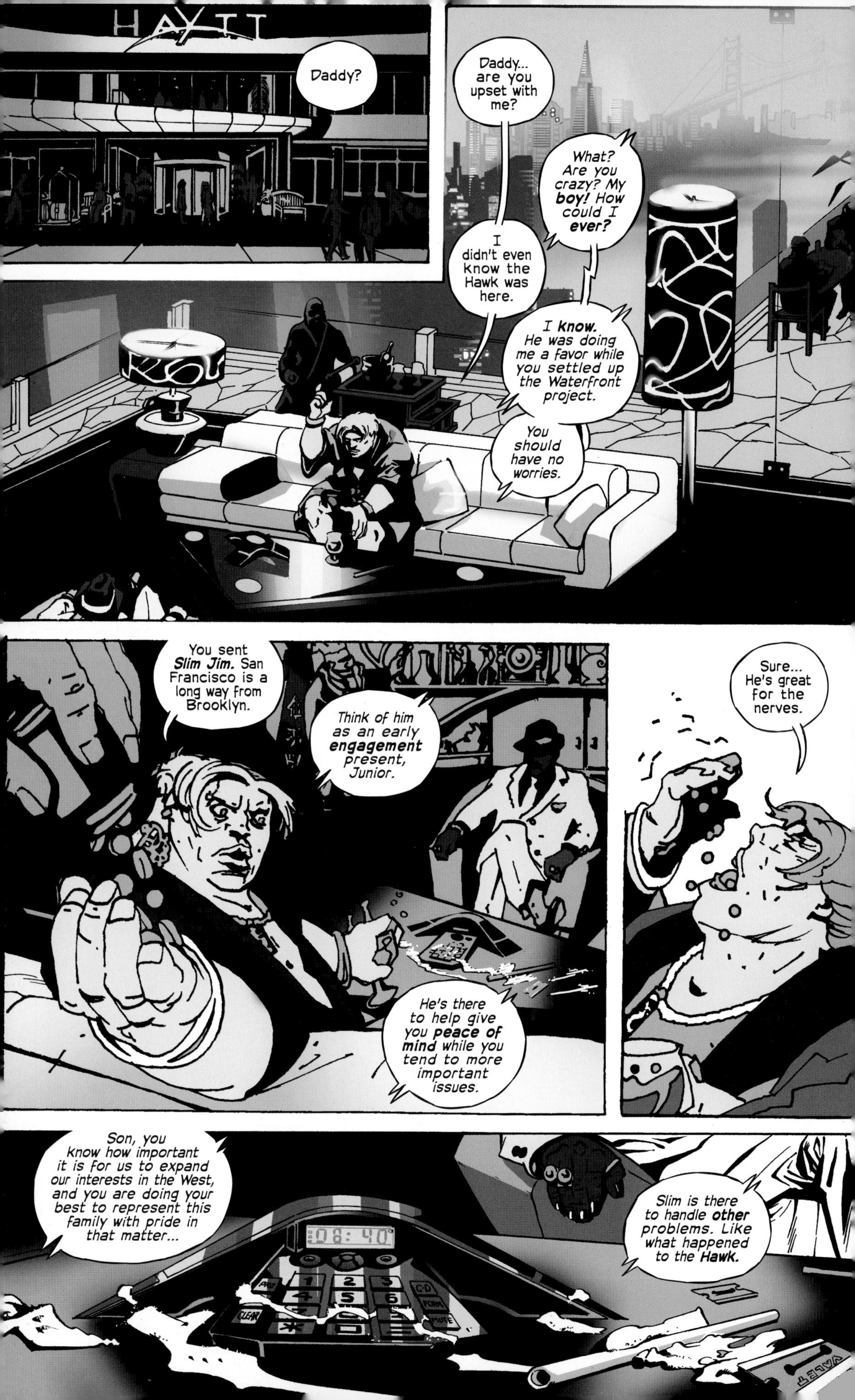
HAYTT
Daddy?
Daddy... are you upset with me?
What? Are you crazy? My **boy!** How could I **ever?**
I didn't even know the Hawk was here.
I **know.** He was doing me a favor while you settled up the Waterfront project.
You should have no worries.
You sent **Slim Jim.** San Francisco is a long way from Brooklyn.
Think of him as an early **engagement** present, Junior.
He's there to help give you **peace of mind** while you tend to more important issues.
Sure... He's great for the nerves.
Son, you know how important it is for us to expand our interests in the West, and you are doing your best to represent this family with pride in that matter...
Slim is there to handle **other** problems. Like what happened to the **Hawk.**
08:40

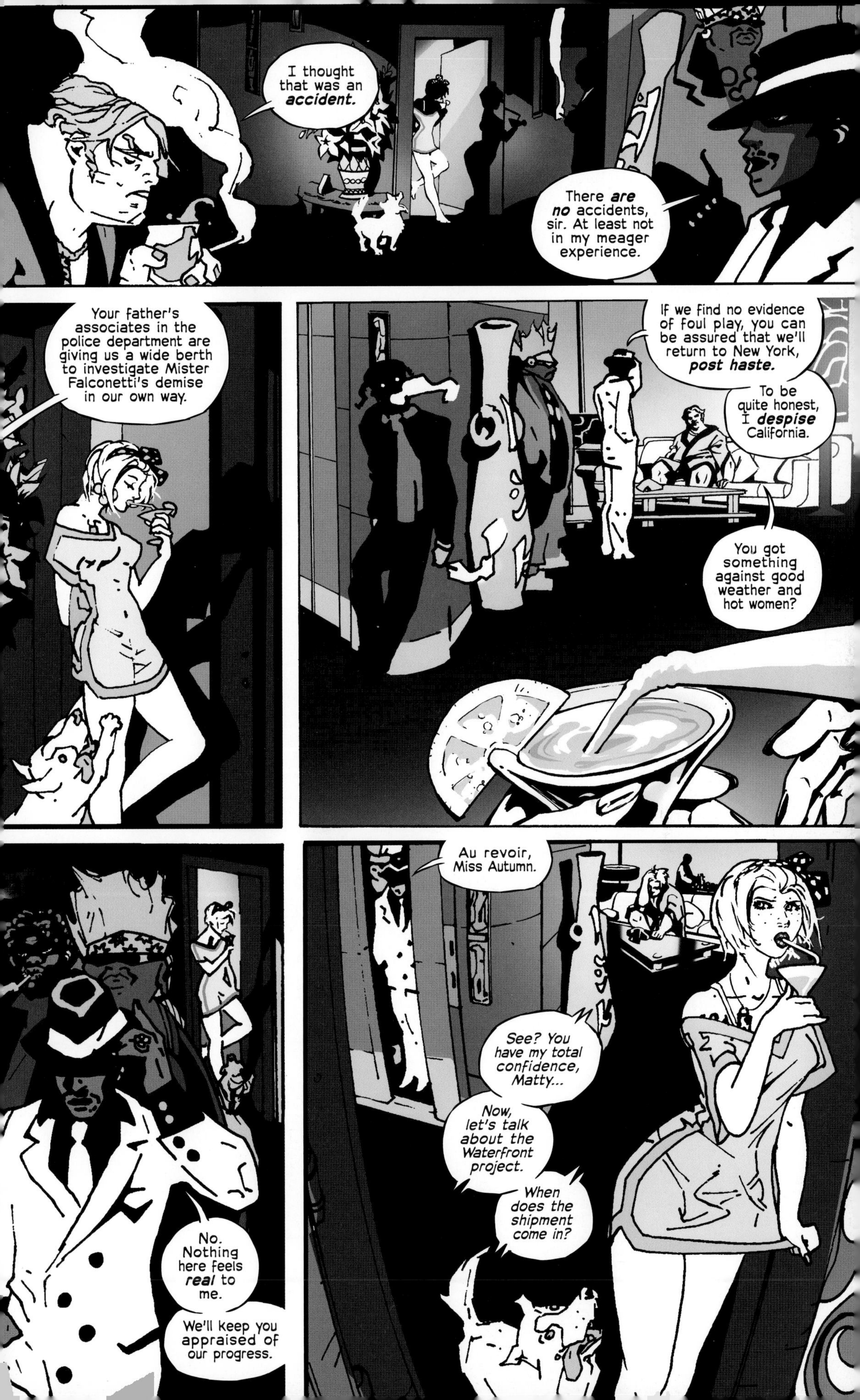
I thought that was an *accident.*
There *are no* accidents, sir. At least not in my meager experience.
Your father's associates in the police department are giving us a wide berth to investigate Mister Falconetti's demise in our own way.
If we find no evidence of foul play, you can be assured that we'll return to New York, *post haste.*
To be quite honest, I *despise* California.
You got something against good weather and hot women?
No. Nothing here feels *real* to me.
We'll keep you appraised of our progress.
Au revoir, Miss Autumn.
See? You have my total confidence, Matty...
Now, let's talk about the Waterfront project.
When does the shipment come in?

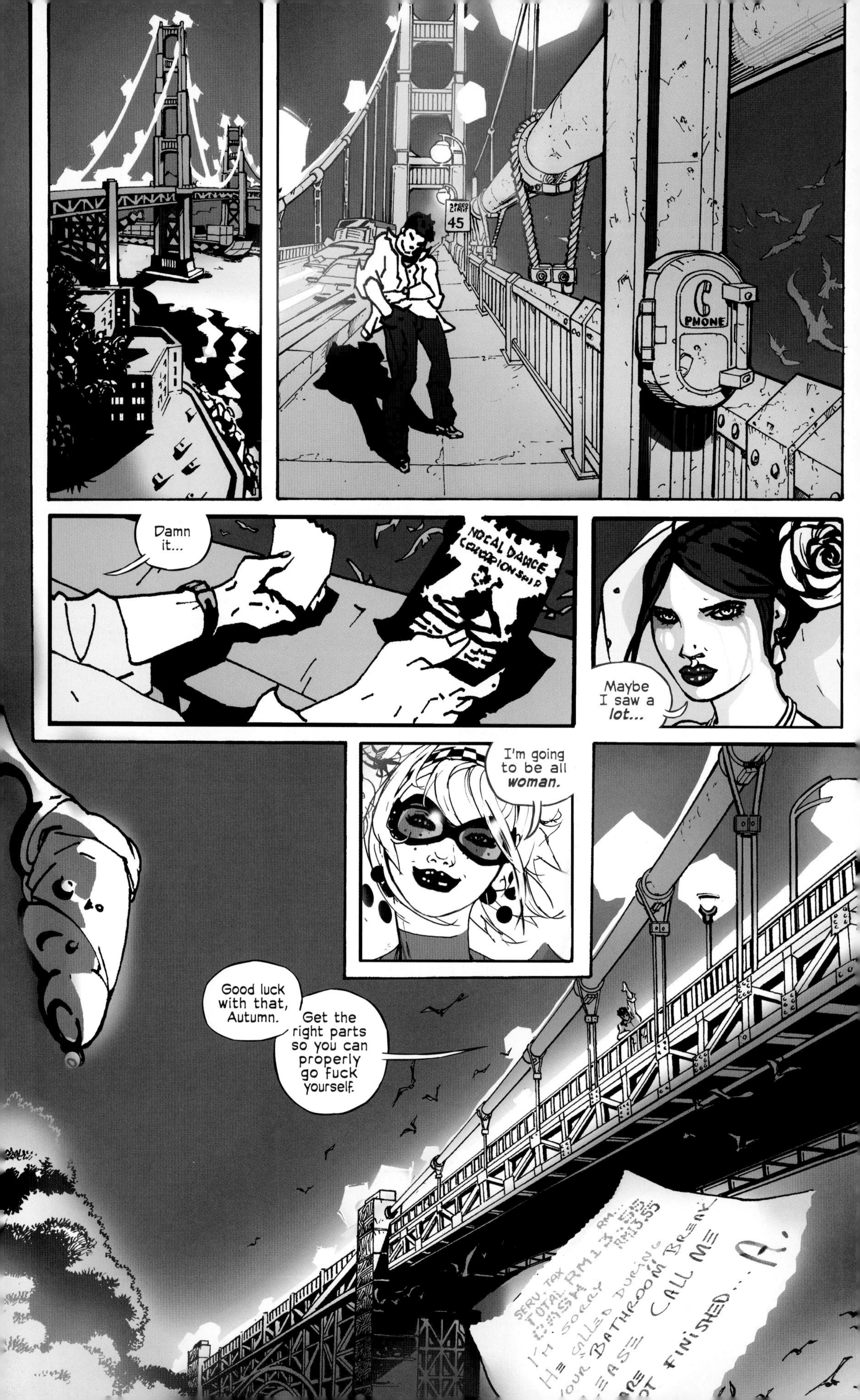
SPEED LIMIT
45
PHONE
Damn it...
NORCAL DANCE CHAMPIONSHIP
Maybe I saw a *lot...*
I'm going to be all ***woman.***
Good luck with that, Autumn.
Get the right parts so you can properly go fuck yourself.
SERV. TAX
TOTAL RM13.55
I'M SORRY
HE CALLED DURING
YOUR BATHROOM BREAK
EASE CALL ME
FINISHED...
R.

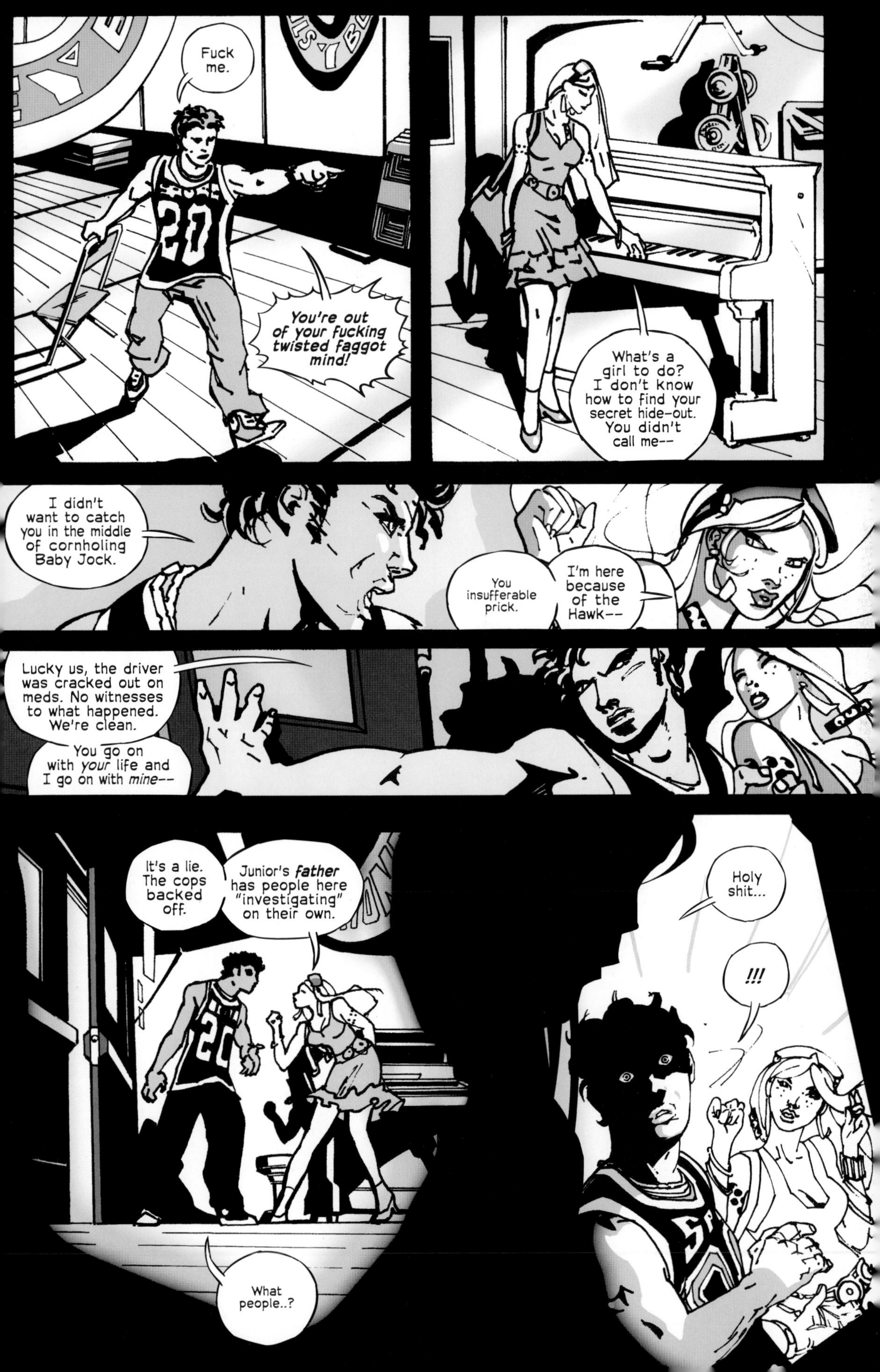
Fuck me.
You're out of your fucking twisted faggot mind!
What's a girl to do? I don't know how to find your secret hide-out. You didn't call me--
I didn't want to catch you in the middle of cornholing Baby Jock.
I'm here because of the Hawk--
You insufferable prick.
Lucky us, the driver was cracked out on meds. No witnesses to what happened. We're clean.
You go on with *your* life and I go on with *mine*--
It's a lie. The cops backed off.
Junior's ***father*** has people here "investigating" on their own.
What people..?
Holy shit...
!!!

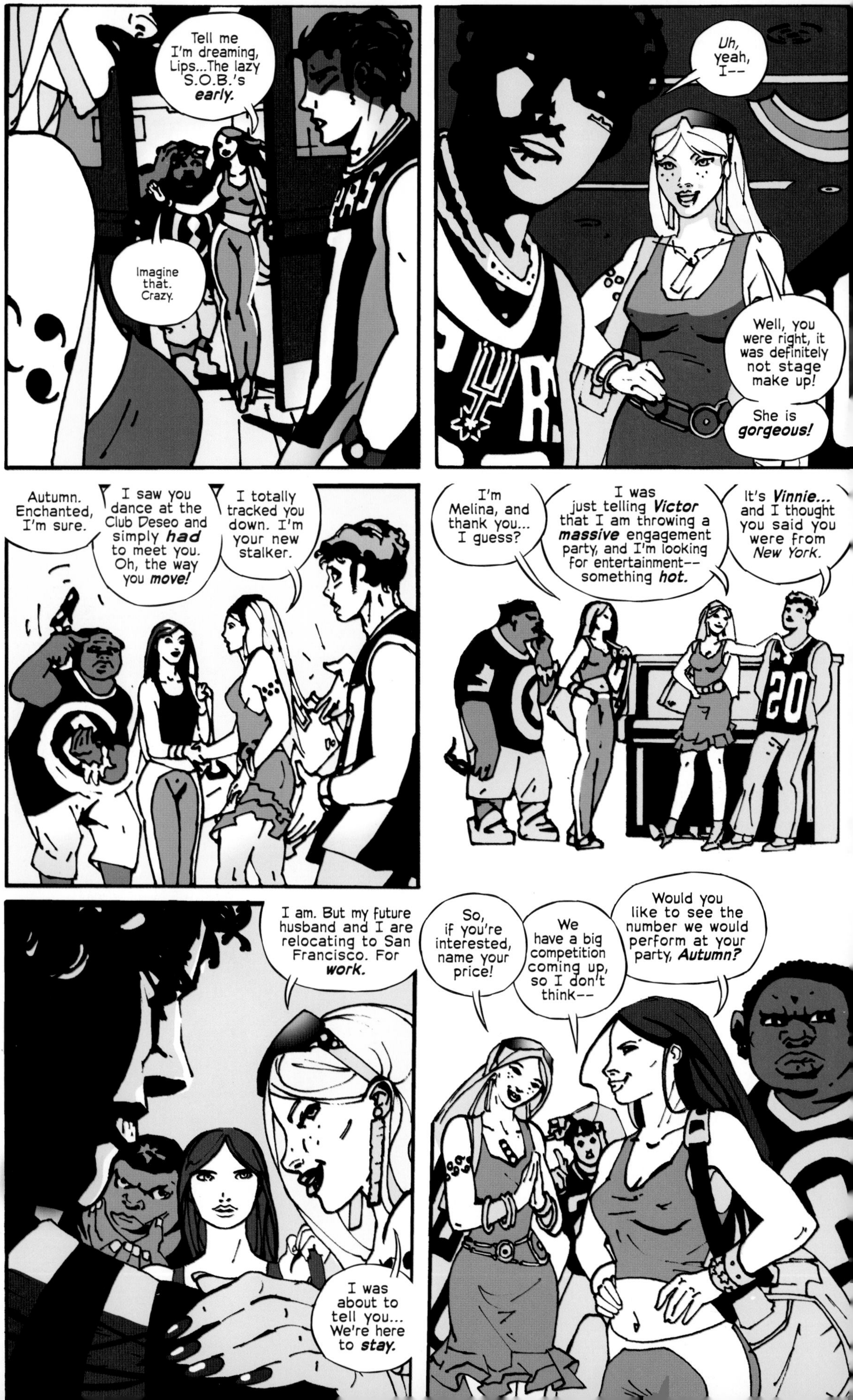
Tell me I'm dreaming, Lips...The lazy S.O.B.'s *early.*
Imagine that. Crazy.
Uh, yeah, I--
Well, you were right, it was definitely not stage make up!
She is ***gorgeous!***
Autumn. Enchanted, I'm sure.
I saw you dance at the Club Deseo and simply ***had*** to meet you. Oh, the way you ***move!***
I totally tracked you down. I'm your new stalker.
I'm Melina, and thank you... I guess?
I was just telling ***Victor*** that I am throwing a ***massive*** engagement party, and I'm looking for entertainment-- something ***hot.***
It's ***Vinnie...*** and I thought you said you were from *New York.*
I am. But my future husband and I are relocating to San Francisco. For ***work.***
I was about to tell you... We're here to ***stay.***
So, if you're interested, name your price!
We have a big competition coming up, so I don't think--
Would you like to see the number we would perform at your party, ***Autumn?***

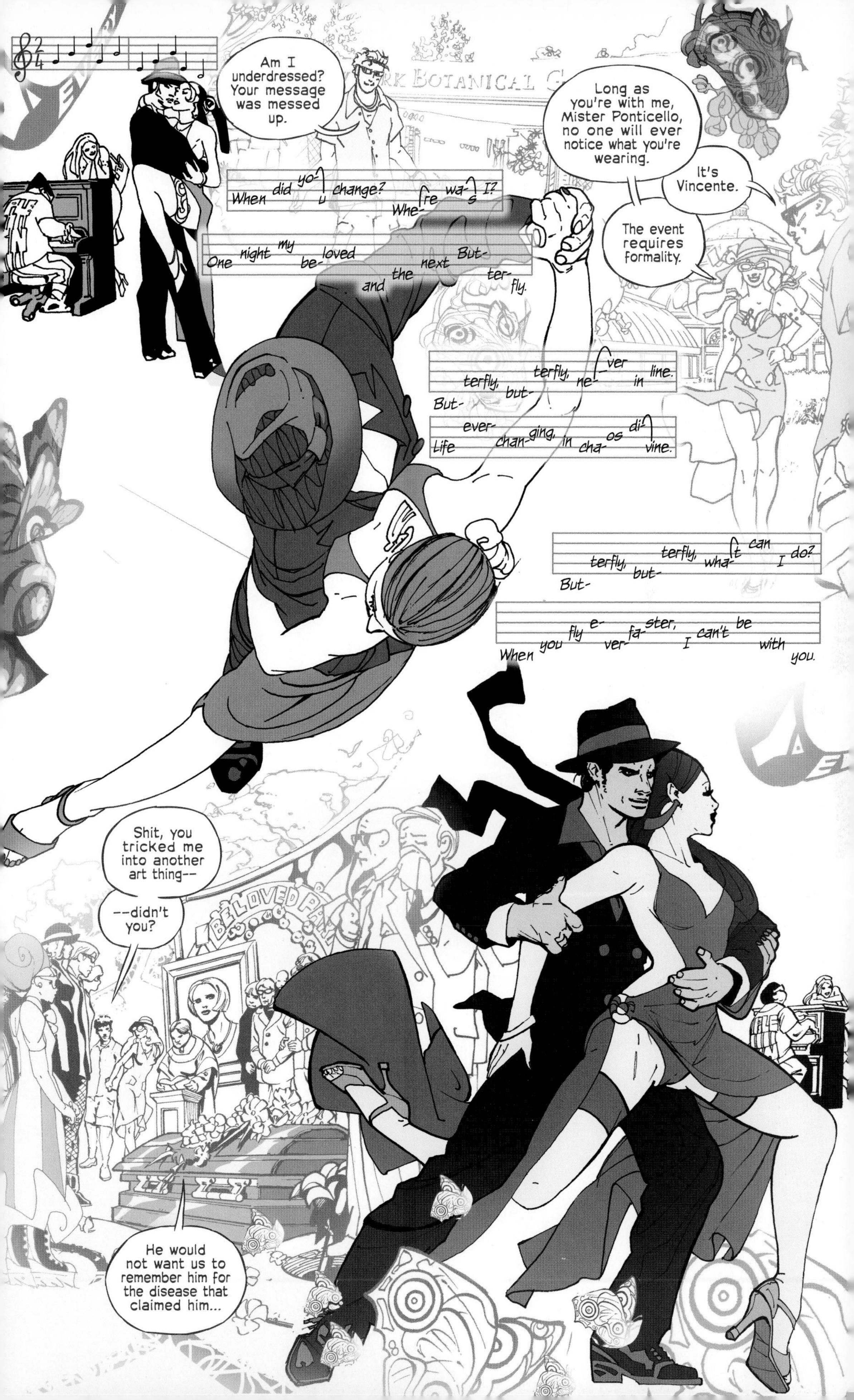

Am I underdressed? Your message was messed up.
Long as you're with me, Mister Ponticello, no one will ever notice what you're wearing.
It's Vincente.
The event requires formality.
When did you change? Where was I?
One night my beloved and the next Butterfly.
Butterfly, butterfly, never in line.
Life everchanging, in chaos divine.
Butterfly, butterfly, what can I do?
When you fly ever faster, I can't be with you.
Shit, you tricked me into another art thing--
--didn't you?
BELOVED
He would not want us to remember him for the disease that claimed him...

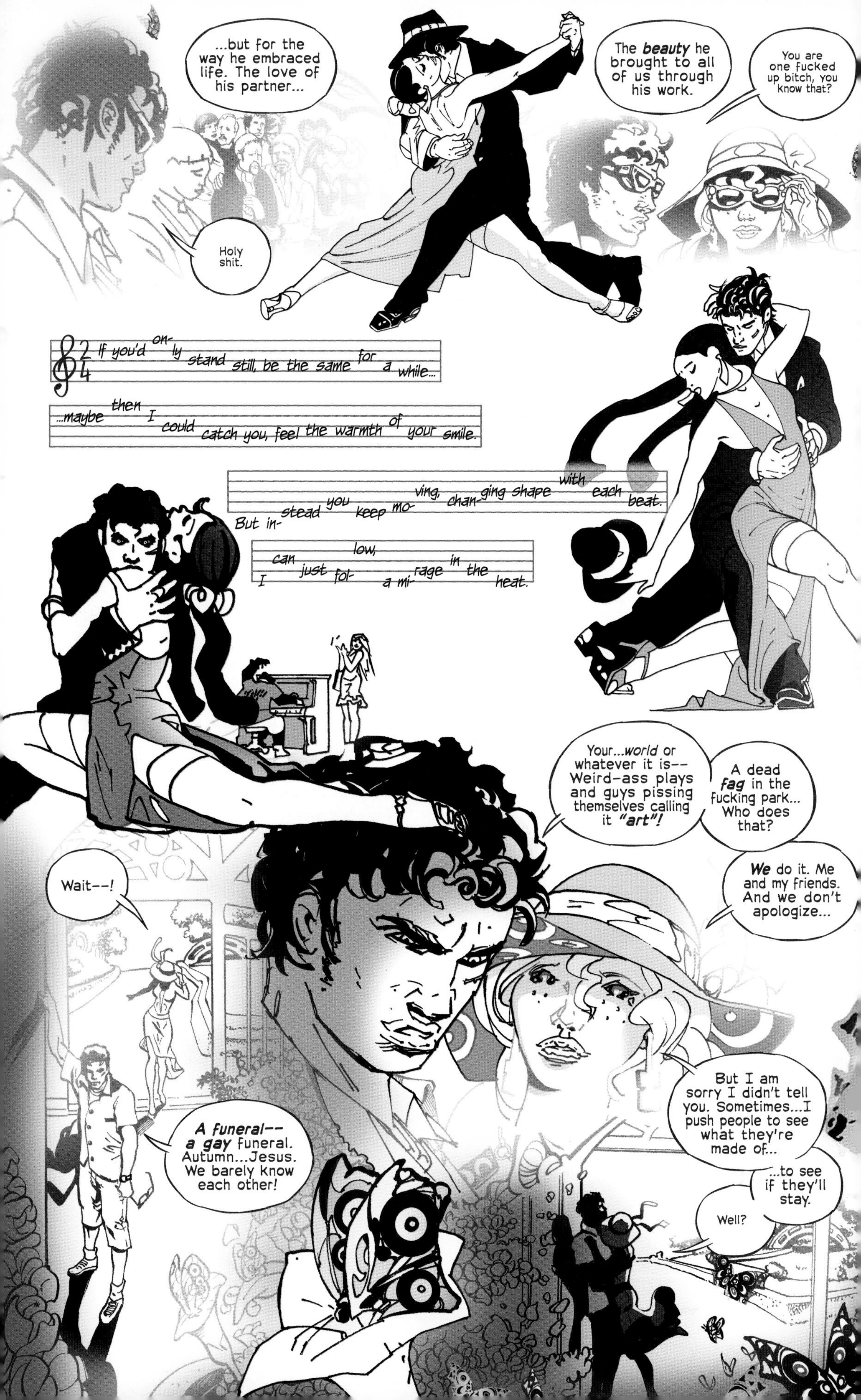

...but for the way he embraced life. The love of his partner...
The **beauty** he brought to all of us through his work.
You are one fucked up bitch, you know that?
Holy shit.
If you'd on- ly stand still, be the same for a while...
...maybe then I could catch you, feel the warmth of your smile.
But in- stead you keep mo- ving, chan- ging shape with each beat.
I can just fol- low, a mi- rage in the heat.
Your...*world* or whatever it is-- Weird-ass plays and guys pissing themselves calling it *"art"!*
A dead **fag** in the fucking park... Who does that?
Wait--!
We do it. Me and my friends. And we don't apologize...
But I am sorry I didn't tell you. Sometimes...I push people to see what they're made of...
A funeral-- a gay funeral. Autumn...Jesus. We barely know each other!
...to see if they'll stay.
Well?

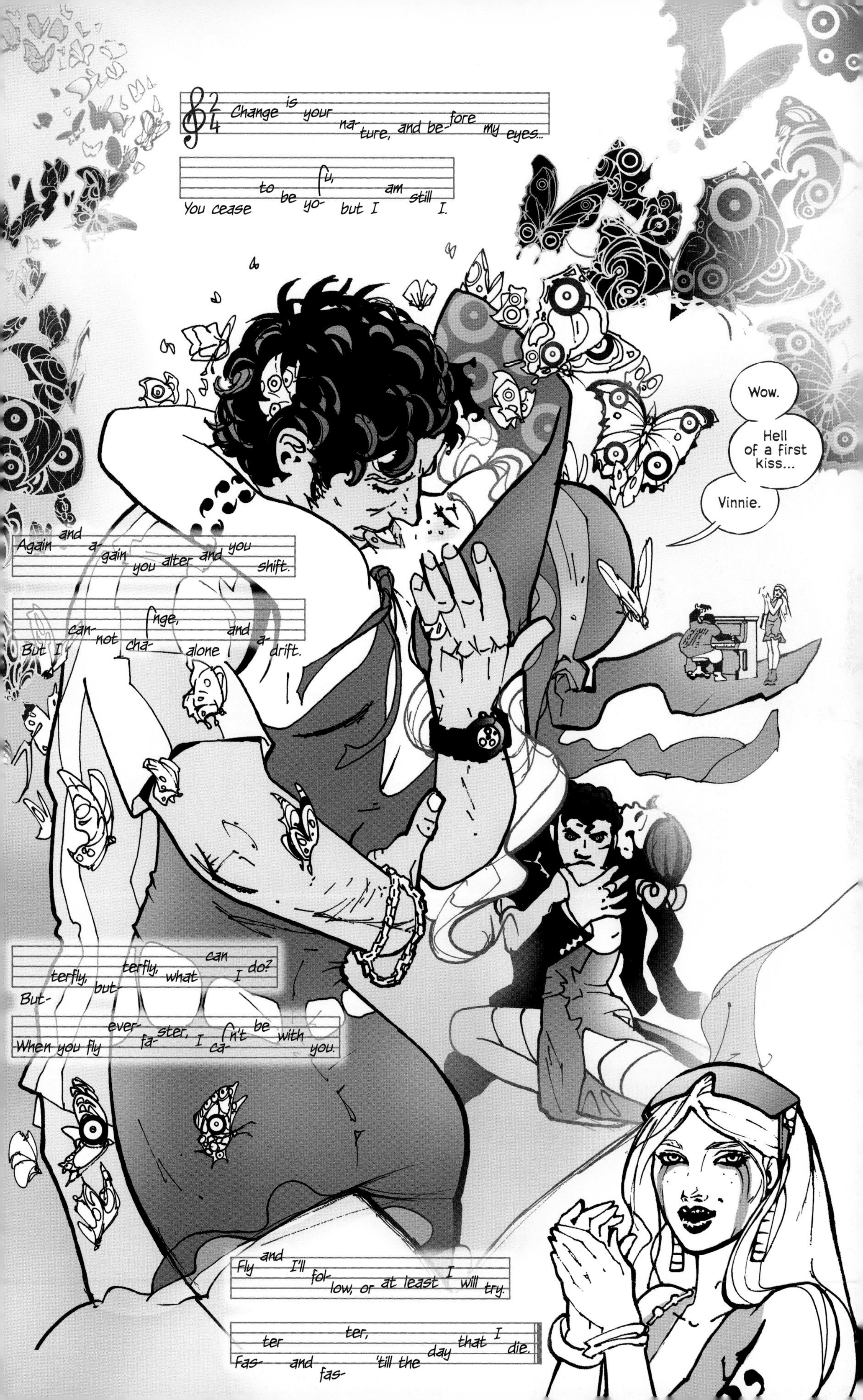
Change is your na- ture, and be- fore my eyes...
You cease to be yo- u, but I am still I.
Wow.
Hell of a first kiss...
Vinnie.
Again and a- gain you alter and you shift.
But I can- not cha- nge, alone and a- drift.
But- terfly, but- terfly, what can I do?
When you fly ever- fa- ster, I ca- n't be with you.
Fly and I'll fol- low, or at least I will try.
Fas- ter and fas- ter, 'till the day that I die.

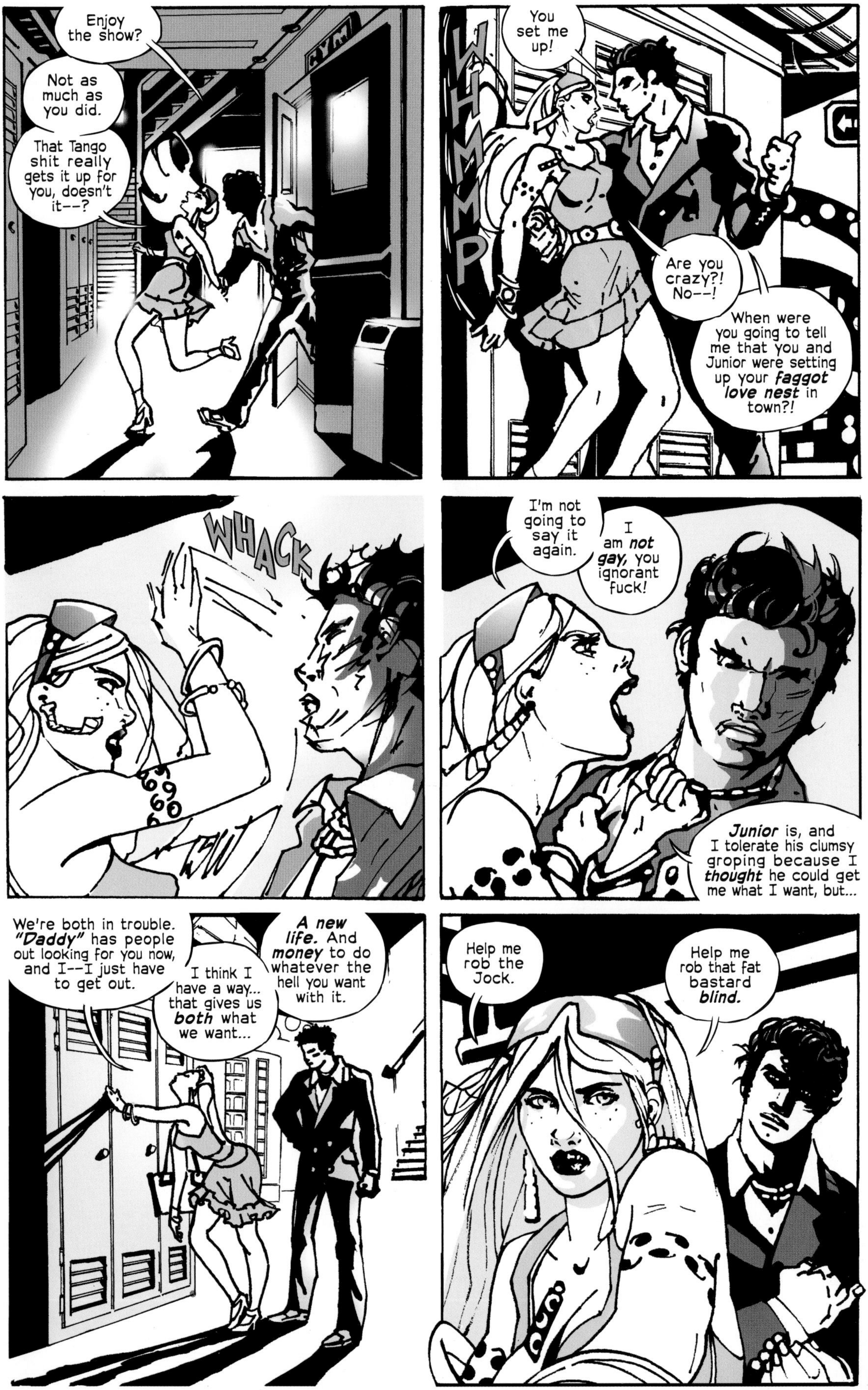
Enjoy the show?
Not as much as you did.
That Tango shit really gets it up for you, doesn't it--?
You set me up!
WHUMMP
Are you crazy?! No--!
When were you going to tell me that you and Junior were setting up your ***faggot love nest*** in town?!
WHACK
I'm not going to say it again.
I am ***not gay,*** you ignorant fuck!
Junior is, and I tolerate his clumsy groping because I ***thought*** he could get me what I want, but...
We're both in trouble. ***"Daddy"*** has people out looking for you now, and I--I just have to get out.
I think I have a way... that gives us ***both*** what we want...
A new life. And ***money*** to do whatever the hell you want with it.
Help me rob the Jock.
Help me rob that fat bastard ***blind.***

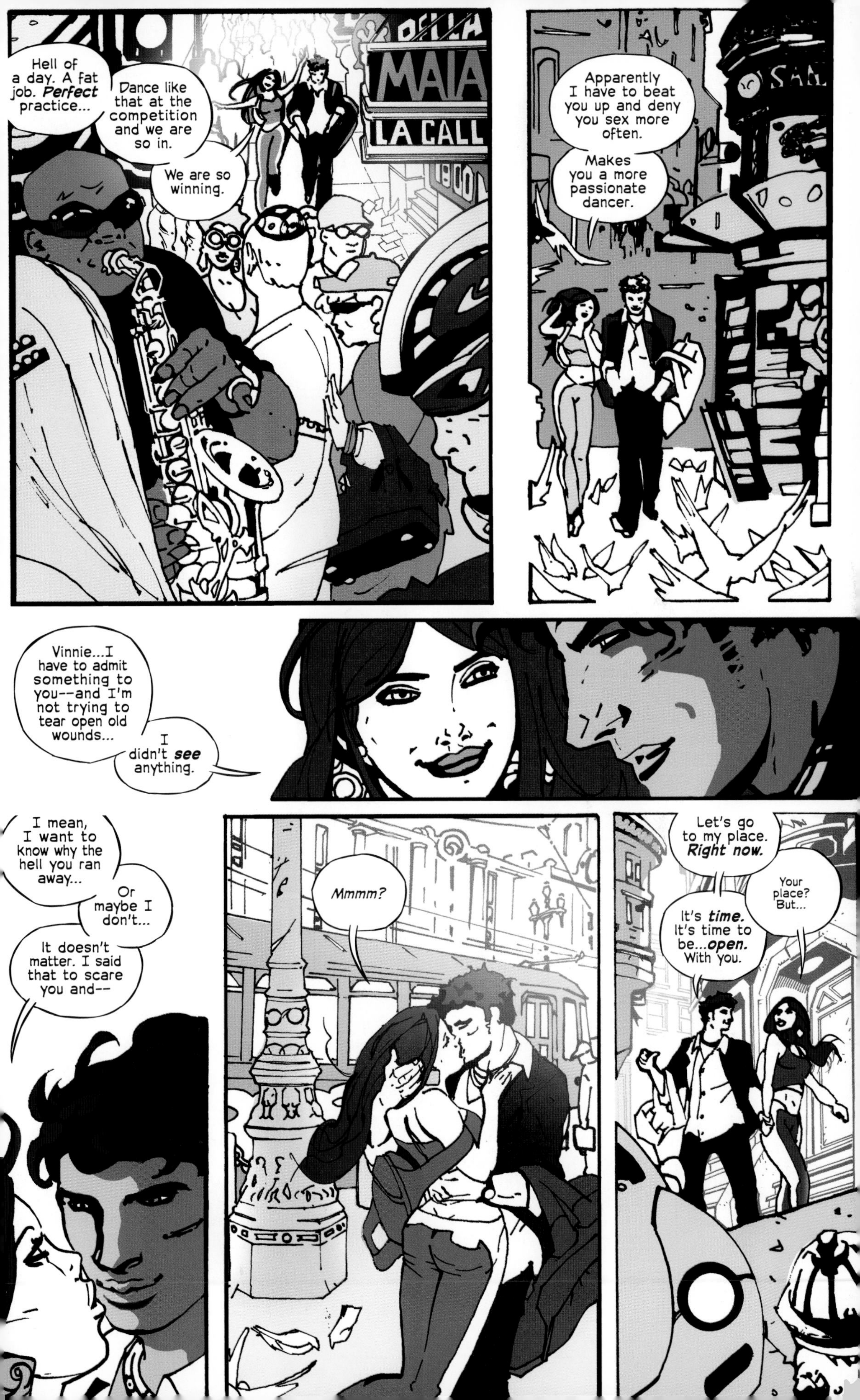
DELLA
MAIA
LA CALL
1900
Hell of a day. A fat job. *Perfect* practice...
Dance like that at the competition and we are so in.
We are so winning.
Apparently I have to beat you up and deny you sex more often.
Makes you a more passionate dancer.
Vinnie...I have to admit something to you--and I'm not trying to tear open old wounds...
I didn't *see* anything.
I mean, I want to know why the hell you ran away...
Or maybe I don't...
It doesn't matter. I said that to scare you and--
Mmmm?
Let's go to my place. ***Right now.***
Your place? But...
It's ***time.*** It's time to be...***open.*** With you.

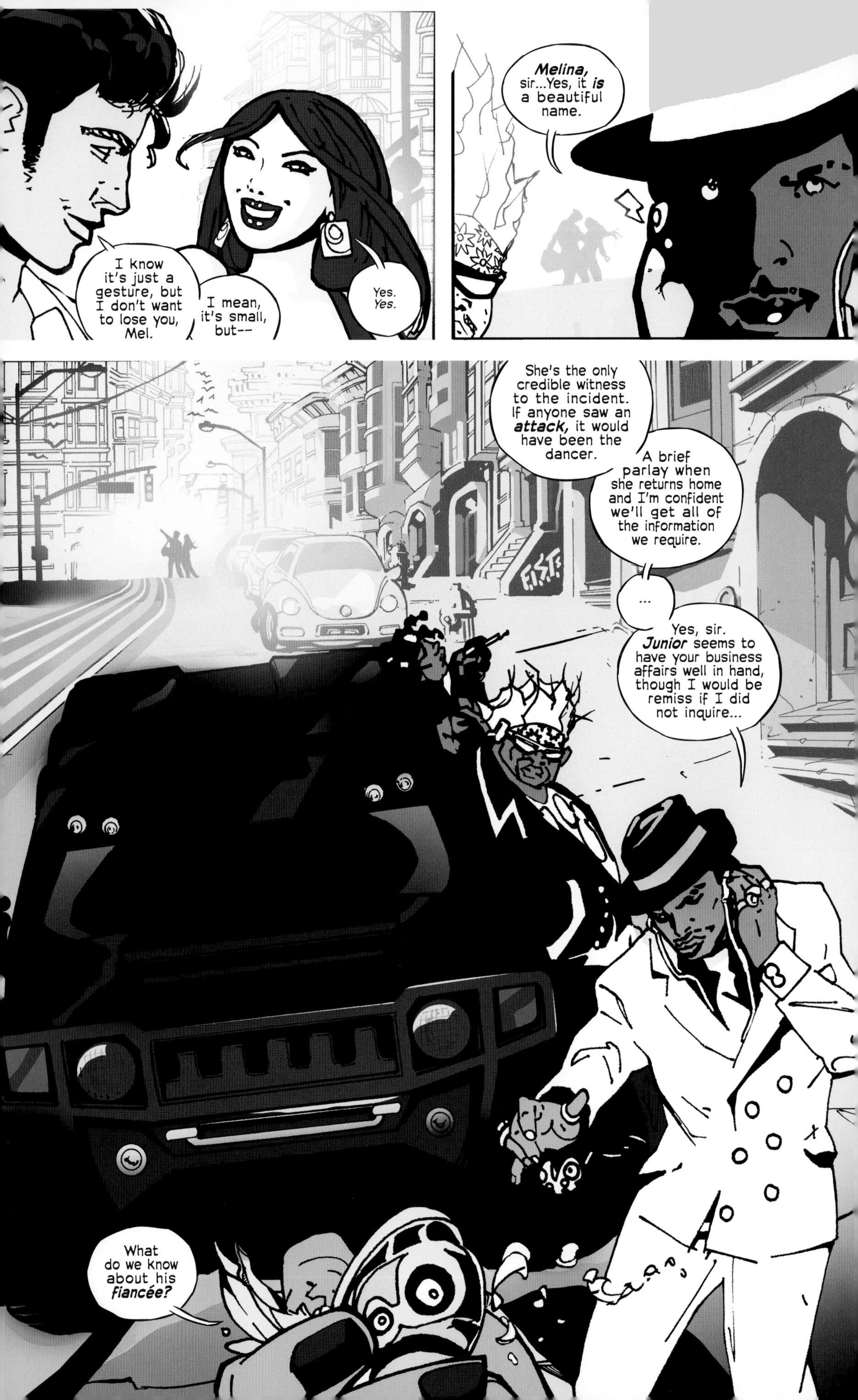
I know it's just a gesture, but I don't want to lose you, Mel.
I mean, it's small, but--
Yes. *Yes.*
Melina, sir...Yes, it ***is*** a beautiful name.
She's the only credible witness to the incident. If anyone saw an ***attack,*** it would have been the dancer.
A brief parlay when she returns home and I'm confident we'll get all of the information we require.
...
Yes, sir. ***Junior*** seems to have your business affairs well in hand, though I would be remiss if I did not inquire...
What do we know about his ***fiancée?***
F.I.S.T.

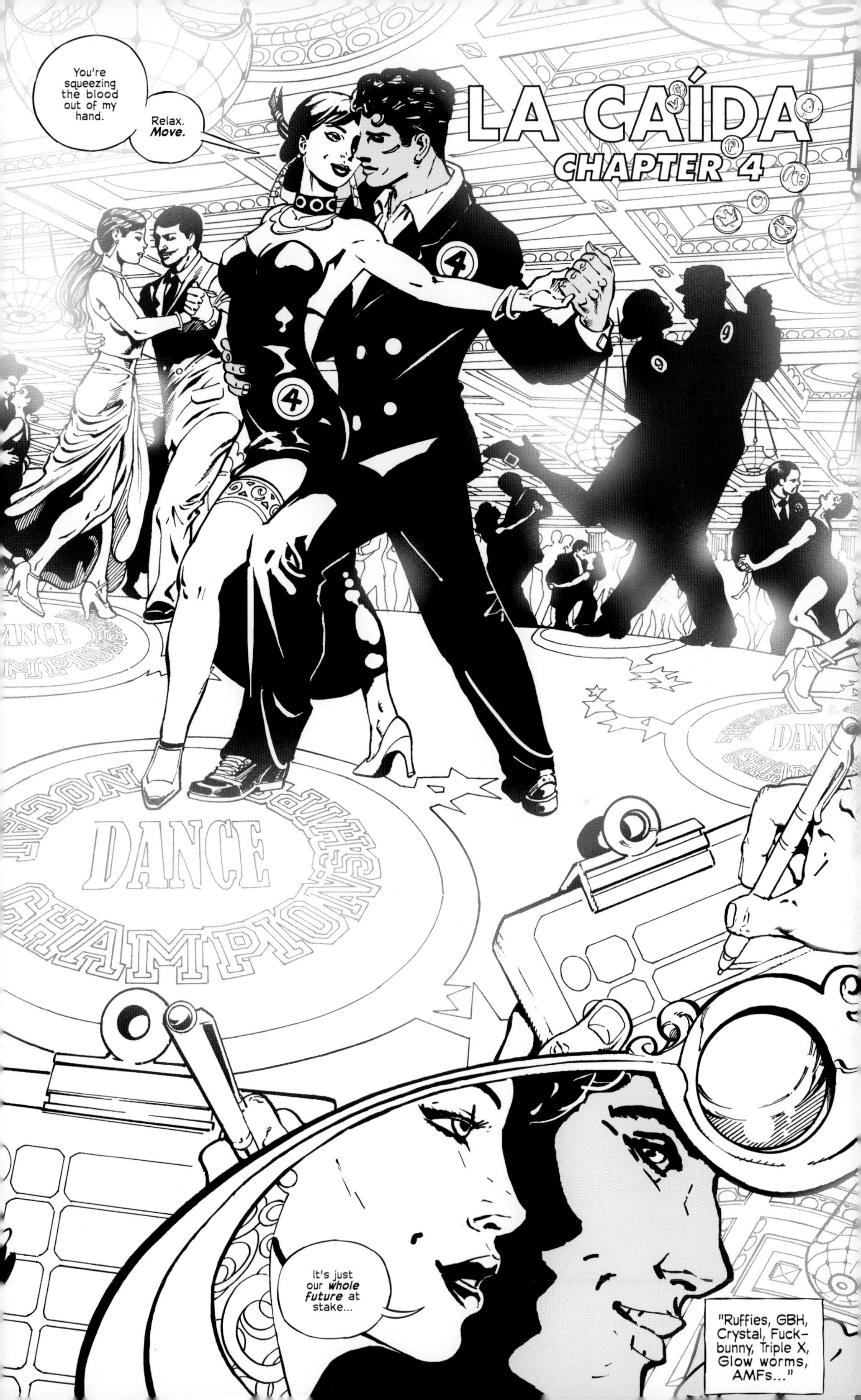

LA CAÍDA
CHAPTER 4
You're squeezing the blood out of my hand.
Relax. *Move.*
DANCE CHAMPIONS
It's just our *whole future* at stake...
"Ruffies, GBH, Crystal, Fuck-bunny, Triple X, Glow worms, AMFs..."

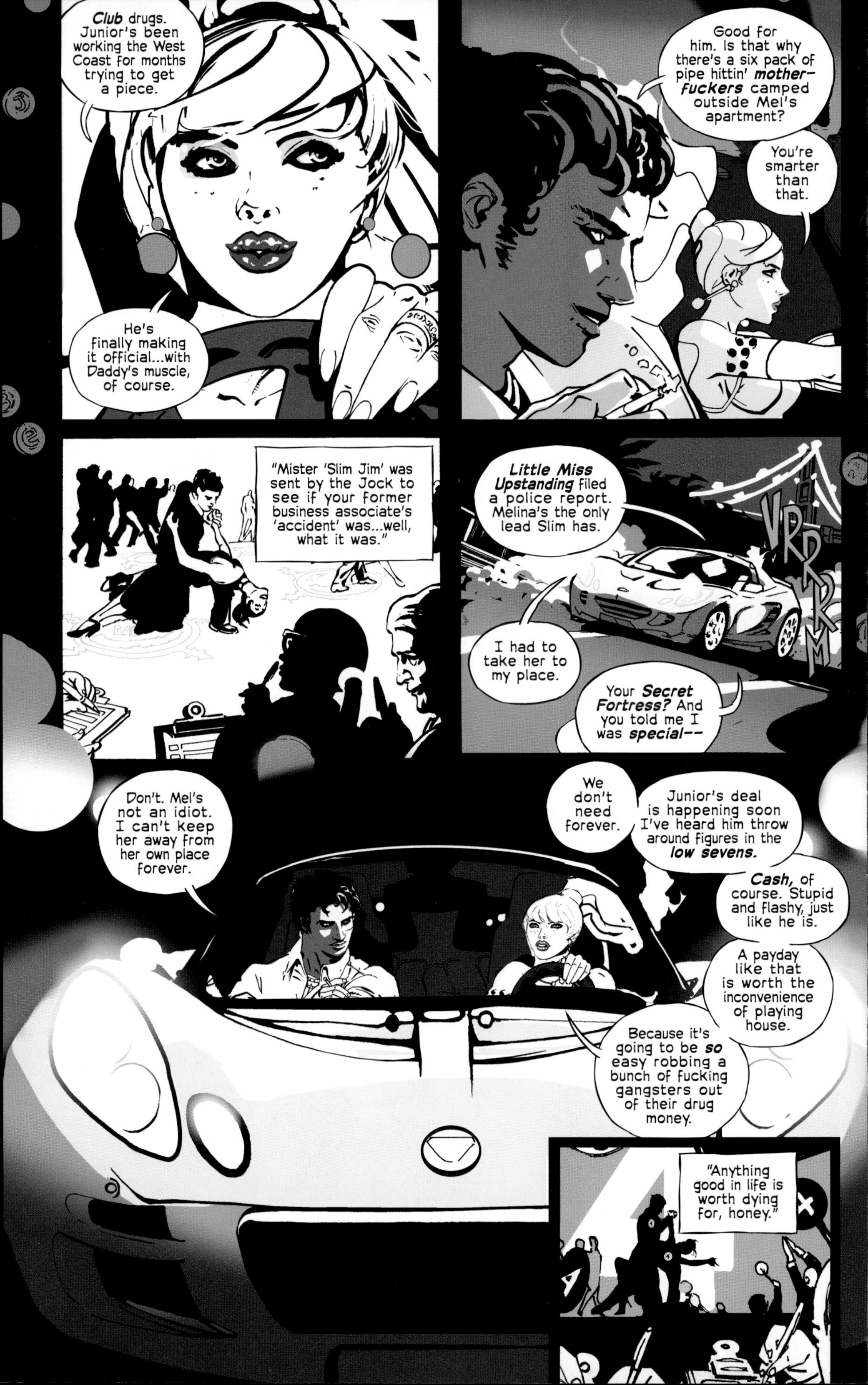

Club drugs. Junior's been working the West Coast for months trying to get a piece.
He's finally making it official...with Daddy's muscle, of course.
Good for him. Is that why there's a six pack of pipe hittin' mother-fuckers camped outside Mel's apartment?
You're smarter than that.
"Mister 'Slim Jim' was sent by the Jock to see if your former business associate's 'accident' was...well, what it was."
Little Miss Upstanding filed a police report. Melina's the only lead Slim has.
VRRRRM
I had to take her to my place.
Your Secret Fortress? And you told me I was special--
Don't. Mel's not an idiot. I can't keep her away from her own place forever.
We don't need forever.
Junior's deal is happening soon I've heard him throw around figures in the low sevens.
Cash, of course. Stupid and flashy, just like he is.
A payday like that is worth the inconvenience of playing house.
Because it's going to be so easy robbing a bunch of fucking gangsters out of their drug money.
"Anything good in life is worth dying for, honey."

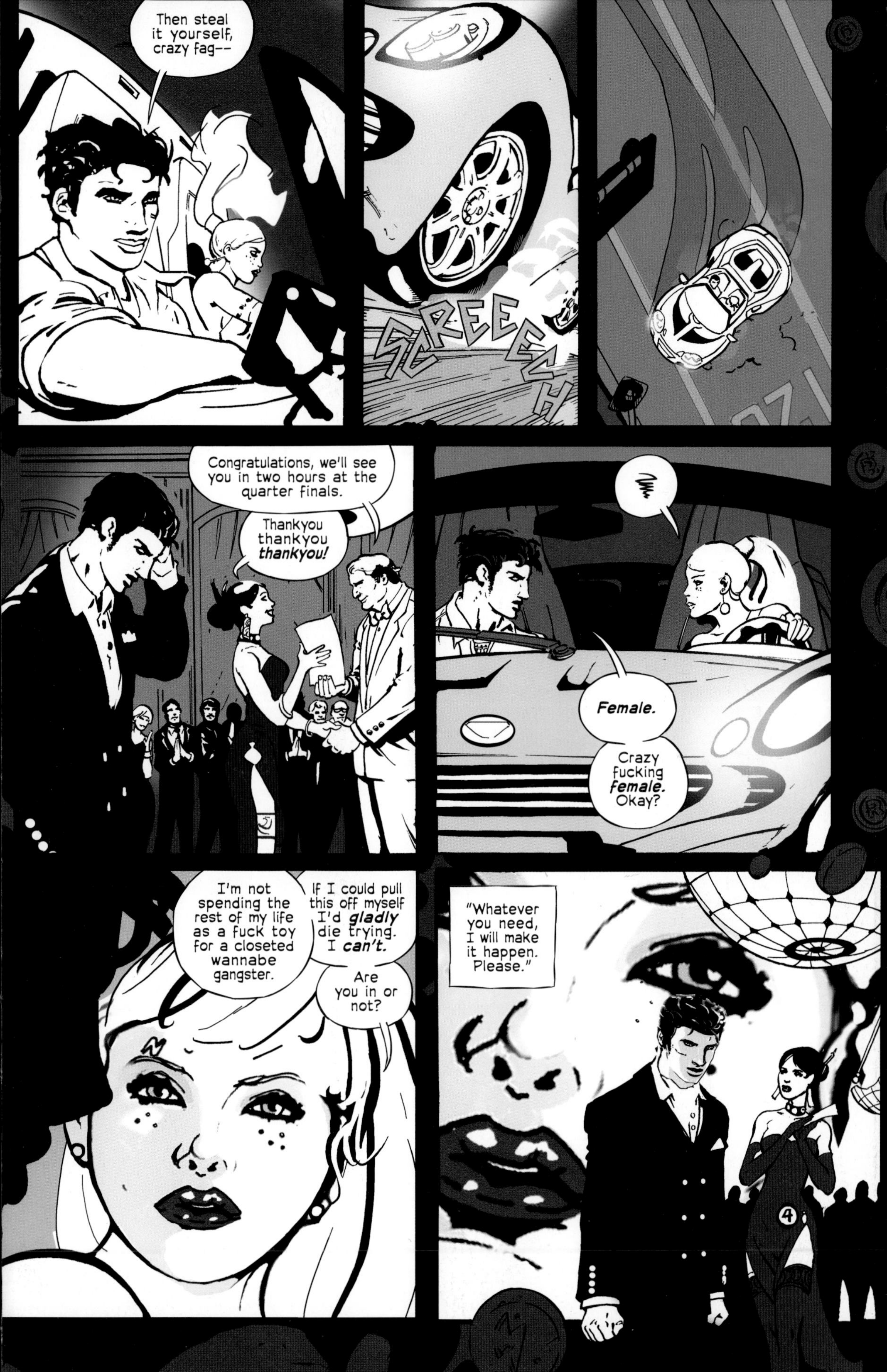
Then steal it yourself, crazy fag--
SCREEECH
Congratulations, we'll see you in two hours at the quarter finals.
Thankyou thankyou *thankyou!*
Female.
Crazy fucking *female.* Okay?
I'm not spending the rest of my life as a fuck toy for a closeted wannabe gangster.
If I could pull this off myself I'd *gladly* die trying. I *can't.*
Are you in or not?
"Whatever you need, I will make it happen. Please."

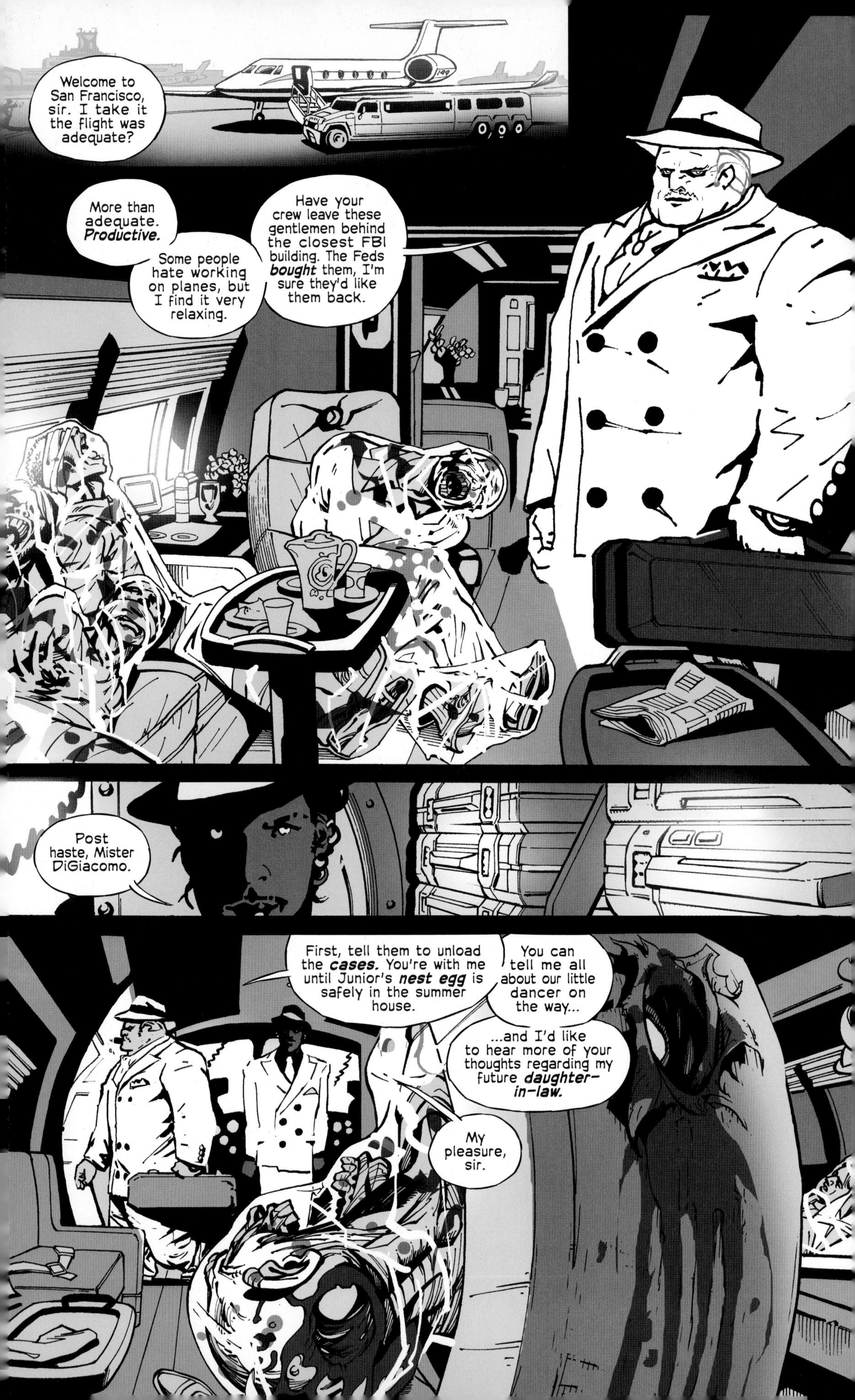

Welcome to San Francisco, sir. I take it the flight was adequate?
More than adequate. *Productive.*
Some people hate working on planes, but I find it very relaxing.
Have your crew leave these gentlemen behind the closest FBI building. The Feds *bought* them, I'm sure they'd like them back.
Post haste, Mister DiGiacomo.
First, tell them to unload the *cases.* You're with me until Junior's *nest egg* is safely in the summer house.
You can tell me all about our little dancer on the way...
...and I'd like to hear more of your thoughts regarding my future *daughter-in-law.*
My pleasure, sir.

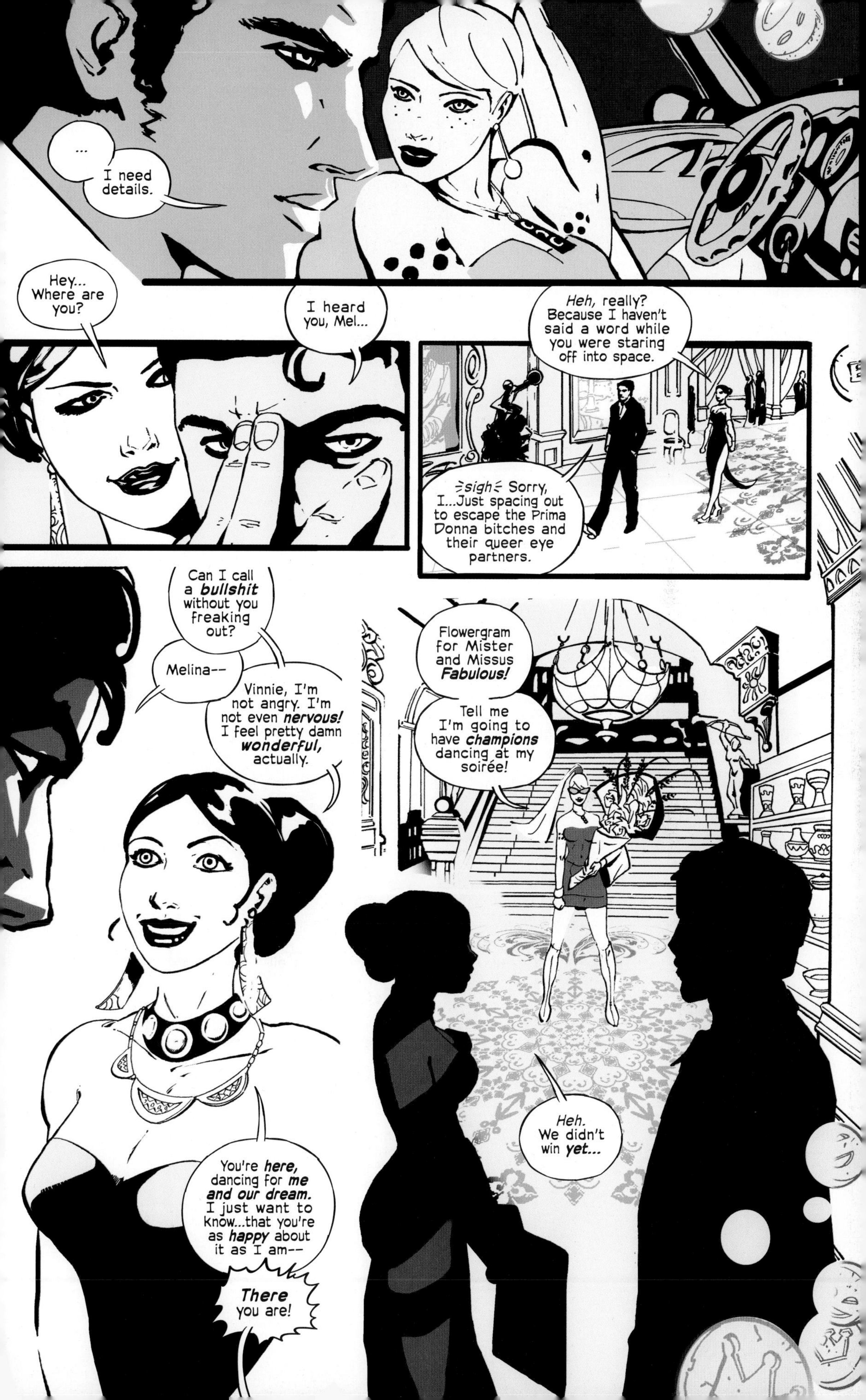
...
I need details.
Hey... Where are you?
I heard you, Mel...
Heh, really? Because I haven't said a word while you were staring off into space.
sigh Sorry, I...Just spacing out to escape the Prima Donna bitches and their queer eye partners.
Can I call a ***bullshit*** without you freaking out?
Melina--
Vinnie, I'm not angry. I'm not even ***nervous!*** I feel pretty damn ***wonderful,*** actually.
You're ***here,*** dancing for ***me and our dream.*** I just want to know...that you're as ***happy*** about it as I am--
There you are!
Flowergram for Mister and Missus ***Fabulous!***
Tell me I'm going to have ***champions*** dancing at my soirée!
Heh. We didn't win ***yet...***

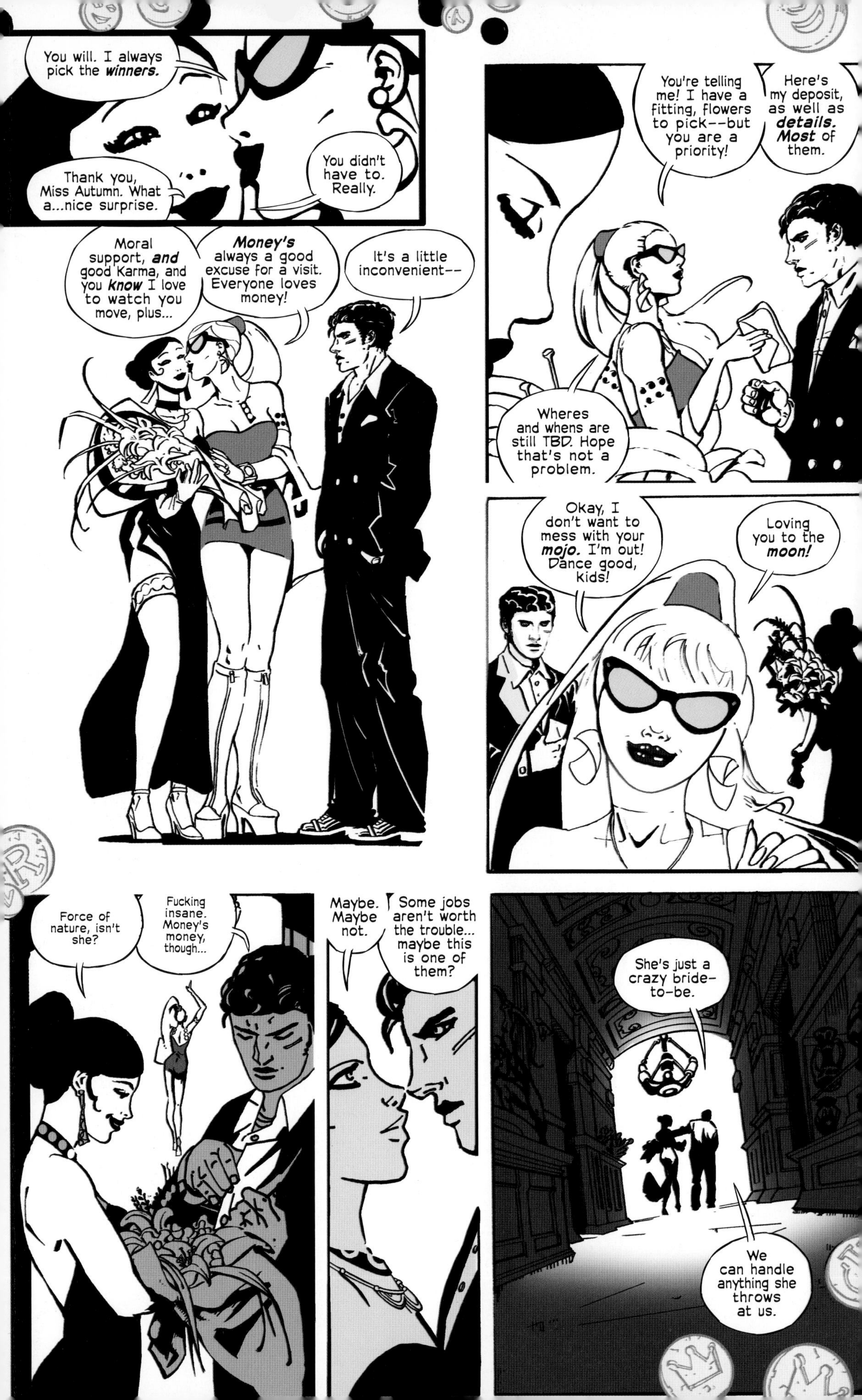

You will. I always pick the *winners.*
Thank you, Miss Autumn. What a...nice surprise.
You didn't have to. Really.
You're telling me! I have a fitting, flowers to pick--but you are a priority!
Here's my deposit, as well as *details. Most* of them.
Moral support, *and* good Karma, and you *know* I love to watch you move, plus...
Money's always a good excuse for a visit. Everyone loves money!
It's a little inconvenient--
Wheres and whens are still TBD. Hope that's not a problem.
Okay, I don't want to mess with your *mojo.* I'm out! Dance good, kids!
Loving you to the *moon!*
Force of nature, isn't she?
Fucking insane. Money's money, though...
Maybe. Maybe not.
Some jobs aren't worth the trouble... maybe this is one of them?
She's just a crazy bride-to-be.
We can handle anything she throws at us.

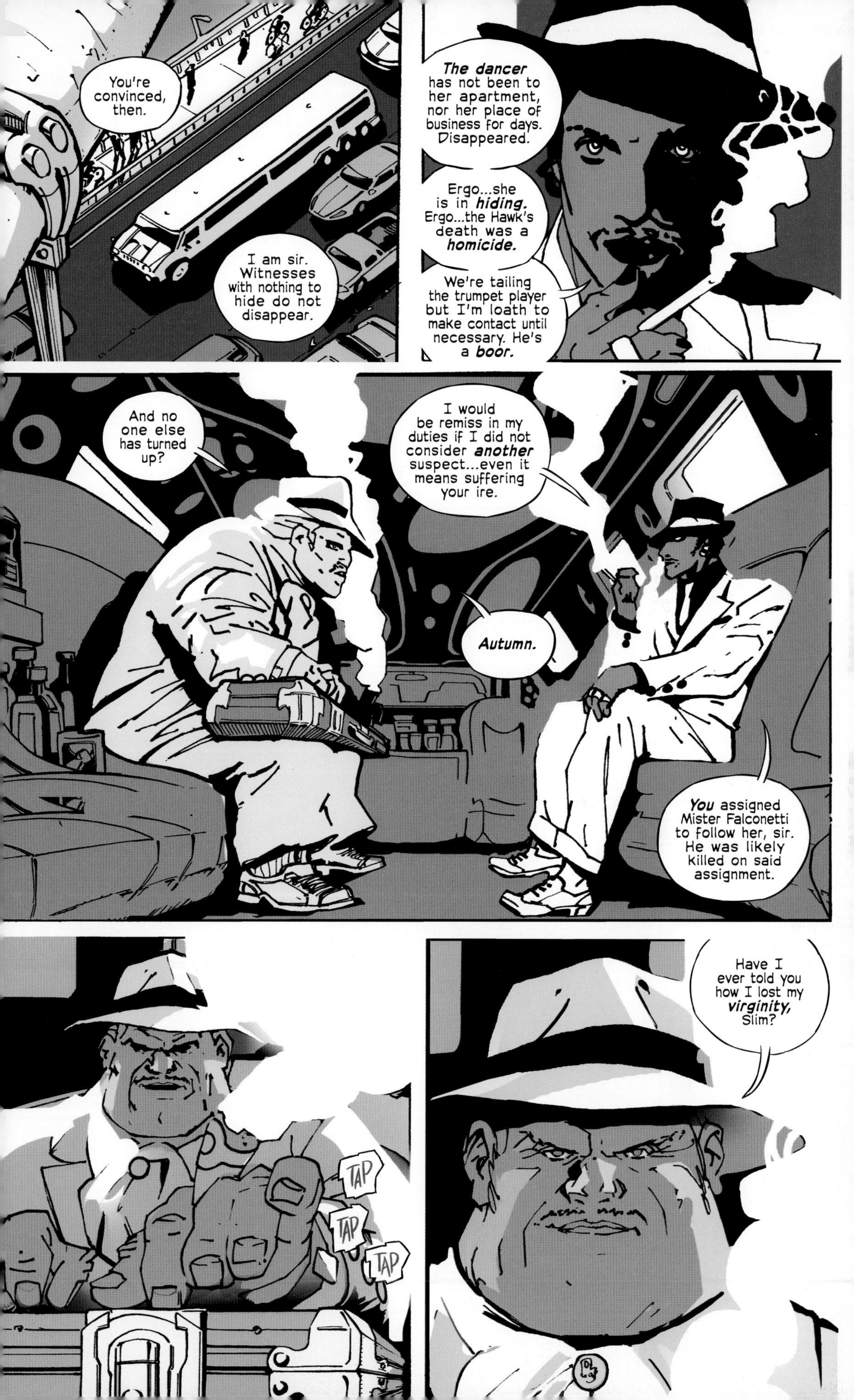
You're convinced, then.
I am sir. Witnesses with nothing to hide do not disappear.
The dancer has not been to her apartment, nor her place of business for days. Disappeared.
Ergo...she is in ***hiding.*** Ergo...the Hawk's death was a ***homicide.***
We're tailing the trumpet player but I'm loath to make contact until necessary. He's a ***boor.***
And no one else has turned up?
I would be remiss in my duties if I did not consider ***another*** suspect...even it means suffering your ire.
Autumn.
You assigned Mister Falconetti to follow her, sir. He was likely killed on said assignment.
TAP
TAP
TAP
Have I ever told you how I lost my ***virginity,*** Slim?

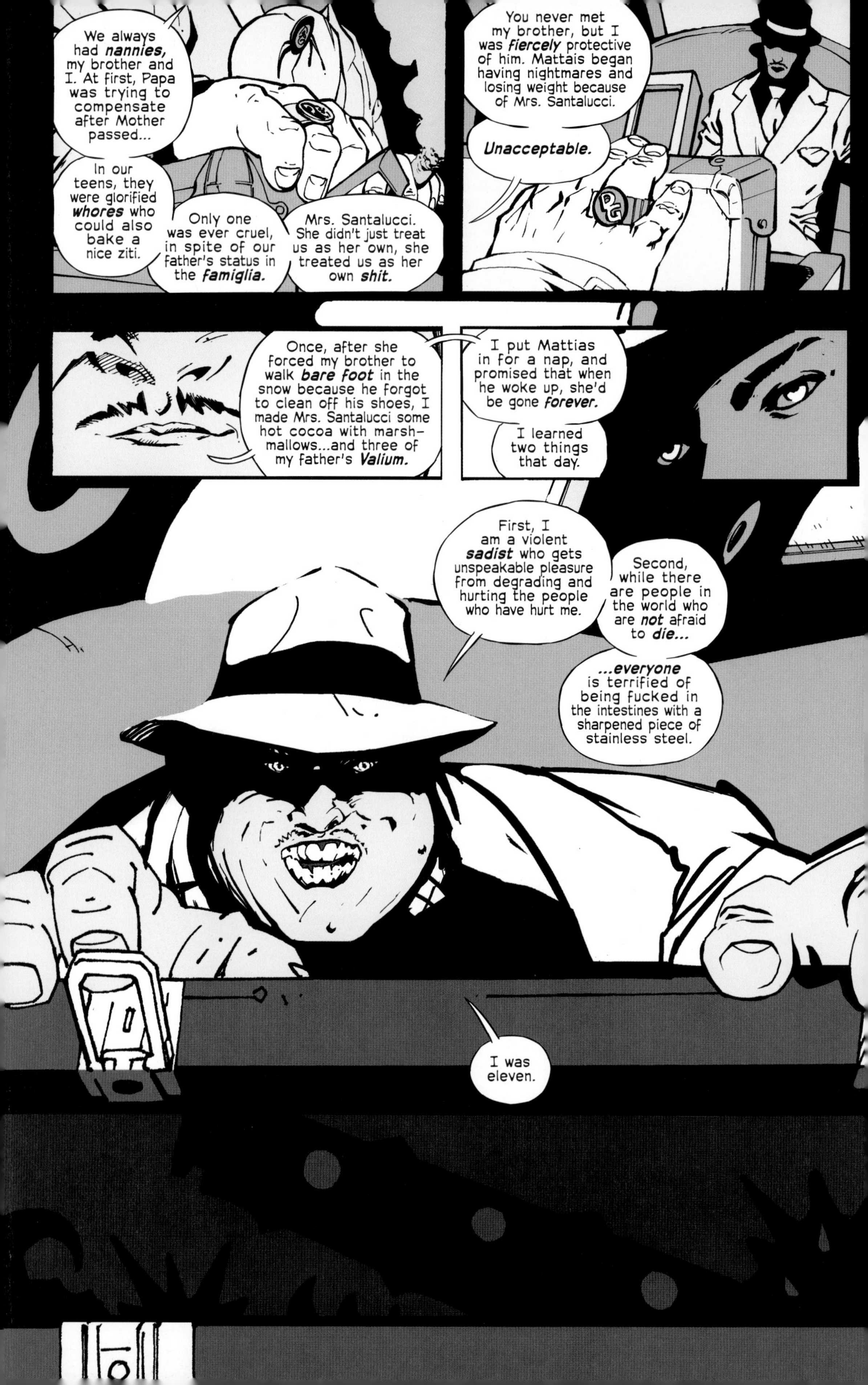

We always had nannies, my brother and I. At first, Papa was trying to compensate after Mother passed...
In our teens, they were glorified whores who could also bake a nice ziti.
Only one was ever cruel, in spite of our father's status in the famiglia.
Mrs. Santalucci. She didn't just treat us as her own, she treated us as her own shit.
You never met my brother, but I was fiercely protective of him. Mattais began having nightmares and losing weight because of Mrs. Santalucci.
Unacceptable.
Once, after she forced my brother to walk bare foot in the snow because he forgot to clean off his shoes, I made Mrs. Santalucci some hot cocoa with marsh-mallows...and three of my father's Valium.
I put Mattias in for a nap, and promised that when he woke up, she'd be gone forever.
I learned two things that day.
First, I am a violent sadist who gets unspeakable pleasure from degrading and hurting the people who have hurt me.
Second, while there are people in the world who are not afraid to die...
...everyone is terrified of being fucked in the intestines with a sharpened piece of stainless steel.
I was eleven.

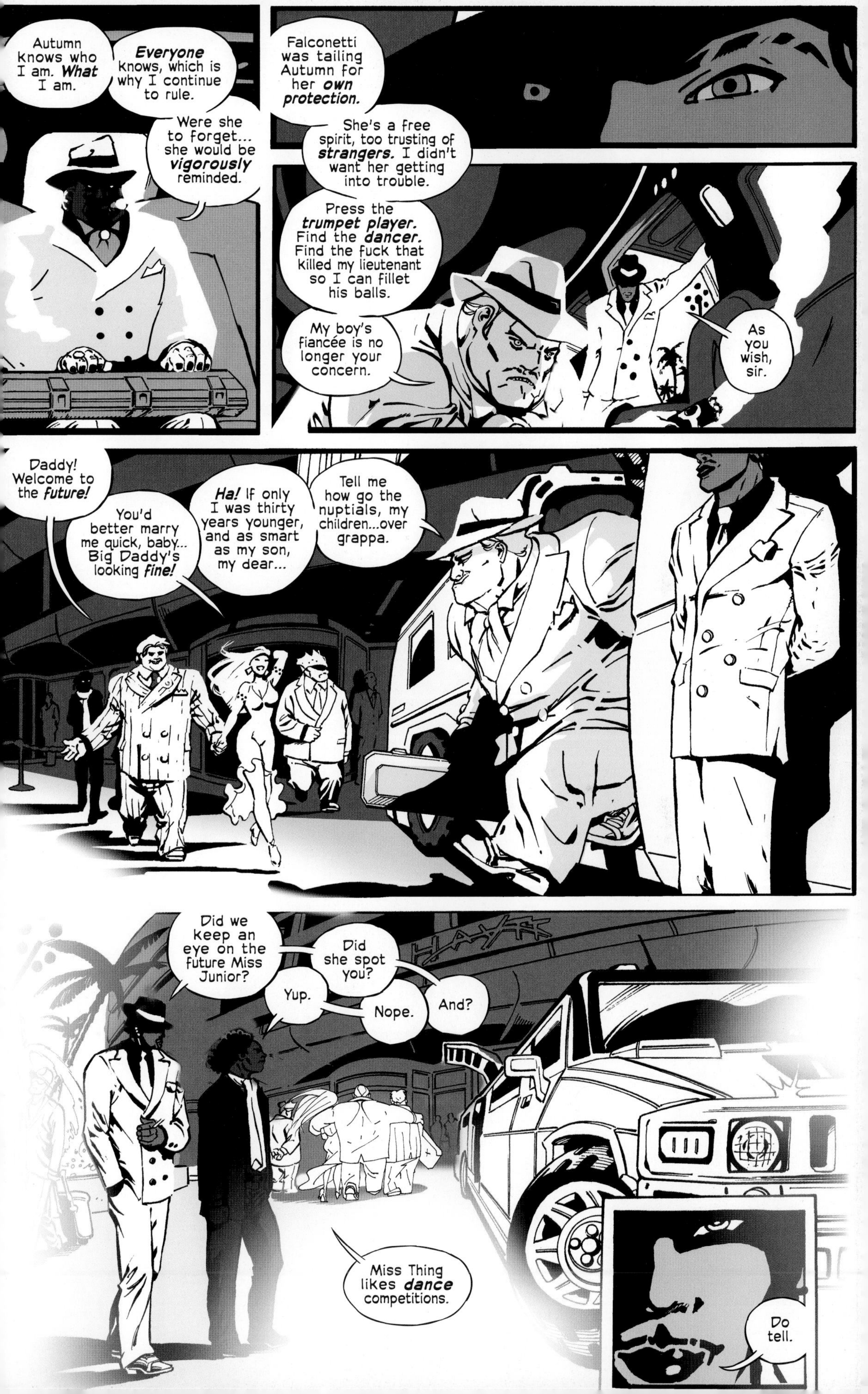
Autumn knows who I am. *What* I am.
Everyone knows, which is why I continue to rule.
Were she to forget... she would be *vigorously* reminded.
Falconetti was tailing Autumn for her *own protection.*
She's a free spirit, too trusting of *strangers.* I didn't want her getting into trouble.
Press the *trumpet player.* Find the *dancer.* Find the fuck that killed my lieutenant so I can fillet his balls.
My boy's fiancée is no longer your concern.
As you wish, sir.
Daddy! Welcome to the *future!*
You'd better marry me quick, baby... Big Daddy's looking *fine!*
Ha! If only I was thirty years younger, and as smart as my son, my dear...
Tell me how go the nuptials, my children...over grappa.
Did we keep an eye on the future Miss Junior?
Did she spot you?
Yup.
Nope.
And?
Miss Thing likes *dance* competitions.
Do tell.

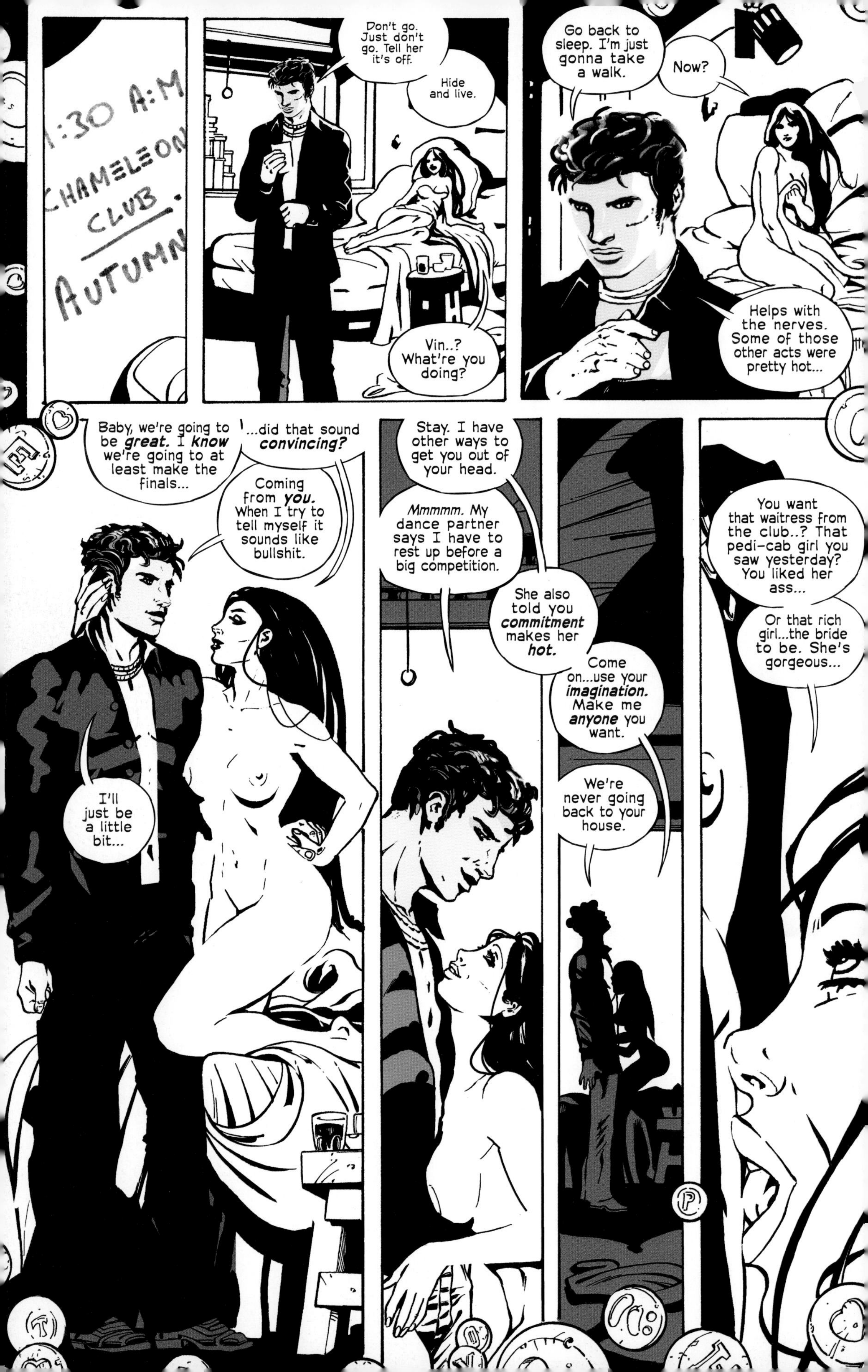

1:30 A:M CHAMELEON CLUB AUTUMN
Don't go. Just don't go. Tell her it's off.
Hide and live.
Vin..? What're you doing?
Go back to sleep. I'm just gonna take a walk.
Now?
Helps with the nerves. Some of those other acts were pretty hot...
Baby, we're going to be **great.** I **know** we're going to at least make the finals...
...did that sound **convincing?**
Coming from **you.** When I try to tell myself it sounds like bullshit.
I'll just be a little bit...
Stay. I have other ways to get you out of your head.
Mmmmm. My dance partner says I have to rest up before a big competition.
She also told you **commitment** makes her **hot.**
Come on...use your **imagination.** Make me **anyone** you want.
We're never going back to your house.
You want that waitress from the club..? That pedi-cab girl you saw yesterday? You liked her ass...
Or that rich girl...the bride to be. She's gorgeous...

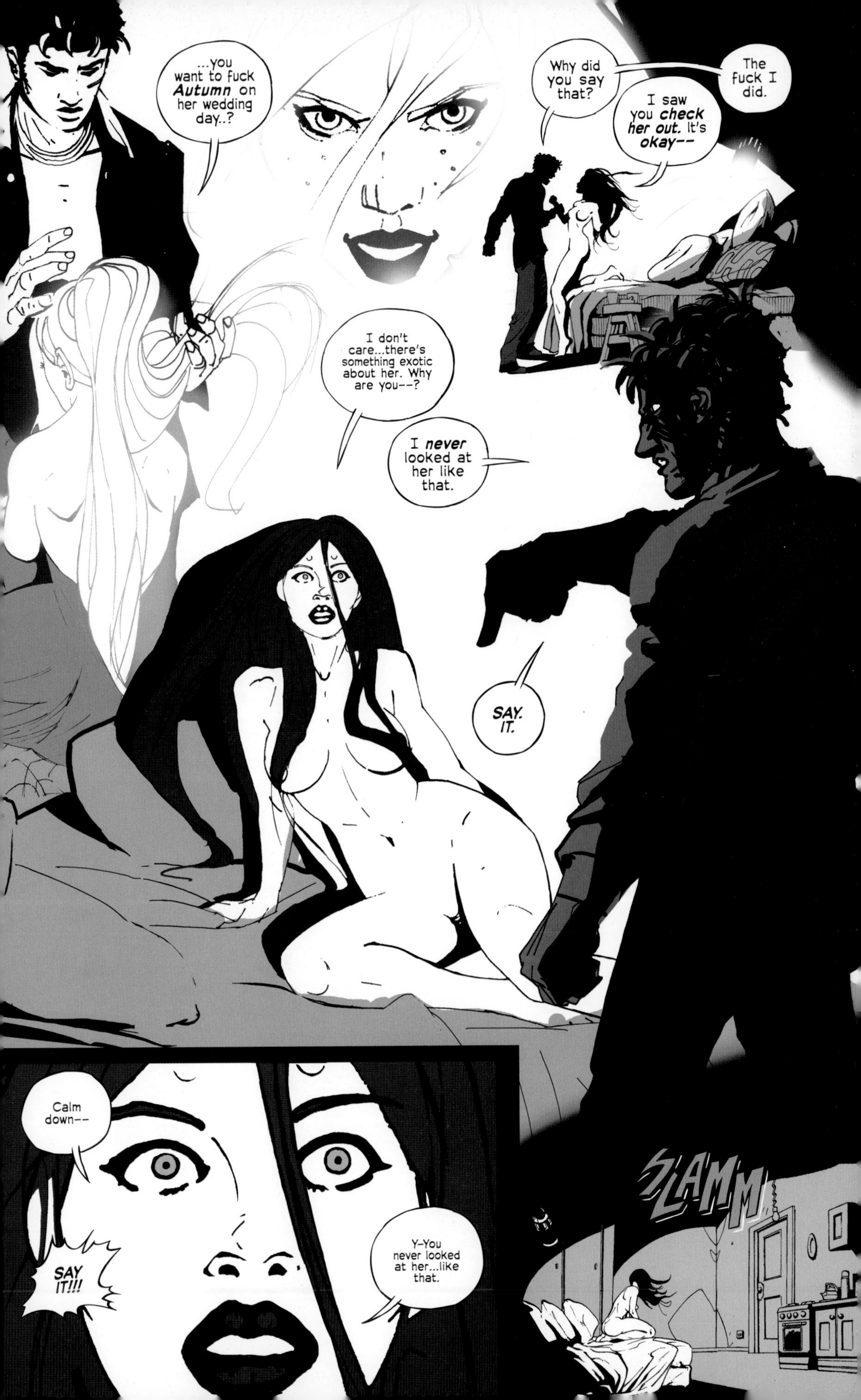

...you want to fuck *Autumn* on her wedding day..?
Why did you say that?
The fuck I did.
I saw you *check her out.* It's *okay--*
I don't care...there's something exotic about her. Why are you--?
I *never* looked at her like that.
SAY. IT.
Calm down--
SAY IT!!!
Y-You never looked at her...like that.
SLAMM

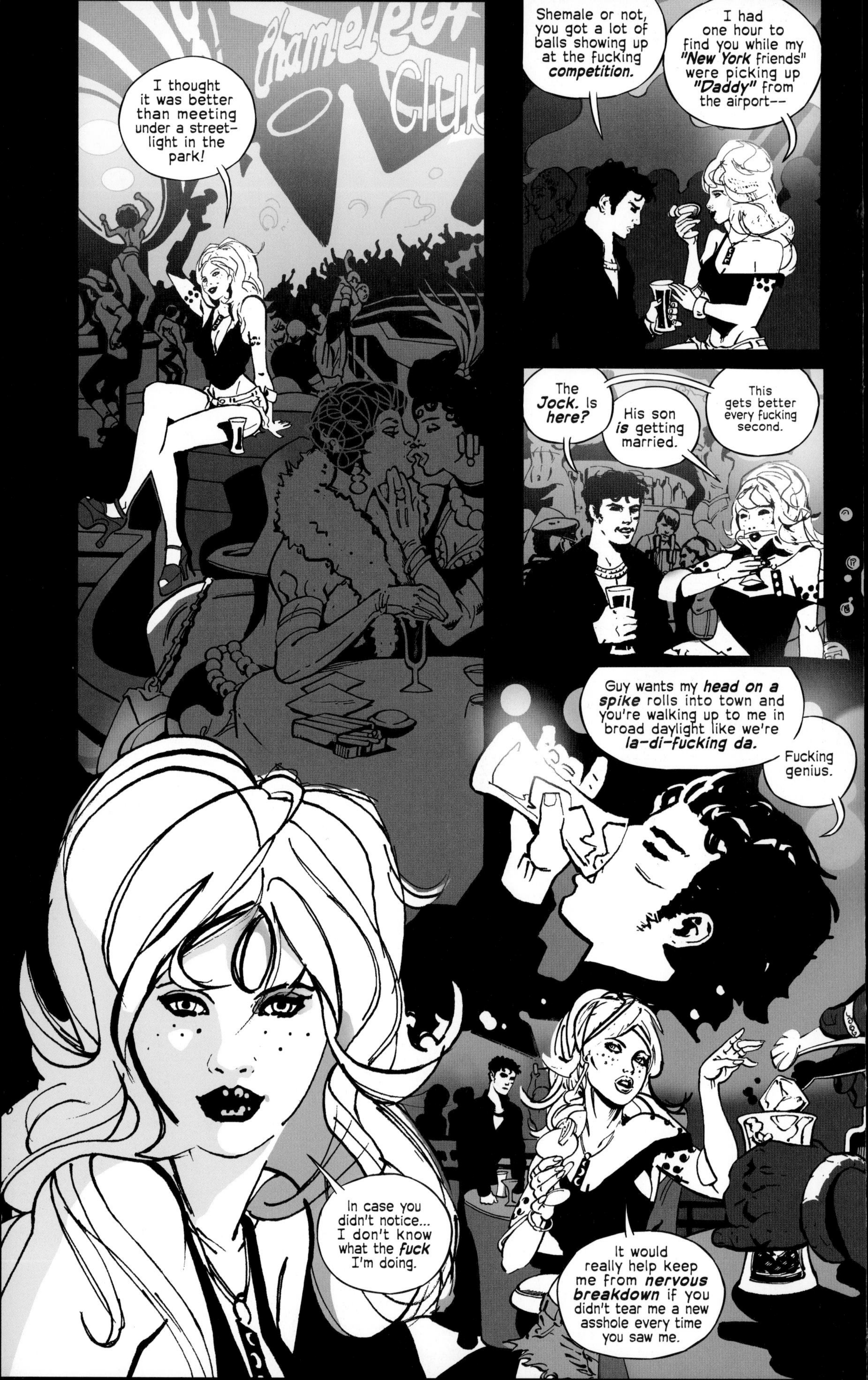

chameleon club
I thought it was better than meeting under a street-light in the park!
Shemale or not, you got a lot of balls showing up at the fucking *competition.*
I had one hour to find you while my *"New York* friends" were picking up *"Daddy"* from the airport--
The *Jock.* Is *here?*
His son *is* getting married.
This gets better every fucking second.
Guy wants my *head on a spike* rolls into town and you're walking up to me in broad daylight like we're *la-di-fucking da.*
Fucking genius.
In case you didn't notice... I don't know what the *fuck* I'm doing.
It would really help keep me from *nervous breakdown* if you didn't tear me a new asshole every time you saw me.

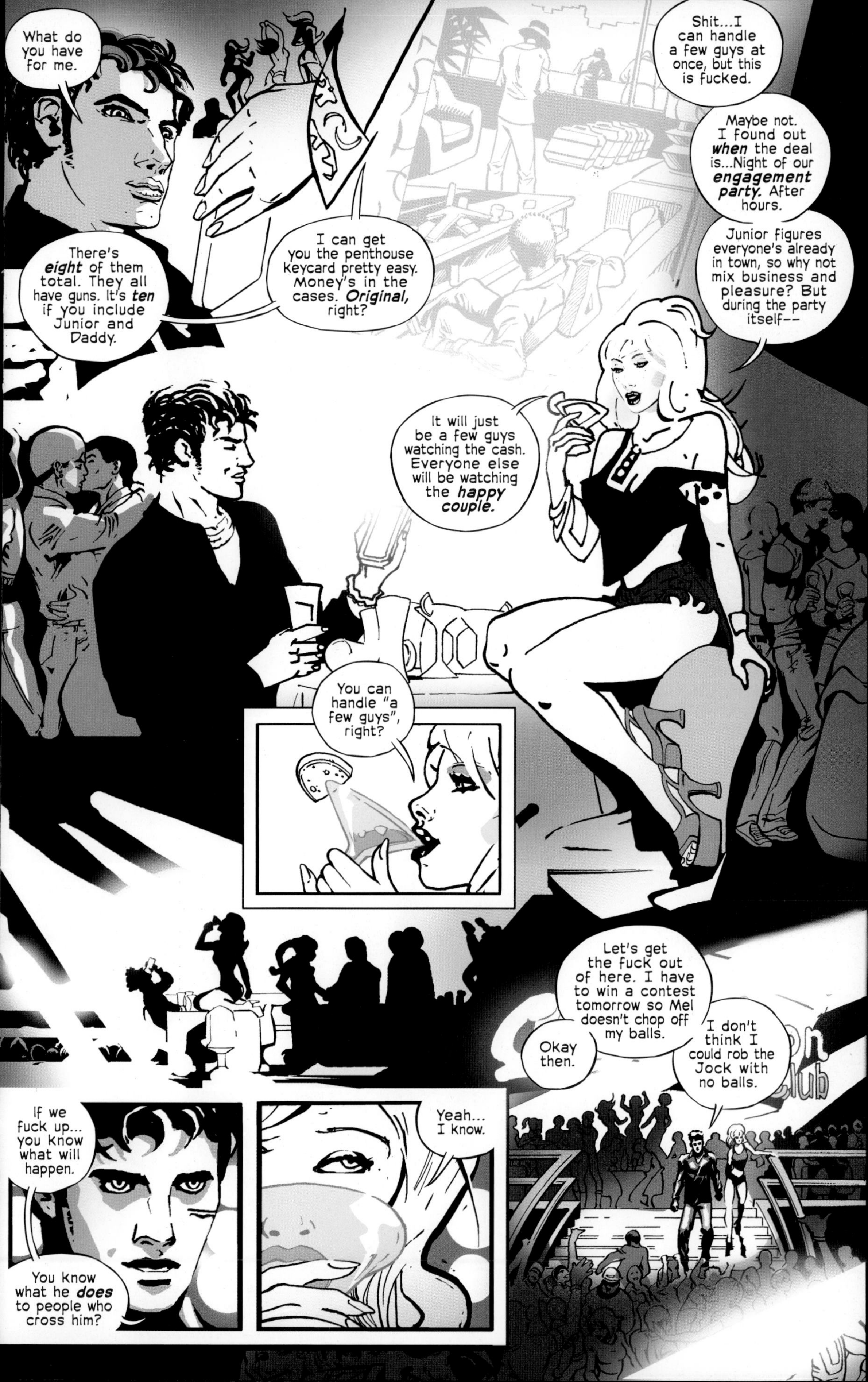
What do you have for me.
I can get you the penthouse keycard pretty easy. Money's in the cases. *Original,* right?
There's *eight* of them total. They all have guns. It's *ten* if you include Junior and Daddy.
Shit...I can handle a few guys at once, but this is fucked.
Maybe not. I found out *when* the deal is...Night of our *engagement party.* After hours.
Junior figures everyone's already in town, so why not mix business and pleasure? But during the party itself--
It will just be a few guys watching the cash. Everyone else will be watching the *happy couple.*
You can handle "a few guys", right?
Let's get the fuck out of here. I have to win a contest tomorrow so Mel doesn't chop off my balls.
Okay then.
I don't think I could rob the Jock with no balls.
If we fuck up... you know what will happen.
You know what he *does* to people who cross him?
Yeah... I know.

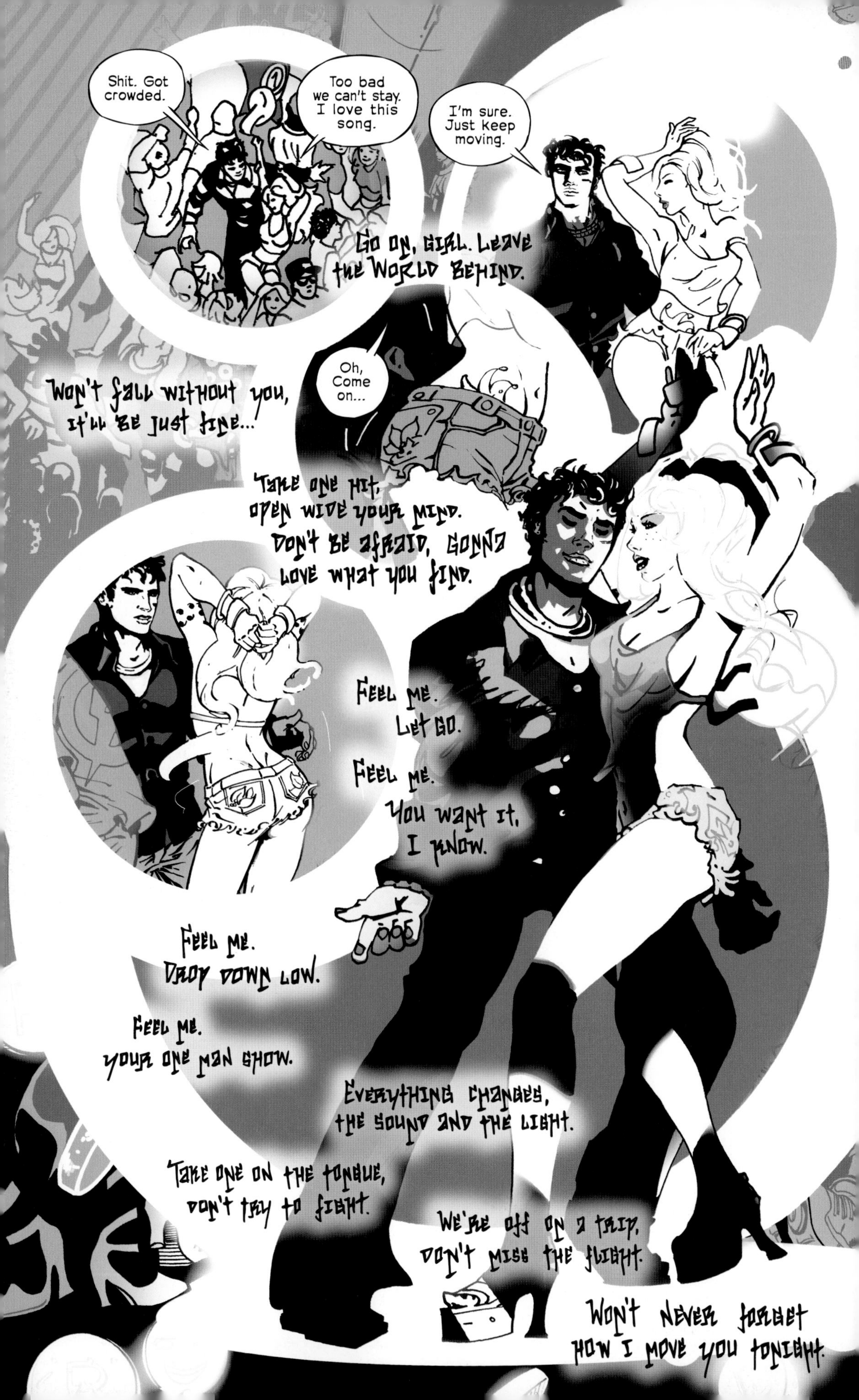

Shit. Got crowded.
Too bad we can't stay. I love this song.
I'm sure. Just keep moving.
Go on, girl. Leave the world behind.
Oh, Come on...
Won't fall without you, it'll be just fine...
Take one hit, open wide your mind.
Don't be afraid, gonna love what you find.
Feel me. Let go.
Feel me. You want it, I know.
Feel me. Drop down low.
Feel me. Your one man show.
Everything changes, the sound and the light.
Take one on the tongue, don't try to fight.
We're off on a trip, don't miss the flight.
Won't never forget how I move you tonight.

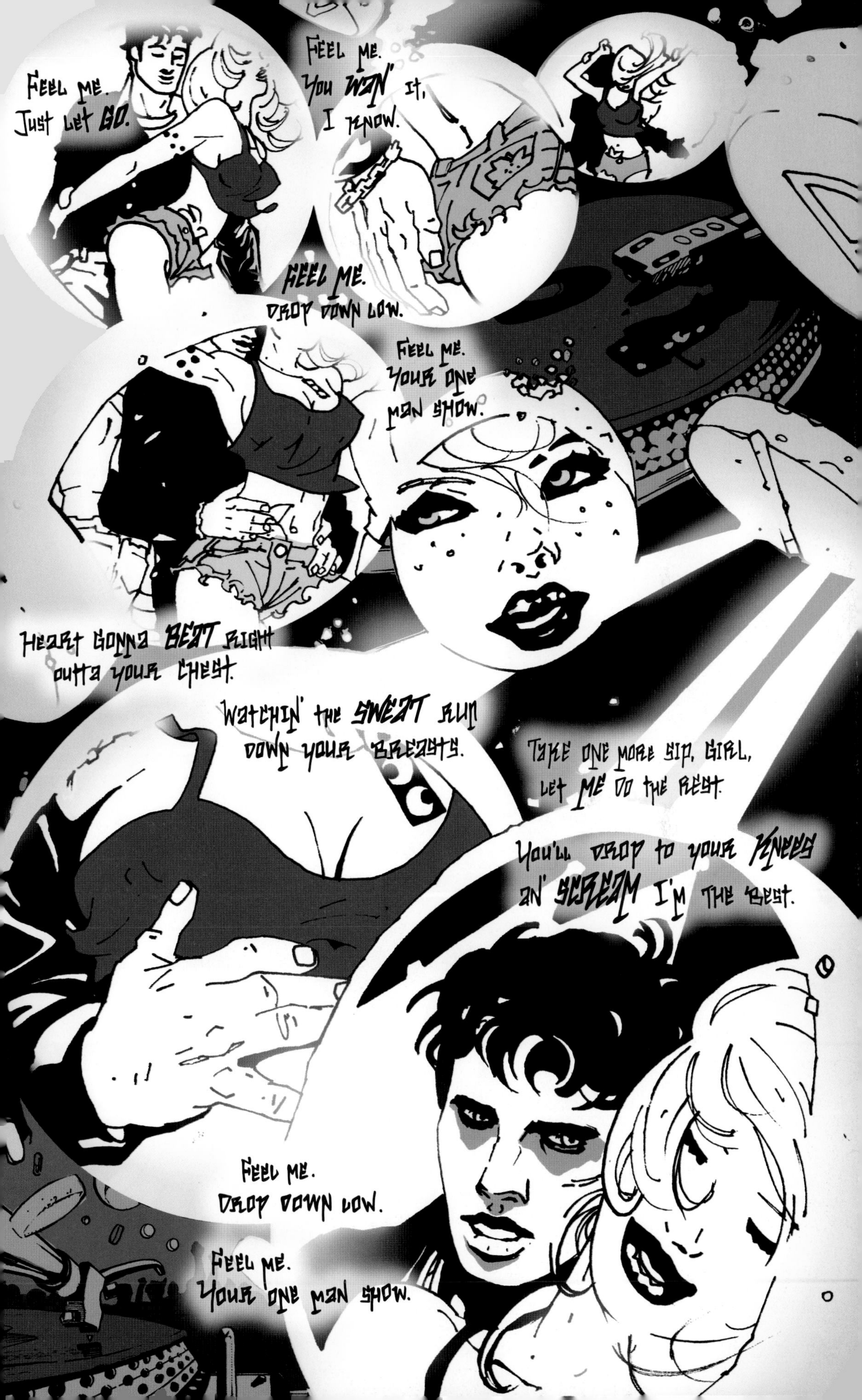

Feel me. Just let GO.
Feel me. You WAN' it, I know.
FEEL ME. DROP DOWN LOW.
Feel me. YOUR ONE MAN SHOW.
Heart gonna BEAT right outta your chest.
Watchin' the SWEAT run down your breasts.
Take one more sip, girl, let ME do the rest.
You'll drop to your knees an' SCREAM I'm the best.
Feel me. Drop down low.
Feel me. Your one man show.

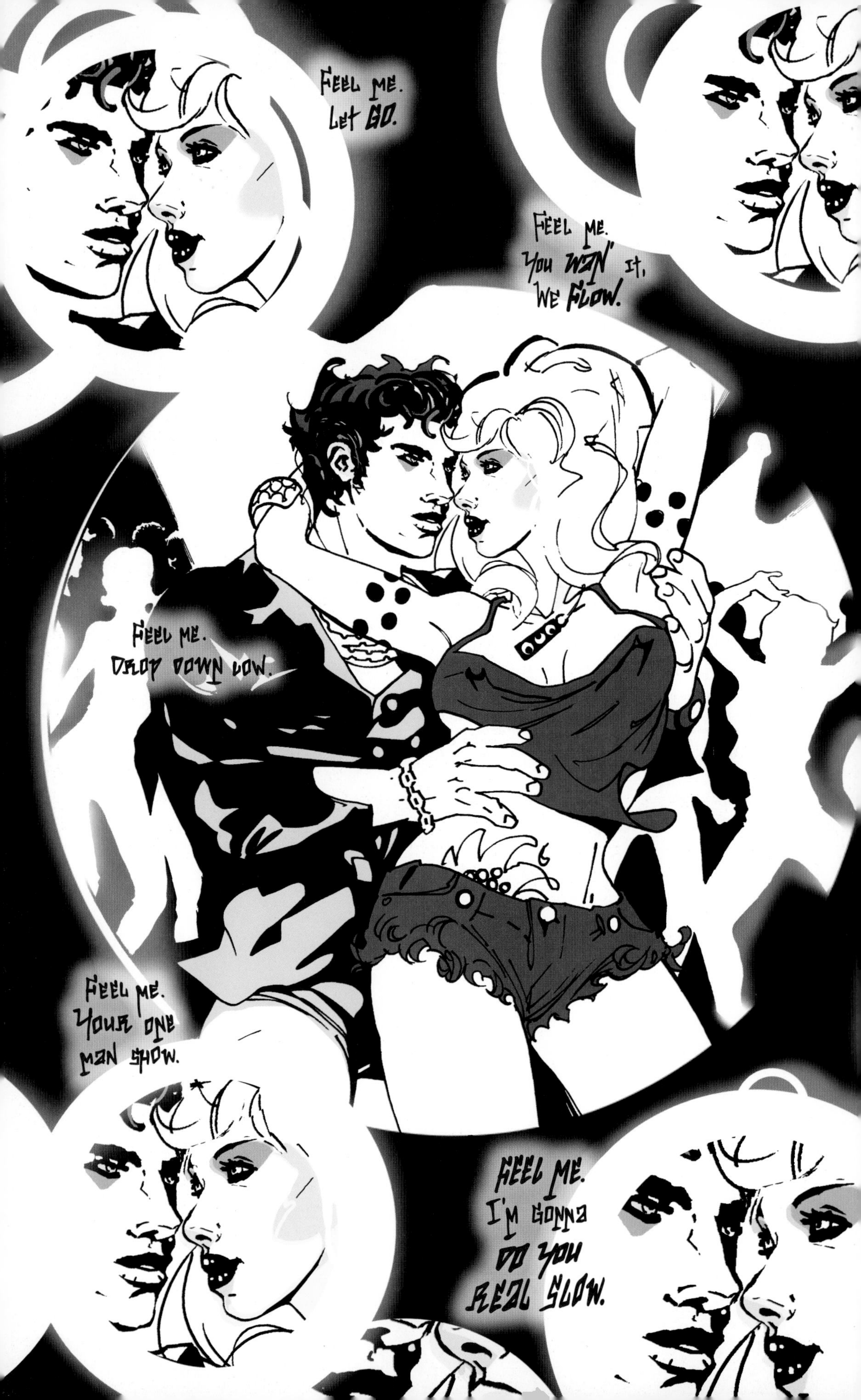

FEEL ME.
LET GO.
FEEL ME.
YOU WAN' IT,
WE FLOW.
FEEL ME.
DROP DOWN LOW.
FEEL ME.
YOUR ONE
MAN SHOW.
FEEL ME.
I'M GONNA
DO YOU
REAL SLOW.

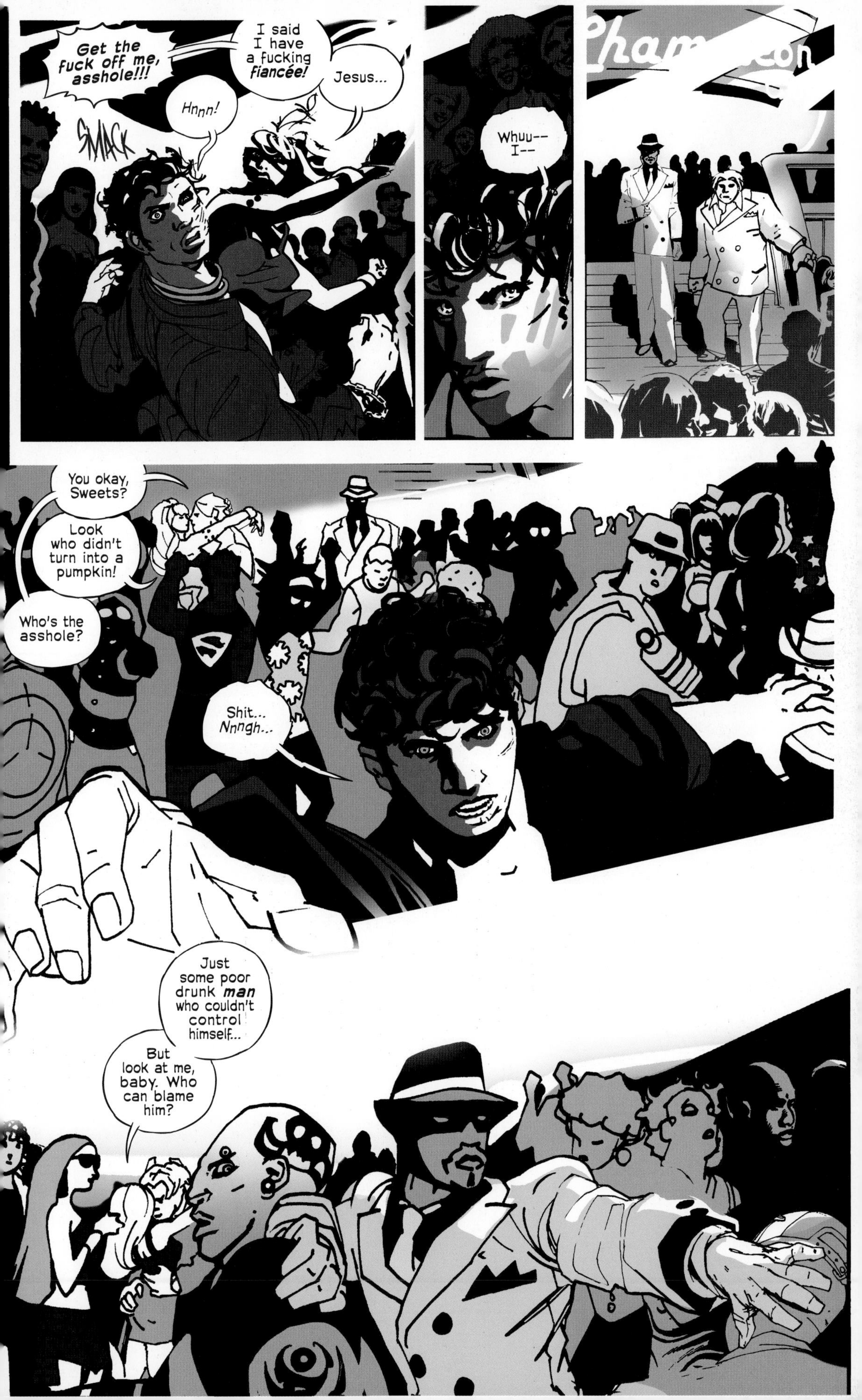
Get the fuck off me, asshole!!!
I said I have a fucking *fiancée!*
SMACK
Hnnn!
Jesus...
Whuu-- I--
You okay, Sweets?
Look who didn't turn into a pumpkin!
Who's the asshole?
Shit... Nnngh...
Just some poor drunk *man* who couldn't control himself...
But look at me, baby. Who can blame him?

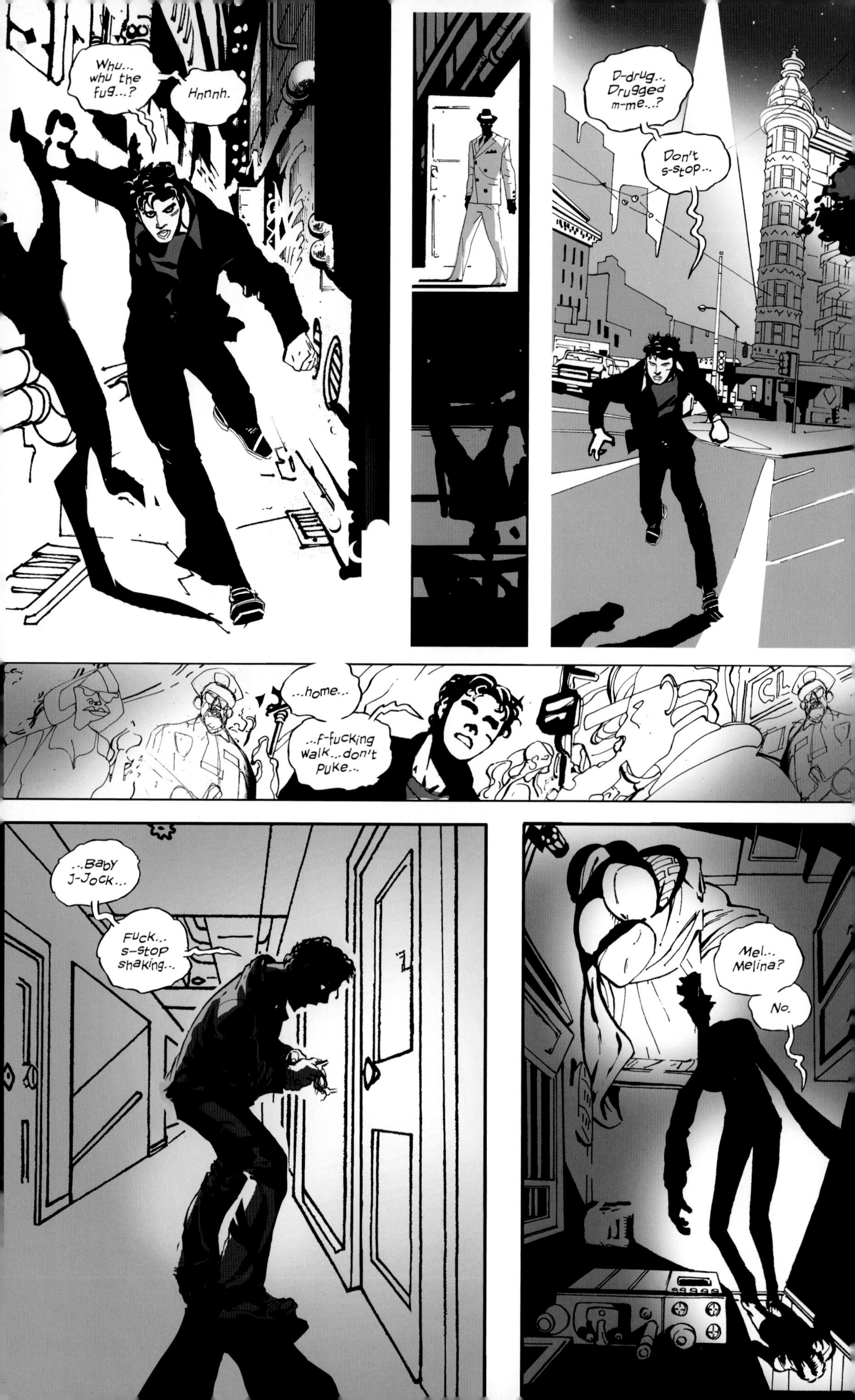
Whu... whu the fug...?
Hnnnh.
D-drug... Drugged m-me...?
Don't s-stop...
...home...
...f-fucking walk...don't puke...
...Baby J-Jock...
Fuck... s-stop shaking...
Mel... Melina?
No.

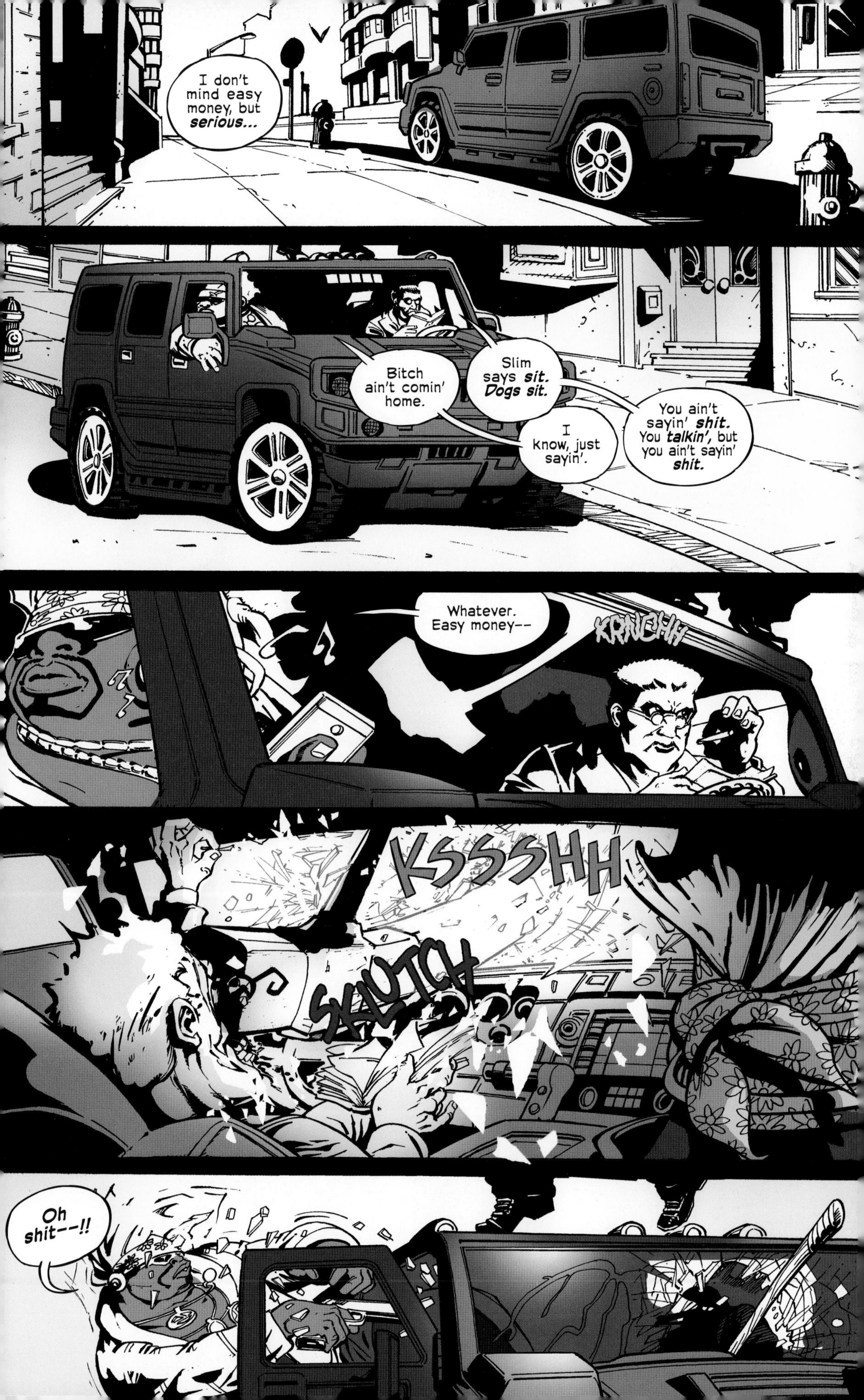
I don't mind easy money, but serious...
Bitch ain't comin' home.
Slim says sit. Dogs sit.
I know, just sayin'.
You ain't sayin' shit. You talkin', but you ain't sayin' shit.
Whatever. Easy money--
KRNCHH
KSSSHH
SKLUTCH
Oh shit--!!

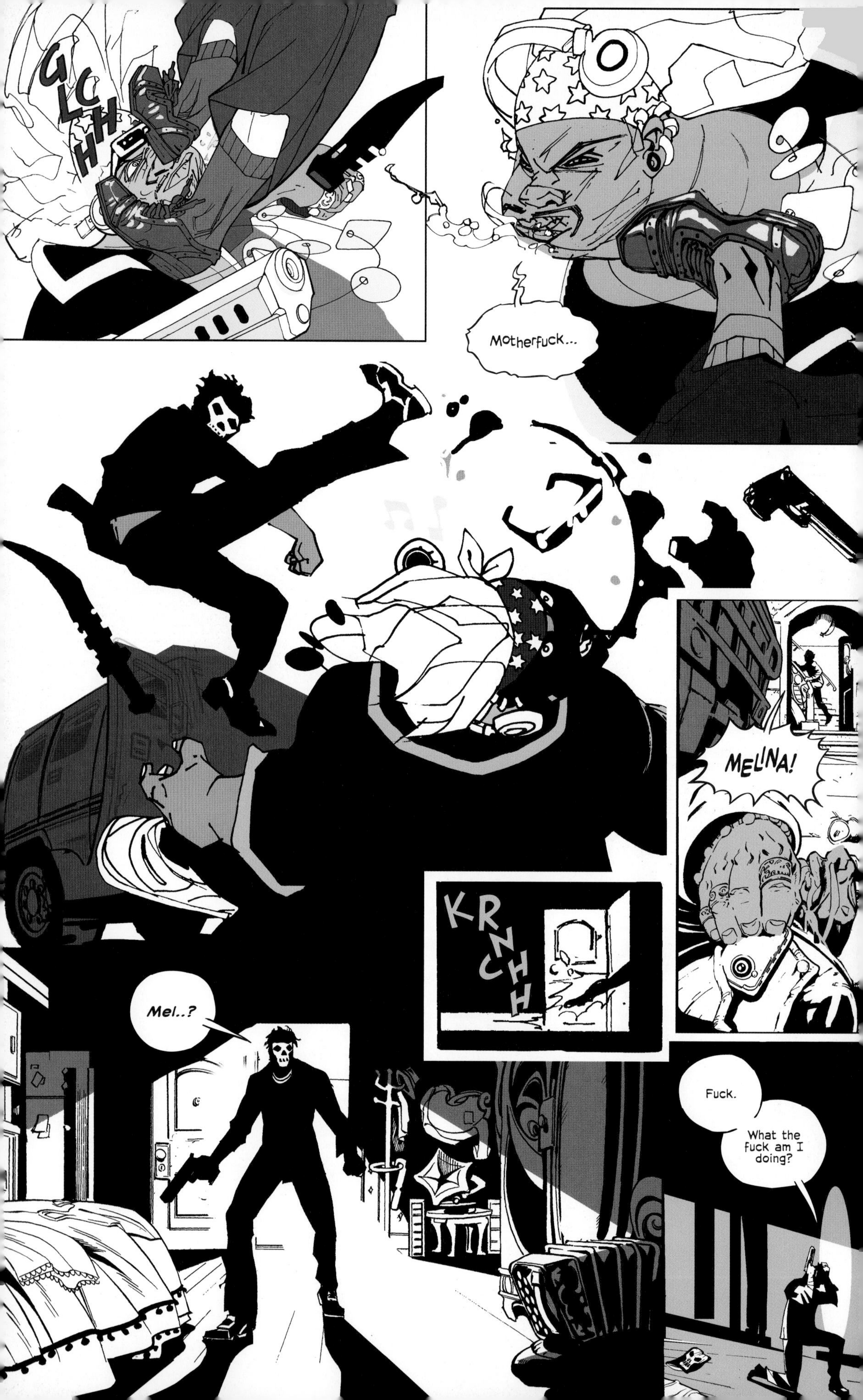
GLCHH
Motherfuck...
MELINA!
KRNCHH
Mel..?
Fuck.
What the fuck am I doing?

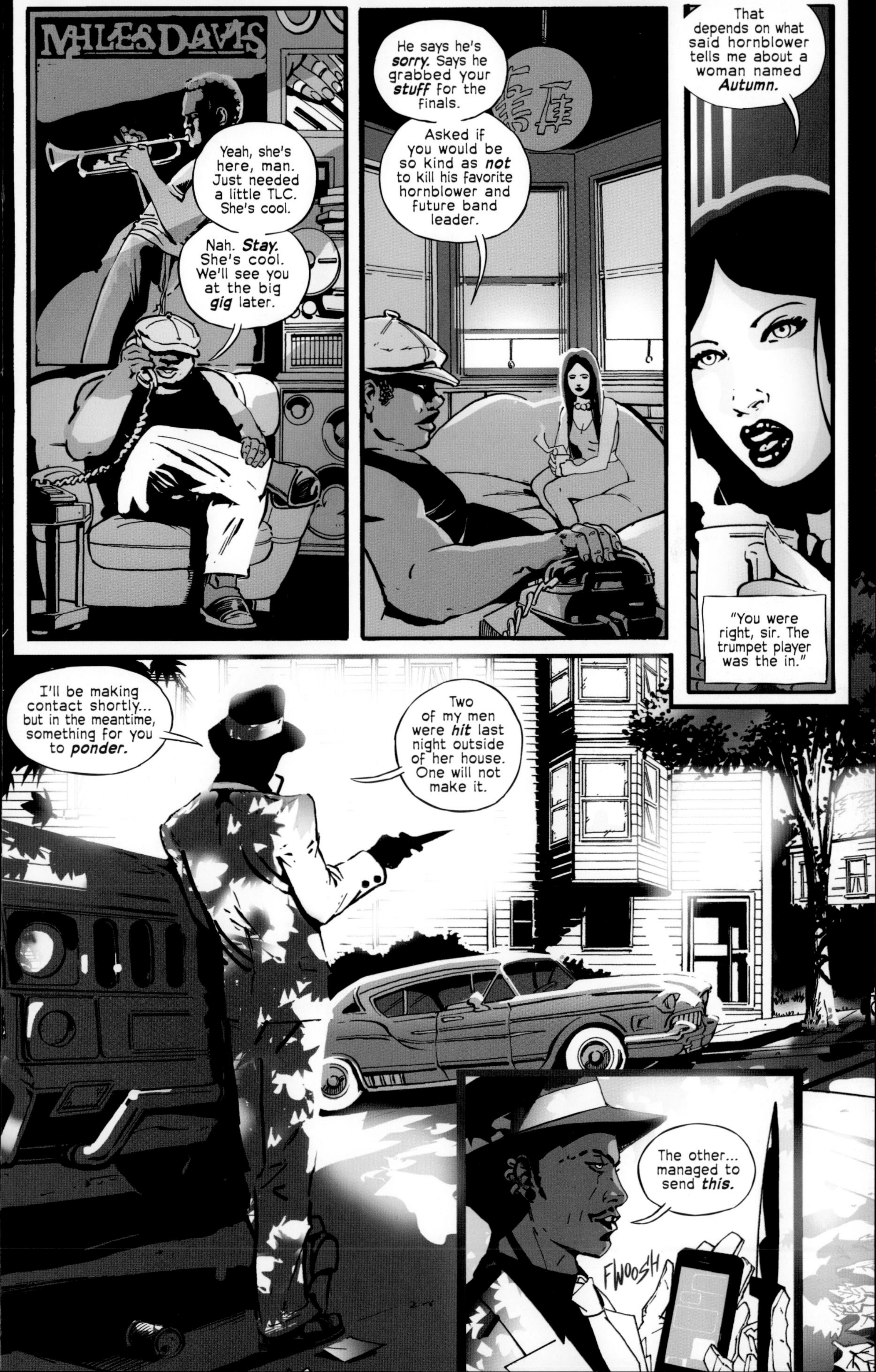
MILES DAVIS
Yeah, she's here, man. Just needed a little TLC. She's cool.
Nah. Stay. She's cool. We'll see you at the big gig later.
He says he's sorry. Says he grabbed your stuff for the finals.
Asked if you would be so kind as not to kill his favorite hornblower and future band leader.
That depends on what said hornblower tells me about a woman named Autumn.
"You were right, sir. The trumpet player was the in."
I'll be making contact shortly... but in the meantime, something for you to ponder.
Two of my men were hit last night outside of her house. One will not make it.
The other... managed to send this.
FWOOSH

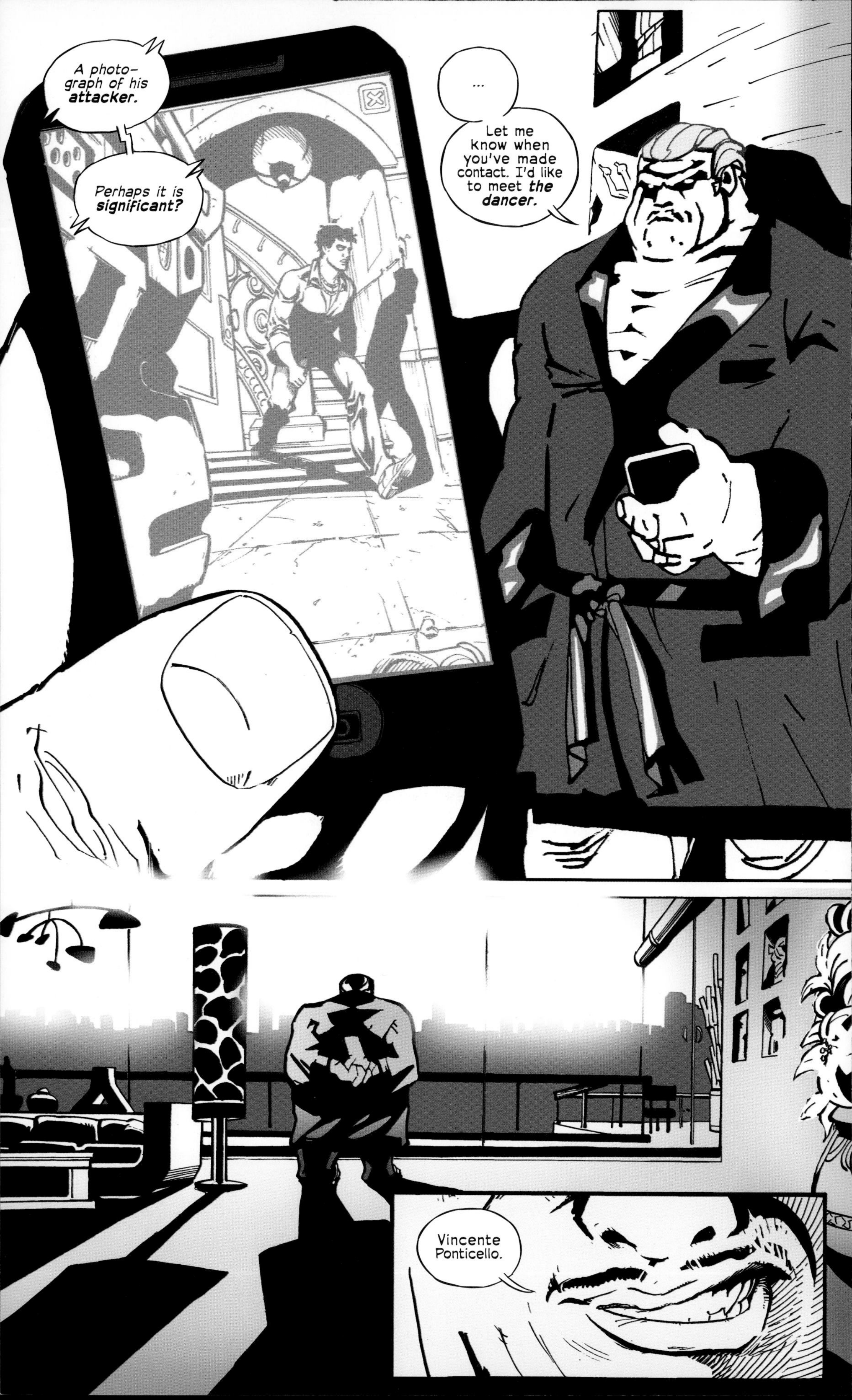
A photo-graph of his attacker.
Perhaps it is significant?
...
Let me know when you've made contact. I'd like to meet the dancer.
Vincente Ponticello.

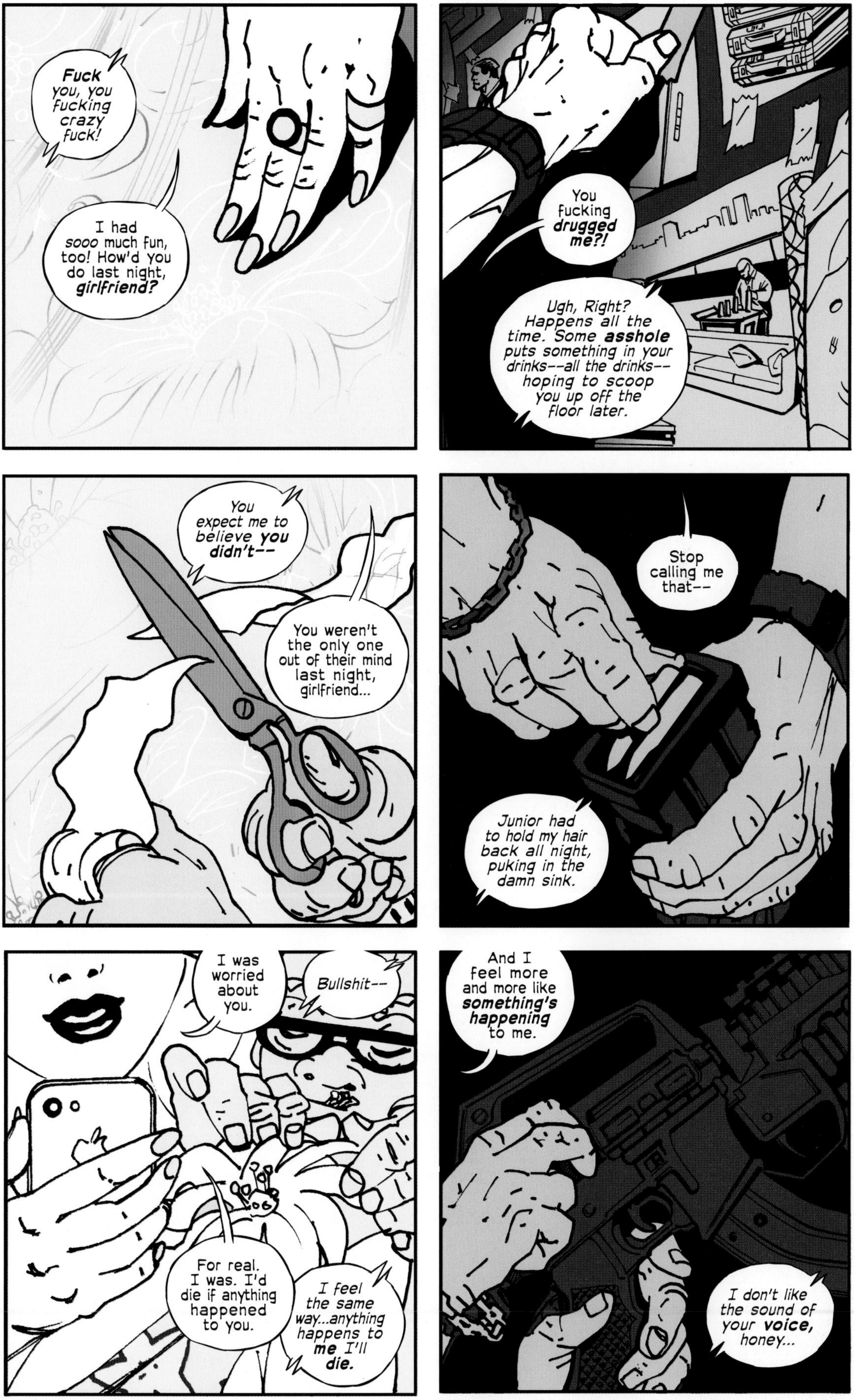

Fuck you, you fucking crazy fuck!
I had sooo much fun, too! How'd you do last night, girlfriend?
You fucking drugged me?!
Ugh, Right? Happens all the time. Some asshole puts something in your drinks--all the drinks--hoping to scoop you up off the floor later.
You expect me to believe you didn't--
You weren't the only one out of their mind last night, girlfriend...
Stop calling me that--
Junior had to hold my hair back all night, puking in the damn sink.
I was worried about you.
Bullshit--
For real. I was. I'd die if anything happened to you.
I feel the same way...anything happens to me I'll die.
And I feel more and more like something's happening to me.
I don't like the sound of your voice, honey...

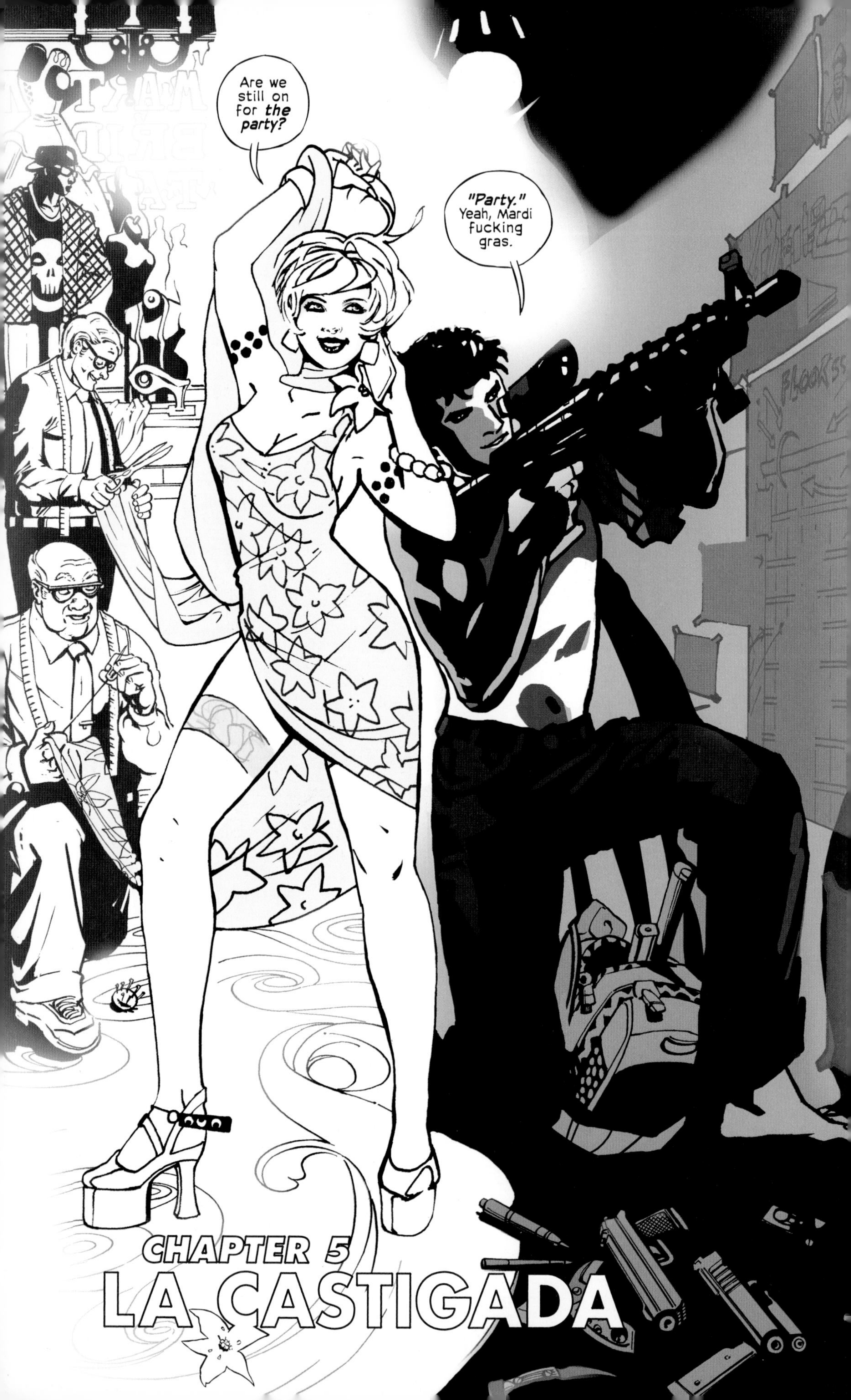
Are we still on for *the party?*
"Party." Yeah, Mardi fucking gras.

CHAPTER 5
LA CASTIGADA

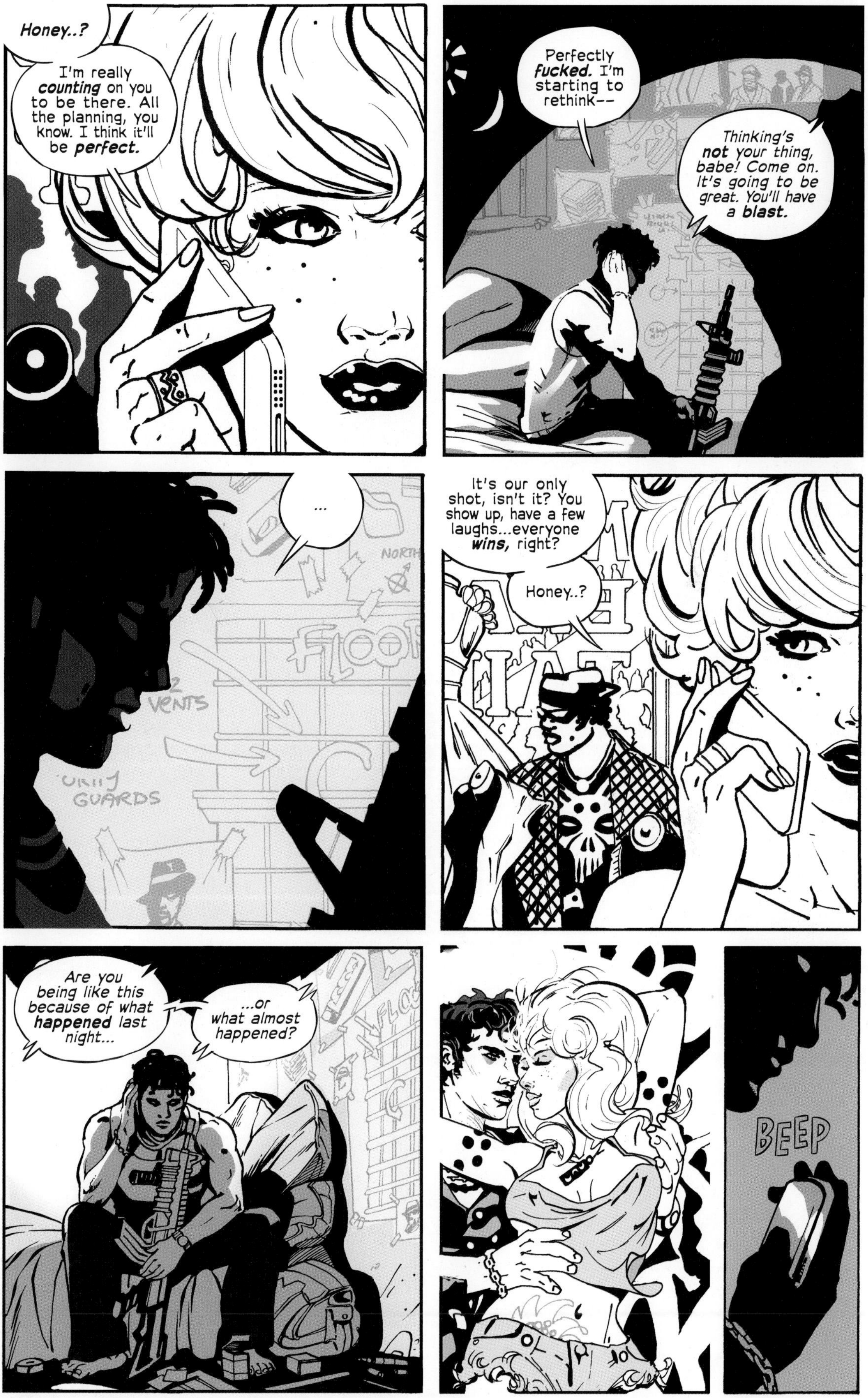
Honey..?
I'm really counting on you to be there. All the planning, you know. I think it'll be perfect.
Perfectly fucked. I'm starting to rethink--
Thinking's not your thing, babe! Come on. It's going to be great. You'll have a blast.
...
2 VENTS
GUARDS
It's our only shot, isn't it? You show up, have a few laughs...everyone wins, right?
Honey..?
Are you being like this because of what happened last night...
...or what almost happened?
BEEP

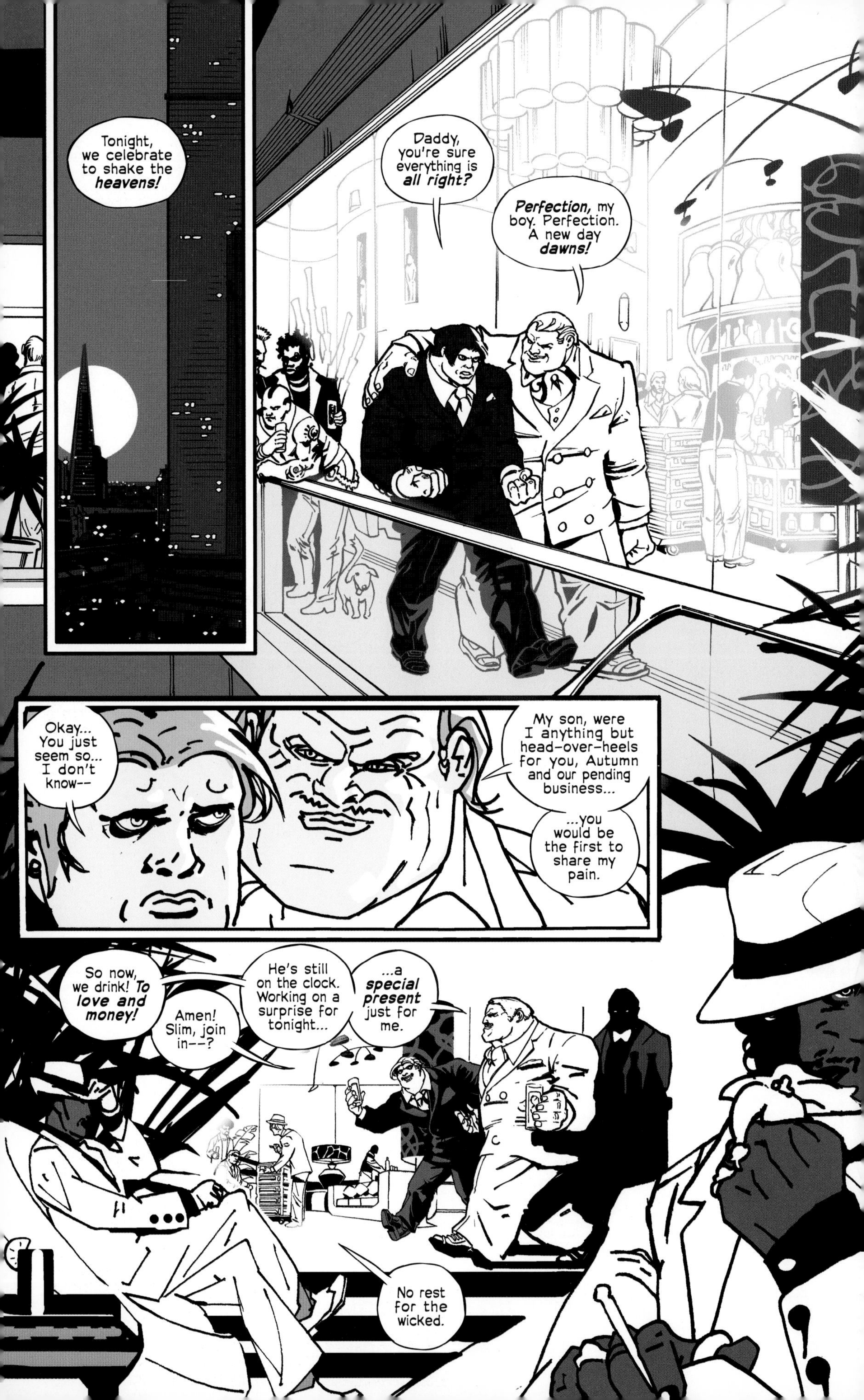
Tonight, we celebrate to shake the ***heavens!***
Daddy, you're sure everything is ***all right?***
Perfection, my boy. Perfection. A new day ***dawns!***
Okay... You just seem so... I don't know--
My son, were I anything but head-over-heels for you, Autumn and our pending business...
...you would be the first to share my pain.
So now, we drink! ***To love and money!***
Amen! Slim, join in--?
He's still on the clock. Working on a surprise for tonight...
...a ***special present*** just for me.
No rest for the wicked.

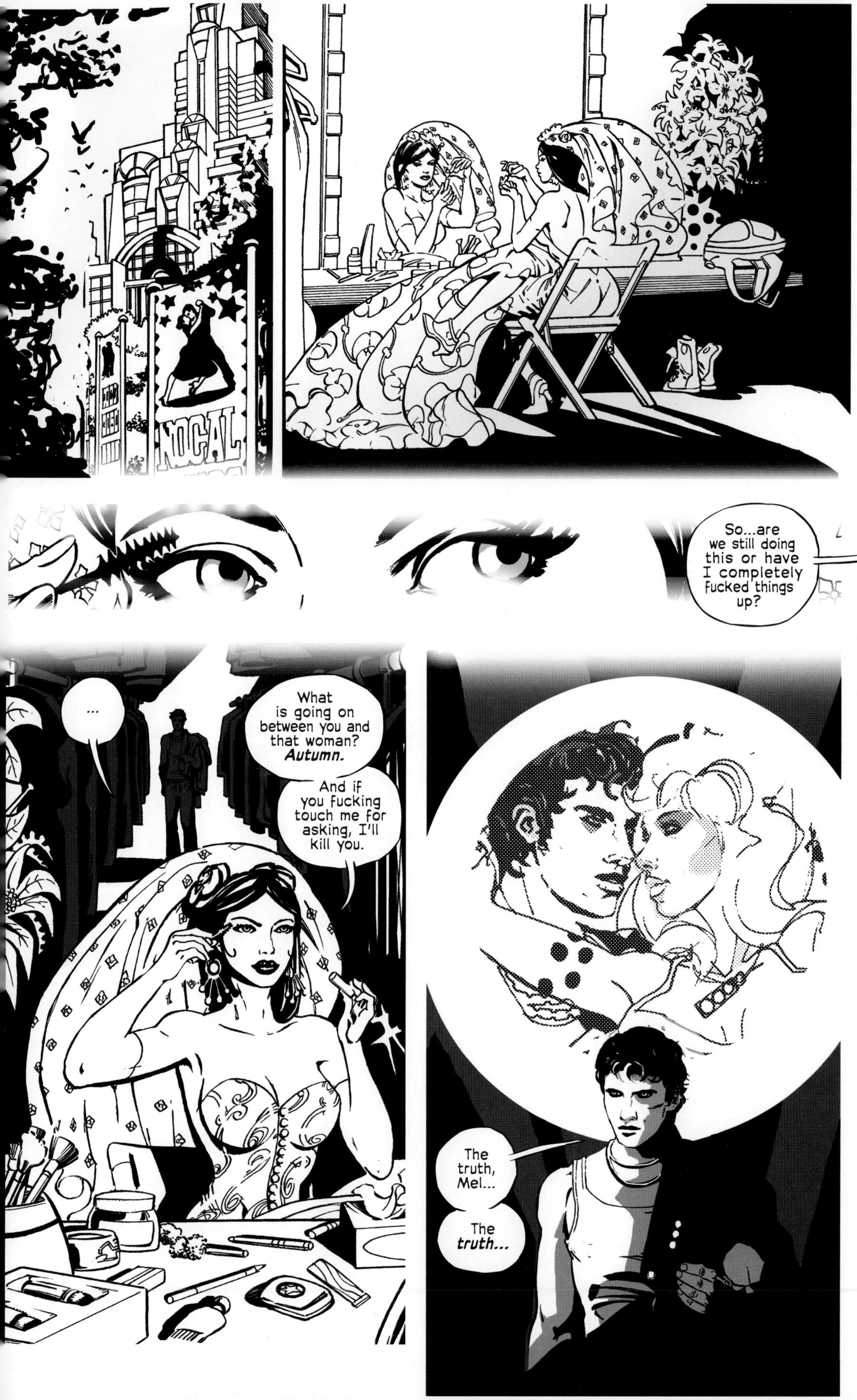
NOCAL
So...are we still doing this or have I completely fucked things up?
...
What is going on between you and that woman? *Autumn.*
And if you fucking touch me for asking, I'll kill you.
The truth, Mel...
The *truth...*

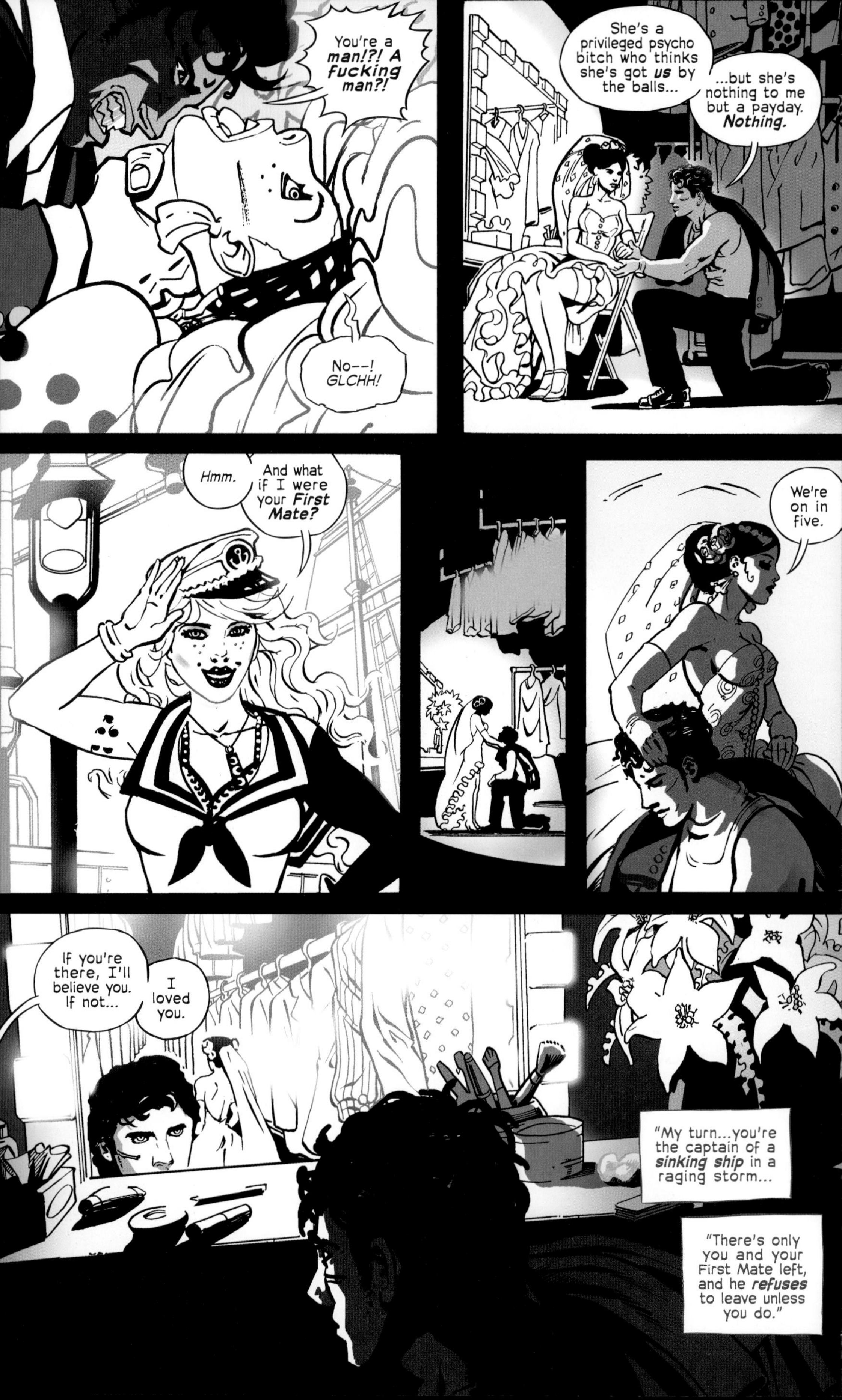
You're a man!?! A fucking man?!
No--! GLCHH!
She's a privileged psycho bitch who thinks she's got us by the balls...
...but she's nothing to me but a payday. Nothing.
Hmm.
And what if I were your First Mate?
We're on in five.
If you're there, I'll believe you. If not...
I loved you.
"My turn...you're the captain of a sinking ship in a raging storm...
"There's only you and your First Mate left, and he refuses to leave unless you do."

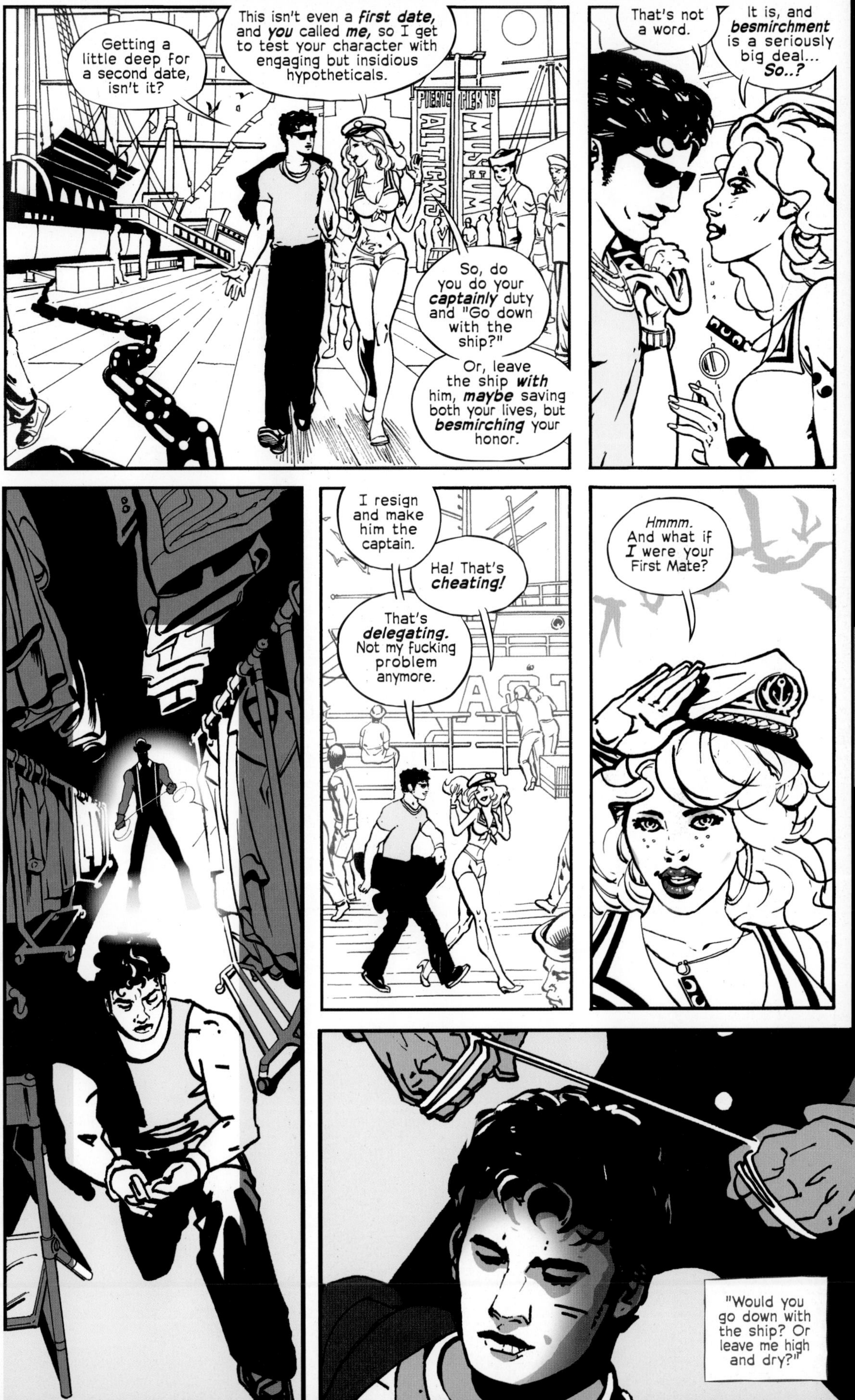
Getting a little deep for a second date, isn't it?
This isn't even a ***first date,*** and ***you*** called ***me,*** so I get to test your character with engaging but insidious hypotheticals.
PIER 15 PIER 15
ALL TICKETS
MUSEUM
So, do you do your ***captainly*** duty and "Go down with the ship?"
Or, leave the ship ***with*** him, ***maybe*** saving both your lives, but ***besmirching*** your honor.
That's not a word.
It is, and ***besmirchment*** is a seriously big deal... ***So..?***
I resign and make him the captain.
Ha! That's ***cheating!***
That's ***delegating.*** Not my fucking problem anymore.
Hmmm. And what if ***I*** were your First Mate?
"Would you go down with the ship? Or leave me high and dry?"

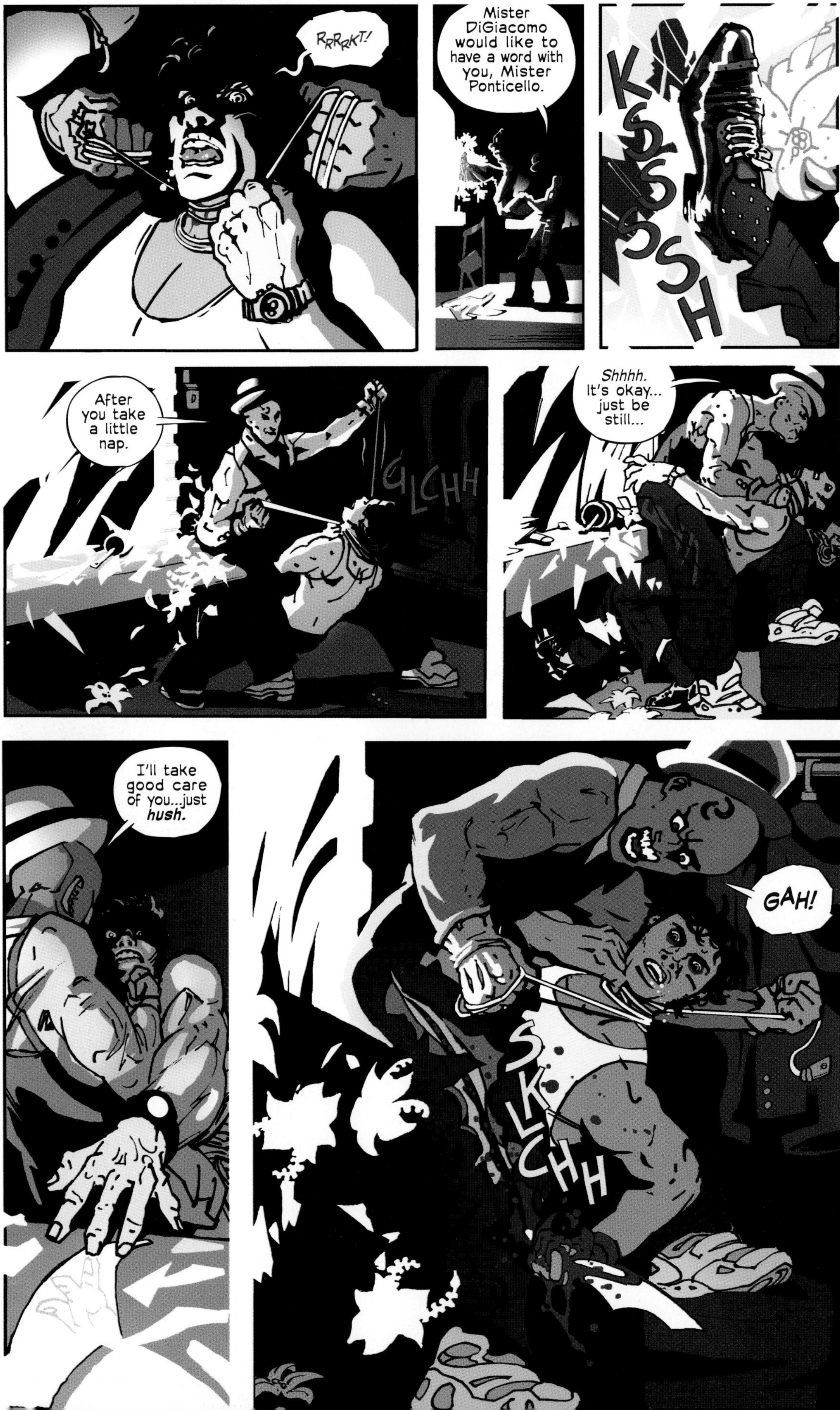

RRRRKT!
Mister DiGiacomo would like to have a word with you, Mister Ponticello.
KSSSSSH
After you take a little nap.
GLCHH
Shhhh. It's okay... just be still...
I'll take good care of you...just *hush.*
GAH!
SKLCHH

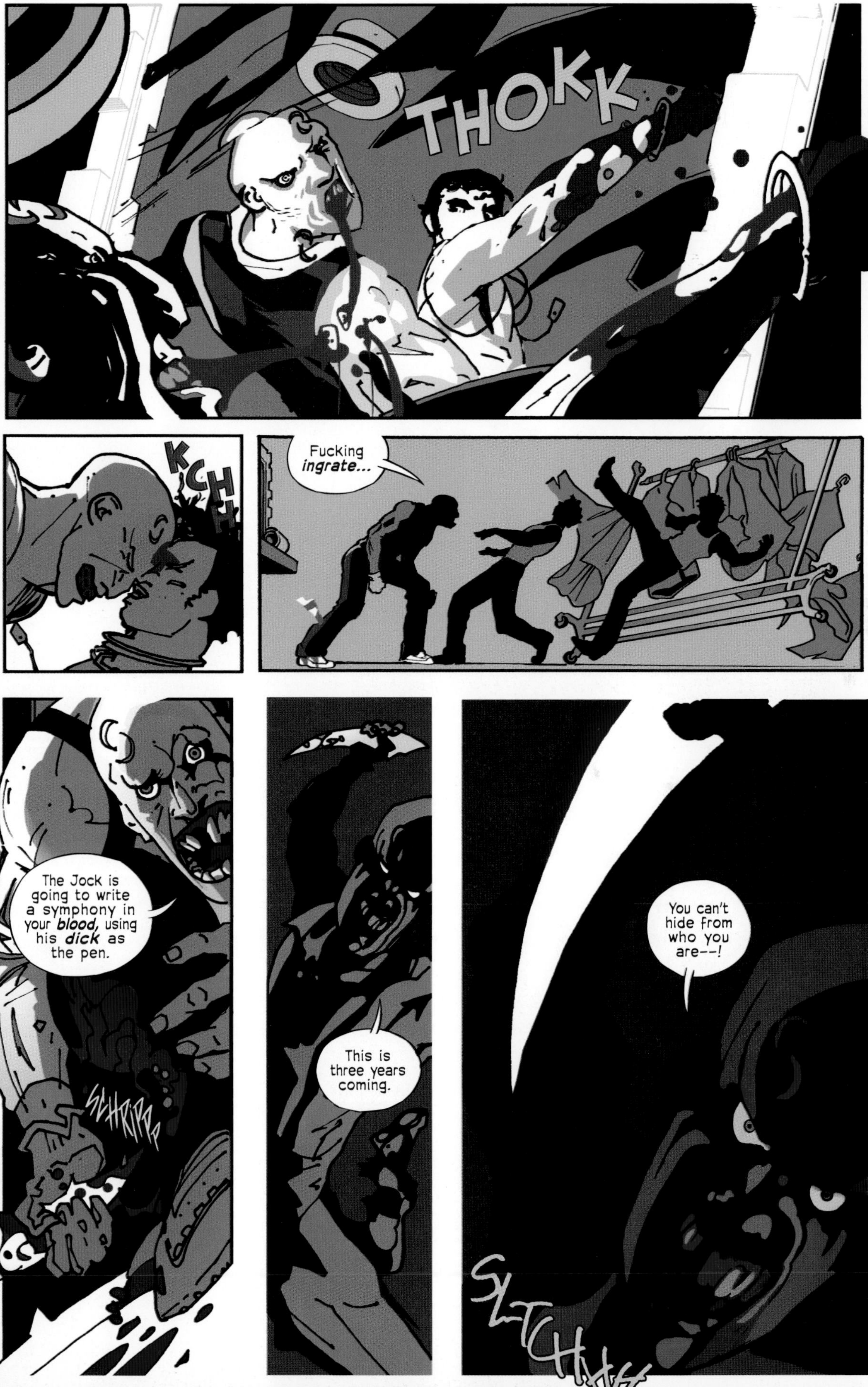
THOKK
KCHH
Fucking *ingrate...*
The Jock is going to write a symphony in your *blood,* using his *dick* as the pen.
SCHRIPPP
This is three years coming.
You can't hide from who you are--!
SLTCHHH

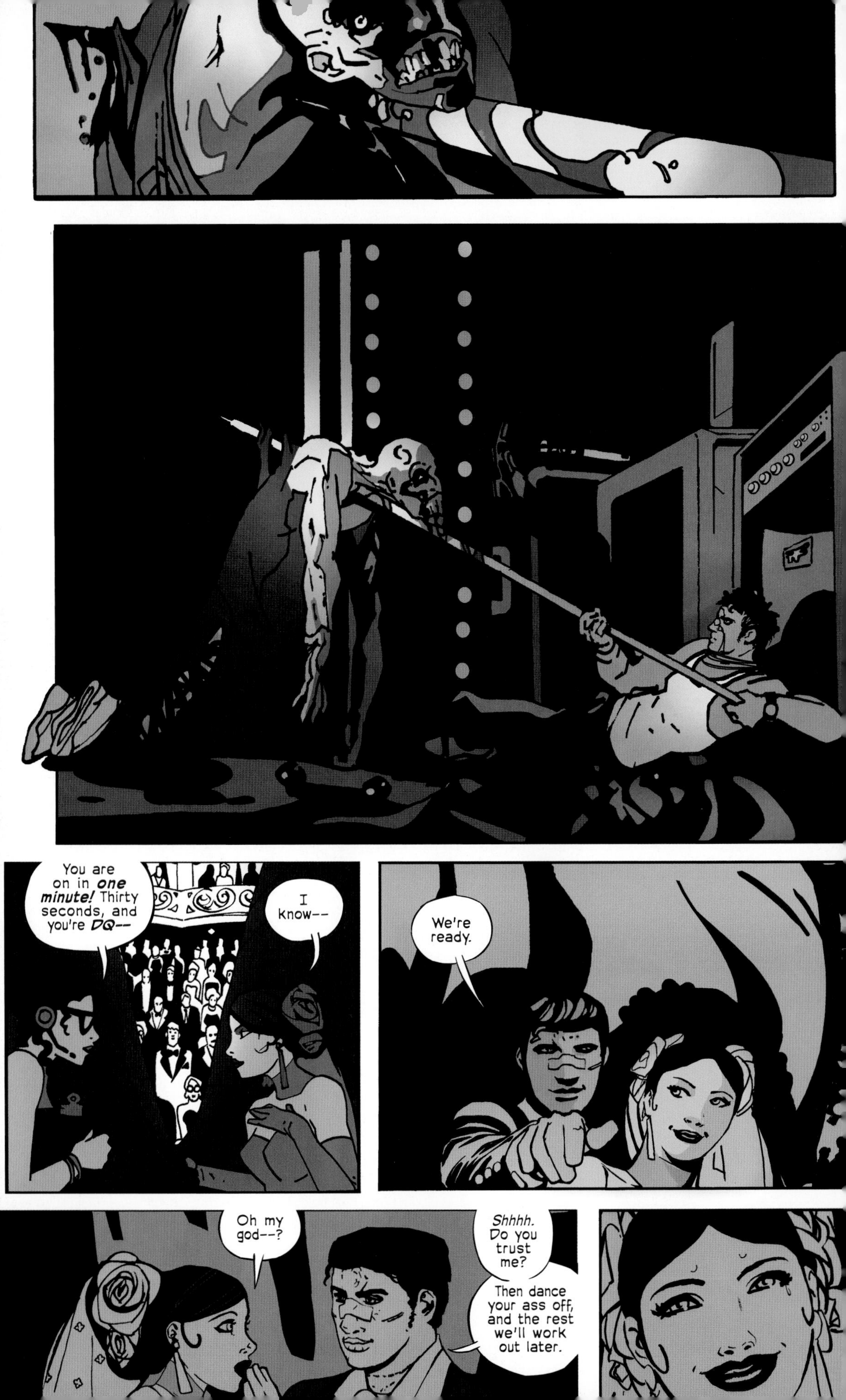

You are on in *one minute!* Thirty seconds, and you're *DQ--*
I know--
We're ready.
Oh my god--?
Shhhh. Do you trust me?
Then dance your ass off, and the rest we'll work out later.

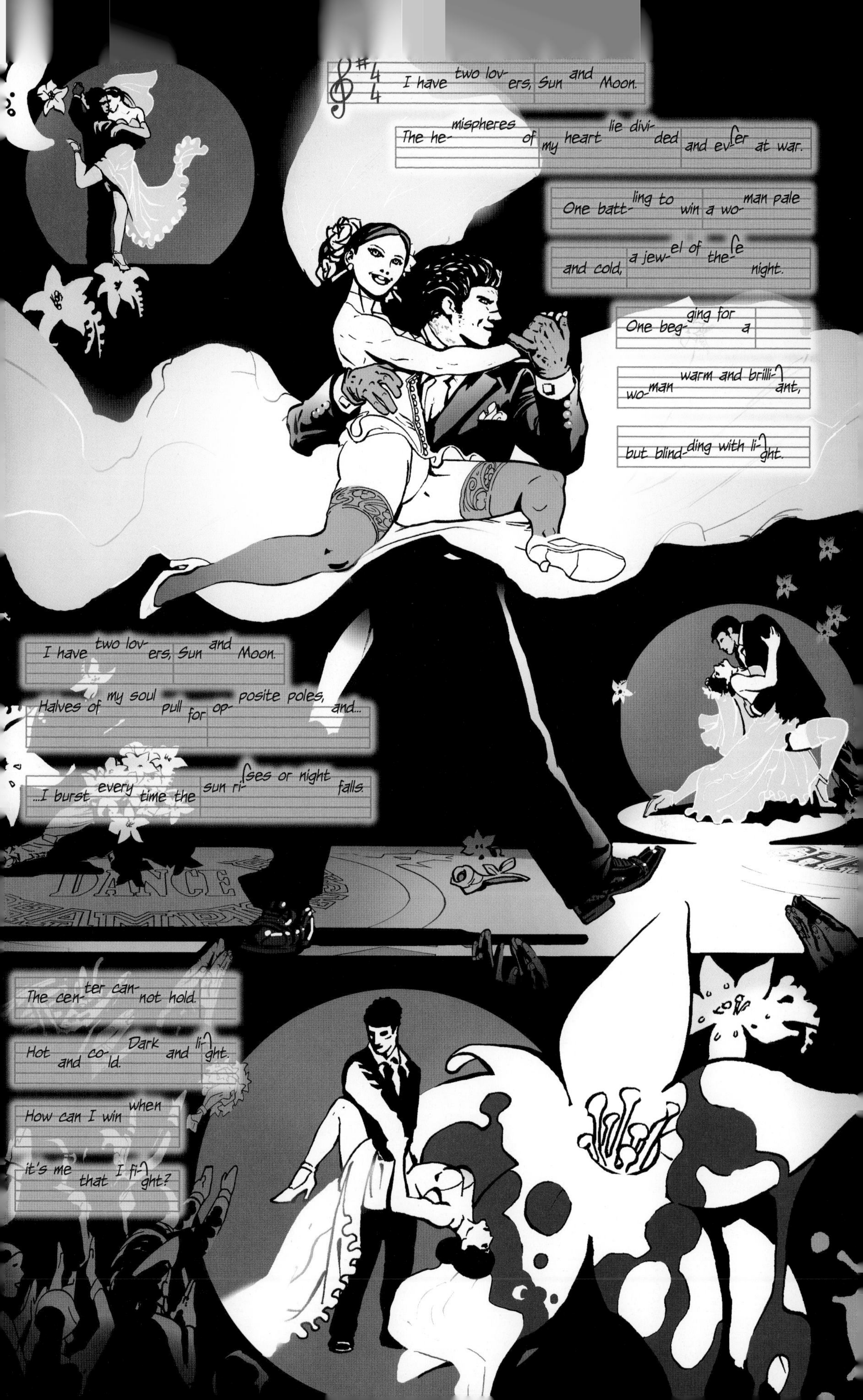
I have two lov- ers, Sun and Moon.
The he- mispheres of my heart lie divi- ded and ev- er at war.
One batt- ling to win a wo- man pale
and cold, a jew- el of the night.
One beg- ging for a
wo- man warm and brilli- ant,
but blind- ding with li- ght.
I have two lov- ers, Sun and Moon.
Halves of my soul pull for op- posite poles, and...
...I burst every time the sun ri- ses or night falls.
DANCE
The cen- ter can- not hold.
Hot and co- ld. Dark and li- ght.
How can I win when
it's me that I fi- ght?

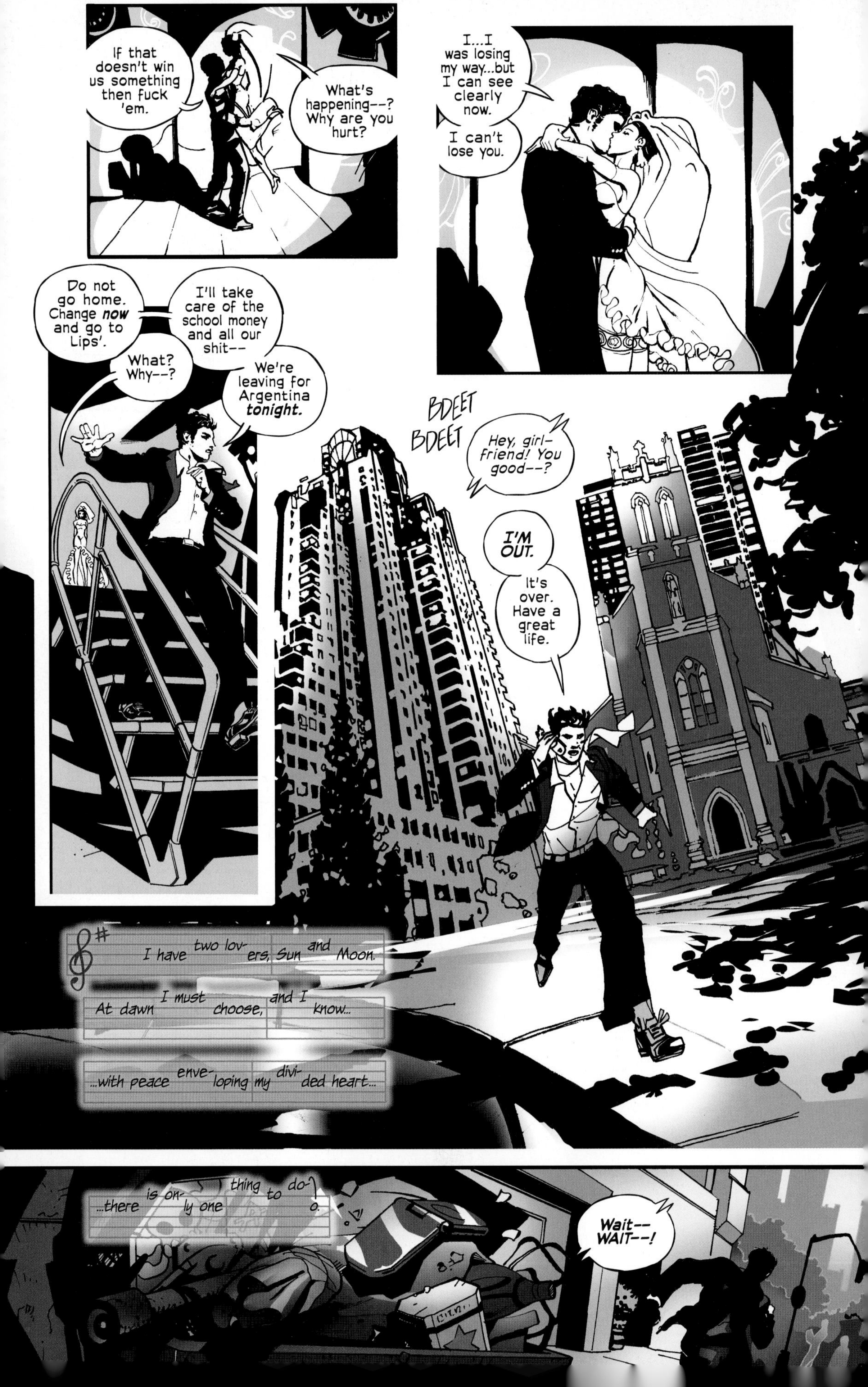
If that doesn't win us something then fuck 'em.
What's happening--? Why are you hurt?
I...I was losing my way...but I can see clearly now.
I can't lose you.
Do not go home. Change *now* and go to Lips'.
I'll take care of the school money and all our shit--
What? Why--?
We're leaving for Argentina *tonight.*
BDEET BDEET
Hey, girl-friend! You good--?
I'M OUT.
It's over. Have a great life.
I have two lov- ers, Sun and Moon.
At dawn I must choose, and I know...
...with peace enve- loping my divi- ded heart...
...there is on- ly one thing to do- o.
Wait-- WAIT--!

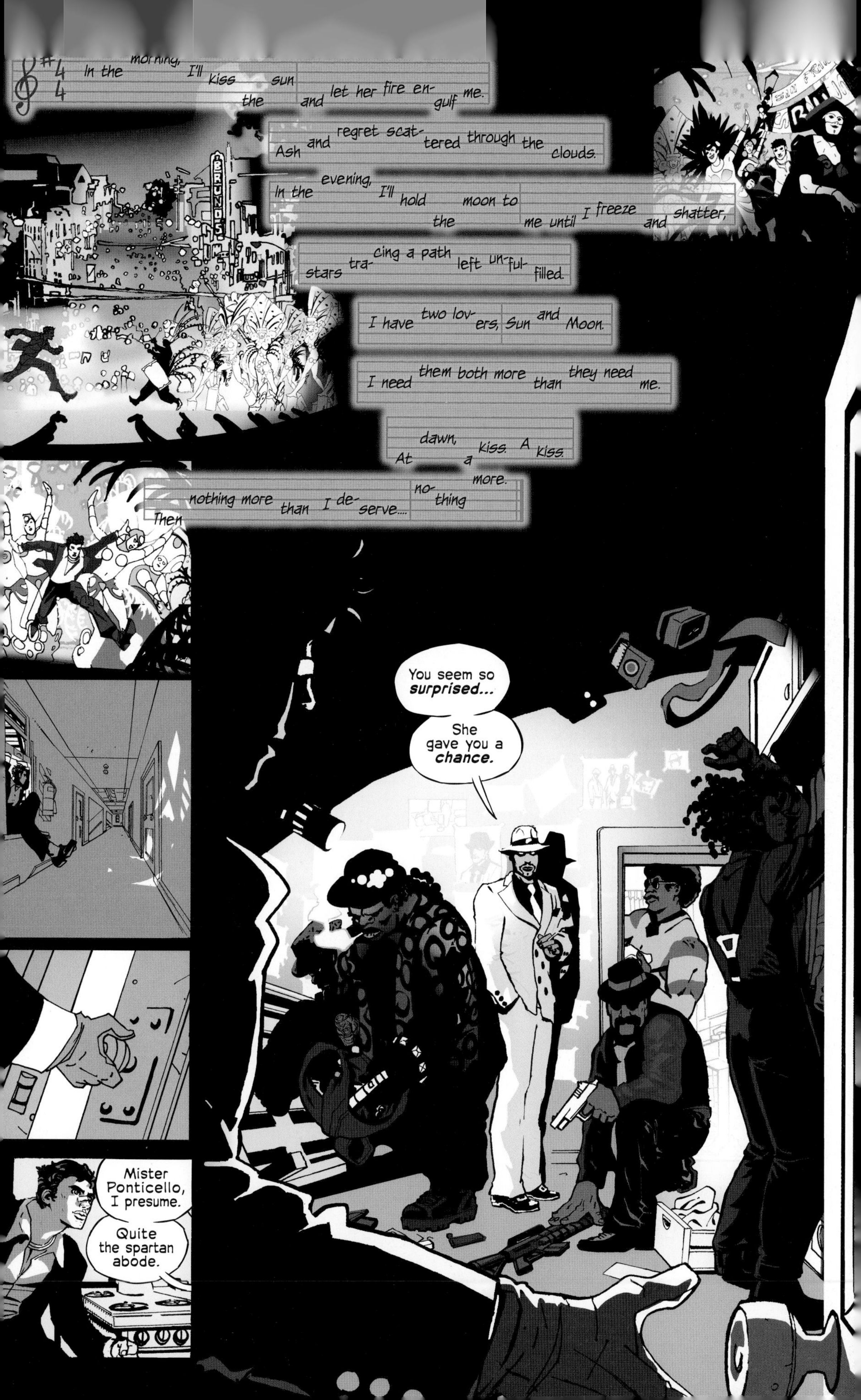

In the morning, I'll kiss the sun and let her fire en- gulf me.
Ash and regret scat- tered through the clouds.
In the evening, I'll hold the moon to me until I freeze and shatter,
stars tra- cing a path left un- ful- filled.
I have two lov- ers, Sun and Moon.
I need them both more than they need me.
At dawn, a kiss. A kiss.
Then nothing more than I de- serve.... no- thing more.
Mister Ponticello, I presume.
Quite the spartan abode.
You seem so *surprised...*
She gave you a *chance.*

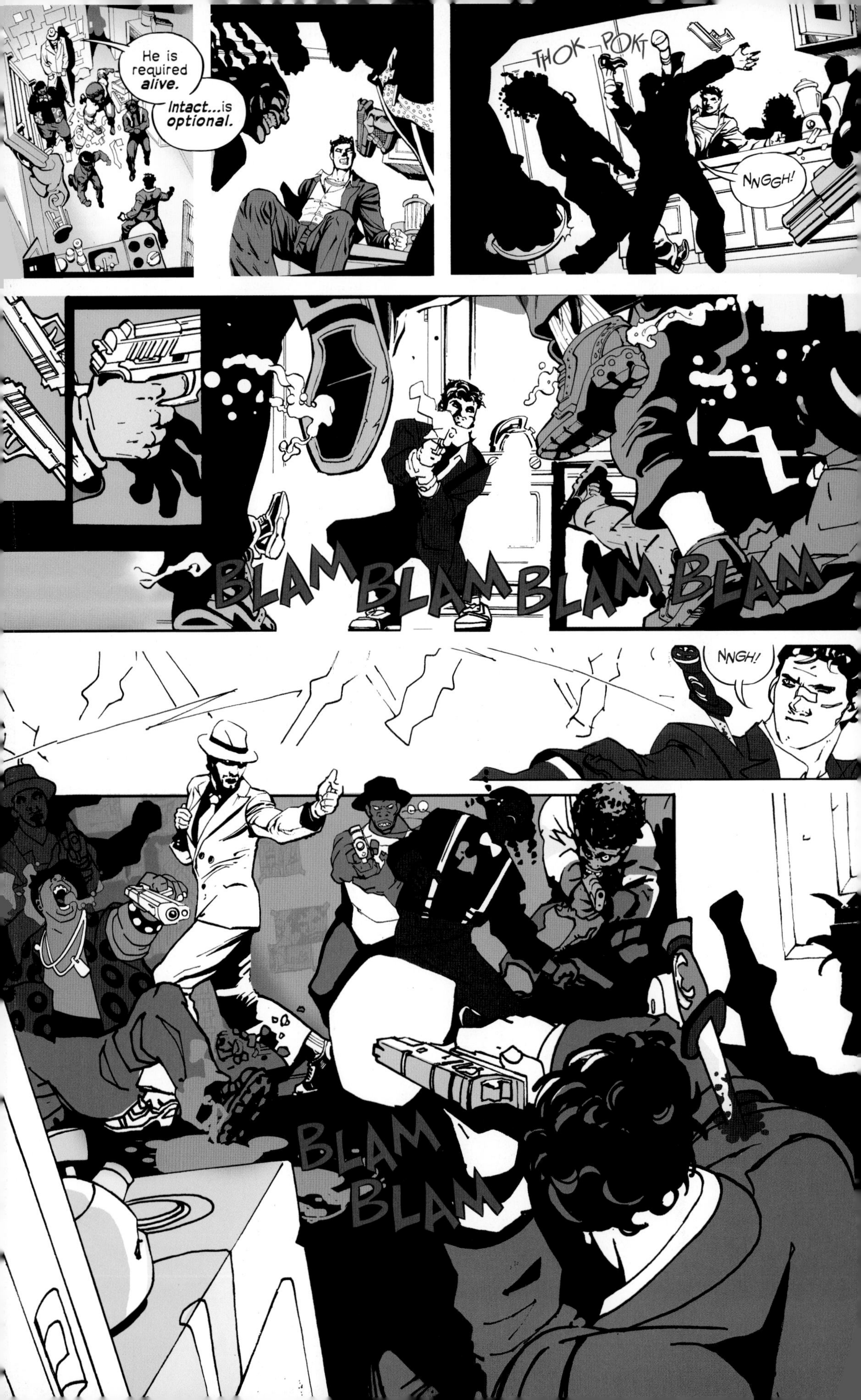

He is required alive.
Intact...is optional.
THOK POKT
NNGGH!
BLAM BLAM BLAM BLAM
NNGH!
BLAM BLAM

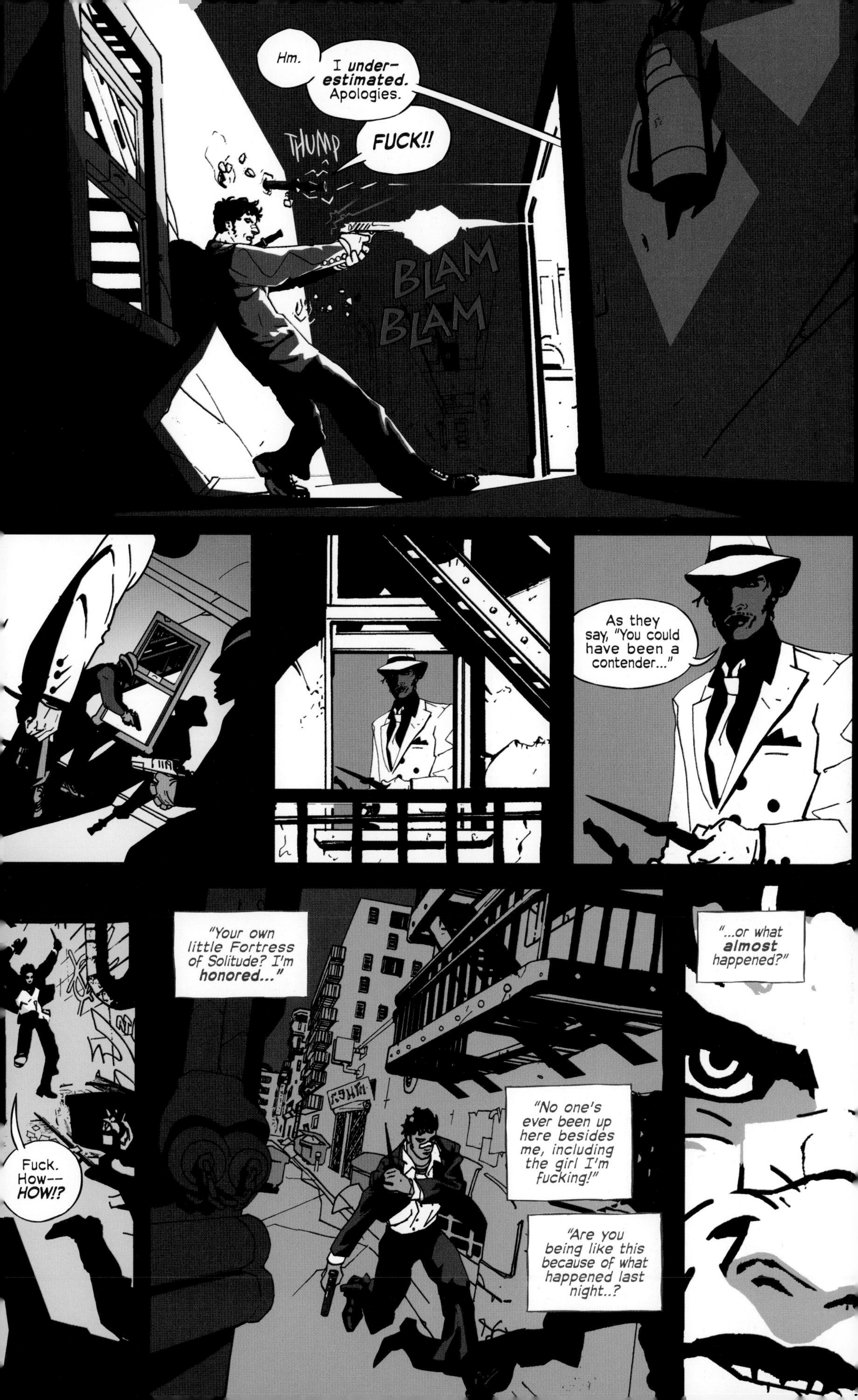
Hm.
I under-estimated. Apologies.
THUMP
FUCK!!
BLAM BLAM
As they say, "You could have been a contender..."
Fuck. How-- HOW!?
"Your own little Fortress of Solitude? I'm honored..."
"No one's ever been up here besides me, including the girl I'm fucking!"
"Are you being like this because of what happened last night..?
"...or what almost happened?"

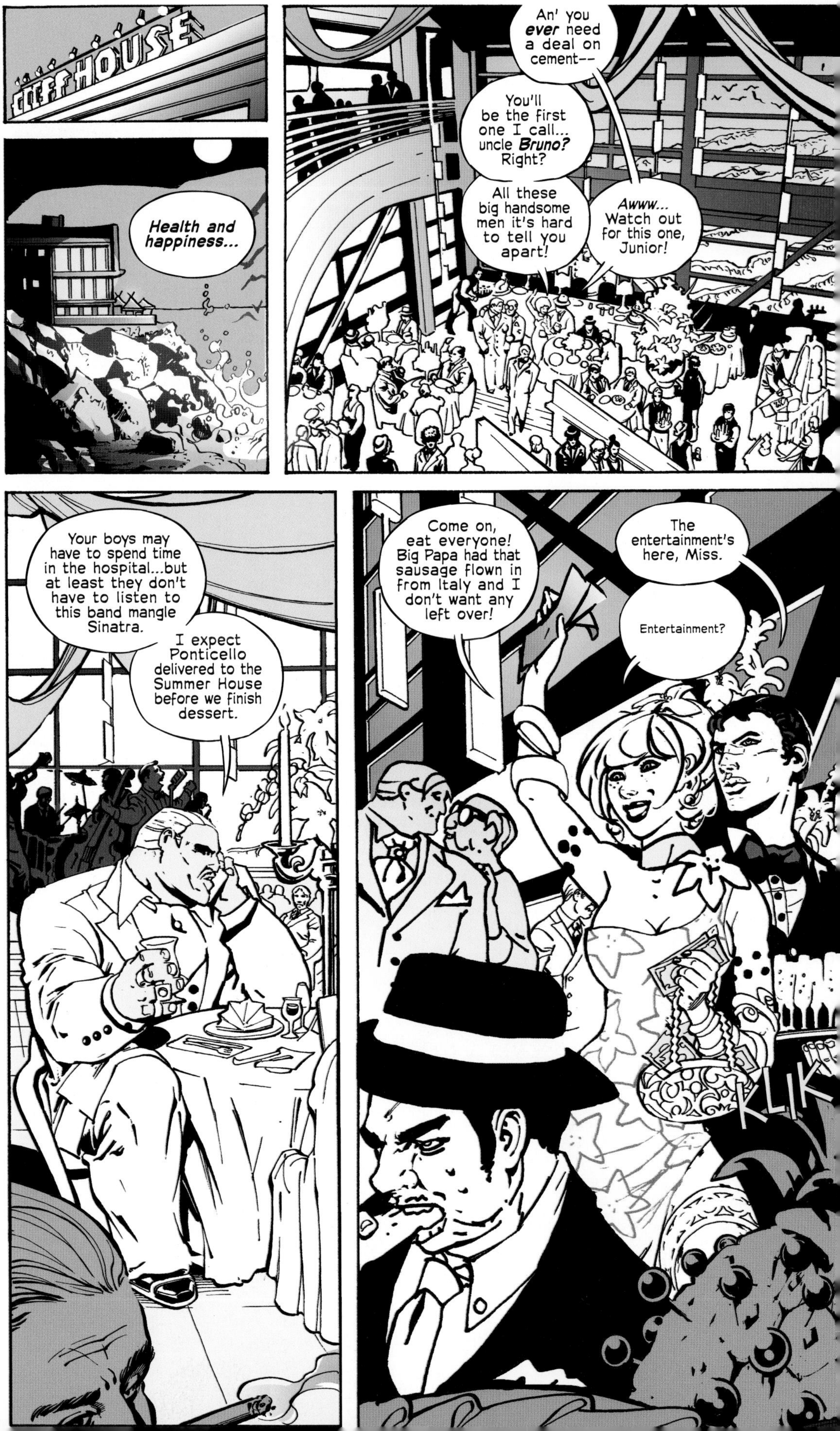
CLIFF HOUSE
Health and happiness...
An' you ever need a deal on cement--
You'll be the first one I call... uncle Bruno? Right?
All these big handsome men it's hard to tell you apart!
Awww... Watch out for this one, Junior!
Your boys may have to spend time in the hospital...but at least they don't have to listen to this band mangle Sinatra.
I expect Ponticello delivered to the Summer House before we finish dessert.
Come on, eat everyone! Big Papa had that sausage flown in from Italy and I don't want any left over!
The entertainment's here, Miss.
Entertainment?
KLIK

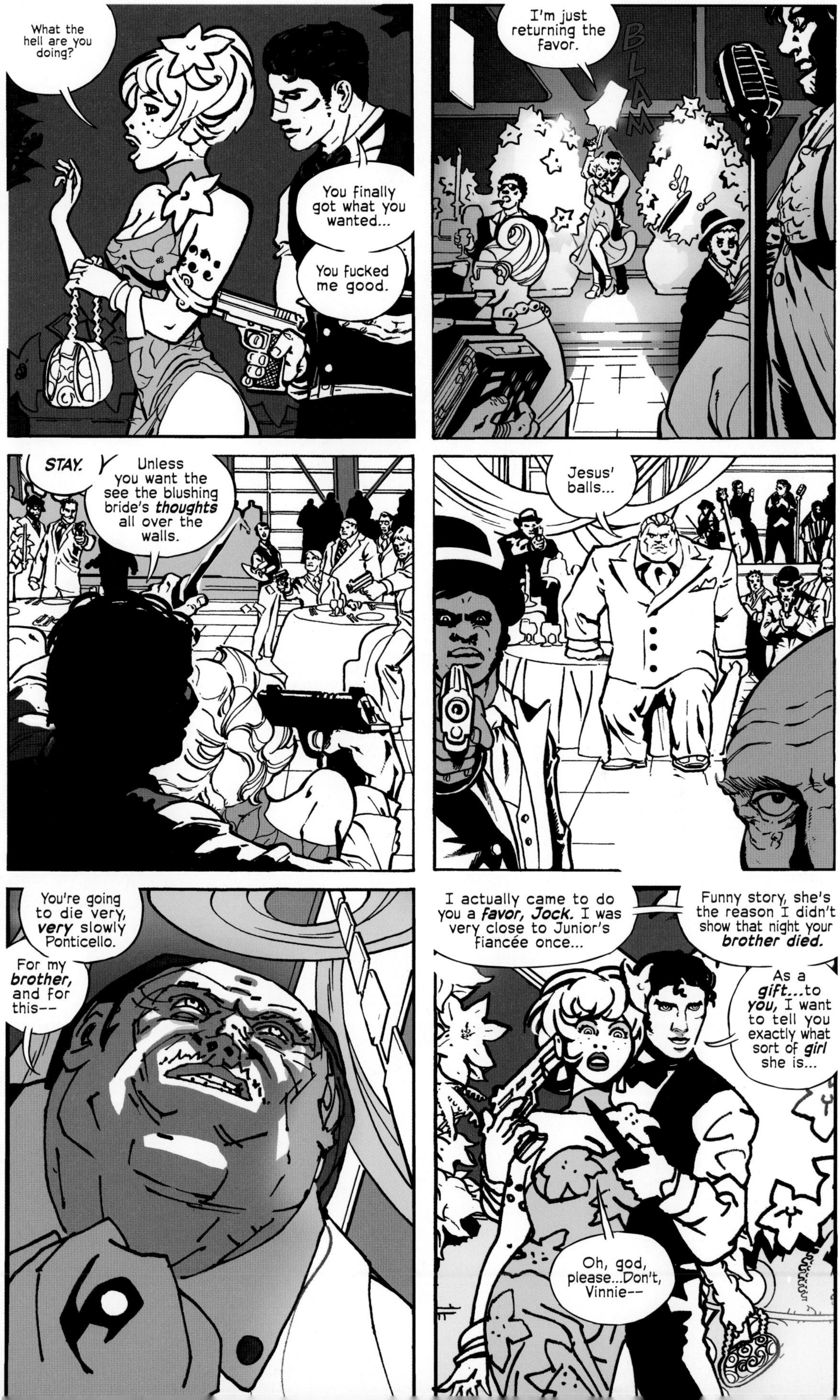

What the hell are you doing?
You finally got what you wanted...
You fucked me good.
I'm just returning the favor.
BLAM
STAY.
Unless you want the see the blushing bride's *thoughts* all over the walls.
Jesus' balls...
You're going to die very, *very* slowly Ponticello.
For my *brother,* and for this--
I actually came to do you a *favor, Jock.* I was very close to Junior's fiancée once...
Funny story, she's the reason I didn't show that night your *brother died.*
As a *gift...*to *you,* I want to tell you exactly what sort of *girl* she is...
Oh, god, please...Don't, Vinnie--

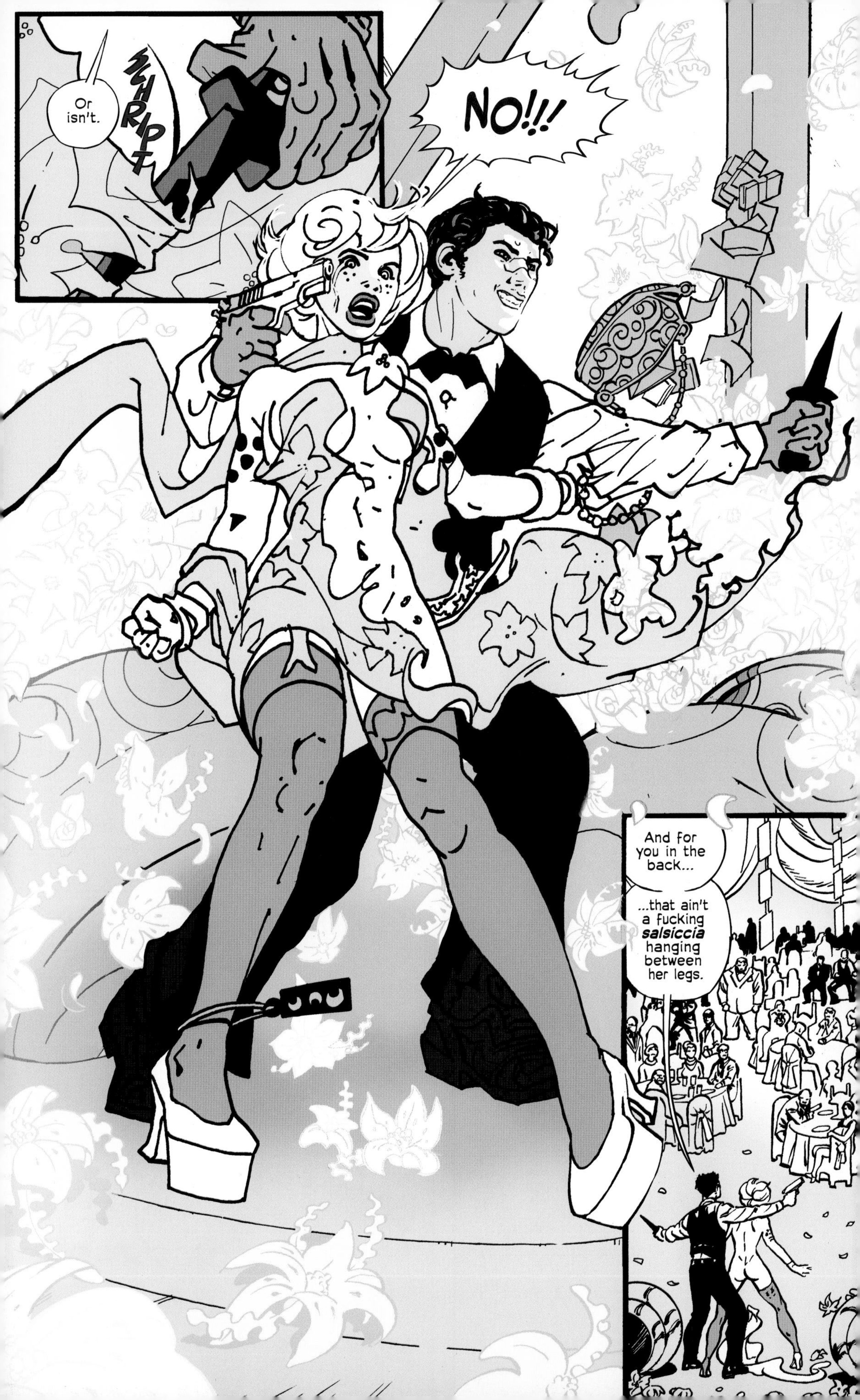
Or isn't.
SCHRIPT
NO!!!
And for you in the back...
...that ain't a fucking *salsiccia* hanging between her legs.

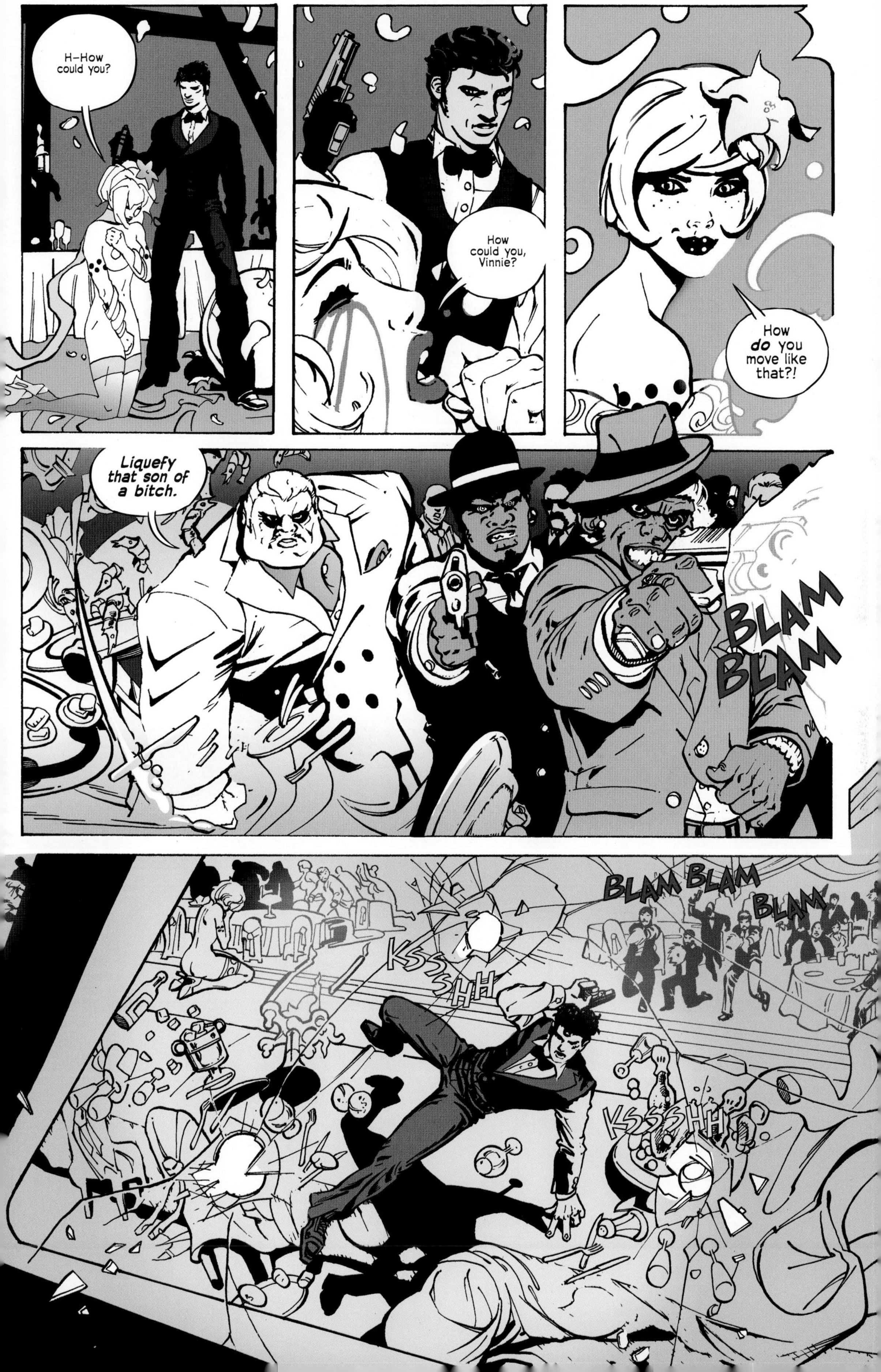
H-How could you?
How could you, Vinnie?
How *do* you move like that?!
Liquefy that son of a bitch.
BLAM BLAM
BLAM BLAM BLAM
KSSSHH
KSSSHH

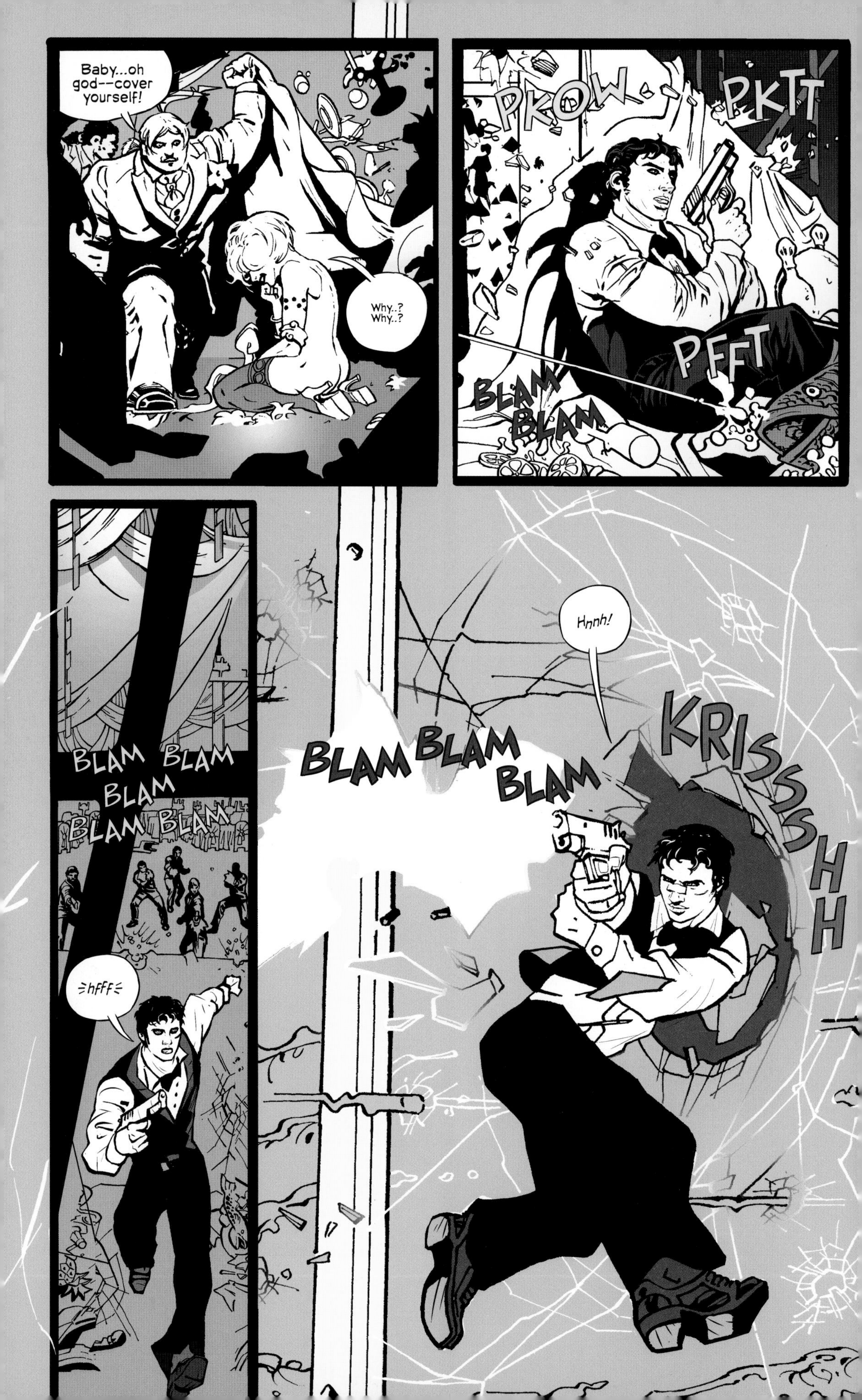
Baby...oh god--cover yourself!
Why..? Why..?
PKOW
PKTT
PFFT
BLAM
BLAM
BLAM BLAM
BLAM
BLAM BLAM
=hfff=
BLAM BLAM
BLAM
Hnnh!
KRISSSHH

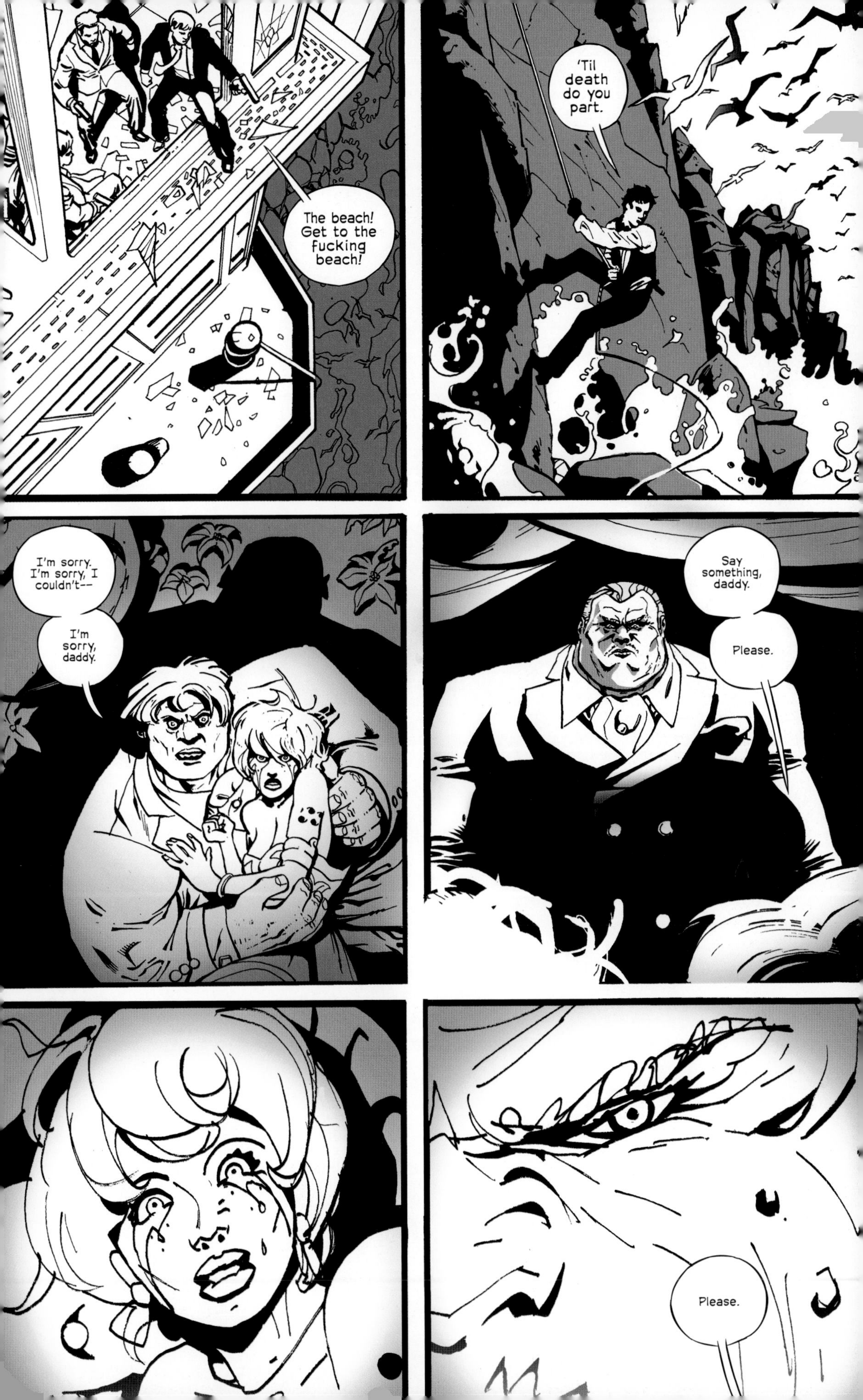
The beach! Get to the fucking beach!
'Til death do you part.
I'm sorry. I'm sorry, I couldn't--
I'm sorry, daddy.
Say something, daddy.
Please.
Please.

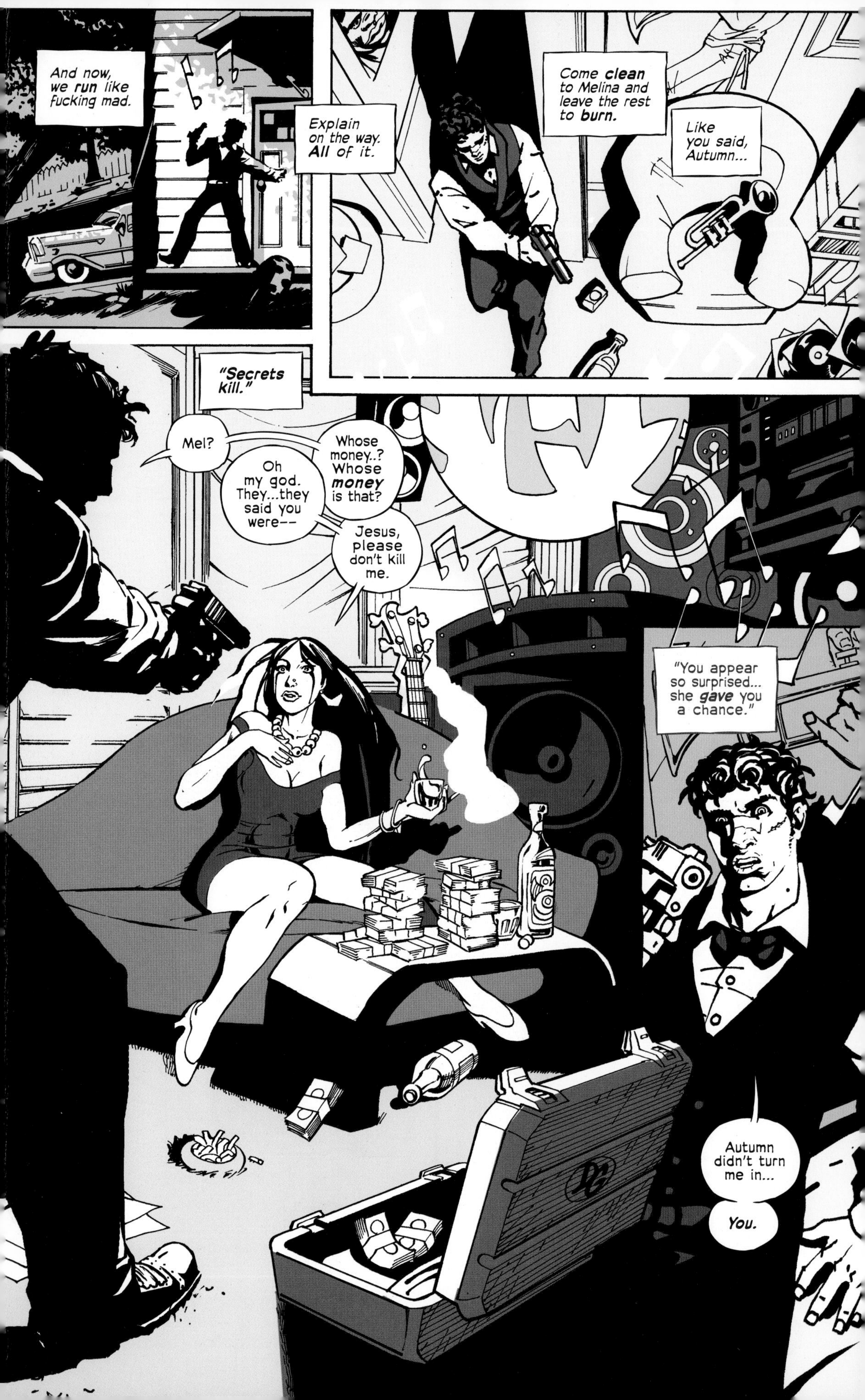
And now, we run like fucking mad.
Explain on the way. All of it.
Come clean to Melina and leave the rest to burn.
Like you said, Autumn...
"Secrets kill."
Mel?
Oh my god. They...they said you were--
Whose money..? Whose money is that?
Jesus, please don't kill me.
"You appear so surprised... she gave you a chance."
Autumn didn't turn me in...
You.

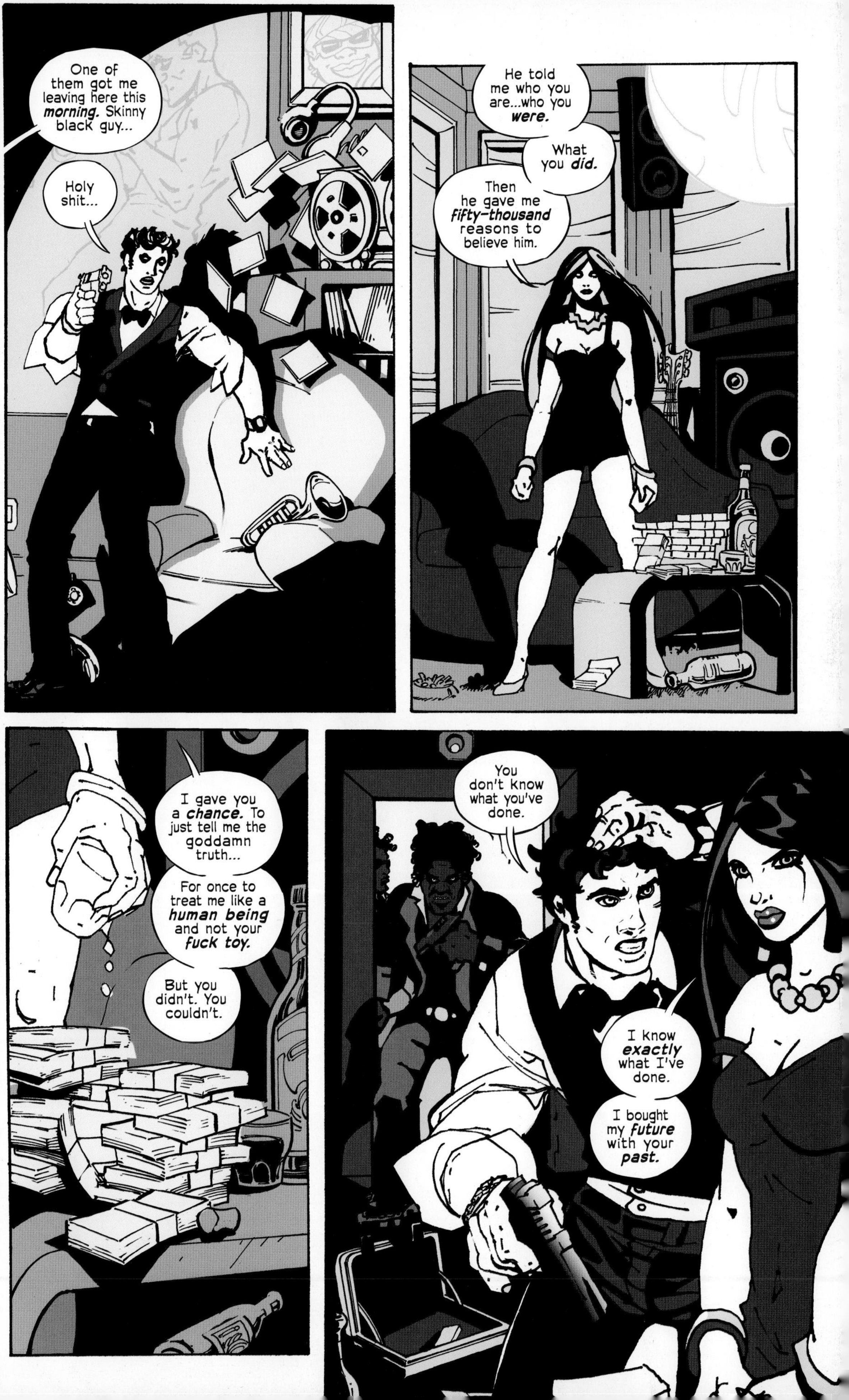
One of them got me leaving here this *morning.* Skinny black guy...
Holy shit...
He told me who you are...who you *were.*
What you *did.*
Then he gave me *fifty-thousand* reasons to believe him.
I gave you a *chance.* To just tell me the goddamn truth...
For once to treat me like a *human being* and not your *fuck toy.*
But you didn't. You couldn't.
You don't know what you've done.
I know *exactly* what I've done.
I bought my *future* with your *past.*

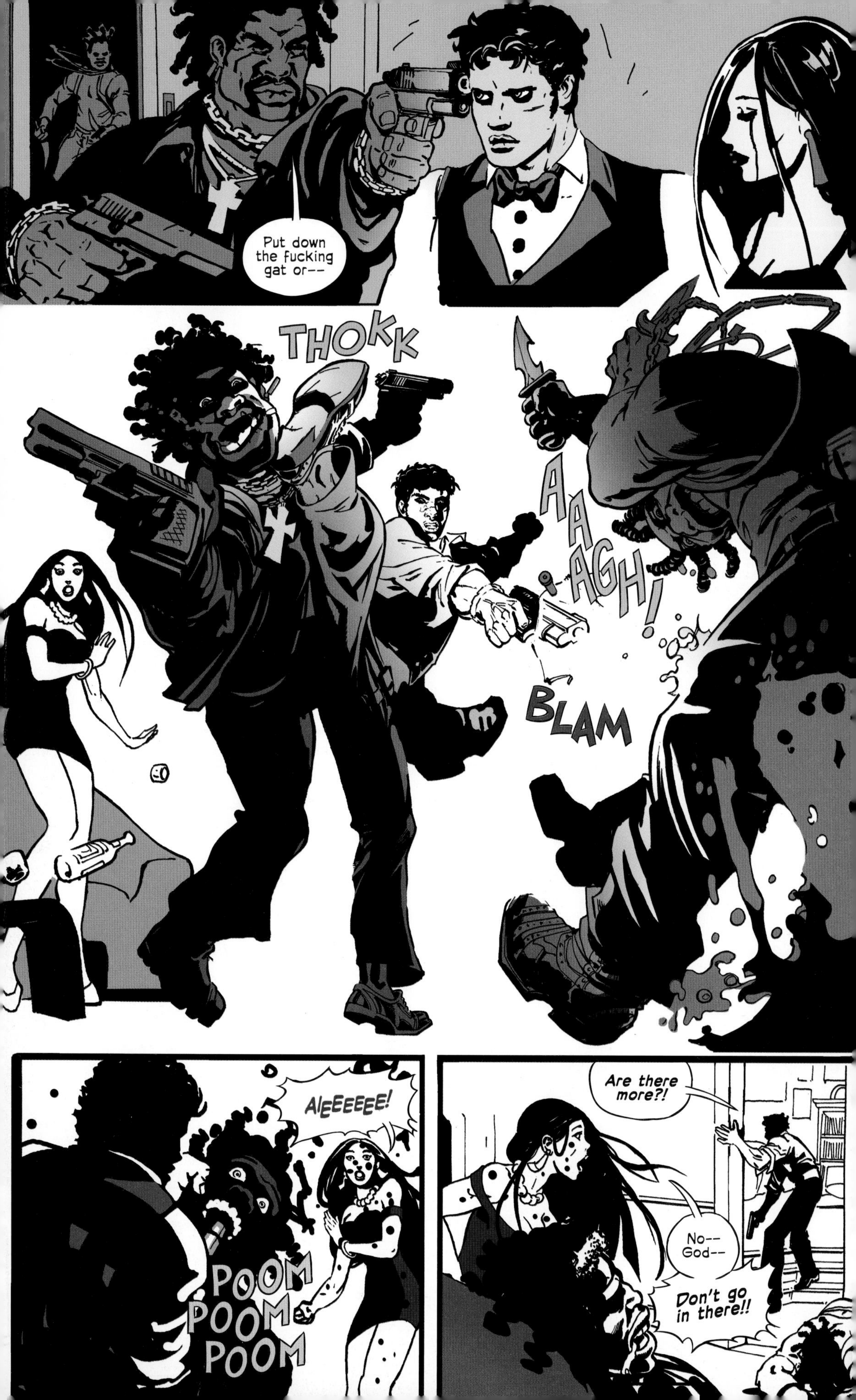
Put down the fucking gat or--
THOKK
AAAGH!
BLAM
AIEEEEEE!
POOM POOM POOM
Are there more?!
No-- God--
Don't go in there!!

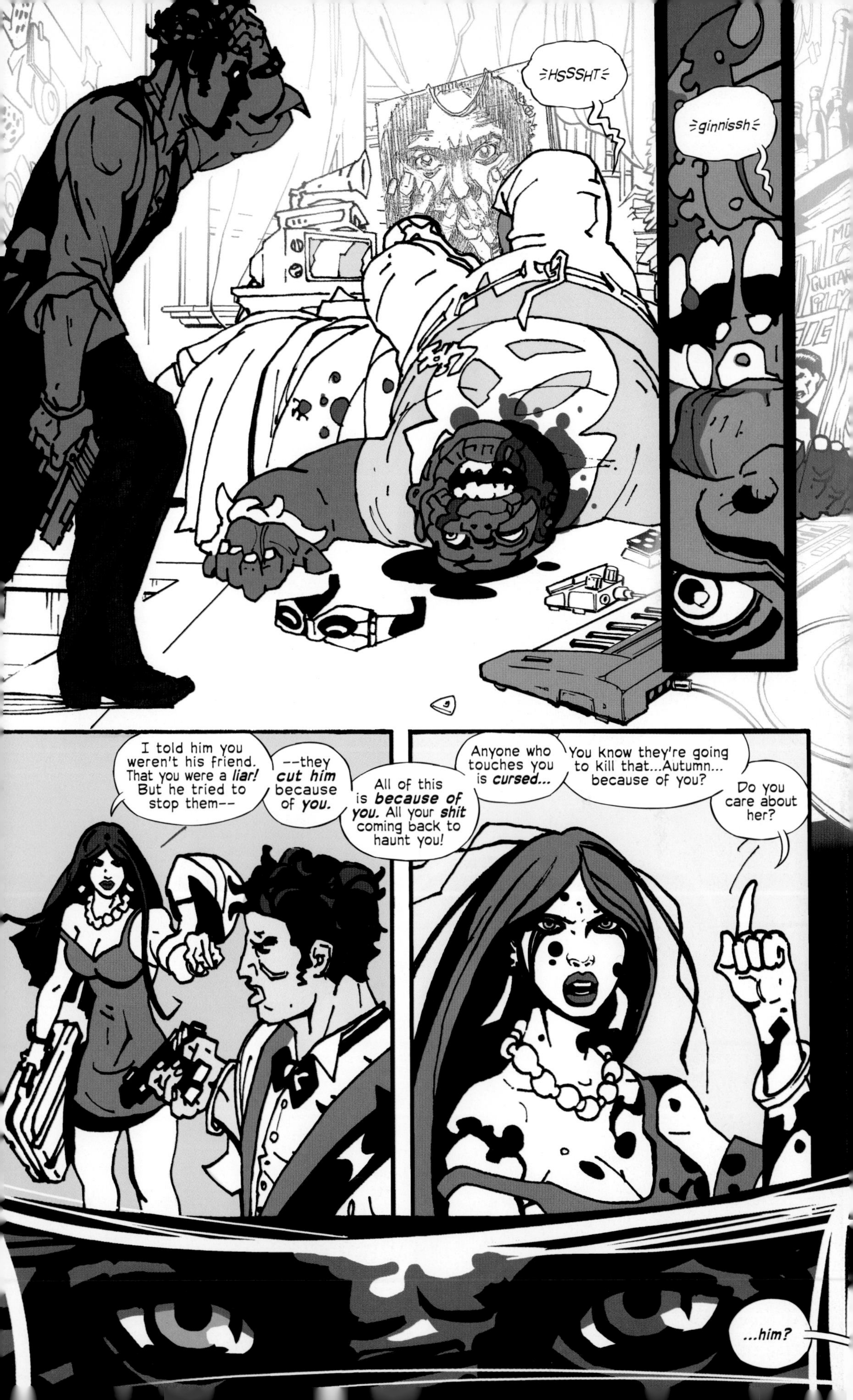
HSSSHT
ginnissh
I told him you weren't his friend. That you were a *liar!* But he tried to stop them--
--they ***cut him*** because of ***you.***
All of this is ***because of you.*** All your ***shit*** coming back to haunt you!
Anyone who touches you is ***cursed...***
You know they're going to kill that...Autumn... because of you?
Do you care about her?
...him?

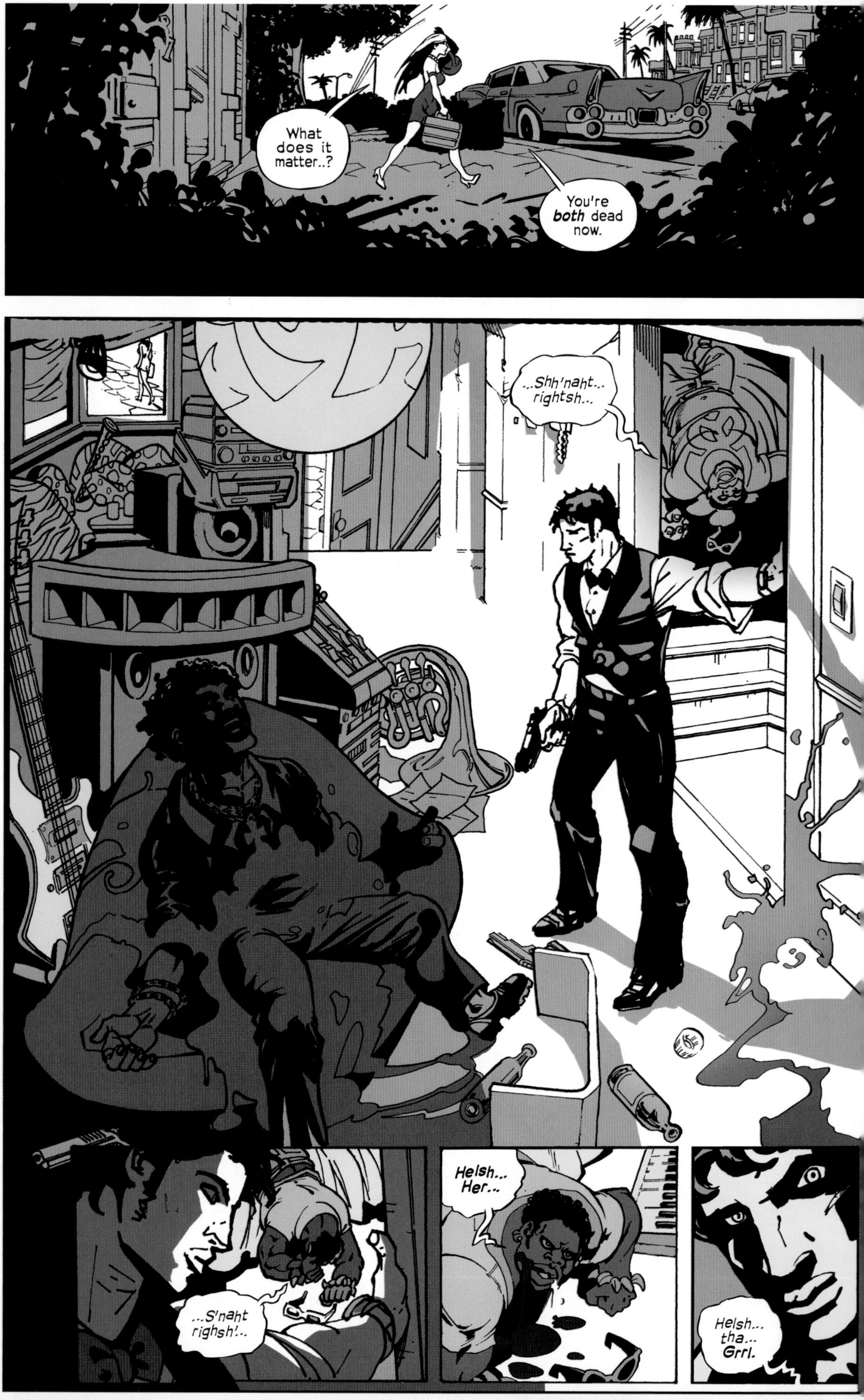
What does it matter..?
You're *both* dead now.
...Shh'naht... rightsh...
...S'naht righsh'..
Helsh... Her...
Helsh... tha... Grrl.

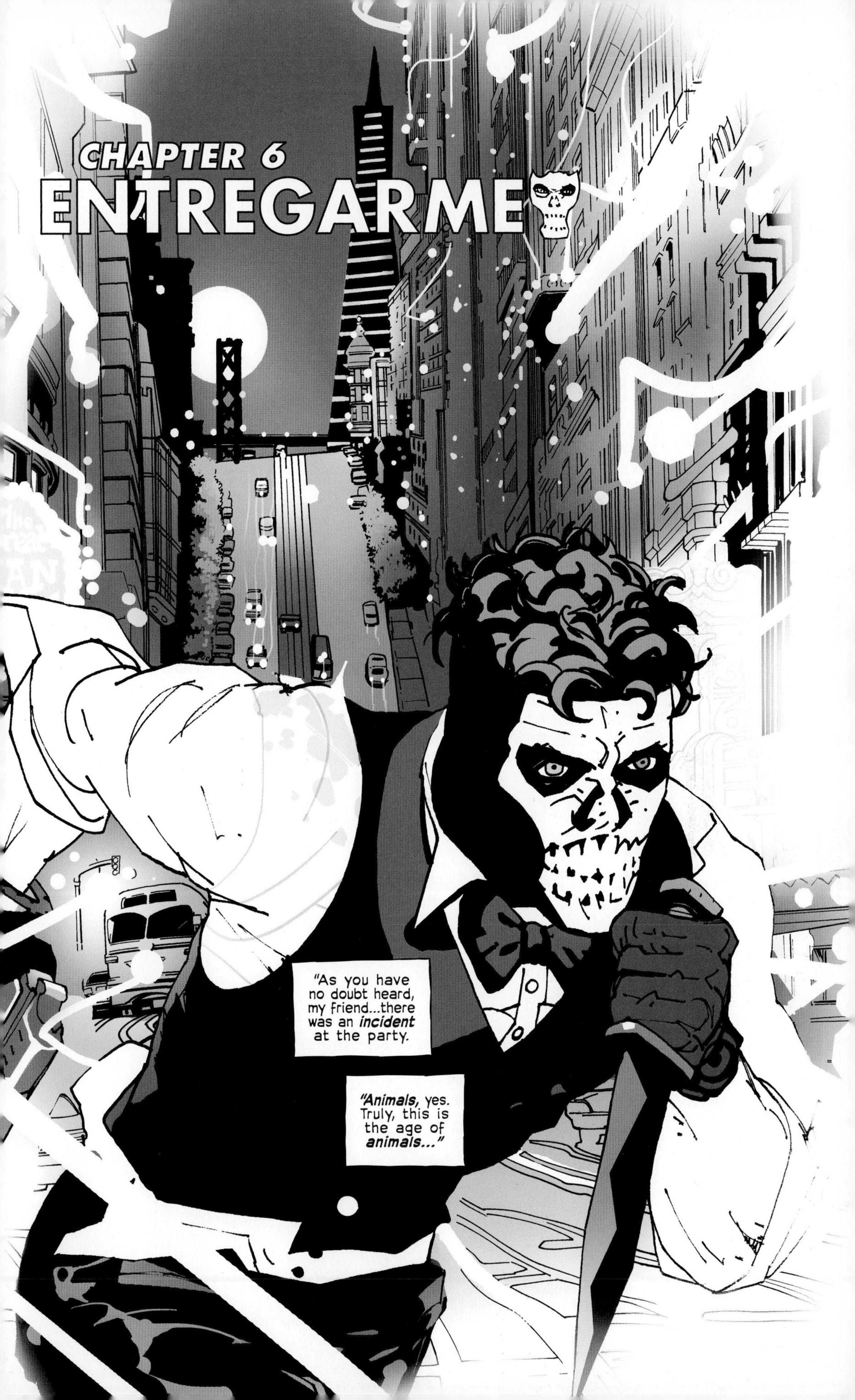
CHAPTER 6
ENTREGARME
"As you have no doubt heard, my friend...there was an *incident* at the party.
"Animals, yes. Truly, this is the age of *animals..."*

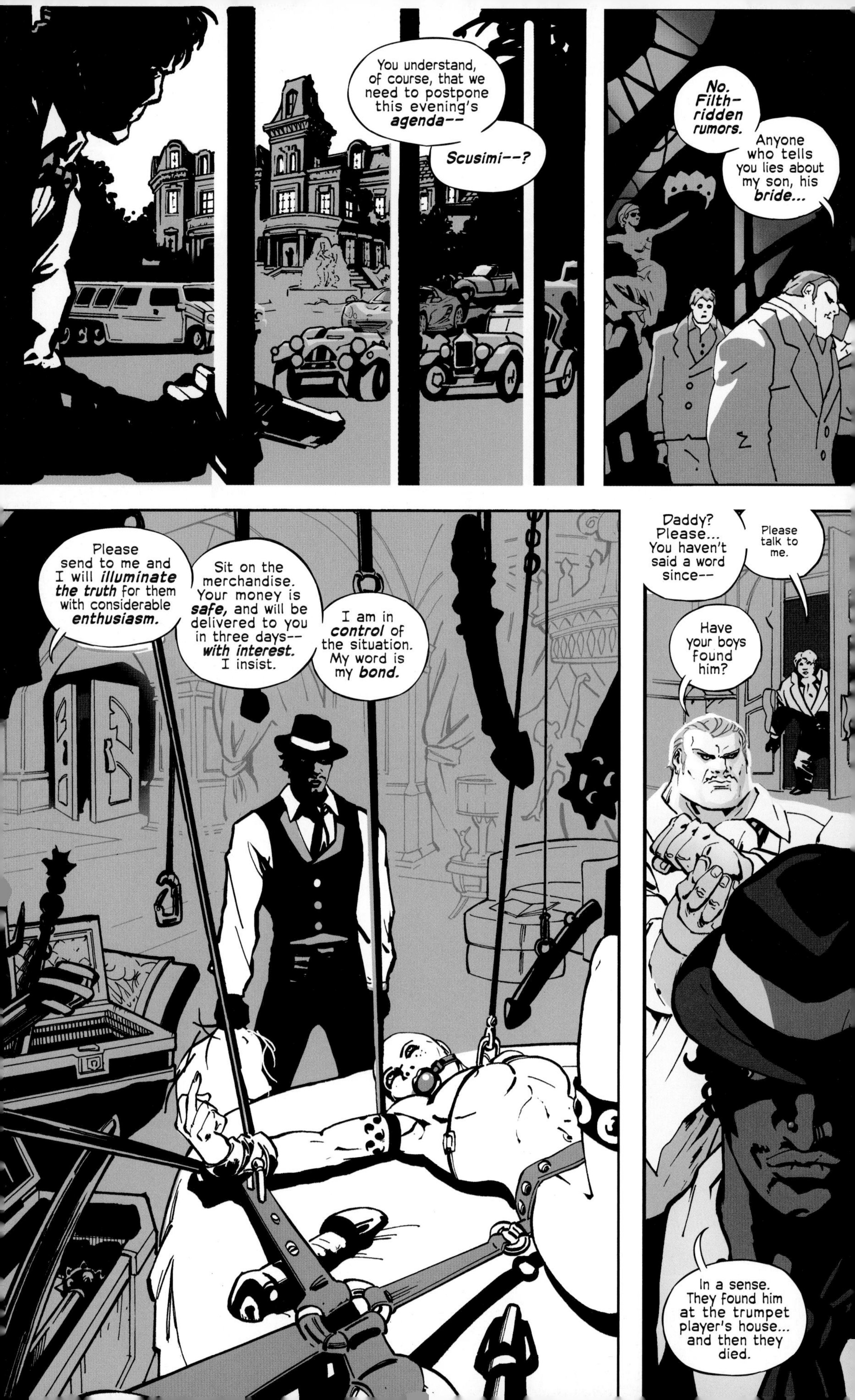

You understand, of course, that we need to postpone this evening's **agenda--**
Scusimi--?
No. Filth-ridden rumors.
Anyone who tells you lies about my son, his **bride...**
Please send to me and I will **illuminate the truth** for them with considerable **enthusiasm.**
Sit on the merchandise. Your money is **safe,** and will be delivered to you in three days-- **with interest.** I insist.
I am in **control** of the situation. My word is my **bond.**
Daddy? Please... You haven't said a word since--
Please talk to me.
Have your boys found him?
In a sense. They found him at the trumpet player's house... and then they died.

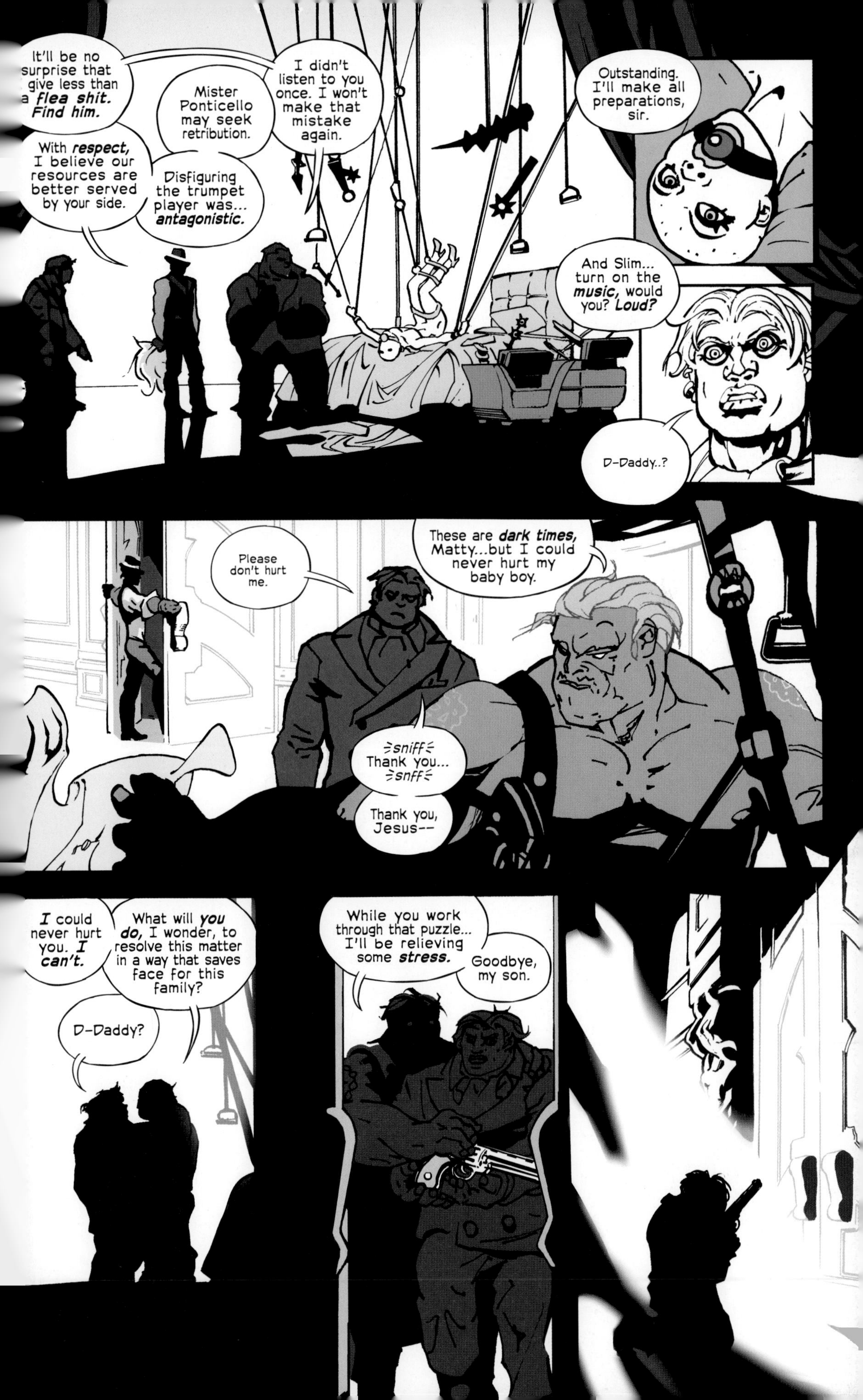
It'll be no surprise that I give less than a ***flea shit. Find him.***
With ***respect,*** I believe our resources are better served by your side.
Mister Ponticello may seek retribution.
Disfiguring the trumpet player was... ***antagonistic.***
I didn't listen to you once. I won't make that mistake again.
Outstanding. I'll make all preparations, sir.
And Slim... turn on the ***music,*** would you? ***Loud?***
D-Daddy..?
Please don't hurt me.
These are ***dark times,*** Matty...but I could never hurt my baby boy.
sniff Thank you... *snff*
Thank you, Jesus--
I could never hurt you. ***I can't.***
What will ***you do,*** I wonder, to resolve this matter in a way that saves face for this family?
D-Daddy?
While you work through that puzzle... I'll be relieving some ***stress.***
Goodbye, my son.

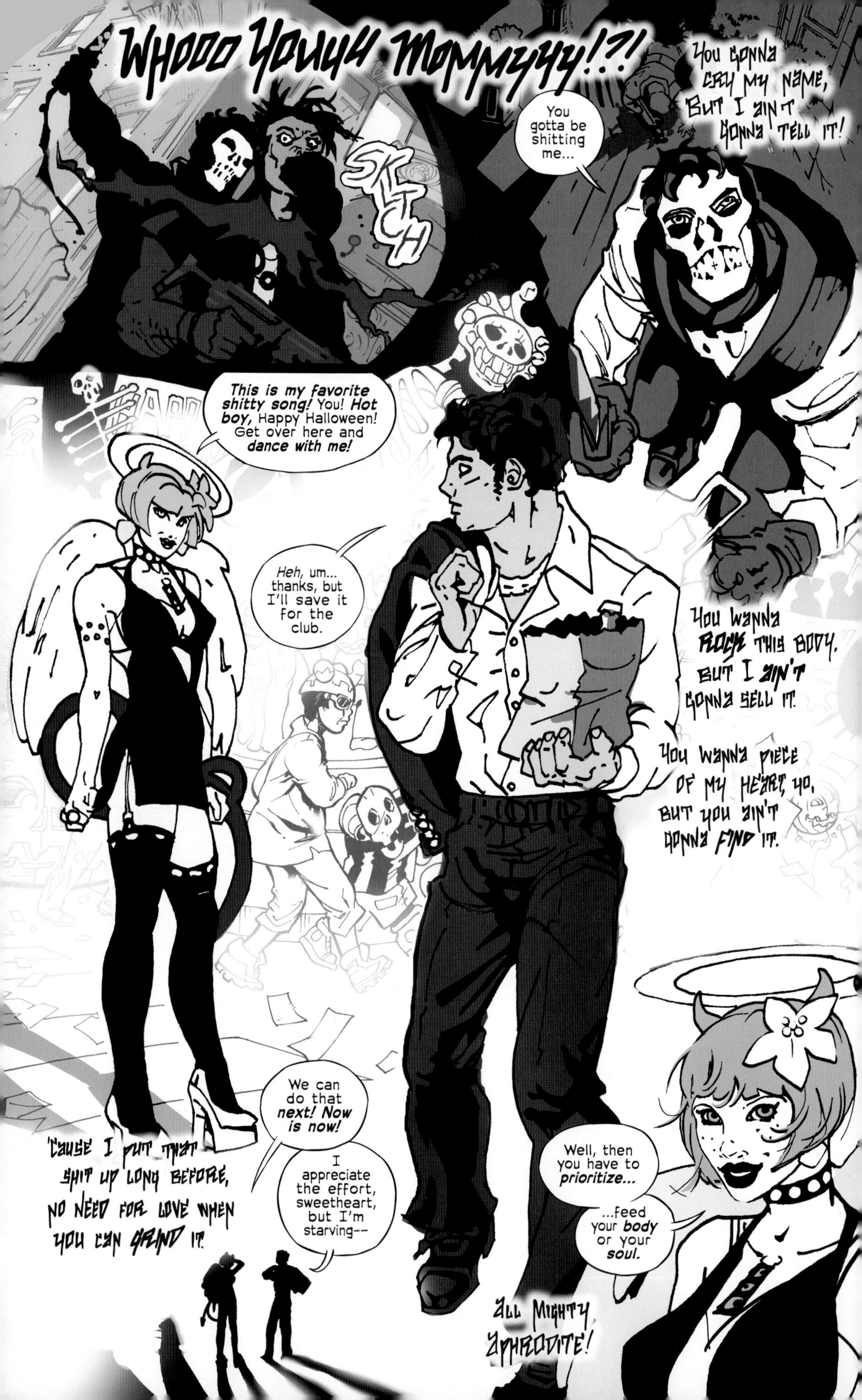
WHOOO YOUUU MOMMYYY!?!
SKLTCH
You gotta be shitting me...
You gonna cry my name, but I ain't gonna tell it!
This is my favorite shitty song! You! Hot boy, Happy Halloween! Get over here and dance with me!
Heh, um... thanks, but I'll save it for the club.
You wanna rock this body, but I ain't gonna sell it.
You wanna piece of my heart, yo, but you ain't gonna find it.
We can do that next! Now is now!
I appreciate the effort, sweetheart, but I'm starving--
'Cause I put that shit up long before, no need for love when you can grind it.
Well, then you have to prioritize...
...feed your body or your soul.
All Mighty Aphrodite!

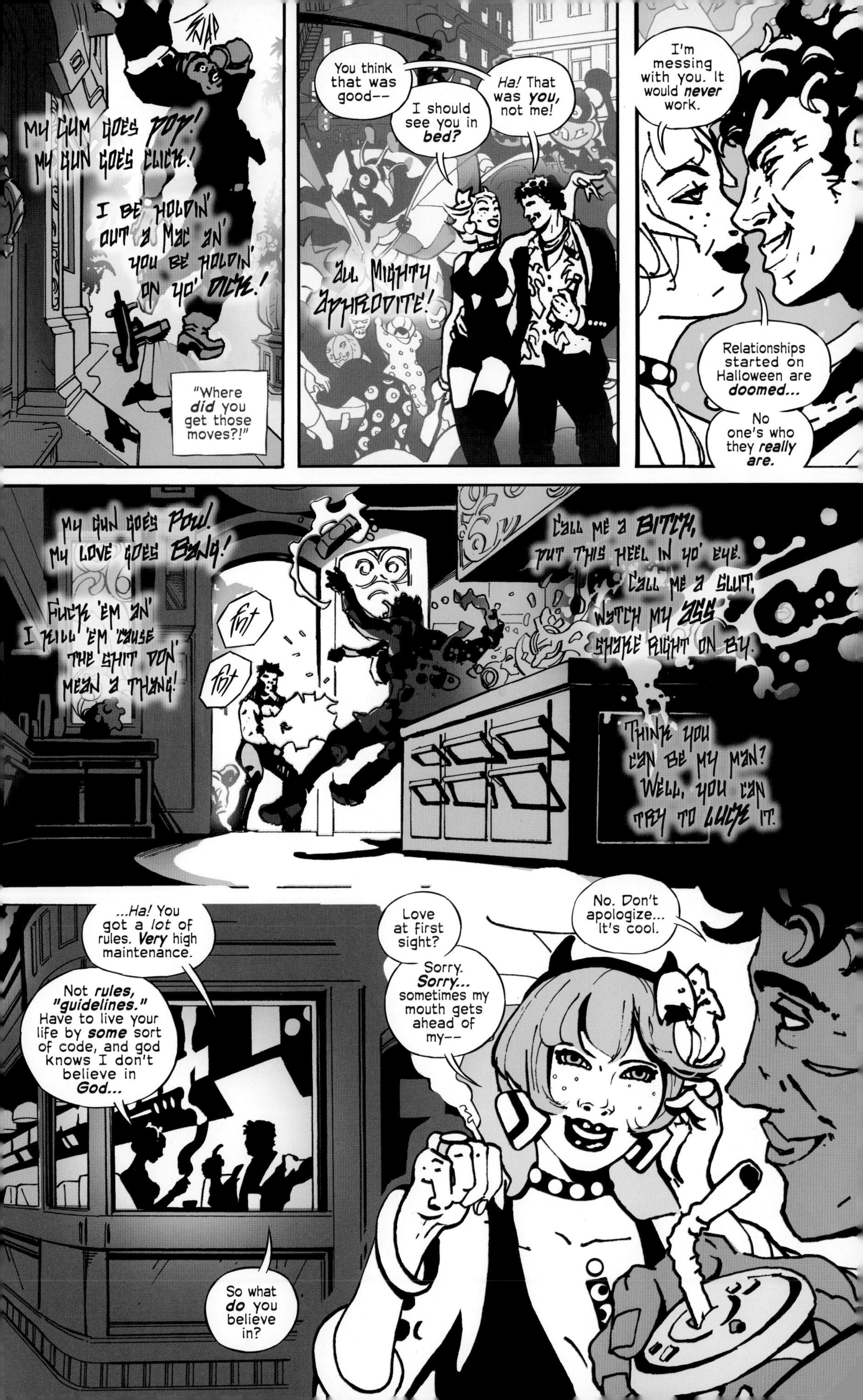
SNAP
MY GUM GOES POP! MY GUN GOES CLICK!
I BE HOLDIN' OUT A MAC AN' YOU BE HOLDIN' ON YO' DICK!
"Where did you get those moves?!"
You think that was good--
I should see you in bed?
Ha! That was you, not me!
ALL MIGHTY APHRODITE!
I'm messing with you. It would never work.
Relationships started on Halloween are doomed...
No one's who they really are.
MY GUN GOES POW! MY LOVE GOES BANG!
FUCK 'EM AN' I KILL 'EM 'CAUSE THE SHIT DON' MEAN A THANG!
FNT
FNT
CALL ME A BITCH, PUT THIS HEEL IN YO' EYE.
CALL ME A SLUT, WATCH MY ASS SHAKE RIGHT ON BY.
THINK YOU CAN BE MY MAN? WELL, YOU CAN TRY TO LUCK IT.
...Ha! You got a lot of rules. Very high maintenance.
Not rules, "guidelines." Have to live your life by some sort of code, and god knows I don't believe in God...
So what do you believe in?
Love at first sight?
Sorry. Sorry... sometimes my mouth gets ahead of my--
No. Don't apologize... It's cool.

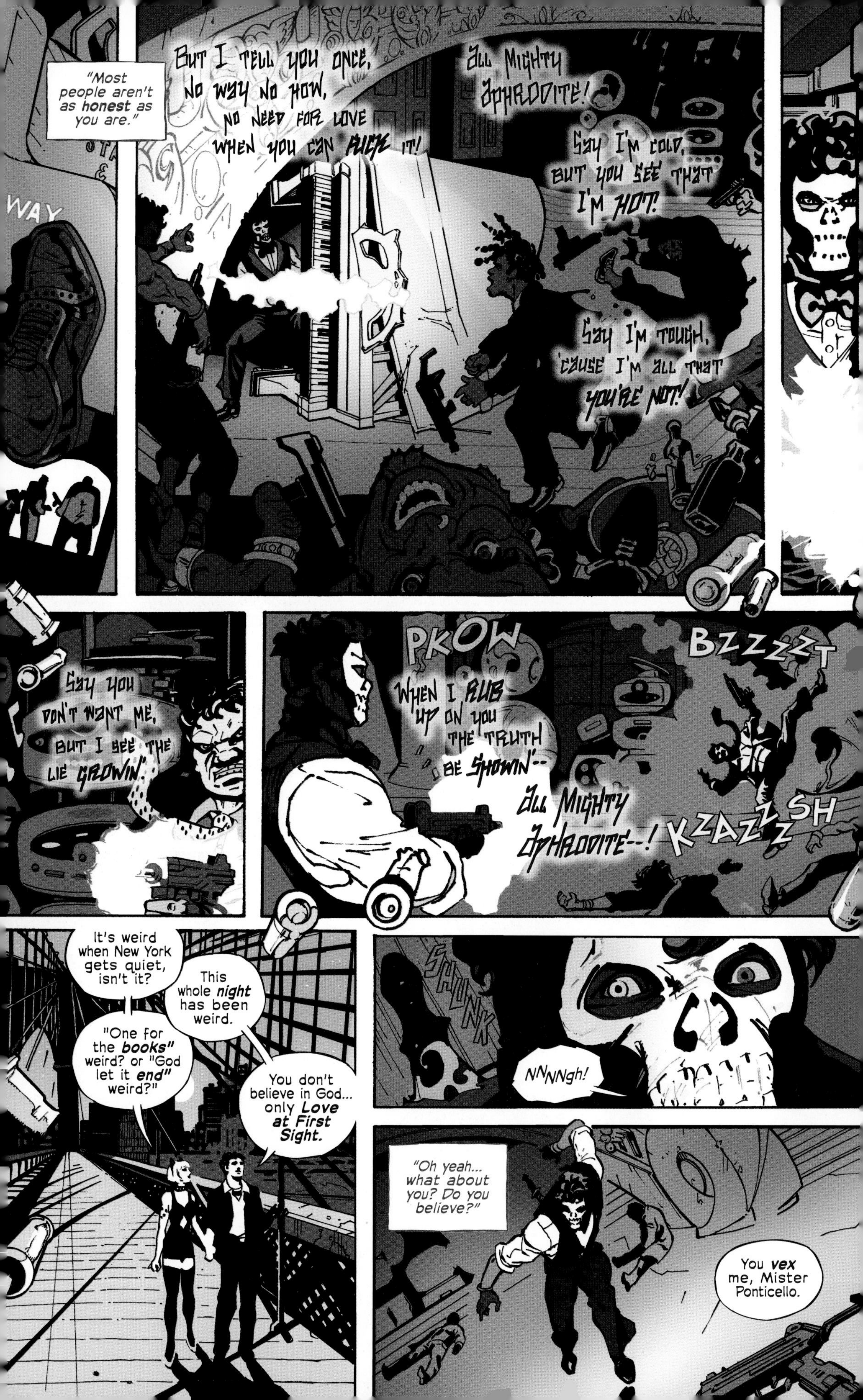
"Most people aren't as honest as you are."
But I tell you once, no way no how, no need for love when you can fuck it!
All Mighty Aphrodite!
Say I'm cold, but you see that I'm hot!
Say I'm tough, 'cause I'm all that you're not!
Say you don't want me, but I see the lie growin'.
PKOW
When I rub up on you the truth be showin'--
BZZZZZT
All Mighty Aphrodite--!
KZAZZZSH
It's weird when New York gets quiet, isn't it?
This whole night has been weird.
"One for the books" weird? or "God let it end" weird?"
You don't believe in God... only Love at First Sight.
SHUNK
NNNNgh!
"Oh yeah... what about you? Do you believe?"
You vex me, Mister Ponticello.

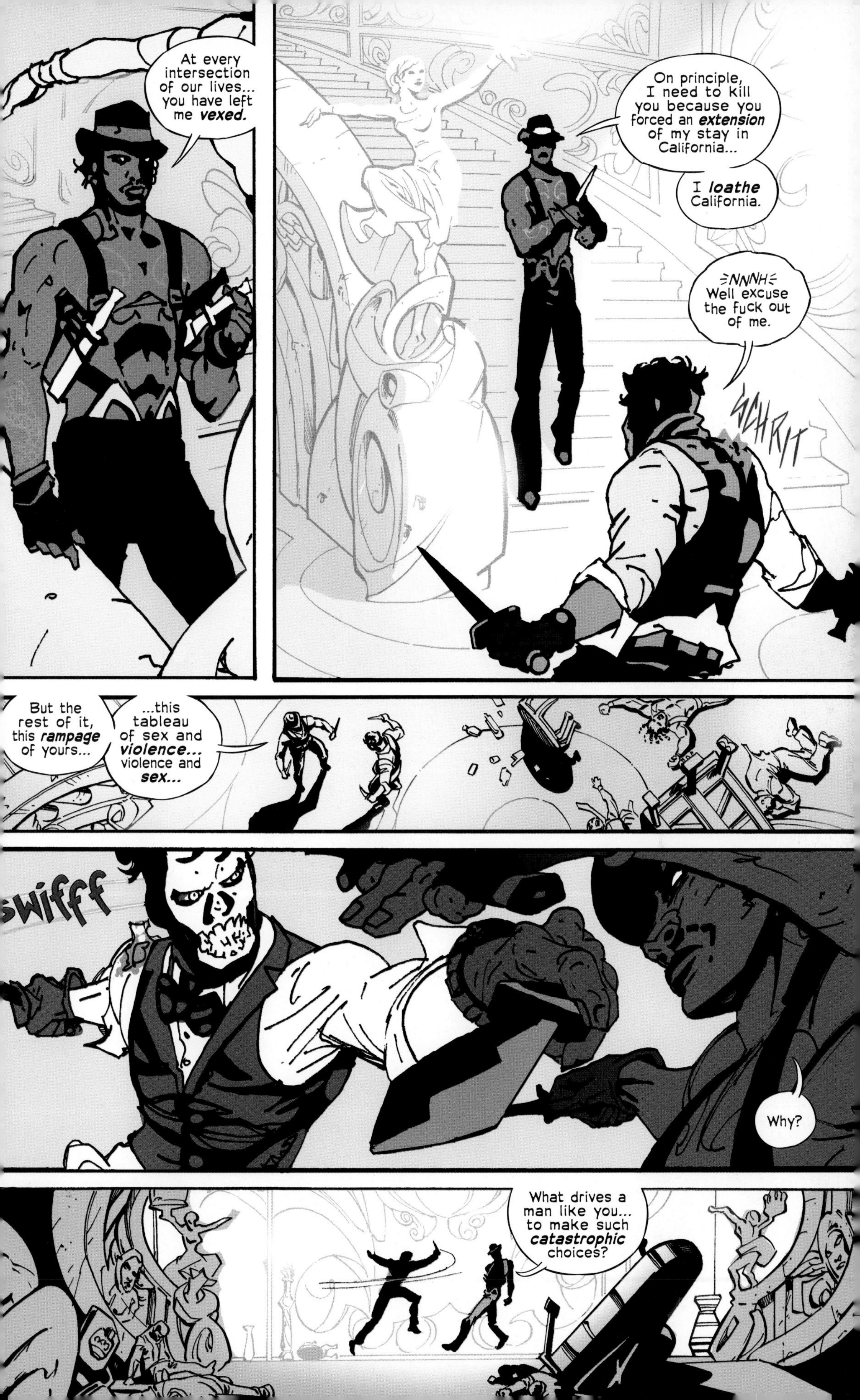

At every intersection of our lives... you have left me ***vexed.***
On principle, I need to kill you because you forced an ***extension*** of my stay in California...
I ***loathe*** California.
NNNH Well excuse the fuck out of me.
SCHRIT
But the rest of it, this ***rampage*** of yours...
...this tableau of sex and ***violence...*** violence and ***sex...***
swifff
Why?
What drives a man like you... to make such ***catastrophic*** choices?

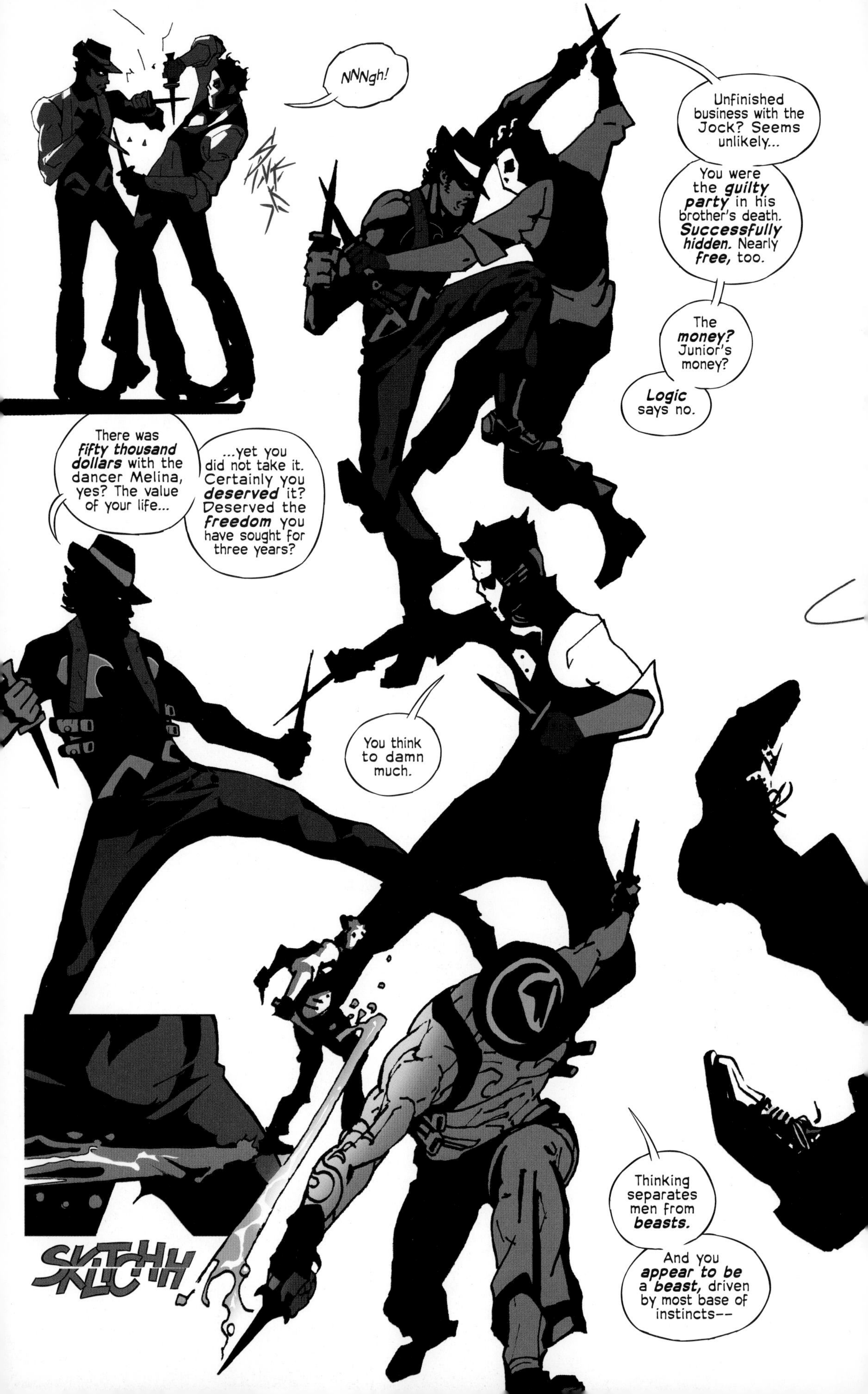
SNIKT
NNNgh!
Unfinished business with the Jock? Seems unlikely...
You were the guilty party in his brother's death. Successfully hidden. Nearly free, too.
The money? Junior's money?
Logic says no.
There was fifty thousand dollars with the dancer Melina, yes? The value of your life...
...yet you did not take it. Certainly you deserved it? Deserved the freedom you have sought for three years?
You think to damn much.
SKLTCHH!
Thinking separates men from beasts.
And you appear to be a beast, driven by most base of instincts--

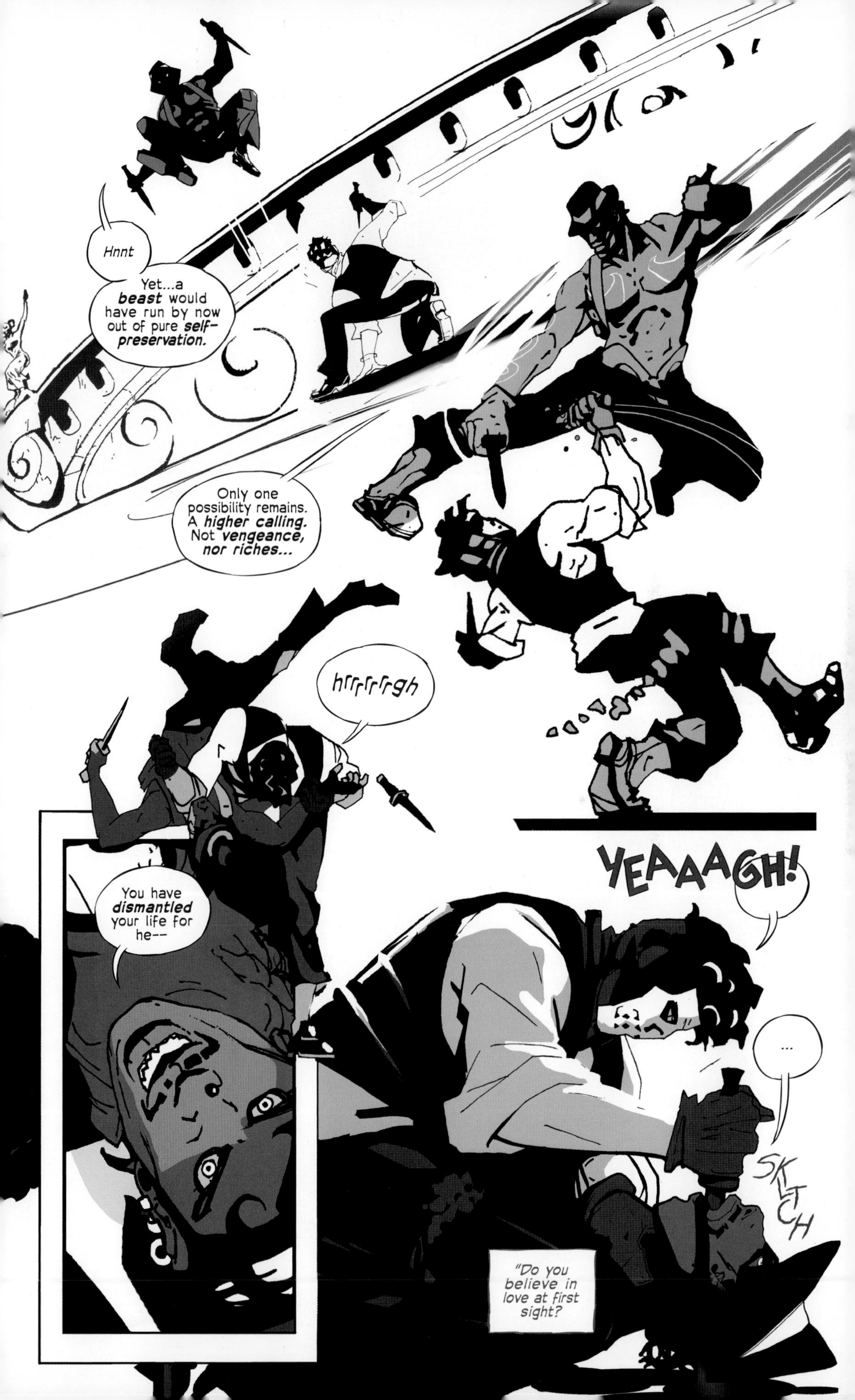

Hnnt
Yet...a beast would have run by now out of pure self-preservation.
Only one possibility remains. A higher calling. Not vengeance, nor riches...
hrrrrrrgh
You have dismantled your life for he--
YEAAAGH!
...
SKLTCH
"Do you believe in love at first sight?

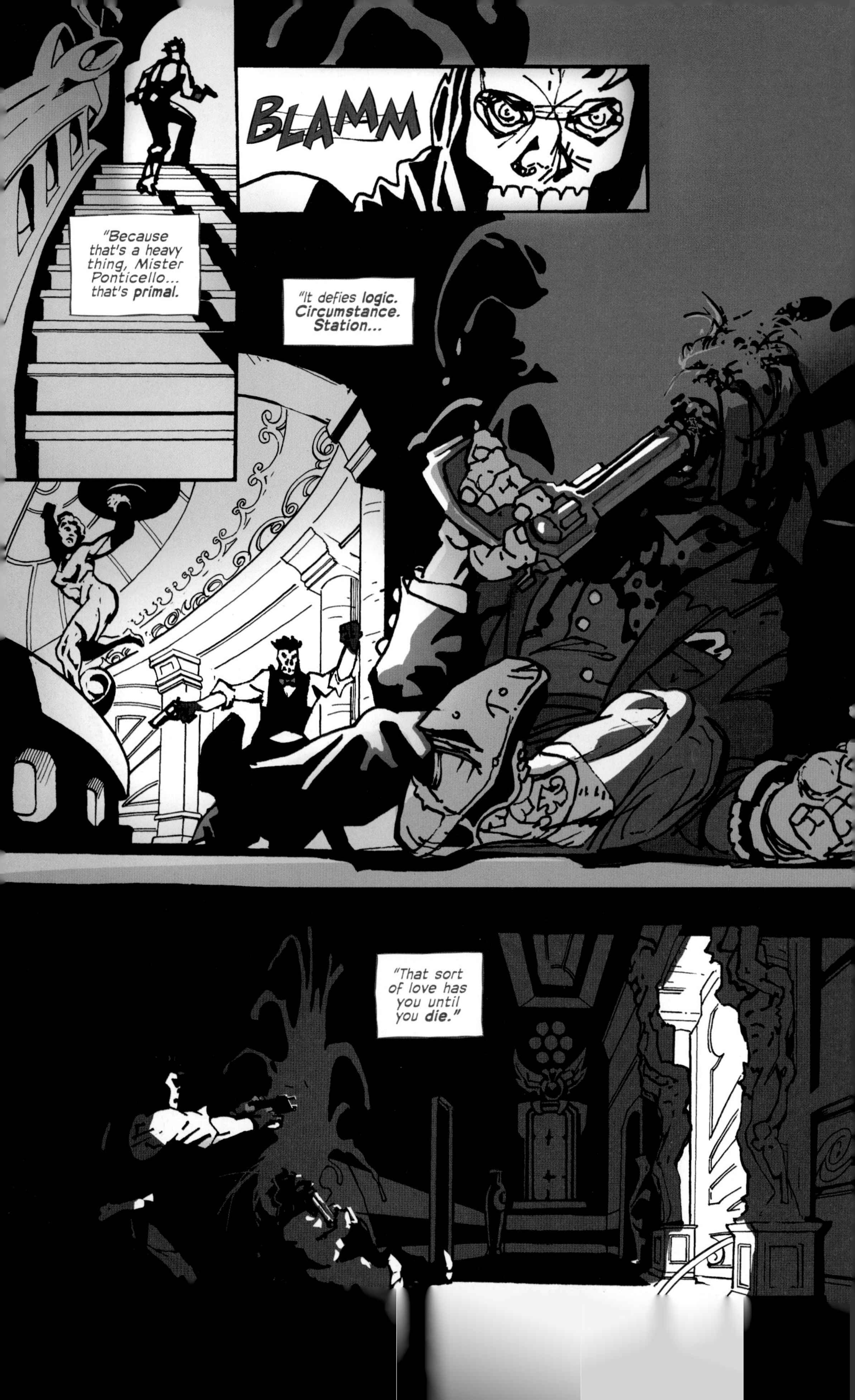
BLAMM
"Because that's a heavy thing, Mister Ponticello... that's **primal.**
"It defies **logic.** Circumstance. Station...
"That sort of love has you until you **die.**"

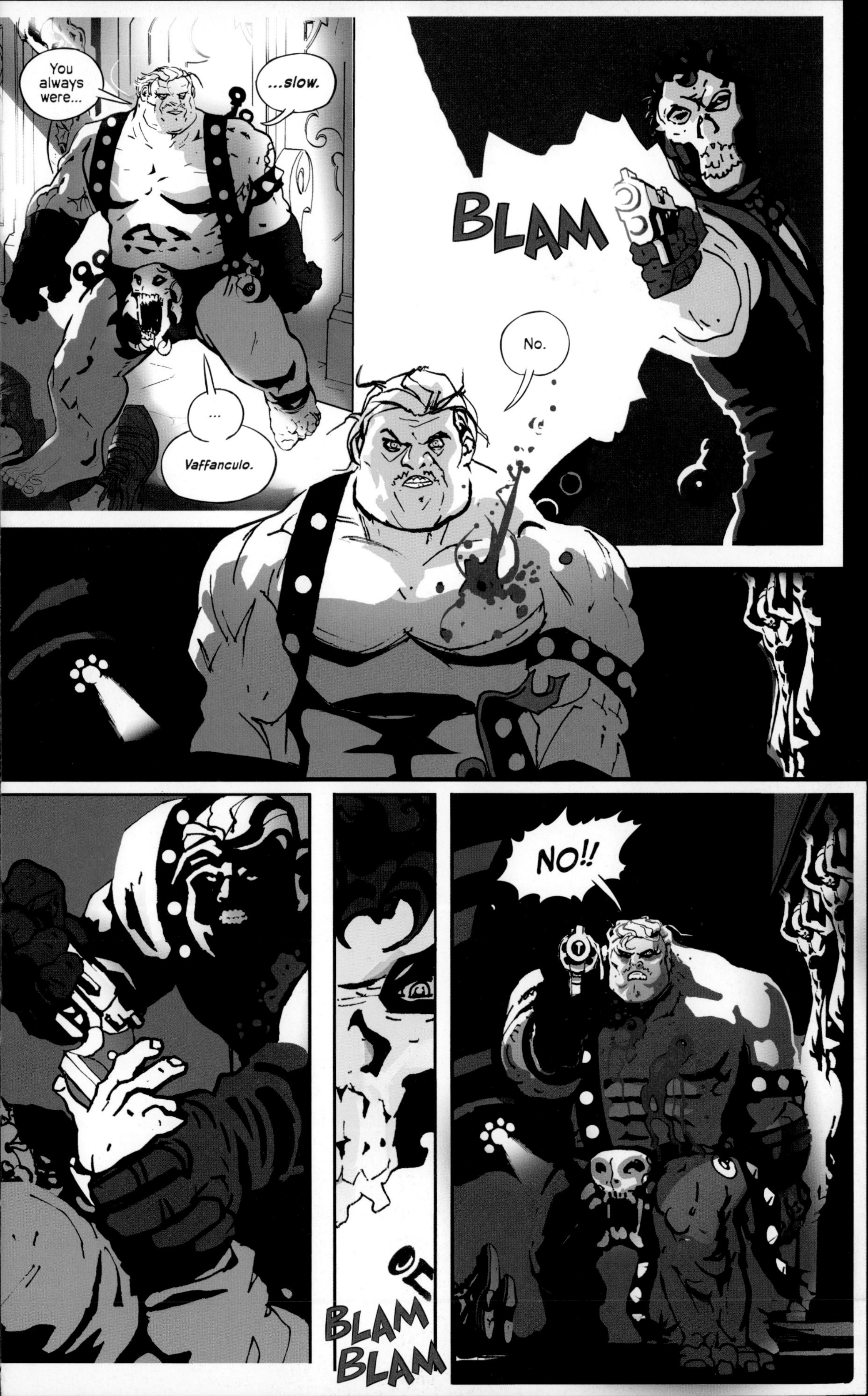
You always were...
...slow.
...
Vaffanculo.
BLAM
No.
BLAM
BLAM
NO!!

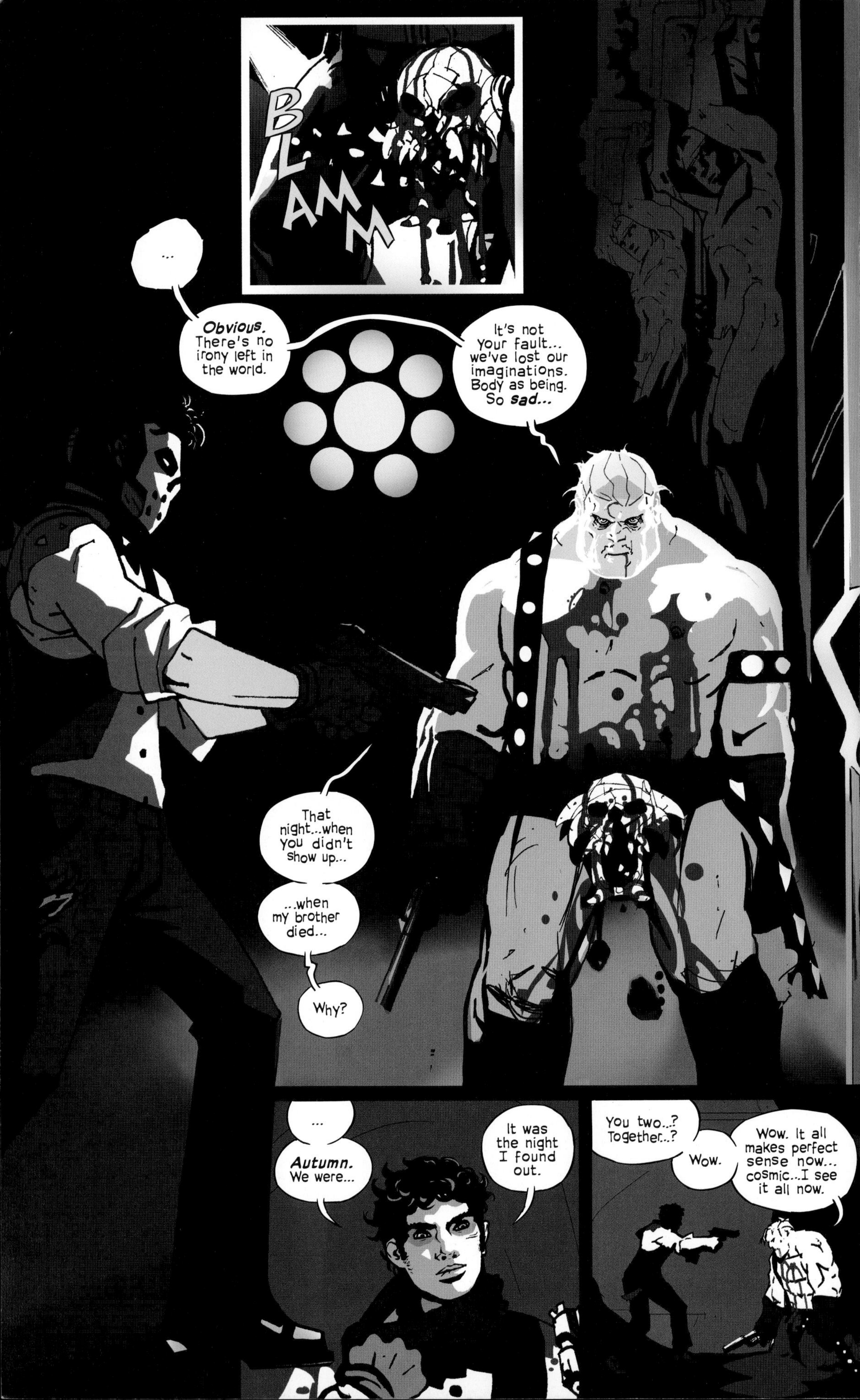
BLAMM
...
Obvious. There's no irony left in the world.
It's not your fault... we've lost our imaginations. Body as being. So *sad...*
That night...when you didn't show up...
...when my brother died...
Why?
...
Autumn. We were...
It was the night I found out.
You two...? Together...?
Wow.
Wow. It all makes perfect sense now... cosmic...I see it all now.

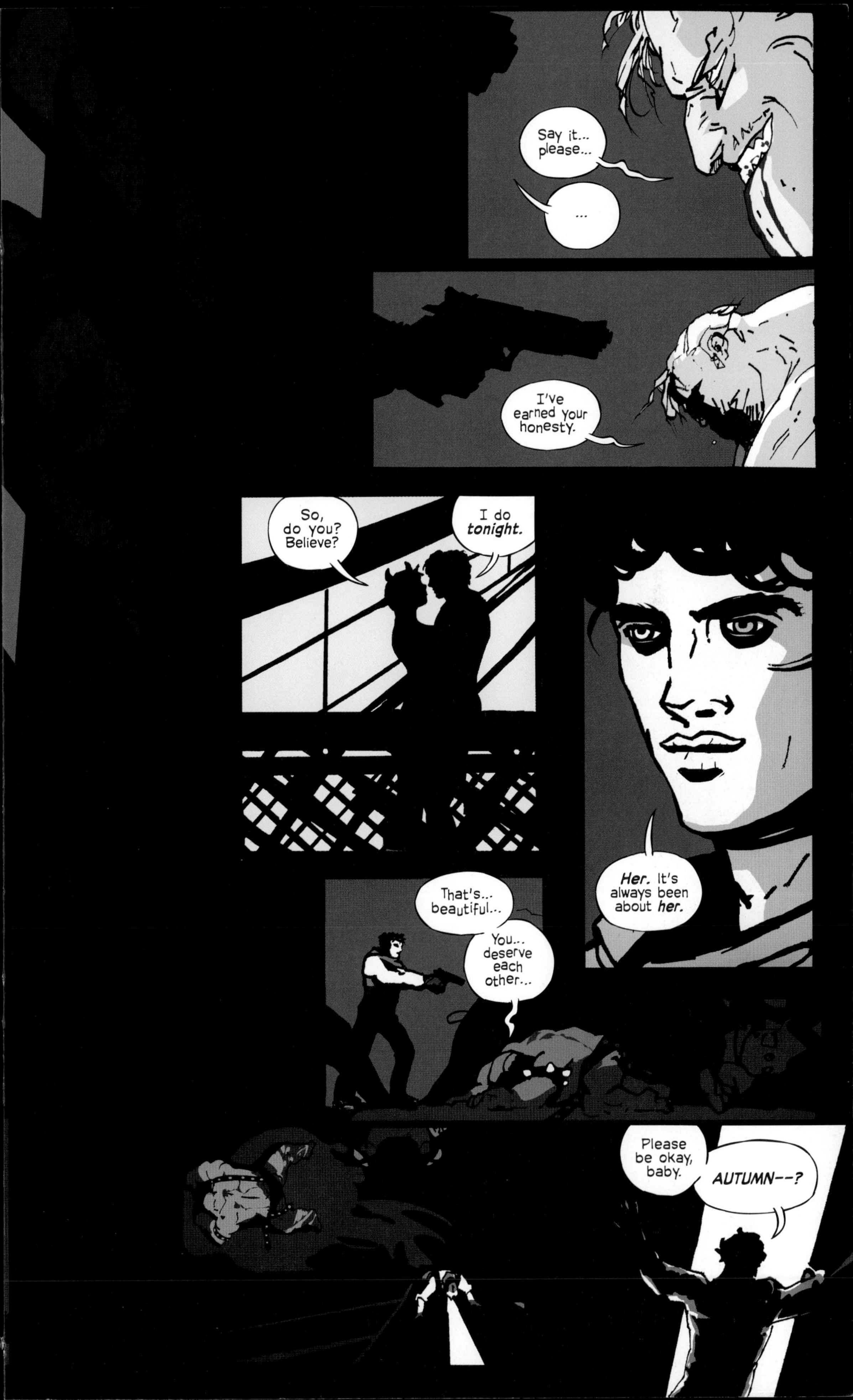

Say it... please...
...
I've earned your honesty.
So, do you? Believe?
I do *tonight.*
Her. It's always been about *her.*
That's... beautiful...
You... deserve each other...
Please be okay, baby.
AUTUMN--?

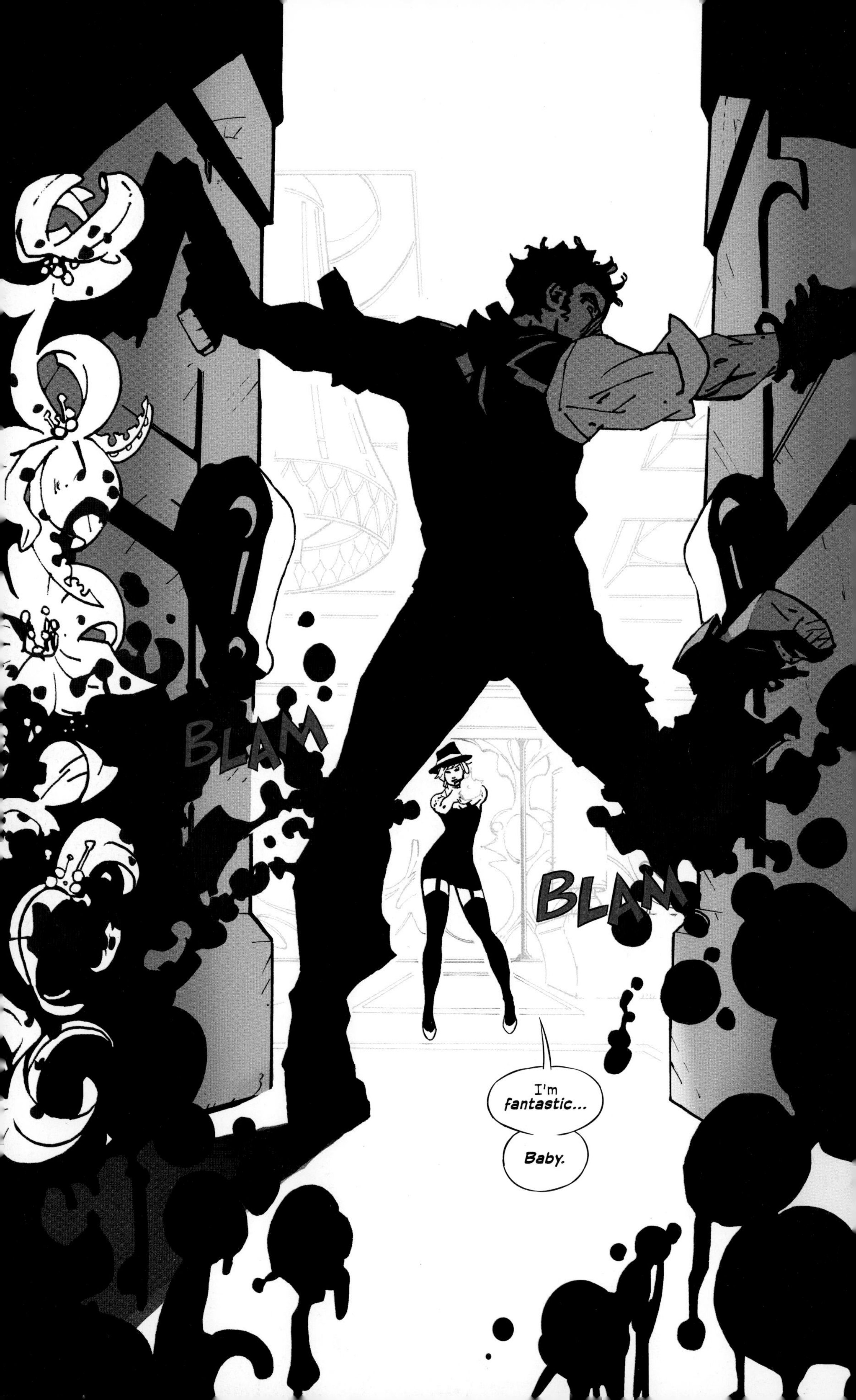
BLAM
BLAM
I'm fantastic...
Baby.

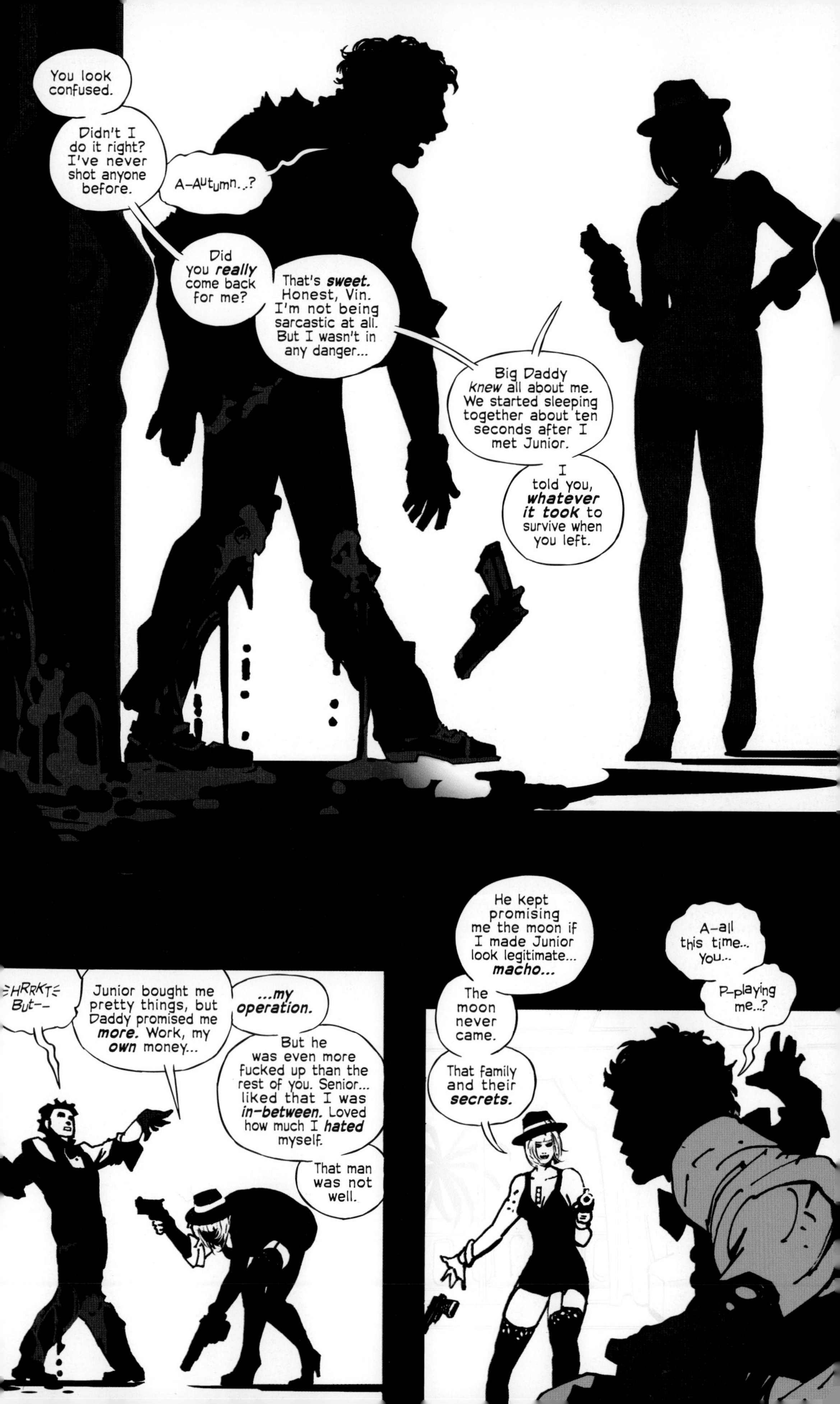

You look confused.
Didn't I do it right? I've never shot anyone before.
A-Autumn...?
Did you *really* come back for me?
That's *sweet.* Honest, Vin. I'm not being sarcastic at all. But I wasn't in any danger...
Big Daddy *knew* all about me. We started sleeping together about ten seconds after I met Junior.
I told you, *whatever it took* to survive when you left.
HRRKT But--
Junior bought me pretty things, but Daddy promised me *more.* Work, my *own* money...
...*my operation.*
But he was even more fucked up than the rest of you. Senior... liked that I was *in-between.* Loved how much I *hated* myself.
That man was not well.
He kept promising me the moon if I made Junior look legitimate... *macho...*
The moon never came.
That family and their *secrets.*
A-all this time... You...
P-playing me...?

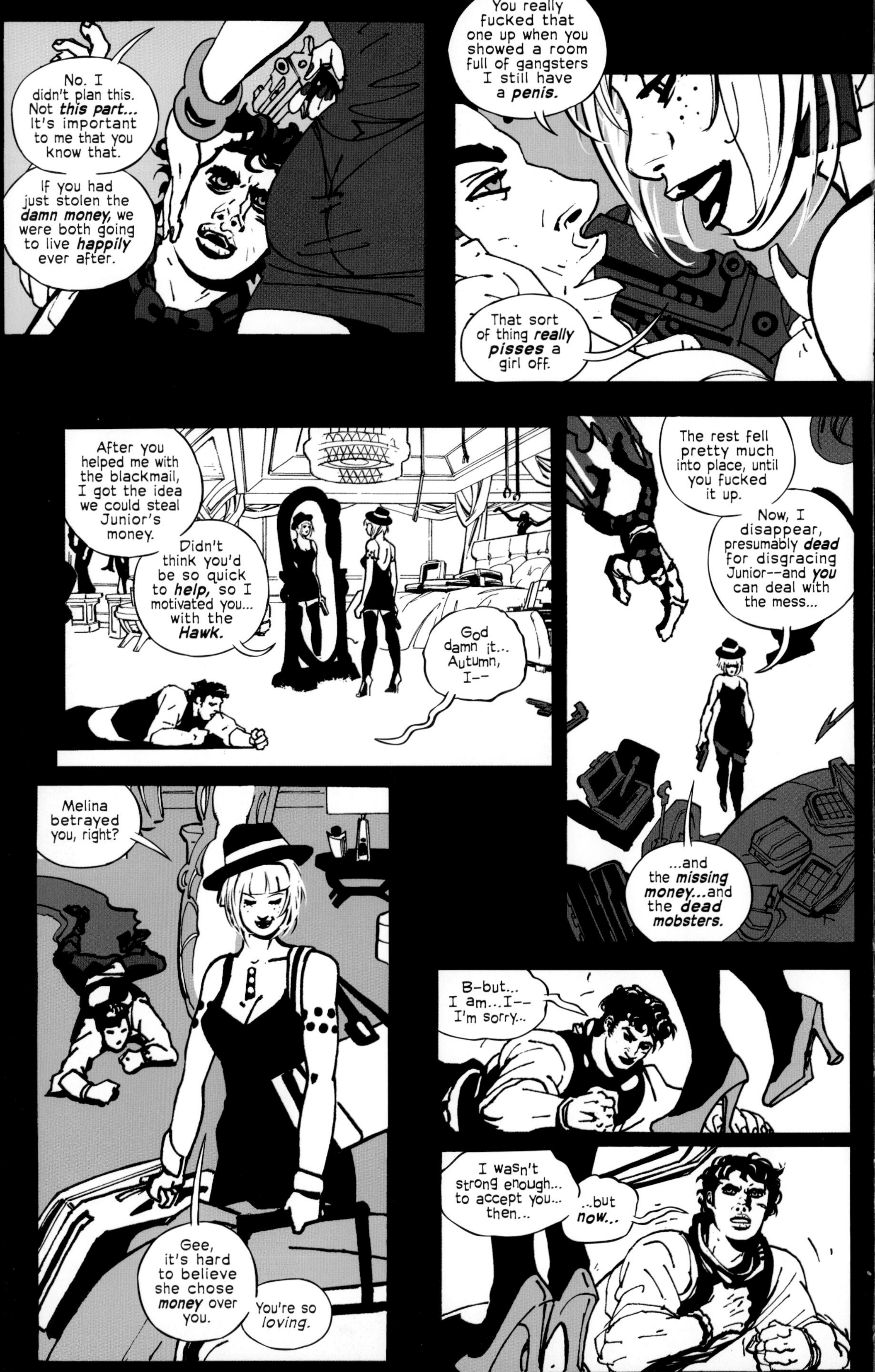
No. I didn't plan this. Not *this part...* It's important to me that you know that.
If you had just stolen the *damn money,* we were both going to live *happily* ever after.
You really fucked that one up when you showed a room full of gangsters I still have a *penis.*
That sort of thing *really pisses* a girl off.
After you helped me with the blackmail, I got the idea we could steal Junior's money.
Didn't think you'd be so quick to *help,* so I motivated you... with the *Hawk.*
God damn it... Autumn, I--
The rest fell pretty much into place, until you fucked it up.
Now, I disappear, presumably *dead* for disgracing Junior--and *you* can deal with the mess...
...and the *missing money...*and the *dead mobsters.*
Melina betrayed you, right?
Gee, it's hard to believe she chose *money* over you.
You're so *loving.*
B-but... I am...I-- I'm sorry...
I wasn't strong enough... to accept you... then...
...but *now...*

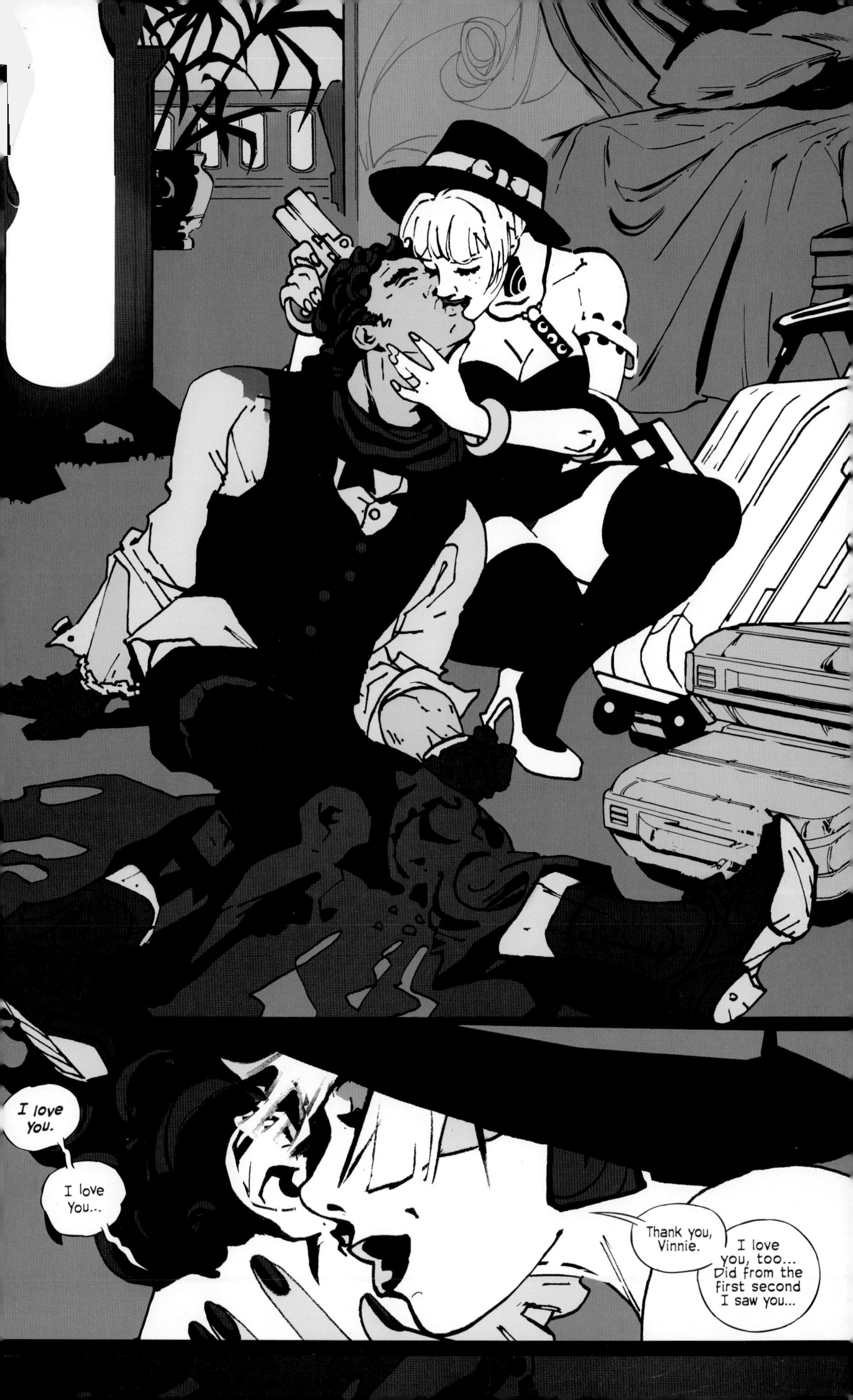
I love you.
I love you...
Thank you, Vinnie.
I love you, too... Did from the first second I saw you...

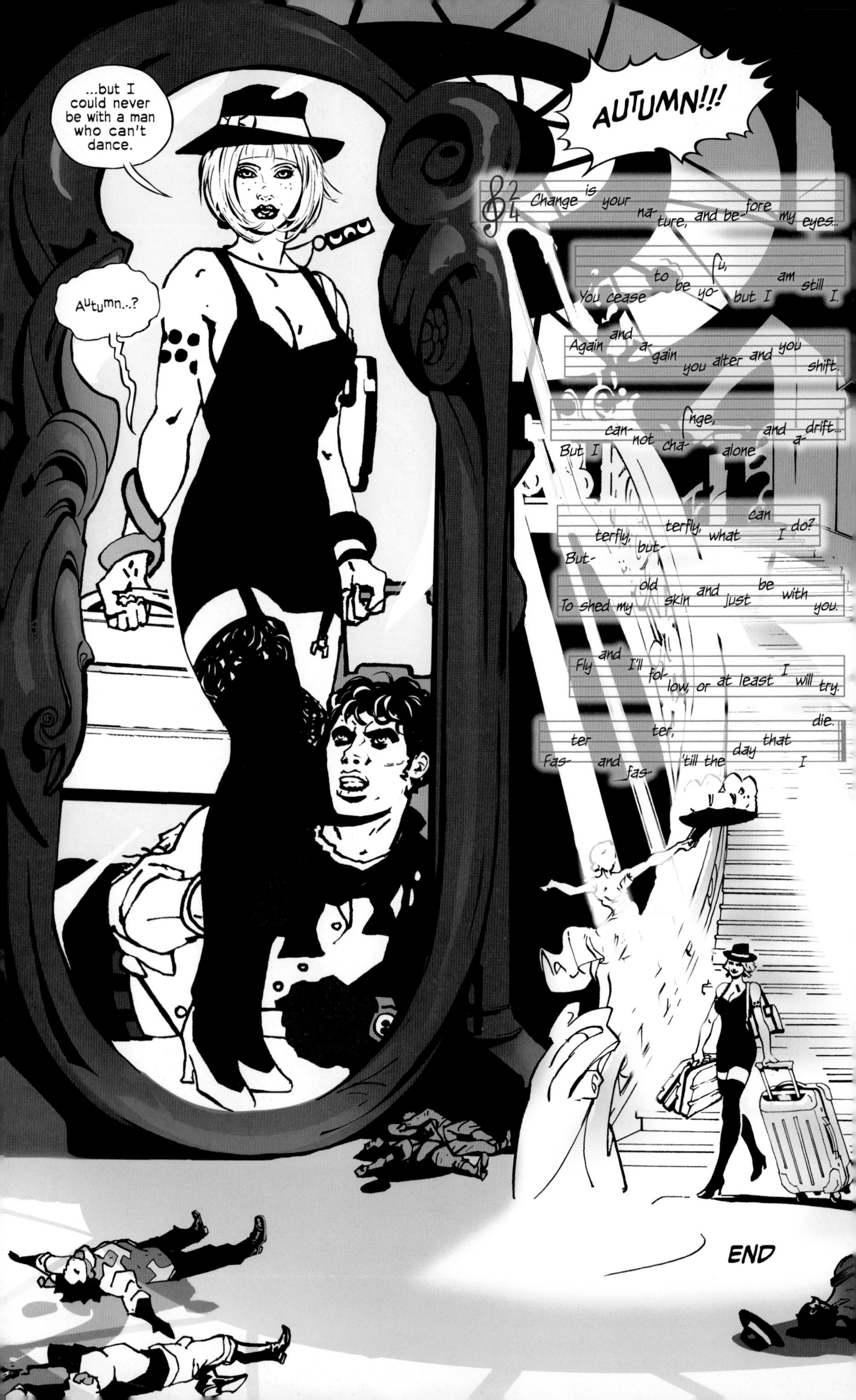

...but I could never be with a man who can't dance.
Autumn...?
AUTUMN!!!
Change is your na- ture, and be- fore my eyes..
You cease to be yo- u, but I am still I.
Again and a- gain you alter and you shift.
But I can- not cha- nge, alone and a- drift...
But- terfly, but- terfly, what can I do?
To shed my old skin and just be with you.
Fly and I'll fol- low, or at least I will try.
Fas- ter and fas- ter, 'till the day that I die.
END